I0823622

Praise for Shona Kinsella

"*Daughters of Nicnevin* is a haunting, ethereal tale of love, sisterhood and magic."
Helen Glynn Jones, author of *The Last Raven*

"Sweeping and evocative, *Daughters of Nicnevin* is lush, earnest, and painfully heartfelt. Every word etches truth in your soul: when it comes to Scottish history tinged with magic, there is no greater authority. Compelling and bone-shakingly real, Kinsella is a beautiful and singular voice."
David Green, author of the *Empire of Ruin* series

"A fiercely independent heroine and a fascinating pantheon of gods [...] Brigit is an admirable protagonist."
Publishers Weekly on *The Heart of Winter*

"[...] the best fantasy novel I have read in a long, long time and, quite honestly, an instant classic in the genre."
A Reviewer Darkly on *The Heart of Winter*

"A wonderfully constructed novel, epic world building and a fantastic story."
TheGrimDarkFiles on *Ashael Rising*

"A strong debut that builds on traditional fantasy... fresh, exciting, and interesting."
Alex S. Bradshaw, *BFS Indie Reviews* on *Ashael Rising*

SHONA KINSELLA

DAUGHTERS OF NICNEVIN

This is a FLAME TREE PRESS book

FLAME TREE PRESS
6 Melbray Mews, London, SW6 3NS, UK
flametreepress.com

US sales, distribution and warehouse:
Simon & Schuster
simonandschuster.biz

UK distribution and warehouse:
Hachette UK Distribution
hukdcustomerservice@hachette.co.uk

The cover is made by Flame Tree Studio, working with the fine and wonderful artist Broci who created the cover for this book. The art is © Broci 2025.
The font families used are Avenir and Bembo.

Flame Tree Press is an imprint of Flame Tree Publishing Ltd
flametreepublishing.com

A copy of the CIP data for this book is available from the British Library and the Library of Congress.

1 3 5 7 9 8 6 4 2

HB ISBN: 978-1-80552-020-7
ebook ISBN: 978-1-80552-021-4

Printed and bound in the UK by CPI Group (UK) Ltd, Croydon CR0 4YY.

Represented in the EU for product safety and compliance by Authorised Rep Compliance Ltd., Ground Floor, 71 Lower Baggot Street, Dublin, D02 P593, Ireland. Contact at www.arccompliance.com

SHONA KINSELLA

DAUGHTERS OF NICNEVIN

FLAME TREE PRESS
London & New York

Part One

Chapter One

Mairead

28th July 1745

The end was in sight.

The old man's rasping breath hitched in his chest, stuttering in time with the flickering light coming from the hearth. Mairead dropped her knitting into the basket by her side and leaned forward, placing her warm hand atop his cold, frail one. He coughed and sighed, his breathing once more settling into an unsteady rhythm, and Mairead squeezed his fingers before letting go and sitting back again. Old Callum's wasted body barely made a hump beneath the blankets and plaids piled upon the bed.

Mairead waited a moment, watching the tiny movement of the blankets as his chest rose and fell, reassuring herself that the moment was not yet upon them. Satisfied, she picked up her knitting once more. The fire crackled in the hearth, the only sound other than the rasp of Callum's strained breathing. Night lay heavy on the village, and most people would be tucked up safe in bed. Even the cattle in the nearby fields were quiet. As she wound the wool around her needles, Mairead filled her mind with the stories Callum had shared about his family, the love and care he held for them, from his one surviving son, all the way down to the littlest grandchild. She softly hummed an old Gáidhlig lullaby as she worked, mentally swapping the words for ones that echoed her intentions. Magic like this, built layer upon layer, could last as long as the wool it was woven with.

Old Callum whimpered and Mairead stood so quickly that her stool almost fell crashing to the floor to disturb the peace of this final night. With a gesture, she stopped it right on the tipping point, then gently placed it back on all three legs without ever touching it. That taken care of, she placed a hand on Callum's brow and murmured to him in a low voice.

"Be at peace, now, *a' charaid.* All will be well."

She could feel the life force within him ebbing away even as she concentrated on it, taking with it a lifetime of pain and loss until all that was left was the love. Of all the passings she had eased, only a handful had ended any differently.

Callum opened eyes the color of a faded spring sky and looked up at Mairead with a lucidity he hadn't shown in days.

"Where's Bernadette?" he asked, his voice creaking like a rusty hinge.

"She had to go home to the bairns. It's late. You don't mind me being here instead, do you?"

"No, no of course not." Callum licked dry lips with what was likely an even drier tongue.

Mairead fetched an earthenware cup of ale from a jug on the dresser and helped him drink. "Careful now, not too quickly," she said, holding a cloth to his chin to catch any drips. "We don't want to start a coughing fit."

Callum waved when he'd had his fill, and Mairead set the cup down and perched on the edge of the bed, taking his hand in hers.

"Do you think she'll be there?" the old man asked, his voice a little closer to the deep, rich tones it had boasted when Mairead first met him a year or more ago.

"Who?"

He turned toward the hearth, avoiding her gaze. "My Lizzie. Will she be waiting for me on the other side, do you think?"

Mairead squeezed his hand, careful not to crush his thin fingers. The truth was that she had no idea what, if anything, waited beyond death, but she had discovered that this was one of the many situations where the person she was speaking to wished for comfort rather than truth.

"I worry sometimes," Callum said, still not meeting her eyes. "She was a good woman, my Lizzie. The kindest heart. Always pious. She must rest in the arms of the angels, surely?" His gaze darted quickly to her face, before settling on the hearth once more. "I can make no such claim for myself. I was hot-blooded in my youth, you see. Did some things I'm none too proud of now."

He swallowed hard. Mairead let the silence draw out, sensing that he had more to say.

"I fear my destination may be a tad warmer and a mite less hospitable."

Mairead thought for a moment, considering how best to answer. It was not the first time she had heard such fears as the end approached and she was sure it would not be the last. Most people spent far more time thinking about the ways in which they had fallen short of their goals, than the good they had done over their lives.

"I don't claim to know the young man that you were," she said at last, "but I believe I do know the man you are now. And that man belongs with his beloved wife."

Callum glanced at her hand, where a thin band of gold gleamed on her fourth finger. "I know it may seem unkind of me, but I do hope your James has a good, long while to wait before you join him."

Mairead gave a tight smile that she hoped Callum would take for grief rather than guilt. She hated lying to people, but it was easier to manage her own life as a widow than an unmarried woman. Whenever she arrived in a new place, the people there accepted her story of a recently lost husband and the need to move away from home to escape the ghost of their life together. When she decided it was time to move on again, they accepted just as easily that she missed her home and was ready to return, the greatest part of her grief in the past. Eighteen months was the longest she had spent in one place in the ten years since she had left her parents' croft.

"How did you and Lizzie start courting?" she asked, deflecting the conversation back to safer grounds.

"Our fathers were elders in the church together and they were always pushing us together. So of course I wasn't interested in her at all."

Mairead listened as Callum told her how they had eventually fallen in love and while he spoke, she absorbed the love and happiness that he shared so freely, storing it to later pour into the shawl she was knitting for his granddaughter, Bernadette, his final gift to her.

His eyes drifted closed and his voice began to trail off. Mairead reached out her senses, feeling the vital part of Callum slipping further away. She leaned over and spoke softly, close to his ear.

"You can go now. You've done enough. You can let go."

She saw the moment when he left, when his body became a shell and whatever had been animating him was gone. A pale, rose-colored mist drifted up from his body, rising out of his pores, it seemed. She watched as it drew together to form the shape of him, the suggestion of a younger, stronger man. The shape looked at her with eyes that were only a hint of the ones she had known, and inclined his head in a gesture of respect, then stood and looked past her. As always at these moments, she had the sensation of a space opening somewhere beyond her shoulder. The shape that had been Callum stared intently at that space, then began to glow with a light that filled the room with feelings of love and joy. Then it was over, and she was alone.

She blinked back tears as she closed Callum's eyes and placed his hands gently on his chest. Whatever the old man had been like in his youth, he was a good man now, and had been one of the first people to make her feel welcome when she arrived in the village. He had taken her on as a housekeeper and given her room and board without ever asking for more than she was willing to give.

Truly, she had planned to move along sooner but hadn't been able to bring herself to leave until he passed. She allowed herself a quiet moment to mourn, to give thanks for the kindnesses he had shown her and the time she had spent with him.

Then she got to work.

She could not spare Callum's family the grief of saying goodbye, but she could spare them the pain of having to prepare his body. First, she warmed some water over the hearth, adding flowers and herbs that she had set aside for this use. Some were included just to mask the smell of death, while others brought protection against misfortune or harmful intent. They would protect his soul until it reached wherever it was destined for, and keep anything malicious from attaching itself to his now-vacant body. While the water warmed and grew fragrant, she took the blankets and plaids from the bed, then stripped Callum and carefully removed the sheet from beneath him.

"I hope Lizzie was waiting for you," she said softly, placing a kiss on his rapidly cooling forehead. As she washed his body and did this last service for him, she found that she was finally able to share her truth with him – now that it could cause no harm to either of them.

"I'm not really a widow," she said, dipping a cloth into the blessed water and gently cleansing every part of the body he had left behind. "I'm what many people would call a witch. I left home when people started to notice that strange things tend to happen around me, and I've been moving around ever since. The Witch Hunters might be gone, but people don't exactly like having us around. No matter that we often make their lives better."

Mairead stopped and straightened, pushing away the bitterness that often rose in her when she thought of how people such as her were treated. Women such as her, really. Male witches were given a great deal more leeway than any woman ever was. She took a few deep breaths and returned to her work.

"I was born this way. I can't help it; I affect the world around me whether I'm trying to or not. So, I had to learn to do it with purpose." She stopped talking as she rolled him onto his side so that she could clean his back. "I thought about telling you, you know. Sometimes you would look at me like you knew there was something more to my story and I could almost believe that it would be safe to show my true self. That you would know me well enough to know that I would only ever seek to do good. But in the end, it just seemed too great a risk. For both of us."

Mairead said no more as she finished the job of cleansing his earthly remains, her heart lighter for the telling of her tale, but at the same time heavier for the loss of this kind soul. She had found that most people were neither particularly good nor particularly bad; most just wanted to get on with their lives in peace. Many would be kind when it cost them little. Fewer were like Callum – kind even when it took effort or left them without. Thankfully, the smallest number of people she had encountered were the opposite – *unkind* even when it took effort for them to be so. Unfortunately, that described her own father.

She wondered if he was still alive. If her mother remained with him on the croft, working her fingers to the bone day after day, alongside a man who denigrated her at the slightest provocation.

There was a reason Mairead had never gone home.

When Callum's body was clean, she wrapped him in a fresh nightshirt and clean bedding, then heated more water to wash the soiled things. There were still two or three hours until dawn, judging from how far the candles in the room had burned down. She might as well do this chore before waking his family with bad news. She set up the washboard and tub in front of the hearth and then brought the mangle through as well – the other rooms of the house were chilly, despite the time of year.

As she knelt on the floor, scrubbing the bedding, only vaguely aware of the body lying a few feet away, her mind wandered back to her father. She hoped that her mother had found a way to leave, to build a life away from him somehow. Maybe he was dead. Perhaps her mother had performed these very tasks for the man who had made both of their lives miserable.

There had always been something different about Mairead, for as long as she could remember. Odd things happened around her. She remembered one spring when she was small, sitting in the garden and wishing the rhubarb was ready to eat. Within moments, the spriggy young stalks had bloomed and become a mature plant ready to harvest, a full season before it should have been. Mairead hadn't understood her mother's horror when she discovered her daughter sitting in the middle of this miraculous growth. Not until years later, anyway.

She could see things that others couldn't. When she was young and insisted that she could see a sprite that played in the spray of the stream near the croft, her parents put it down to an active imagination. Her mother thought it charming until the night she had woken them, screaming because she saw some vast, black beast prowling around the croft in the dark. By the time she saw the bloodied ghost of a warrior traipsing across the fields, causing birds to take flight and small creatures to flee, she knew to keep the experience to herself.

If that had been all, perhaps things would still have been all right, she mused as she worked soap through the bedding, idly casting a protective charm over it as she worked, so that it would bring some peace and good health to whichever household it ended up in. *But of course, there was more.*

Whenever she wished for something strongly enough, the world would somehow shift to bring her desire to her. When she was young that was awkward, but manageable. When Millicent Ferguson had a new doll that Mairead coveted, it went missing and somehow turned up in their woodshed – a place Millicent had certainly never been. Mairead had played with the doll until she grew bored with it, then had returned it, claiming to have found it by the side of the road. As she had gotten older, however, that particular facet of her magic had proven far more problematic. When she had spent a summer pining after Millicent herself, only for the girl in question to start following her everywhere, sitting outside her home at all hours of the day and night, refusing to eat unless Mairead ate with her...well, that had been difficult for all involved.

It was around that time that her father had finally noticed that more strange things happened around his daughter than around the rest of the village combined. He had confronted her and, when she couldn't explain it to his satisfaction, he had beat her black and blue with his belt. In her fear and pain, she had somehow sent it all bouncing back at him. His own violence hit him threefold.

By the time they had both recovered from that, he was terrified of her, which only made him all the angrier, and she knew that she had to find a way to control her power. He never lifted his hands to her again, but that didn't stop him taking his fury out on her mother, spitting at her and calling her 'Satan's whore', when he didn't use his fists. Her mother begged her not to act against him, convinced it could only make matters worse.

Mairead spent her last few years in her parents' home learning to keep an iron control over her will. Otherwise, she had no doubt, her father would have dropped dead.

As she fed the bedding through the mangle, squeezing as much water out of it as she could, she forced thoughts of her parents away. They had made their choices and so had she, and that was all there was to it.

In the decade since she had left home, she had met three others like her. Each had taught her something of what she was and how she could use her innate connection with the world to improve her life, as well as the lives of those around her. In the end though, she had learned the most from a healer who was not born with any power. Instead, this woman had trained and practiced and honed her instincts and her connection, until the potions and tinctures that she made with such love and care provided far more relief than could be explained by ingredients alone. Until she could pour enough of that love and care into a patient to help bones knit and wounds close.

Mairead had trained beneath her for eighteen months before it became obvious that they were now living in the healthiest town in the Highlands, and she knew that the time had come to move on.

By the time all the washing was done and folded on a stool, waiting to be hung out on the line, the square of sky she could see through the window was beginning to lighten to gray and she knew she could put it off no longer. She stood by Callum's side once more, saying a final farewell of her own, before holding her hands over him and muttering a quick incantation to cast a light glamour over him, just enough to soften the ravages of his final days, to allow his family to remember him as he had lived rather than as he had died.

She lifted the washing and carried it out to the small yard behind the house. She glanced around furtively to make sure that no one was stirring in any of the other houses that shared this plot of ground, before gesturing for the wooden pegs to move themselves from their bag to the line to secure the bedding as she hung it.

Without warning, something tugged at her awareness, pulling at her senses in a way that wasn't entirely comfortable. She stopped what she was doing, head raised, all of her senses on high alert. There it was again. It felt almost like someone plucking at her sleeve to get her attention, though it was coming from miles and days away. Somewhere to the north-east, she thought. Toward Inverness.

She stood still for several long moments, waiting to see if it would happen again. When it didn't, she finished hanging the washing, all the while pondering what had just happened. It felt almost as if something – or someone – was reaching for her, calling out to her. It was not dissimilar to the feeling of meeting another witch, the recognition that came when their powers touched each other. But she had never experienced that at a distance before.

Shrugging it off as best she could, she opened the gate between Callum's house and the seamstress's next door and let herself out onto the street. Birds sang a greeting to the dawn, and farther away cattle were lowing. Lamps were lit behind windows as she made her way along the street, the village slowly waking around her.

The plucking sensation came again, just as she reached the small house that Bernadette shared with her husband and children. Mairead nodded once, decisively. She knew which direction she would be traveling in when she left here.

She lifted her hand and knocked gently at the door.

Bernadette opened the door a moment later, still in a nightgown and robe, her hair wrapped in a scarf. She looked at Mairead, her eyes filling with tears as understanding broke over her. "He's gone, isn't he?"

25th July 1745

Dear Lord G________,

I write to inform you that the Roman son has landed upon our shores this very week. He comes with full intent to right the wrong done to his family and restore his father to the place which God intended for him. He is calling upon all true and faithful men of Scotland to join him.

He is, however, extremely unprepared. He promises aid from his cousin in France once the undertaking is begun, but we know how fickle that personage can be. We have urged him with all due love to return to the Continent until such aid has been forthcoming, but he is bound and determined to proceed.

He plans to make his way to Glenfinnan and beseeches you to join him there. It would be well if you did attend, even if only to persuade him to delay his plans.

Your Faithful Friend,
S__________ of Glen________

Chapter Two

Constance

30th July 1745

Constance's shoulders ached as she kneaded the dough, especially the left one, which had never been quite right since she had injured it in a childhood fall. Oatmeal dust drifted in the air, knocked up from the scarred wooden surface of the table. With a sigh of relief, she scooped the dough up and dropped it into the skillet before flicking a cloth over it to let it rest. She stepped back and almost tripped over the child who had crept up behind her as she worked.

"Elspeth! What are you doing there? I could have hurt you!"

"Sorry, Mama." Her six-year-old daughter looked up at her with wide eyes. "I wanted some bannock."

"It's not ready yet, love," Constance said, wiping her hands on her apron. "How about some porridge?"

Elspeth gave her a solemn nod and climbed into a chair at the end of the table.

Constance spooned some porridge out of the pot hanging over the hearth fire and mixed in some milk to cool it. "You're up early," she said, placing the bowl gently in front of her daughter. She glanced at the door leading toward the other room in the small cottage, where she had left the children sleeping while she got to work. "Did the baby wake you?"

Elspeth shook her head. "Simon and Janey are still asleep." She spooned up some porridge and blew on it before carefully nibbling at some from the tip of the spoon. "I heard Da talking to the mans outside. They were loud."

"Men," Constance corrected gently. She lifted the skillet and placed it at the edge of the fire, where the flames were less intense. *Who could be paying a visit so early in the day?*

The door banged open, and Iain came in, stomping mud and straw off his boots as he came. Simon sent up a wail from the other room and Constance fought the urge to scold Iain for his noise. Instead, she gritted her teeth and went to fetch the baby.

"He's here," Iain said as soon as she returned, Simon cradled against her shoulder and Janey trailing behind, rubbing sleep from her eyes. "It's starting."

"Who's here?" Constance settled Janey at the table and put some porridge out to cool for her, then handed Simon to Elspeth so she could flip the bannock in the skillet without having the baby too close to the fire. It was far easier to do all of this while the children were still abed, but there was no point trying to point out to Iain how he had made her morning harder. He would likely just look at her like he was a puppy she had just kicked for no reason, an expression that often made her want to kick him in reality.

Iain dropped into the chair by the hearth, seemingly oblivious of the fact that he was now in her way as she tried to organize breakfast. "Prince Charles Edward Stuart. He plans to raise his father's standard at Glenfinnan. The uprising is upon us."

Constance stepped over Iain's legs to retrieve the skillet, and tipped the bannock out onto a wire rack to cool, before serving her husband a large portion of porridge and finally retreating to the table, where she took Simon from his sister and put him to her breast.

"What does this mean?" she asked, trying to get her thoughts in order. "Will Clan Gordon rise?"

"It could go either way – men of Gordon fought on both sides the last time. Even if the duke declares for the Hanoverians, there are plenty of men in the clan still loyal to the Stuarts," Iain said around a mouthful of porridge. "And no shortage of men in the duke's own household willing to lead them. John Gordon brought the news. He thinks we should prepare to be called to arms."

Constance said nothing. There had been rumors of another rising for years, but she hadn't truly believed they would come to anything; it had been so long since the last attempt. "What will happen? If the men of Kilmartin are all called to arms?"

Iain scraped his bowl clean of porridge before answering. "Then we'll go. We'll follow the prince for as long as necessary."

"But it's almost the harvest," Constance said, switching Simon to the other breast. "How will we gather in the food if half the village are gone?"

Iain shrugged and got to his feet. "Those who are left behind will just have to manage."

Constance handed the bucket of vegetable scraps to Elspeth and ushered her out to feed the pigs and goats, so she could scrub the floors while Simon and Janey napped. Her stomach rumbled, reminding her that she hadn't eaten yet today – all the disruption in the morning had distracted her and she had forgotten. She looked at the bucket of water she had warmed and sighed. She would find time to eat later.

She dragged the bucket over to the door and knelt by the muddy footprints Iain had left that morning. She began her scrubbing there so it should be mostly dry by the time Elspeth came back in. As she got to work scrubbing the floorboards clean, she grumbled to herself. "Just have to manage… How on God's green earth does he think fewer people can manage the work that already takes every hand in the village to do?"

That was the problem with all of these lairds and their high and mighty ideals – they never spared a thought for the practicalities of it all. She could understand their sense of duty and how they could feel obligated, crofter to laird to king. But didn't they understand that duty went the other way too? Didn't a laird have as much of a duty to see his tenants fed as he did to provide taxes and men to the king?

As she crawled backward across the floor, pulling her bucket with her and scrubbing until her hands and shoulders and back ached with it, she briefly wished she was back in the blackhouse she had grown up in – smaller and in some ways more easily tended than the cottage she lived in now. The floor was smaller and took less work to maintain, for one thing. She stifled a laugh, knowing that her mother would swat her with her own scrubbing brush if she knew of the ungrateful thoughts in Constance's head.

Iain was a cousin of the duke. Not in the main family line, not close enough to have a place at the castle, but close enough to have a two-room cottage with a separate barn, and a larger parcel of land than most. Close enough to be the main tenant of the area known as Kilmartin, and to have crofters and tenants beneath him who looked to him for guidance and help. By marrying him, Constance had moved up in the world, secured her children's future, and made her father proud. Still, she might have thought twice about it if she'd known she'd be left to somehow manage all of this while he went off to play at being a soldier, even if marrying him had bought her a certain amount of disguise and freedom.

She sighed and sat back on her heels, pushing stray wisps of hair out of her face. In front of her, the brush continued to scrub on its own, moving in the same careful circles that Constance had been using. She stared at its movement, entranced for a moment. What could her life be if she didn't have to spend so much of it hiding who she truly was?

The sound of small, skipping footsteps and a nonsense song alerted her to Elspeth's return in plenty of time for her to grab the scrubbing brush and get back to work herself.

"All done," Elspeth said in a singsong voice as she tiptoed across the newly cleaned floor. "Da said I could play with the calves after I've done lots of chores."

"Did he now?" Constance got to her feet with a wince as she straightened her hips and back, then carried the bucket of water to the door and sat it outside; she would take it across the yard to pour away later.

"So can I have more chores?" Elspeth looked up at her hopefully.

"Hmmm." Constance put her hands on her hips and feigned thoughtfulness. "Well, we need some firewood cut, but I think you might be a bit small yet for that job. I've already cleaned the floor and tidied away from breakfast..."

"Please, Mama? Please?"

Constance looked around the room until her gaze fell on the basket she used for gathering food. "I know. You can take that basket and go and fetch me some carrots for the stew. Do you remember which rows are ready?"

"Nearest the house?" Elspeth asked, dashing across the room and hooking the basket over her arm.

Seeing how small Elspeth looked holding it made Constance's heart ache. As someone who had never cared much for children, and certainly had never dreamed of the day she would have her own, the deep preciousness of them, the constant urge to protect them and fend for them had taken her completely by surprise. "That's right," she said, pushing the emotion away. "First two rows nearest the house. Watch out for dandelions too, bring back some leaves if you can."

"Yes, Mama." Elspeth was off out the door before Constance could think of anything else she needed.

She stood in the middle of the room, thinking for a moment. Simon and Janey would likely wake soon, so she could do the weeding and thinning in the vegetable garden after they were up. There was still laundry to be done and the stew to be started. Her stomach growled again. First, food.

She quickly fetched herself a cup of ale and a slice of bannock, which she slathered with butter, before sitting at the table to eat. A few moments of peace, then she would get on with the next job on her never-ending list of things that needed done.

Iain came home late that night, long after the children were in bed, when darkness was beginning to settle over the land. Constance was waiting for him in the chair by the hearth, mending stockings and humming a quiet tune. In these moments, she could almost appreciate her life, even if it were not what she would have chosen for herself.

Unlike that morning, Iain came in quietly. He slipped out of his boots on the doorstep and clearly tried not to wake the children. From the exaggerated care he showed, he was also clearly worse the wear from drink. No doubt he and John and half the other men of the village had been at the whisky and talking of revolution all evening.

Constance suppressed a sigh and an eye roll and carefully placed her mending in the basket at her side. "Is there news?"

"Aye, though not news I'm pleased to share." Iain walked gingerly across the room and leaned against the table, his voice thick with whisky.

Constance could smell the peat on him from where she sat. *He'd best not get any closer to the fire or the fumes coming from him will be enough to catch light.* "What's happened?"

"That turncoat Ruairidh Cameron has left to join the new Watch company in Braemar. Took a couple of the other young lads with him."

"Whatever possessed the boy? He's barely old enough to sign up!"

Iain rubbed a hand across his face, weariness beginning to overcome the drink. "No doubt his grandfather filling his head with stories of the '15. Marr did the cause no favors with his poor leadership. Apparently Ruairidh told his ma that if it came to a fight again, it would be better to be on the winning side this time."

Constance shook her head. "The idiot child would be better not to fight at all."

Iain snorted. "It's funny to hear you calling him a child, you being only eight years older yourself."

"Aye, well. Some of us were born older."

"I cannae argue wi' that." Iain moved to stand by her side and laid his hand heavily upon her shoulder. "Mayhap the heads of Clan Gordon will share the lad's thoughts and not call us up this time."

"We'd all be well to stay out of it," Constance muttered, shrugging his hand off and rising to begin the tasks of getting ready to retire for the night. "What difference does it make to the likes of us whose pampered behind sits atop a throne in London?"

Iain gasped. "Constance! How can ye say such a thing?"

"It's true," she snapped, tired of all the many things she had to pretend about. "Neither Stuarts nor Hanovers have done anything to put food on our table or clothing on our backs. Is the King Across the Water going to come back from Rome and suddenly make everything well with the world? They're no better than children squabbling over a toy, with no thought for who gets hurt in the process."

Iain stared at her, his expression appalled. "Never say such a thing in my hearing again," he said at last. "And if you value me at all, you'll never speak this way in anyone else's hearing either."

Constance leaned on the table, her fists pressing into the wood. Every muscle in her body felt taut as she struggled not to let her power escape with her fury. How dare he? What gave him the right to tell her what she could and couldn't say – what she could and couldn't *think* in reality. If she didn't need him…if she could live her life as she chose… But no matter what she wished for, she did need him. She took slow, even breaths, pushing her anger, and her magic, back down into her core, where it roiled inside of her.

"I'm sorry," she said, forcing her voice to sound like she meant it. "I'm just frightened."

Iain softened straight away, as she knew he would. He loved to play the protector to her weak little woman. He came over and put his arms around her, pulling her roughly to his chest. She gritted her teeth and pressed her face against him, as much to smother her anger as to show affection.

"I should have thought," he said into her hair. "Of course you would be. I'll do everything I can to return to you, my love. You and the bairns will be safe here."

"What if you don't make it back? What if the Watch come while you're all gone? You know they've taken liberties in the past, when circumstances allowed. How will I keep the children safe? I don't know what to do without you." Constance felt sick at this betrayal of herself.

"The pope himself supports the Stuarts' claim to the throne. We're fighting on the side of God. He will keep us all safe. You must have faith."

She could not bring herself to answer such nonsense, so she simply nodded, then pulled away and began tidying up the table.

"Leave that," Iain said, pulling at her waist. "Come and show your husband how you will miss him when he is gone."

"There is still work to be done," she said. She pushed him away gently but firmly.

"And it will still be so in the morning. It is the work of a wife that's needed from you now." He grabbed her waist again, pressing his groin against her hip.

She could see from the stubborn set of his jaw that there would be no denying him. "As you wish," she said with a sigh, and allowed him to pull her through to bed.

Later, as he lay snoring beside her, and she stared into the darkness near the ceiling above, her body aching where he had been less than gentle, tears leaked from her eyes though she made no sound. Surely there could be more to her life than this charade? Iain was not a bad man, not really, but she did not want *any* man. She did not want marriage and obligations and some man always, always, telling her what to do and what to think and what to be.

Her grandmother had tried to step outside of the role that society forced upon her and had been hanged for it. Constance had learned that lesson well – her mother had made sure of it. *Don't stand out, make yourself smaller, make them like you, never draw attention.* Sometimes she wondered if her grandmother had gotten the better of it – a few years of living as her true self, then death. Not this endless misery of twisting herself into the shape that was expected of her, with only years of the same to look forward to.

She rolled onto her side, looking at the children. The girls were asleep in the bed against the opposite wall, Simon tucked safely into the crib alongside them. There were some consolations to this life she was forced to live, after all. She must think only on that.

Although she focused her mind on the children her aching heart called out into the world for someone like her to find her, someone she could be her true self with. Surely there must be someone like that out there, somewhere?

Chapter Three

Mairead

6th August 1745

Mairead walked along the grass verge at the side of the road, picking brambles from the bush and eating them as she went. Several days of heavy rain had delayed her departure after Old Callum's funeral, but now the sun was out, and she was underway. Bernadette had tried to persuade her to stay, to build a home there, but the call that had come to her from the north-east had continued to pull at her, and she knew she could not rest until she answered.

She had folded her heavy traveling cloak into a wrap to carry the few belongings she had taken with her: two changes of clothing, her medicinal supplies, some food and water for the journey. She wasn't sure how far she would be walking. Days, at least. She had a little money with her – enough to pay for a meal and a place to sleep in an inn or two, if her path took her past any.

She walked until she came to a crossroad. One road went roughly north to south, while the one she was on continued from west to east. She stopped and glanced along both roads, making sure that she was unobserved, before pulling a cloth-wrapped bundle from a pocket in her skirt. She unwrapped the cloth to reveal a stone with a hole in the middle, through which a piece of cord was laced. After glancing around again, she allowed the stone to drop so that it hung from the cord, which she held lightly between thumb and forefinger. The stone swung in small pendulum movements.

"Be still," Mairead said softly.

The stone ceased its movement.

"Please show me the way to go to find the source of the call."

The stone began to swing again, moving in small circles that gradually grew wider. After a moment of this, it pulled sharply to the left, pointing up the road that headed north. The stone strained at the end of the cord, as if being pulled in that direction.

"Thank you," Mairead said.

The stone dropped back to hang motionless at the bottom of the cord. Mairead carefully wrapped it once more in the soft cloth and tucked it back into her pocket, before turning onto the road leading north.

She used the same method to find her path many more times that day, before the falling darkness forced her to find a place to rest. As dusk filled the sky, she realized that she would have to spend the night outdoors and began to look for some shelter, however meager, hoping that it wouldn't rain overnight. It wouldn't be the first time she'd been caught out like that, but it was never enjoyable.

Off to the side of the road, she spotted a formation of rocks that would give her shelter on two sides, surrounded by springy heather, which would serve well as a mattress for the night. She made her way over to it and tucked herself into the space, sitting with her back resting against one of the rocks. She pulled some dried meat from her wrap and chewed at the edge of it, worrying at it the same way she worried at the inside of her lip when she was anxious.

She *was* anxious. Something in the air spoke of tension and danger. Whatever it was didn't seem to be close, was not an immediate threat, but it was there. A hint of blood on the air. Now that she had stopped long enough to pay attention, it occurred to her that she had been feeling this all day, at the edges of her awareness. She wondered for a moment if it was wise to spend the night here after all, out in the open, unprotected. But then, what else could she do? Walk all night?

When she had finished chewing on the dried meat, she took a drink of spring water from the stoppered bottle she carried and tried to relax. Tension lingered in her body; her muscles were tight and beginning to ache. She huffed out an exasperated breath. Sleep would not come until she had investigated this unrest.

Mairead sat cross-legged, arms resting on her thighs, and closed her eyes. She took several deep breaths, drawing the cool, late-summer evening air into her lungs, pulling it down, down, down, picturing the lightness of the breeze filling her extremities, connecting her to all who breathed this same air. The breeze rippled her hair, lifting stray strands away from her face and neck. As she breathed in and out, in and out, she sent a part of her awareness to drift with the breeze, just as part of the wind joined with her, in her lungs, in her blood. Mairead relaxed her grasp on that piece of herself, allowing it to float on the eddies of the air, to drift up and away from where she sat in the heather. Her internal vision doubled, and all at once she could see both the swirl of colors playing across the backs of her eyelids as well as the top of her own head, as if looking down upon herself from above.

She let the currents in the air carry her away, as she looked out over the land, seeking the source of her discomfort. The wind carried her to the north, soaring over mountains and drifting over forests. Badgers moved below, snuffling about on their own secret business. For a time, an owl soared alongside her, wings spread as it effortlessly rode the currents in search of food. It wasn't long before it spotted something below and plummeted. She passed over crofts with firelight coming from inside, and others with no signs of life.

Nothing she saw shed any light on the feeling of tension and danger in the air, until she was blown a little more to the west, passing over a low range of hills to expose a steep-sided valley, where a small group of tents sat on the bank of the river, with men and campfires all around. On the edges of the group, men lay wrapped in their plaids, sleeping, or trying to, while others ate and chatted by the fires. Out in the darkness, Mairead sensed the alert minds of guards, patrolling the valley and watching the hills. Above the central tent flew the royal standard of the House of Stuart.

Mairead gasped, and her awareness snapped back into her body, where she waited many miles away. She scrambled backward, for a moment worried that she had been discovered, the urge to flee shooting along her limbs. It was only when the rocks were against her back that she remembered all that happened and knew that she was safe. From the rebels, anyway.

Another uprising was underway. No wonder she had smelled blood on the air – plenty of it would be spilled in the days to come, and the land around here remembered the previous attempts to restore the Stuarts to the throne.

Her heart began to slow, her breathing becoming steadier as she accepted that the danger was far away. She would have to be sure to avoid them on the road, even if it meant taking a roundabout route to whatever was calling to her in the north-east. She took another piece of dried meat from her pack, and nibbled at it. The salty, smoky taste did as much as the act of eating to ground her back in her body.

Fatigue crashed down upon her, and she was reminded that traveling such as she had done was not without cost. Her limbs weighed twice as much as usual, and she had no sooner finished eating than tiredness overcame her. She curled up in the heather, pulled her shawl tight around her shoulders and was asleep within moments.

When she awoke, the moon was near the horizon, huge and orange, and for a moment she did not know where she was. Something small rustled in the heather near her head and she jerked upright, peering around with bleary eyes. Was that what had awoken her? A field mouse or shrew or something? Her head thudded sickly, as if there had been too much whisky before sleep, and her stomach churned. Aftereffects of the magic she had performed.

Just as she was about to lie down again, hopeful for some more sleep before dawn, a ball of light danced past the rocks she had curled up beside, first flitting one way and then the other. Mairead stared at it, trying to wake enough to process what she was seeing. At the center of the light was a flame, though it was attached to nothing that would burn. It was around the size of her thumb and seemed to move with intent, though what that intent was, she couldn't possibly begin to guess. It danced toward her and hovered a handspan from the tip of her nose, before bobbing off over the top of the rocks and across the expanse behind them toward a copse of pines.

Mairead rubbed her eyes hard and then opened them, blinking. The will-o'-the-wisp was still there, dancing around the edge of the trees, casting its light much farther than could be explained by its size.

"What do you want?" Mairead muttered, not expecting a response.

It danced back toward her, then went toward the trees once more.

Mairead shook her head, the deep ache making her feel weak. She began to lie down once more, then saw another ball of light, this one with a faint blue tinge, rather than the warmer, yellower glow of the first. The blue wisp darted across the road she had been walking and after the first one, toward the trees.

Mairead stared at them, her headache temporarily forgotten. She knew better than to follow a will-o'-the-wisp; there were more than enough tales of travelers being led astray into bogs or marshes, or worse, never to be seen again. The wisps were dangerous. Or at least they could be – like all fae, they were so far removed from humans and human concerns that they were unknowable. Whether it was through mischief or indifference, they had led many a person to their doom.

Of course, there were the other stories, far rarer, but told in awed whispers all the same. Stories of those who were brave and true, who had followed a wisp to their heart's desire. Mairead didn't know what her heart's desire was, but she doubted it could be found in a copse of pines on this lonely stretch of road.

As she watched, another wisp appeared and another, until there was a small group of them, dancing and twirling around the edges of the trees.

The faint sound of a clarsach carried across the night air, which had fallen unnaturally still. Mairead strained her ears to hear it, the music ethereal and haunting. The wisps paired off and began to dance together in elaborate moves that somehow echoed the longing of the music, the sense of yearning and hope.

Before she knew she had made a decision, Mairead was on her feet, stumbling toward the trees, drawn on by the music and the beauty of the wisps.

What are you doing, you fool? she admonished herself, but it made no difference; her body was responding to something more powerful than her own thoughts.

The wisps parted as she approached, seeming to usher her within the circle of the trees, where she staggered to a halt and fell to her knees. Before her, seated on a fallen tree trunk, with a clarsach between her thighs was the most beautiful woman Mairead had ever seen. Her skin glowed, casting a light all its own across the grass at her feet. Tattooed vines and flowers climbed from one foot and spiraled around her leg, only to disappear beneath the short slip that she wore. So much of her skin was bare, it was almost as if she were naked, so immodest was her dress. Her features seemed to shift and change so that Mairead couldn't quite capture her image, and some distant part of her mind thought that perhaps this was for the best.

Long, delicate fingers plucked the strings of the harp, pulling enchanting music into the air. The wisps danced, and Mairead's pulse danced in her throat in time with them. Something about the woman in front of her pulled at her senses in a similar manner to meeting another witch, but this was so much more powerful; it overwhelmed her natural reticence until all she wanted was to sit at the musician's feet until the end of time.

After moments or hours or centuries, the long, delicate fingers stilled, the strings allowed their notes to fall to silence, and the woman focused her gaze upon Mairead for the first time since she stepped between the trees.

"Well, hello there," the musician said, her voice as melodic as the harp she carefully placed on the ground by her feet. "Where did you come from?"

Mairead looked up at her, not quite able to meet her gaze. "I was sleeping, out near the road. But then I heard...you play *beautifully*."

The woman smiled and Mairead felt like her heart was going to stop in her chest, and dying at that moment would be fine with her. The wisps, which had been dancing around and between the trees, all began to settle on the branches, as if watching what would happen next.

"I'm sorry that I disturbed your rest."

Mairead shook her head. "Not at all. Sleep cannot compare with this."

The woman cocked her head to one side, studying Mairead. "You're one of mine, aren't you?"

"One of..." Mairead shook her head. "I don't understand."

"You are a witch, are you not? Born with a caul, I assume, since you would not be able to see me now, if you didn't have second sight."

Mairead could only stare at her, dumbfounded. Slowly, she nodded.

"I am Nicnevin," the woman said with a grin. "Queen of Witches."

Mairead sank forward into a bow, letting her forehead touch the grass at the fae queen's feet. *Nicnevin! Here, in front of me? Am I dreaming?* She surreptitiously pressed her hands into the ground, hard enough to feel the soil beneath the grass grind into the lines of her fingers. It certainly felt real.

"Rise," the musician, Nicnevin, said with a laughing lilt. "Can I assume you have heard of me?"

"Yes, my lady," Mairead said, eyes on the fae's feet.

"It probably wasn't *all* true." Nicnevin laughed. "Tell me, what brought you to be sleeping by the side of the road?"

"I'm simply traveling, my lady," Mairead said. "I realized that I wasn't going to reach the next town before night fell and decided that here was as good a spot as any to camp for the night."

"And where are you traveling to?" The strings of the clarsach shivered, as if Nicnevin had lightly run her fingers over them, though she had not moved.

Mairead thought for a moment of evading the question, but for all she knew the fae witch already knew the answer. Perhaps she was even the one who had called Mairead to the north-east in the first place.

"I do not know, my lady. I felt something, like someone reaching for me, from somewhere north-east of here. I was going to find out what it was."

A night bird twittered in the branches above and Nicnevin's gaze lifted, seeking it out. Mairead felt a weight lifted from her, though it was not entirely a feeling of relief.

"There is another like you, and not like you," Nicnevin said, still peering up toward the branches, and behind them the stars. "She is alone and in pain. I can feel her. I can feel all of you, when I try."

"All witches?" Mairead asked.

Nicnevin looked at her again and gave a solemn nod. "From the first time they use magic, knowingly or otherwise. There are fewer now than there once were."

"Because of the trials?" Mairead asked, fear of the answer weighing upon her shoulders.

"In part, though very few of the people who were killed in the trials were truly witches. Many of our kind went into hiding or found ways to disconnect themselves from their magic. The true legacy of the trials is the fear that they instilled in people who otherwise would have given little thought to witches. So many of our kind have been killed as children by parents who fear them."

Mairead's mind flashed to her father, to the lash of his belt and the burning fury that had built in her with his violence.

"I see you know something of that," Nicnevin said softly, her eyes searching Mairead's face. "I am sorry for your pain."

Mairead took a deep breath and forced her shoulders down and her neck straight, holding her head high. "It is in the past."

A red-tinted wisp floated down from its place amongst the branches and hovered between them, just in front of Mairead's face. It made a noise, a sound like the wind blowing through a hollow log, almost musical.

"Hold out your hand," Nicnevin said.

Mairead glanced away from the wisp to the fae queen.

"It wants to give you a blessing."

"A blessing?"

"It is quite safe, I assure you," Nicnevin said with a wry smile.

Mairead swallowed and looked back to the wisp, still hovering in front of her face. It made the same sound again and bobbed impatiently. Slowly, she lifted her right hand, palm upturned until it was just below the wisp. The wisp settled onto her palm, setting her skin atingle. The flame felt neither hot nor cold, but it made the skin of her arm rise into goosebumps, and a shiver wound down her spine, bringing cold prickles in its wake.

The wisp made the noise again, a series of notes this time that was almost a tune. Sparks flew from it to whirl around it before sinking into Mairead's hand. She felt them merging with her, the magic of them touching her own. Suddenly her heart was overflowing with gratitude though she had no idea what the wisp had actually done. She was surprised to feel tears escaping from her eyes and trickling down her cheeks.

"Thank you," she whispered, not sure what she was thanking it for.

The wisp hooted again then took off, flitting up into the air and disappearing beyond the trees.

"What was that all about?" she asked, looking back to Nicnevin, who was watching with a soft expression.

The fae shrugged. "It saw your pain and felt for you. What it gave you is between the two of you, but you'll know when the time is right. Perhaps that exchange is why you were drawn here tonight, why you discovered us."

Mairead frowned. "Wasn't I meant to?"

"Not specifically. I knew there was a witch nearby, but my presence was cloaked. Only one such as you, born under a caul, would be able to see through it. I was simply marking the full moon in the company of the wisps."

"I'm sorry for intruding," Mairead said, heat rising to her cheeks.

Nicnevin shook her head. "I am always pleased to meet one of my witches. And you are particularly…intriguing." She sighed. "I sense troubled times coming to these lands. I do not know what lies ahead, but I believe there will be upheaval for all. I cannot turn the tides of fate, but if there is some way that I can help those like us, know that you may call upon me."

"I don't—"

Before Mairead could finish, Nicnevin had disappeared, there one moment and gone the next, leaving no sign that she had ever been there. A delicate run of notes on the vanished clarsach shivered in the air and then was gone.

Chapter Four

Mairead

10th August 1745

As days of walking passed, Mairead's encounter with Nicnevin began to seem more and more like a dream – something that could not possibly have happened. She doubted her own memories and let the magic of it all fade.

The call from the north-east became a constant irritant against her skin, the need to get there as quickly as possible driving her to walk until exhaustion overcame her at the end of each day, until she could simply go no farther, before sleeping like the dead, and waking to do it all again the next day.

On the fifth day after she met – dreamed? – Nicnevin, she rounded a bend in the rutted cart track she was following and stumbled to a halt. Filling the path ahead of her was a band of men, all armed, mostly with farming implements, though some few had swords, and all wore wicked-looking daggers at their belts. Their leader stopped in the middle of the track and raised his hand, signaling for those behind to stop.

"What have we here?" he asked in Gáidhlig.

"Just a traveler," Mairead answered, in his own language.

"Well, she's a Highlander, at least," the man next to him said in a low voice.

"Where are you traveling to?" the leader said, studying Mairead carefully.

She was glad of her travel-worn clothing and less than tidy appearance. "I'm looking for work," she said, trying to figure out the safest story to tell these men. Would thinking she was a widow make them feel sorry for her and let her pass? Or make them see her as prey?

"You're just wandering the Highlands alone, looking for work?" the leader said, a mocking tone to his voice. "I suppose it's just coincidence that you decided to explore just at this particular moment in time? Who are you reporting back to?"

Mairead let her shoulders drop forward, pulling herself in upon herself to look smaller. "I don't know what you're talking about," she said, allowing a tremor to sound beneath her words. "I don't report to anyone. I don't know anything about anything. I just—" she let a small sob hitch her words, "—I just needed to be somewhere else for a while. Please don't hurt me."

The leader continued to look at her with suspicion, but the man at his side softened and stepped forward.

"Don't worry, lass, we'll not see any harm done to you." He moved to her side and placed a heavy hand on her shoulder.

Mairead thought it was part attempt at comfort, and part ensuring that she did not attempt to escape.

"Tell us who you are and how you came to be here," said the leader, "and if you tell us the truth, we'll let you be on your way."

And how will you know if I don't? Mairead thought but did not say. She had to hide the steel in her heart beneath the softness they expected to see.

Mairead covered her face and began to cry, allowing her grief for Old Callum to come to the surface, using it to give her performance a feeling of veracity.

"John, can ye no see ye're frightening the girl?" the man beside her said. "At least let her have a drink of water and a moment to calm herself."

The leader sighed. "Fine."

Mairead watched through her fingers as he turned to the men behind them and ordered them to keep watch – and their distance – while he and Iain found out what she knew. *So, the kind one is called Iain.*

Iain handed her a handkerchief, which she pressed to her eyes, noting the careful stitching around the edge. There was something in it…something familiar. Before she could figure out what it was, John, the leader of the group, thrust a waterskin at her and bid her drink.

"Now," he said, his voice soft but firm, "tell us who you are and how you came to be here. No more delays."

"My name is Mairead Ferguson," she began, handing back the waterskin, letting him see her hand tremble a little. "My husband died in the spring. I tried to keep going with the croft on my own but... everywhere I look there are reminders of him and it's...it's just too much. I miss him too much. So, I decided to go away for a while, find work and somewhere to stay for a time."

John studied her intently before glancing up at the overcast sky. Above them, gulls wheeled, calling to one another in their harsh voices. "You just abandoned your croft?" he asked without looking back at her.

Mairead shook her head, setting her plaited hair swinging against her back. "My husband's younger brother is looking after it. He'd been staying with us for a while before James..."

"What of your other kin?" John asked. "Why not go home to your parents or the like? Why seek out work where you don't know anyone?"

"I needed to be away," she said quietly. "I just want a fresh start, somewhere new, where I'm not surrounded by reminders of my husband dying slowly and in pain. Please, just let me pass."

John and Iain looked at each other, some unspoken communication passing between them. John glanced over his shoulder at the men behind him, some of whom were taking the opportunity to sit down or to eat and drink, while others were spread out, watching over the path in both directions.

Mairead counted thirty-two of them, including John and Iain, some of them scarce more than boys.

"Fine," John said at last with a sigh. "Though I'd not advise you to keep traipsing through the countryside at the moment. There may be other bands of men about, and I cannot say that they would all treat you right."

Mairead lowered her gaze in an effort not to roll her eyes. As if any woman needed warning that men might be dangerous! "I'll settle down as soon as I find somewhere that I can be of use," she said.

Iain cleared his throat. "Might be we can help with that," he said. "If you keep on this track a half day or so, you'll come to a stone cottage with a barn. Beyond that another half hour's walk, is Kilmartin village. They're like to need the help."

"Thank you," Mairead said, touched despite herself at this effort he was making to help, though she had no intention of stopping anywhere until she found the source of the call, the witch who needed her, if Nicnevin was to be believed.

She stepped forward, but John caught her arm, his fingertips digging painfully into her flesh.

"If we see you again, I shall not release you so easily," he said, his voice pitched low enough that she doubted anyone other than Iain could hear him. "Don't give me cause to name you a spy."

Mairead yanked her arm away, glaring at him. "I have no interest in who you are or where you go," she snapped. "I'll be sorry indeed if I see you again."

He clenched his jaw, and for a moment she could see his thoughts warring on his face, his desire to punish her for speaking to him so, against his desire to be on his way without further delay. His better nature – or the urgency of his business – won out and he snarled at her to be on her way.

Mairead tightened the wrap she had made from her cloak, nodded at Iain by way of farewell, and set off, moving past the rest of the group of men, avoiding eye contact with any of them. Her power churned inside her, making her blood and bones fizz and spit like fat on the fire. She kept tight control of it, determined not to allow any sign of it to escape, no matter how much she wanted to show that John just how little she thought of him.

She forced down the old, familiar frustration at having a power that should help her, keep her safe, yet so often limited her instead. Her magic would keep her safe from two or three people who meant her harm, but she couldn't defend herself from a group this size all at once, and if she showed any hint of being a witch, well, they would as like as not tell themselves they were justified in doing whatever they wished to her.

She was very aware of their presence at her back, like a weight against her senses, though she refused to look around. She would not give them that much power over her, to leave her cringing and fearful. She walked at a brisk and steady pace, head held high, and as the morning passed, her awareness of them lessened, eclipsed by the pull that she had been following for so many days.

She was drawing close to the source.

It added an urgency to her steps, pulling her on faster and faster, until she was holding her skirt out of the way as she ran. She rounded a bend and stumbled to a gasping halt as a stone cottage with separate barn appeared before her, just as Iain had described.

Standing between the two buildings was a woman with a bucket in one hand, while the other shaded her eyes as she gazed back at Mairead. She looked to be around the same age as Mairead, though she carried an air of responsibility and grief, which made her seem older.

Mairead could feel the power radiating from her even as they studied each other across the width of the yard. The hairs on her arms all stood on end, and she felt her own power surge in response. This was the witch she had been searching for.

She hesitated for a moment, unsure of the best approach to take. She had learned the hard way that the common ground of being a fellow witch was not always enough to make one welcome. Then she remembered the village that Iain had told her about.

"Excuse me," she called to the woman, who still stood with her bucket, staring back at Mairead. "Can you tell me if this is the right road for Kilmartin?"

The woman shook herself, set the bucket down at her feet, and moved closer to Mairead, though she still kept some distance between them. "Aye," she answered, wary. "It lies half an hour or so down that way. Visiting family, are you?"

"Looking for work," Mairead answered, keeping her voice light. "I met some men on the road, they suggested that there might be work to be found in the village."

"Did they now?" The woman studied her as if weighing her up. "What men were these?"

Mairead took a step closer, making sure not to move too suddenly. "There was a group of them, but I only got two names. John and Iain. It was Iain who suggested I might find work in the village."

The other woman heaved a sigh. "Of course it was." She glanced down the road in the direction of the village and then back at the cottage behind her.

Mairead followed her gaze and noticed for the first time that a crib woven from willow twigs was sitting on the ground outside the door to the house, with a pudgy baby arm waving around from within it.

"I was about to make some tea. Would you care to join me? I can tell you a little of what to expect from the village before you get there."

"That's very kind of you," Mairead said, "but I wouldn't want to be a bother."

"It seems only fair since my husband is the one who sent you here. Come on in," she said with a jerk of her head.

Mairead stepped over the boundary from the cart track she was following and onto the path, which led through a gate and onward to the door of the cottage. The woman turned and headed toward the house, speaking over her shoulder as she went.

"My name is Constance," she said. "Constance Gordon. Iain is my husband. I'm surprised he sent you here, just at the moment. Things are a little...unsettled."

"I think he took pity on me," Mairead said. "His friend John was not so kind."

Mairead's toe caught on a rock sticking out of the dirt of the yard and she stumbled forward, almost crashing into Constance, who turned and caught her arm to steady her. The touch sent waves of sensation crashing over Mairead, startling her for a moment. They stood close together, gazes locked, and Mairead felt her heart pounding at the base of her throat.

"I…uh, sorry. Thank you. I tripped."

Constance stared at her and the moment stretched out between them until the baby in the basket by the door began to cry. Constance jerked as if slapped and turned away. "I should have warned you, the ground is a little uneven here."

Mairead gave a quiet laugh. The ground was uneven, true enough, but she felt as if the whole world was tilting beneath her feet every time she looked at Constance. Was it only a case of her magic responding to that of the other woman? If her senses were anything to go by, Constance was the most powerful witch she had ever encountered.

They made it to the door without further incident, and Constance scooped up the basket with the baby inside and led the way through the door and into the interior of the cottage. Inside, Mairead found herself standing in a large room with a hearth at one end, with chairs on either side. Close by was a large table with more chairs, and early preparations for a meal. On one side of the hearth, the wall was lined by a large dresser filled with the items needed to feed a family. On the other side, a door led to another room.

On the floor, in front of the table, two children were playing with a stack of wooden blocks, the older one building a tower, which the younger child then took great delight in knocking down. Constance set the basket down close to the other children then set about heating water for tea.

"Can I help with anything?" Mairead asked, feeling out of place and awkward in a way she rarely did when arriving somewhere new.

The baby began to fuss, and Constance sighed. "Don't suppose you've any interest in changing his clout while I sort the tea?"

This was something of a test, Mairead realized. Did Mairead really want to help or was she just being polite? Would she help if it meant getting her hands dirty with the kind of chore that few people wished to do? Was she someone who could be of use in a village such as Kilmartin, or did she think herself above the tasks that keep a household – and a village – running?

"Of course," she said with a smile. She went to the basket and lifted the baby, settling him in the crook of her arm. "You're a bonnie lad, aren't you? Shall we get you clean and dry?"

"Thank you," Constance said. She gestured to shelves lining the wall behind Mairead. "You'll find a basket over there with fresh clouts and in the smallest pot by the hearth there's warm water and a cloth for cleaning him."

The older of the two girls playing on the floor was now staring shyly at Mairead. "Mama, who's this?"

Constance looked at Mairead and quirked an eyebrow. Mairead suddenly remembered that she hadn't given her name. Heat rushed to her cheeks.

"I'm Mistress Ferguson," she said, smiling at the child before looking up to Constance. "Mairead Ferguson. I'm pleased to make your acquaintance."

Their eyes met and Mairead felt pinned to the spot by Constance's gaze. She had to wrench herself away, to turn to the shelves and seek out the clouts for the baby. He wriggled and fussed in her arms, a comforting weight, grounding her to the reality around her and not the magnetic pull of Constance's eyes.

She busied herself changing the baby, talking to him in a soft voice. She watched Constance from the corner of her eye as the other woman stoked the fire to heat water and then added dried herbs to a teapot. The older child was staying close to her mother now, while the middle one continued to play with the wooden blocks, banging them together and singing a nonsense song.

When the tea was served and the two women settled at the table, Constance took the baby and began to feed him. "You said you were looking for work? What kind?"

"Well, I grew up on a croft, I've some knowledge of healing and birthing, I've been a housekeeper and a seamstress. I can turn my hand to most things and what I don't know, I learn quickly." Mairead rested her elbows on the table and leaned forward. "Would you know of a position that might suit?"

Constance studied her for a moment until the fire popped and the baby twitched before beginning to wail. Mairead waited as his mother soothed and settled him.

"You'll not find much coin to spare around here," Constance said, reaching for her tea and carefully sipping it while trying not to hold the cup over the baby's head. "We're a small village without much outside trade."

"I'd work for room and board," Mairead said quickly. "I've not much use for coin myself. More often than not, I trade for what I need."

Constance was quiet again, seemingly trying to reach a decision about something. At last, she said, "Go on into the village tonight. We don't have an inn – not enough travelers passing through – but if you call at the house with the blue door and tell them Mistress Gordon sent you, they'll give you a bed and a meal for the night. Come back and see me in the morn, and we'll talk some more."

"I will, thank you." Mairead drank the last of her tea and then stood. "Is there anything I can do for you before I go? To repay you for the tea?"

"The company was payment enough. I'll be seeing you tomorrow then."

Chapter Five

Constance

11th August 1745

Constance was up with the dawn and bustling around the cottage, cleaning and preparing food for the children, trying to get as much as she could done before they woke. Her stomach was aflutter with anticipation, and she didn't know why. Or at least she tried to tell herself she didn't.

Another witch! At least, she thought that's what she had felt when she met Mairead the day before, but other than her grandmother, she had never known another, and Grandma had died when she was a bairn. There was definitely something there though, that feeling like lightning was in the air whenever she looked at the other woman. She could ask her…or maybe not. If she was wrong, if Mairead was not like her at all, she could be inviting trouble down on herself.

She could hear her mother's voice in her head. *Keep quiet. Keep small. Go beneath notice. That's how you stay safe.*

She had been making herself small her whole life. She couldn't risk it all now, just because she thought she might finally find a friend. Someone she could be herself around.

What if she doesn't come back?

The thought stopped her in her tracks, leaving her standing still, spoon poised to stir the porridge. Surely, Mairead would come back. Wouldn't she? Constance replayed their conversation in her head. She had certainly suggested that she would have some work for Mairead, or would at least help her find some, but maybe she should have been clearer, maybe she should have just made the offer outright then and there. But she had wanted to have some time to think it over. She hated making decisions on the spur of the moment.

She had thought about it all evening and long into the night, but no matter which way she turned it, it seemed that Mairead was an answer to her problems, witch or not. If she was willing to work for room and board, and she had grown up on a croft, then she should be able to help with some of the jobs that Iain had abandoned while he went off to play at rebellion. And if she also proved to be pleasant company, all the better.

"Mama," Janey said, stumbling into the room on sleep-clumsy legs. "Birdies noisy."

"Yes, they are, aren't they?" Constance scooped her daughter into her arms and gave her a quick but heartfelt hug before depositing her at the table. "What do you think they're saying to each other?"

"Hmmm." Janey put her chin in her hands and looked deep in thought. "They say, 'where worm, me hungy'."

"I'm glad we don't have to eat worms for breakfast," Elspeth said, coming to sit beside her sister at the table. "They're all wiggly and slimy."

"Oh dear, I was planning to make worm stew for dinner," Constance said, shaking her head. "I suppose I'll have to think of something else now."

She spooned porridge into bowls while the girls giggled and came up with different ways to eat worms. In these quiet moments with the children, she almost forgot about Mairead and all of the possibilities she seemed to promise. Almost.

After they had all eaten and washed and dressed, Constance wrapped Simon to her chest with a shawl, handed Janey a basket of wooden pegs, and carried the laundry on her hip out into the yard. She told herself that she was not waiting for Mairead, choosing to do chores close to the house, where she could watch the road, that it made sense to hang the washing early and check on the cattle later. Elspeth had taken a bucket of scraps to feed the goats and chickens, and the cattle could fend for themselves for the time being.

Constance set the basket down on a stool that she kept near the line to make it easier to hang the washing with Simon strapped to her. She lifted the first item out only to turn and see Mairead standing at the gate, as if by magic. Constance had seen no sign of her on the road when she had stepped out of the house. Not that she had been looking, of course.

"*Madainn mhath*," Mairead said with a shy smile. "May I come in?"

"Of course," Constance answered, feeling heat begin to work its way up her neck. "I didn't expect you so early."

Mairead glanced at the sky, which was a bright, crisp blue, the sun just beginning to warm the air. "I'm sorry, I can come back later if you like? I'm used to rising early, but I didn't think."

"No, not at all." Constance felt a tug on her skirt as Janey grabbed a handful of it and peeked out from behind her legs. "The children tend to make sure I rise early too. How did you get on in the village last night?"

Mairead grinned. "Mistress Croaker said to tell you that she'll have your kirtle ready by Sunday, if you wish to stop by for it after midday. She also said that she's not helpless and you should spend less time worrying about old women who know how to take care of themselves."

Constance snorted a laugh and lifted a hand to shield her eyes from the sun as she looked past Mairead in the direction of the village. "Her husband died this winter gone. Iain and I try to keep an eye on her, help with repairs and what have you."

Mairead glanced over her shoulder and then stepped into the yard. "She was very kind. And had the best rabbit stew I've ever eaten. Can I help with the laundry?"

"I'll manage, thank you." With a flick of her head, Constance indicated over her shoulder to the house. "Why don't you set your belongings down inside for the moment, while we talk?"

Mairead gave her a searching look and Constance had to use all the stillness she had learned in her life not to crumple under that gaze. Something about the other woman made the breath catch in her chest. *Send her away. It's too dangerous to keep her close. She can see too much of you.*

Before the thoughts could force words from her mouth, Mairead broke eye contact and turned to the house. Air rushed back into Constance's lungs and suddenly she was aware once more of the sun upon her skin, the weight of Simon wrapped against her chest, birdsong mixed with the noises of the livestock, the faint scent of the lemon balm she mixed into the soap from the washing she was hanging. She shook her head, chasing the thoughts away. There was nothing dangerous here, just an offer of help that she could scarce afford to refuse.

Mairead returned after only a moment, but the respite had been enough for Constance to gather herself. Mostly. She was careful to keep her focus on the washing she was hanging as a way to avoid looking at Mairead.

"As you saw on the road here, my husband and most of the men from the village have gone…traveling…for a time. I don't know when they'll be back." *Or how many of them will make it back.* "But there's a harvest to be brought in and a village to prepare for the winter and there are not enough capable hands to do the work. You said yesterday that you were willing to work for room and board. Is that still the case?"

Constance glanced at Mairead but carefully avoided meeting her eyes.

"It is. I can sleep in a barn or outbuilding if that's easier." Mairead spoke with a gentle lilt, her accent not pinpointing her roots.

"That won't be necessary." Constance turned back to the washing, only to see that she had already hung everything. Janey had wandered a few feet away and was crouching, drawing shapes in the dirt with a stick, and she could hear Elspeth laughing from somewhere on the other side of the house. "My husband has the largest holding in the area – we're responsible for producing a significant amount of the food needed by the village, and I take that responsibility seriously. If you're willing to help me ensure that everyone here eats this winter, I will gladly give you space to sleep in my home."

"I would be pleased to help." Mairead dipped her head in a gesture of respect, which made Constance uncomfortable. "Where would you like me to start?"

Constance spent the rest of the morning giving Mairead a tour of the property, explaining where things were kept and what the routines of the holding were. The children followed them around, watching Mairead and pointing out important matters like a line of ants on the ground, or the gate that they were not allowed to climb on, or the funny noises the goats made. Constance found herself caught between being frustrated with the constant interruptions and charmed by the details that her daughters considered important. Mairead treated each thing pointed out by the children with the same gravity she showed Constance, displaying not a hint of impatience. Constance took the opportunity to study the other woman's face as she crouched beside Janey and Elspeth to look at a scattering of small flowers growing around the base of a fence post.

Either Mairead was very good at hiding her true feelings, or she actually enjoyed the children's company. Constance could not yet decide which it was, but she knew which one she hoped for. Mairead was an enigma. She wore simple but well-made clothing and had none of the hungry look of someone who has fallen on hard times. She seemed to take in everything that Constance told her, asked pertinent questions, showing her understanding of what needed done, and carried herself with a confidence that suggested whatever her needs were, she could meet them on her own terms. She bore little in common with the occasional travelers and itinerant workers who had passed through Kilmartin before.

So what had brought her here?

"Forgive me for asking," Constance said as they made their way back in the direction of the house. "It's not common to see women traveling alone the way that you are. How did you come to be here?"

Mairead looked at her for a moment and seemed reluctant to answer. Concern prickled up Constance's back, warning her that something here wasn't right.

Mairead sighed then said, "My husband died. It wasn't quick. I needed to be somewhere else, somewhere that I wasn't surrounded by memories."

"What about your family?" Constance asked, thinking of her own mother. They didn't always see eye to eye, but if anything ever happened to Iain, she knew that her mother would be there to help her through it all.

Mairead pressed her lips tight and shook her head.

"I'm sorry for your loss," Constance said softly, glancing at the other woman and wondering how much of a loss it really was. There seemed nothing to disbelieve about Mairead's story, but still some instinct niggled at her, telling her there was more here than she was being told.

In the days that followed, the two women settled into an easy rhythm, finding that they worked well together. Mairead took on any chore asked of her and several that weren't, and she did each one to a high standard. Her patience and enthusiasm with the children never waned and Constance decided that she didn't care what the full story behind Mairead's journey was; she was just very glad to have her around.

In the evening, when the work was done, they would sit by the fire together, talking quietly or sometimes just watching the flames in companionable silence. Constance had grown more certain that Mairead was like her, that she had magic of her own, but she had no idea how to bring it up – or even whether or not she should. If her instincts were wrong, she would be risking exposure. And even if she was right, Mairead might not know about her powers, or she might hate and fear them, thinking they were evil as so many would have them believe. And even if Mairead knew all about her powers and was happy and comfortable talking about it with Constance, she still might betray Constance at a later date. Just because there hadn't been a trial in years, didn't mean there would never be another.

And yet, despite knowing all of that, the pull to tell her was strong. The chance, however small, that she might finally have someone in her life that she could be entirely herself with filled her with a yearning she had long since thought abandoned.

Proclamation

On this day of 19th August 1745 I, Prince Charles Edward Louis Philip Casimir Stuart, do raise my father's standard at Glenfinnan in Scotland. I assert before God that my father, James Francis Edward Stuart, is the rightful king of these lands, as chosen by God himself and confirmed by Pope Clement XI, God's voice on Earth.

I call upon all faithful and true subjects of the crown to join me in removing the Hanoverian Pretender to the throne, and restoring my father, King James III and VIII.

None of my father's subjects need fear retribution for what has been done by necessity in his absence and only those who stand against us now shall know our enmity.

Chapter Six

Mairead

26th August 1745

Two weeks had passed since Mairead moved into Constance's home and she was surprised by how comfortable she had become. The children were a regular source of delight, the two girls both intelligent and kind-hearted and the baby full of wonder and play. That day had dawned clear and bright, a break from the drizzle that had persisted for the last few days, and over breakfast Constance announced that they would be making a trip to the village as soon as the morning chores were complete. There was food to deliver and supplies to be traded for.

"I thought we could all go," Constance said as she broke a piece of bannock off and handed it to Simon, who was sitting on her knee, grabbing at everything within reach. "It's a challenge to keep the children occupied while also making sure everything gets to where it should be and we get everything we need, all by myself. And it would give you a chance to meet some people. Get to know the village."

Mairead smiled, watching the baby mash the bannock with his hard little gums. "That sounds good."

While Mairead tidied away the breakfast things and fed the animals, Constance gathered everything they needed for the day and got the children ready. They met in the yard outside the house an hour later. Constance was standing by the side of a small cart, hitched to the shaggy pony that usually wandered the fields with the cattle. Elspeth and Janey sat amongst the sacks and baskets loaded into the cart, while Simon dozed contentedly, wrapped in a shawl and tied to his mother's chest.

Constance turned to look at Mairead as she came around the side of the house and smiled at her. Her face lit up. The warm August light caught the lighter, golden strands of her hair, making them seem to glow. Her hazel eyes were almost green in the sunlight and for a moment Mairead drew up, struck for the first time by the thought that Constance was beautiful.

"Ready?" Constance asked, quirking an eyebrow.

Mairead could only nod, flustered as she was by the sudden realization that more than their shared magic might be drawing her to the other woman.

They set off, walking along the track to the village side by side, Constance leading the pony. "He can probably pull us all, even with the full load," she said, glancing at Mairead. "But it's a pleasant day to walk, and this way we can save his strength for the journey home."

"I like to walk," Mairead said. "There's something freeing about knowing that your own two feet can take you anywhere you might care to go."

"Did you walk all the way here?" Constance asked. "From...?"

"From home," Mairead said, neatly sidestepping the question of where she came from. "I did, yes, so half an hour to the village is no challenge at all. How many people live in Kilmartin? I didn't get much sense of the size of it when I visited before."

Constance tipped her head to the side, seemingly in thought. "There are about twenty families in the village itself and about the same again scattered around the outskirts. We've no inn, and no church or school since the minister died and no one came to replace him. We do have a farrier, who'll do some other blacksmithing if you ask him kindly, though he'll grumble about it. We have a healer whom you'll likely meet today, and Mistress Croaker is our seamstress. She oversees the making of tweed as well, though I doubt we'll have the time for that this year. Not until winter is upon us, at least."

Mairead watched as worry descended over Constance's face. They hadn't spoken much of the fact that the local men had all 'gone traveling'. Mairead thought it likely that the group she had met on the road were on their way to join the Bonnie Prince and his uprising, though she supposed it was possible they were on the other side of things. Either way, it seemed unlikely that they would return soon – unless the rebellion was quashed early, but if that were the case then likely many of them wouldn't return at all.

"Where do you get supplies from?" Mairead asked in an effort to pull the other woman's thoughts away from her worries.

Constance glanced over and gave her a slight smile that suggested she knew exactly what was going on. "We grow, mend and make most of what we need here, and we all work together to look after each other. A couple of times a year, the farrier or the healer will travel to Inverness to get supplies that they need. Sometimes people will go with them, but both of them are usually willing to take coin and collect things people might need. And there are a few pedlars make a point of passing through."

"Are there many horses in the village?" Mairead asked, looking down at the rutted dirt road beneath her feet. The grass in the center grew high and the bushes and undergrowth on either side encroached upon the path. This was not a road that saw a great deal of traffic, especially wagons.

"Not too many. A few ponies, like Angus here."

"But you have a farrier?"

Constance chuckled. "I'm so used to having him now, I forget that it's unusual. Mr. Calhoun is Irish. He came to Scotland in '15, a young lad, planning to join the uprising. By the time he got here though, the rebellion had been put down. He met some Gordons and ended up working for the duke and his brother, and he still does. He used to live closer to Gordon Castle but then he met his wife at a dance in Inverness. She grew up here and didn't want to leave, so he came to her. He visits the castle once a month to check on the horses and Fyvie Castle every three months or so. And of course, sometimes he gets called away in between times."

"He must be a skilled farrier if they have him travel rather than use someone closer," Mairead said, ducking her head slightly as she passed beneath an overhanging branch.

"He's good with horses and reasonably so with people. I'd guess there's more to it than that, but it's not my place to pry if he doesn't want to make his business known."

Mairead looked at Constance and raised an eyebrow. "That's an unusual position to hold, especially from someone who obviously feels an obligation to the people in the village."

Constance met her gaze briefly before looking away, a tight smile on her face. "We all have parts of ourselves and our lives we'd rather keep private. I simply extend others the same courtesy I would hope to receive."

This was obviously a sore point – Constance's manner had changed completely, as she took on a more distant air than she had maintained since that first day they had met. Mairead wondered if the part of herself that the other woman kept private was her magic, or if there was more to it than that. The air had thickened between them and try as she might to think of another conversational gambit, she could not quite break the silence. Every comment she thought to make or question she thought to ask curdled in her mouth before it had a chance to escape.

They walked on in strained silence until Elspeth asked for a story. Glad of the opportunity to shatter the awkwardness that had developed, Mairead launched into a story about a lonely little robin who made friends with a squirrel.

By the time they reached the village, the odd tension between them had dissipated, and both Mairead and Constance were laughing as the story Mairead was telling grew more and more outlandish, with Elspeth and Janey shouting out suggestions for how it should continue. The dirt road they had followed here continued right through the middle of the village, which was formed mostly of terraced stone cottages with thatched roofs. Each had some garden space with vegetable beds growing neatly, while a few chickens and goats wandered free.

At the far end of the main part of the village there was a larger stone house with a smithy attached, open at the front with the forge on display. On the opposite side of the road there was a large timber building, which looked newer than the rest of the buildings Mairead had seen in the area but somehow looked forlorn and empty.

"Is that the church?" she asked, pointing to it.

Constance looked at the building, which stood almost twice as high as the stone cottages that lined the road. "Aye, it is. It served as the schoolhouse too; the old minister taught the local children their letters and sums, at least enough of both so that they could run a household and read the Bible. He was a kind man."

"When did he pass?" Mairead asked.

"Two years ago." Constance reached out to help first Elspeth then Janey down from the cart. "Mistress Croaker found him, collapsed at the altar, when she went in to pray one morning. Best we could tell, his heart had given out the night before."

"What a pity," Mairead said, her voice soft. "And he was never replaced?"

Constance shook her head. "We informed the presbytery of course, and they said they would send someone to take over the parish, but they never did. I suppose we're just too small a community to matter. The church elders hold services most weeks, and there's a traveling minister who stops by a few times a year, performs weddings and christenings. We generally take care of burials ourselves." Constance shrugged. "It's not ideal, but we do what we can. And they do say that God helps those who help themselves."

Mairead turned to see a woman with bright red hair, partially covered by a cloth cap, walking toward them, a small boy toddling along at her side and holding onto her skirt.

"Good day to you, Constance. How are you and your delightful children?"

Constance set her shoulders and fixed a smile to her face. "Good day, Roisin. We're well, thank you, and you? Samuel seems to be bigger every time I see him."

Roisin laughed. "I swear he grows every time I look away. Thank the Lord for Mistress Croaker helping out, or I would never be able to make him clothes quickly enough to keep up with him."

Mairead looked down at the child, presumably Samuel, who wore well-made wool trousers and a linen shirt, smarter and more expensive than anything she would expect to see on such a young child in a simple farming village like this. He looked more like a laird's son. She glanced over at Elspeth and Janey, who were both wearing simple wool smocks, despite the fact their parents were likely higher up the social hierarchy than any other families around here.

"I see you have a friend visiting?" Roisin said, looking pointedly at Mairead.

"Oh dear, where are my manners? Roisin Murphy, this is Mairead Ferguson." Constance glanced at Mairead. "Mistress Ferguson is a relative of my husband's. She's staying with us for a time."

"It's a pleasure to meet you, Mistress Murphy," Mairead said, lying through her teeth. Something about Roisin got her hackles up and while she might have no reason to dislike her as of yet, she had no doubt that something would come to light sooner or later. Her instincts were rarely wrong.

"How lovely. Is your husband traveling with you, Mistress Ferguson?" Roisin asked, reaching down to rest her hand on her son's head.

"My husband passed away recently," Mairead said, looking away.

"Oh, I'm so sorry for your loss." Roisin did actually seem flustered, Mairead had to give her that much. "Are you…do you have children?"

Mairead pressed her lips together and shook her head. She could sense Roisin struggling to think of the right thing to say and felt a momentary flash of guilt, as she always did when it came to lying about this. She had never grown comfortable with it, though the need for such deception remained.

"We've brought plenty of onions and carrots, if you're needing any," Constance said, breaking the awkwardness. "Oats, eggs and butter too."

"I can give you two good-sized trout for some eggs. Fergus caught them yesterday, nice and fresh."

Mairead crouched to talk to the children while Constance and Roisin bartered. She should probably pay attention, get more of a sense of what items were given value here, but her skin was prickling with discomfort and something, some sense of danger, was pulling at her attention. While she chatted with Elspeth and Janey, she scanned the village, looking for some hint of what was making her so uncomfortable.

The sensation reminded her of when she had been on the road, that same night she encountered Nicnevin, when she had traveled with the wind and learned of the arrival of the Stuart forces. But it couldn't be anything to do with them; they were miles and days from here and had no logical reason to travel in this direction. Janey was saying something that Mairead had missed the start of.

"Hmm?" she said absently, stretching her senses as far as she could. She could find nothing to explain her sudden discomfort, but felt a sense of capable calm wash over her as Mistress Croaker approached the cart, a broad smile lighting her face.

Mairead allowed herself to be distracted and soothed by the other woman's arrival, noting quickly how happy and comfortable the children were in her presence. As they chatted, more people came out and gathered around the wagon, some carrying baskets or cloth bags of things they were hoping to exchange for the supplies that Constance had brought, while others seemed to be just taking advantage of the opportunity to catch up with their friends and neighbors.

As Mairead allowed her gaze to drift over the gathered villagers, she noted that there were only two men in the group – one who looked eighty if he was a day, and the other a middle-aged man who walked with a limp and had one arm strapped to his side. He hoisted young Samuel up with his good arm, talking quietly with Roisin. There didn't appear to be any boys over the age of twelve or so. It seemed that the band she had met traveling really were the majority of the men and older boys from the village. No wonder Constance was worried about how they were going to get the harvest in, not to mention the rest of the work that needed to be done before winter.

"What have we here?" A harsh voice rang out, cutting through the babble and drawing everyone up short. Three men stood across the cart track leading back toward the Gordon cottage. All three looked disheveled and unkempt, carrying a suggestion of lawlessness, and the middle figure, the older of the three, carried a gun, which he swung by his side in such a way as to draw the eye, without quite pointing it at anyone.

"Is it market day?" he asked, seemingly sure that he now had everyone's attention.

The man standing with Roisin handed her son to her and stepped forward. "Can we help you gentlemen with anything?" he asked, his voice gruff, but his tone polite.

Mairead looked around the crowd; everyone seemed on edge, but no one was outright fearful. Mistress Croaker gently pushed Janey and Elspeth behind her so that her body was between them and the strangers, while Constance gave her a worried look.

"We're with the Black Watch," the apparent leader of the strangers said. "On our way to meet up with the rest of our company, but we thought to stop the night somewhere, have a hot meal and a warm bed."

"I'm afraid we've no inn here," the village man said. "What direction are you headed? Might be we know of somewhere on your route that would better suit your needs."

The stranger glanced at his companions before answering. "We don't feel much like continuing our journey today. I'm sure what hospitality you have here will be enough for us."

The village man gestured with his free arm. "You can see we've little enough to share here, with only a space on the church floor for you to sleep. Surely you'd be more comfortable pressing on to somewhere larger, with an inn?"

"Looks to me that you could do with a few extra men around the place," said the younger man to the left of the gun-wielding intruder. His face wore a definite leer. "Help you manage all these womenfolk."

The tension in the air increased, a few of the women letting out small gasps, or stepping back, hands raised to their chests.

"We're in need of no such thing. I believe it's time for you *gentlemen* to be on your way."

The gunman raised his rifle, pointing it directly at the village man. "Where are the rest of your men?"

"None of your business," he growled.

Before Mairead had even noticed her moving, Constance had stepped forward and laid a hand on his arm. "Peace, Fergus," she said in a soft voice, then louder, "Some of our men are out in the fields and with the sheep and what have you, seeing to chores outside the village. A number of them have gone to a cattle market and will be gone for a few days. So, you see, we are not short of men, they'll be with us again soon enough."

The gunman scratched his head and peered up at the sky, where a flock of birds wheeled overhead, calling to one another. One of the children in the village crowd was crying softly, an adult voice quietly soothing them. Mairead took hold of Elspeth's and Janey's hands and gently pulled them over to the cart.

"I'm not quite sure I believe you," the gunman said, finally looking back at Constance.

Mairead tensed. There were only three of them. She could probably disable them magically, but could she do it without everyone realizing what had happened? That they had a witch in their midst? She began to pull her magic into her hands, ready to act if necessary.

Constance put her hands on her hips, every inch the imposing lady of the area. "I'm not sure I care what you believe. You've come into our village, pointed your gun at us, demanded what we don't have to share, and then insulted us. Is this the behavior that's expected from men of the Black Watch? What would your commanding officer have to say about all of this?"

Dear Lord, what is she thinking, antagonizing them like that? Despite her fear, Mairead couldn't help but be a little impressed at the strength and fearlessness Constance displayed. She crouched beside Elspeth and Janey in the shadow of the cart, no longer able to see what was going on.

"I have a very important job for you two," she murmured, leaning in close to them. "Can you crawl beneath the cart and wait there until Mama or I tell you to come out?"

"Why is the man angry?" Janey asked, looking worriedly in the direction of where her mother stood, facing down the gunman.

"I don't know, petal, but don't you worry. I'm going to help Mama sort it all out. Now, you two crawl under there, all right?"

"Come on, Janey," Elspeth said, taking her sister's hand and pulling her to the ground. "Just like hide-and-seek."

"Good girls," Mairead said, a weight shifting from her shoulders. "Just like hide-and-seek. Remember to be nice and quiet."

With the children safely settled beneath the cart – except for Simon, who was still strapped to his mother's chest – Mairead began to edge her way around the outskirts of the crowd.

There seemed to have been some further exchange between the gunman and Constance as he was in the middle of an angry retort.

"...entirely the business of the Watch, if the men of this village are traitors to the crown, as I suspect."

"I have told you already where they are," Constance said, her voice growing strained.

"Well, then, if your story is true, then there should be no problem with us staying a few days. When they return from the...cattle market, was it?...then we'll be on our way and no harm done."

Mairead made it to the front of the crowd just in time to see the look of worry pass between Constance and the village man who had first spoken to the outsiders.

"Very well. Beds will be made up for you in the church, and we'll make sure an evening meal is brought to you there. There's a well behind the farrier's," she said, pointing. "You're welcome to draw water to refresh yourselves from your journey. Fergus, can you help our *guests* get settled?"

Fergus regarded the Watch men with a stony expression, then looked back at Constance and heaved a sigh. With a grunt and a jerk of his head he gestured for the three men to follow him, then turned and headed for the church.

Mairead moved straight to Constance's side. "Are you well? You handled that admirably."

Constance looked at her with fear written across her face, before visibly shaking it off and straightening her shoulders. "Where are the girls?"

"Under the cart. When he pointed the gun at Fergus, I thought it best to get them out of sight."

Constance let out a deep, shuddering breath and headed straight toward the cart. "Thank you."

Mairead followed in Constance's wake as she pushed through villagers who stood in worried huddles, and crouched beside the cart, her skirt trailing into a puddle. Simon stirred in his wrap and began to fuss as the girls crawled out from beneath the cart and into their mother's arms.

Mairead looked around and noticed that the village women were still milling around, seemingly waiting for someone to tell them what to do. No doubt that duty would fall to Constance. It seemed that a lot was falling to her in her husband's absence.

Mistress Croaker appeared at Mairead's side. "These men are trouble," she said in a low voice.

"Do you think they're truly with the Black Watch?" Mairead asked, watching as Constance stood and moved through the crowd, speaking softly, touching arms and backs with comforting pats.

Mistress Croaker shrugged. "It's not beyond the Watch to bully and threaten when they can get away with it. Equally, it wouldn't be the first time that some bad actors have pretended to an authority they do not hold in order to take advantage of folks." She sighed. "All that to say, I don't know. All remains possible."

Mairead thought hard. If the men, whoever they were, stayed together in the church building away from the eyes of the village, then perhaps she could do something to resolve this situation. But what?

It would have to be handled delicately; if they really were members of the Watch, then anything untoward happening to them might well bring scrutiny to the village that they could scarce afford. So, the men had to leave here, happy and well, and content that there was no reason for the Watch to pay any further visits. If, however, they were bandits masquerading as the Watch, they needed to be convinced that it would cause them too much trouble to try and take anything that wasn't given freely.

Short of all the village men coming home unexpectedly, she wasn't sure how either could be achieved.

She glanced over again at Constance, who was gazing worriedly at the church building, then turned to Mistress Croaker. "Let me fetch you some water from the well, while we're here."

"That's kind of you, Mistress Ferguson, but there's no need. Fergus brought me over a bucket this morning."

"Then it'll save you a trip tomorrow," Mairead said with a smile at the older woman. "As long as you have another bucket?"

Mistress Croaker sighed. "Well, if you're determined, I do, in fact. It's inside by the fire. I'll just have a quick word with Constance while you do that."

Mairead gently squeezed Mistress Croaker's forearm, and headed straight for her house, ducking under the low lintel and into the dim interior. She stood for a moment, allowing her eyes to adjust, surprised to notice just how much the noise from outside was dampened. In here, you could barely tell that half the village was assembled only feet away. The seamstress's house was more modest than the Gordon cottage. Mistress Croaker had only one room. A large table took up much of the space in the middle, fabric and sewing tools piled neatly on its surface and oil lanterns burning at either end. A neatly made bed was in one corner, the curtain around it drawn back to let air – and heat – move freely in the small room. On one side of the hearth was a dresser with crockery and cooking supplies and a wash bowl with matching ewer. Between the dresser and the hearth, Mairead spotted the bucket she had come in for. As she crossed the room to fetch it, she glanced at a pot with some porridge sitting beside the fire, no doubt left over from Mistress Croaker's breakfast.

She remembered Constance telling the men that an evening meal would be brought to them. *Could I cook for them and weave some magic into the food? Something that encourages them to leave and to forget all about us?*

She stepped back outside with the bucket, mind racing with thoughts of ingredients that might support such magic, lend their energy to hers.

"I was looking for you," Constance said, stepping in front of her. "I didn't know where you'd gone."

Mairead blinked, her thoughts pulled back to the present. "My apologies, I should have let you know. I'm just fetching some water for Mistress Croaker." Mairead looked straight at Constance, the sunlight falling upon her face. She looked anxious. Angry. Suspicious. "Should I not? Have I done something wrong?"

Constance sighed. "No. No, you haven't." She looked over her shoulder at the church, a haunted expression touching her eyes. "It's just that, between you and these men, we've seen more strangers in the village since Iain left than we have in the last six months. It worries me."

"Did you think I had gone to speak with them? Help them somehow?" Mairead was hurt. She had thought that there had been the beginnings of a bond between them, some trust that might have been the beginnings of a friendship. *Or something more.*

Annoyance flashed in Constance's eyes. "Can you blame me? Truly? You arrive here with no real explanation of why you would be traveling through here when the village is quite remote and lies on no major road, you tell me that you met my husband and the other men from the village on your way here, and two weeks later men claiming to be from the Black Watch appear and begin menacing us and demanding to know where all the men are. Can you truly tell me there is nothing suspicious about that chain of events?"

Mairead let her indignation ebb away. "Well. When you put it that way." She placed the bucket on the ground by her feet and straightened to look at Constance directly. "I am in no way involved with the men who have come here. And I do have an explanation for why I'm here, rather than any other place. But that is best kept for your ears only, I think."

Constance looked around and Mairead followed her gaze. Some of the village women had gone, presumably returned to their homes and the many tasks that no doubt required their attention. Others still lingered by the cart, perhaps waiting for Constance to carry out their trades, perhaps just waiting for advice, or some direction from her.

Beyond them, Fergus was leading the strangers into the church building, his posture tense with anger. The gunman swung his rifle at his side, his face smug as he cast a look back over the village.

"I might know a way to get them to leave," Mairead said, leaning toward Constance and speaking softly. "But I'll need you to trust me. And I'll need to trust you. Perhaps with my life."

Chapter Seven

Mairead

Mairead stood perfectly still, waiting, though her heart thundered in her chest. She hadn't really intended to say that, hadn't meant to put so much trust in Constance yet. But if not now, then when? If she was going to take a chance and share her magic with the other witch, then what better way to do so than in service of the village she so clearly cared for?

Constance broke eye contact first, looking over her shoulder to where the village women lingered by the cart. "I'll be back in a moment. Could someone keep an eye on the girls while I show Mistress Ferguson to the well?"

Elspeth and Janey were involved in some kind of energetic game with the other children from the village, something that involved lots of hopping and skipping and screeches of laughter. Mairead was pleased to see that they had all recovered quickly from any alarm over the Watch men and their gun.

"I'll watch them," Mistress Croaker said from where she stood chatting with a woman whose name Mairead did not yet know.

"Thank you," Constance said. "I won't be long." The other woman waved that off and Constance turned to Mairead. "Follow me."

Neither of them spoke as she led the way along the road and behind the farrier's house, to the side of a stone well, above which a metal pail hung from a simple pulley system.

Constance made a point of checking to make sure there was no one in hearing distance then stepped close to Mairead and said, "Very well then, tell me what you mean."

Mairead bit her lip and squeezed her hands together, willing them to stop trembling. "I think you and I have something in common," she began, keeping her voice low and looking off past Constance's shoulder, too anxious to say all of this while meeting her eyes. "Something that sets us apart from others. I have some small...abilities...that most people do not have. I think I may be able to use those abilities to find a solution to the problem of today's visitors. But it would be best done without the knowledge of the rest of the village."

"You speak in riddles," Constance snapped. "Be clear."

Mairead released a shaky sigh, then extended her hand in the direction of the well, without touching anything. She extended her will and focus until she could almost feel the rough fibers of the rope against the palm of her hand, feel the weight of the bucket rest upon the muscles of her arms, although her arm stopped a good foot short of where the rope hung.

Constance looked at the well and gasped as the bucket began to lower, seemingly of its own accord. Mairead searched the other woman's face for any signs that she was about to scream, or run, or lunge at her.

Constance turned back to face her, a brief flash of wonder and joy passing over her face before the mask of the person she had to be settled into place once more. The pull from her, which Mairead had followed all the way here, increased, almost driving Mairead to her knees. In that moment, she knew she would do almost anything for the woman standing in front of her.

"How do we get rid of them?" Constance said, focusing on the most pressing matter.

Mairead stepped closer to the well and took the rope in hand, drawing up a bucket full of water as she spoke. There was nothing to be gained by taking any further chances. "It's not certain that this will work, so be aware of that. I've never attempted a working quite like this before."

"Understood," Constance said, glancing back toward the road and making a *hurry up* gesture.

"I believe that if I cook their evening meal, with the right ingredients, I could weave enough of my will through it that it would make them...

pliant. Suggestible. Enough that they could then be persuaded to leave and not return."

Constance crossed her arms over her torso.

"In case you're worried, I swear to you upon my life that this is the first magic I have worked since arriving here, and I will never use my abilities to influence anyone from the village."

"I know," Constance said absently, looking away. "What do you need?"

Mairead transferred the water from the well bucket to the one she had carried from Mistress Croaker's home. "I'll need to gather some plants, if they grow around here, and then I need time and privacy to work. I'll also need help figuring out what to tell them so that they don't return."

"I'll take care of that. Give me a list of the plants you need, and I'll let you know whether they can be found locally. Now let's find you some space to work."

In the end, Mairead was able to gather all of the plants and herbs that she needed, and Constance gave her some salted meat and drippings to make a meal for the strangers. After that, Constance had explained to the villagers that they must be accommodating, following the requirements of hospitality as expected of all Highlanders, and give these men from the Watch no cause to doubt them.

Bridie, the woman who had watched the girls, offered to see to the supplies for the visitors, but was happy enough to offer her hearth to cook at instead after a quiet word from Constance.

As the sun sank toward the horizon, Mairead entered Bridie's home, while Constance worked to keep everyone busy, putting on an appearance of normality for their guests, who watched them from the church steps, with Fergus looming nearby.

Mairead hung a pot from the tripod over the hearth fire and added some water and the salted meat and drippings. As she cleaned and chopped the vegetables and herbs, she chanted over them, focusing her will into the food.

"My will is your will, hear me and obey."

As well as onions and carrots and some other roots, she added a handful of sloe berries, some crushed elderflowers, nettles, and dandelion leaf.

"My will is your will, hear me and obey."

All the ingredients added, Mairead pulled over a low three-legged stool and sat by the hearth, stirring the pot and pushing her magic into the meal. Doubt niggled at the back of her mind. She wasn't sure if she could make this work. Truth be told, she wasn't sure that she *should* make this work. Overriding someone's own will was a questionable thing to do… but then hadn't these men, with their gun and their claims of authority, chosen to override the will of the village by refusing to leave when asked? Was this magic really any worse than that? No one would be threatened or intimidated here, just gently encouraged to leave. Surely that was less harm in the world than would be caused by these men reporting the villagers as Jacobites?

Mairead shook her head, trying to shake the thoughts away. Now was not the time for doubt. She had to concentrate, or she would undermine the working herself. After a few deep breaths to center herself once more, she allowed the rhythm of her chanting and the stirring movement of the spoon to pull her into a state somewhere between sleeping and waking, where her access to her magic was at its strongest.

She had no idea how much time had passed before a knock at the door roused her, but the small house was filled with a mouth-watering smell from the food, and her own stomach growled loudly.

"Is the food ready?" Constance called from outside. "Our visitors are hungry."

"Yes. Yes, it's ready." Mairead looked down at the pot and hoped fervently that this would work. Then she wrapped some fabric around the handle and hoisted it from above the flames.

She carried the pot carefully outside, ducking beneath the lintel and climbing the two stone steps up to the road, Constance by her side.

"Are you sure about this?" Constance asked in a low voice, eyes trained on the church where the three men still sat on the steps.

"As sure as I can be." Mairead glanced at the other woman. "There's still time to change your mind. The food is only half of the spell."

Constance pressed her lips together at that word. *Spell.* It clearly made her uncomfortable. So even if she knew what she was – and Mairead couldn't imagine how she could possibly be unaware of the vast store of power that lay under her skin – then she can't have accepted that part of herself. But she hadn't run screaming from Mairead either. There had been no mention of the devil's work or any such nonsense, so Mairead still had hope.

"We must do what is necessary to protect the village."

"It would be best if we could get them inside," Mairead said, her breath beginning to show the strain of carrying the heavy iron cauldron. "Where we're less likely to be interrupted."

"Leave that part to me."

They left the road and crossed the low grass that lay in front of the church building. The sun was low in the sky and Mairead shivered as they moved into the shadow of the building, a feeling of foreboding crawling up her spine. She almost turned back then, almost told Constance that they could find another way, but the other woman was already speaking, and the plan was in motion.

"Gentlemen," Constance said as they reached the bottom of the stairs, "Mistress Ferguson here has made a lovely meal for you. If you'll step inside, there are dishes and cutlery in the cupboard at the back of the building, and I believe you may even find some wine left over from the last wedding celebration we held here."

The leader of the men looked at her with a lazy leer, and Mairead thought he would simply refuse to move and insist on being served out here. That wouldn't make things impossible, but it would certainly be more difficult. But then he got to his feet, slowly, making it clear that he was only moving because he had decided to and that he would do so in his own sweet time. He stretched, his shirt lifting to show a strip of pale skin and coarse dark hair on his belly.

"Seòras, Garett, you heard the lady. Let's go eat."

The two younger men scrambled to follow his lead, and Mairead let go of a pent-up breath as she and Constance followed them inside. Fergus moved to come along but Constance met his eyes and shook her head slightly. The village man frowned but held back as requested. *How is she going to explain that to him later?* Mairead wondered, glancing back at him before she crossed the threshold into the church.

As a child, after she was old enough to understand what she was, she had spent one long summer absolutely terrified of the church at home. Her parents' croft was a little too far out for regular worship, but her father always dragged them along for high days and holy days. Mairead had always dreaded it; he made her scrub until her skin was raw and wear her best dress and shoes that pinched, which he made her squash her feet into for two years after they stopped fitting.

The summer after he had taken his belt to her and she had sent it back at him threefold, he told her over and over that she was Satan's child and that God would strike her dead, that He would send her to Hell to burn for all eternity for her wickedness. He repeated these things so often that she started to believe him and got it into her head that the next time he dragged her to church, God would see her and set her on fire there and then. She had been almost catatonic with fear on All Saints' Day when her father forced her through the door to the stone building, with its angels and gargoyles looming down from the walls.

Of course nothing had happened, other than the boredom of sitting through the dour minister's sermon, uncomfortable in her itchy dress and too-small shoes.

Perhaps because it was built from wood, or perhaps because the overbearing presence of her father was absent, this church felt much lighter than any she had been in before. She could imagine this as a place of joy and peace where the community could come together to celebrate life. Candles had been lit in large stands placed in each corner of the room, giving a warm glow to the interior despite the lingering twilight outside. There was no hearth to warm the building, but it wasn't terribly cold at this time of year, and sleeping in here wrapped in a plaid would be comfortable enough.

Of course, if their plan worked, no one would be sleeping here tonight.

"Take a seat, and I'll fetch the bowls," Constance said, gesturing at a row of wooden chairs lining the walls.

Mairead walked after her. The muscles in her arms were beginning to ache, and her hands complained where a fold in the fabric wrapping the hot metal handle was digging into her fingers.

"You can set it down there," Constance said, laying her hand on top of the cupboard at the back of the room.

Mairead groaned as she hauled the cauldron up onto the cupboard, then let it go with a sigh and rubbed her hands together to ease the ache. She turned and almost tripped over the gunman, who had appeared right behind her.

"Aren't you a pretty little thing?" he said, grinning wide enough to display a few missing teeth and let her get a whiff of his reeking breath.

Mairead stepped back sharply and glared up at him.

"We are both married women," Constance said curtly. "And our husbands do not take kindly to other men sniffing around their wives."

"Well now, maybe your husbands shouldn't go off and leave you all alone, then."

"I will ask you to stand back once, sir, and if you fail to do so you will discover that he has not left me helpless."

The man looked from Constance to Mairead and leaned a little closer then sniffed in a great loud breath and turned away. "That dinner smells fine. I suggest you serve it before it gets cold."

With that, he wandered back over to where the younger two were watching, rapt expressions on their faces. Mairead's qualms about using her magic on these men reduced to all but nothing in light of their ill-mannered and threatening behavior.

She and Constance exchanged a look as the other woman took bowls and spoons from the cupboard, as well as a dusty bottle of wine. Mairead served a portion of the stew into each bowl, while Constance pulled the cork from the wine bottle, then they turned and walked side by side to the group of men.

They silently handed the food over, Mairead squashing down the urge to tip it into their laps. Instead, she concentrated on repeating her chant in her mind, pushing her will carefully toward the men.

My will is your will, hear and obey.

She felt it when the magic began to take root, when the men began to succumb to her will. It happened with one of the young ones first; he had shoveled his food down as if he hadn't eaten for a week, and as he sat the empty bowl on the chair beside him, his posture subtly changed, the line of his shoulders softened, the defiant jut of his jaw shifted. Mairead felt the thread that connected them settling into his mind. She waited patiently for the others to join him, keeping up the chant in her mind, letting Constance bustle around and talk and cover for her distraction.

It took only a few moments more for the other two to settle beneath her influence. Soon all three of the men sat still and quiet, waiting, peaceful.

"I hope you've figured out what to tell them," Mairead said softly, glancing at Constance.

"Just how much can you convince them of?" Constance asked.

Mairead shook her head. "I don't know. I've never tried anything like this before. It's probably safest to keep it simple."

Constance nodded, chewing at her lower lip. For a moment, she stood, gazing into space, then she nodded decisively, straightened her spine, and spoke. "Tell them that they're well-rested, that they slept the afternoon away and now they're eager to resume their journey. Tell them that they saw nothing of interest here, that it's no more than a few houses huddled together and not worth visiting again."

Mairead repeated all of that to the men, pushing her will into the words, *hear and obey* echoing in her thoughts. She felt the suggestions sink into the minds of the younger two, but there was some resistance from their leader, some part of him that pushed back against her influence. Mairead pushed a little harder, repeating the instructions with more of her will pressing behind her words.

This time, she felt the idea settle over the mind of the leader. Now she just had to persuade him that it was his own desire. But that might be better done indirectly.

She stepped back beside Constance and leaned in to murmur, "I think they're just about ready. When they start to seem a bit more alert, try to convince the leader to stay."

Constance gave her a sharp look. "But we want them to leave!"

Mairead nodded. "We need him to think it's his idea – and unless I'm wrong, he's the type of man who will not accept being corrected by a woman."

"Clever." Constance gave her an appraising look, as if seeing her in a new light.

They waited quietly while the men sat in trancelike peace, until suddenly the leader stood and looked around, blinking and confused.

Mairead nudged Constance, who stepped forward, wringing her hands as if worried. "Are you sure you want to leave tonight?" she said, injecting just a hint of dismissiveness into her tone.

The leader frowned and touched his forehead. "Is that what I said?"

"Well, yes," Constance continued. "But wouldn't it be more sensible to wait until the morning? I mean, there are all sorts of dangers around."

The gunman drew himself up to his full height and put on such a patronizing look that Mairead wanted to smack it right off his face. "Me and my boys are more than capable of taking care of ourselves. Gratifying though it may be to have you worrying your pretty little head over us, if I wanted advice from a woman, I'd have wed when my ma wanted me to."

Mairead gathered up the man's greatcoat from where it lay thrown across a few chairs. "Well, if you're certain, then we'll wish you a safe journey," she said, holding the coat out to him.

He stepped forward and took it from her, knocking over the wine bottle he had placed on the floor. It rolled across the floor, dribbling wine from the neck, until one of the younger men stooped and picked it up. He held it out to Constance with an apologetic look. Constance reached for it, but the leader grabbed it first, winked at her, then held it to his lips and tipped it up, gulping down whatever was left.

Mairead suppressed a shudder at the thought of guzzling wine down so quickly. *What a waste.*

The gunman handed the empty bottle to Constance with a smirk. "Don't suppose you've any more of that stuff lying around? It's not too bad at all."

Constance shook her head. "I'm afraid not."

There was a pause. The men just stood around, looking vaguely confused. Mairead could feel her influence over them beginning to wane and gave Constance an urgent look.

"Well then, if you're determined to be off, perhaps we could escort you to the edge of our land?" Constance said, hooking her arm through the gunman's after he slung his rifle over his shoulder by the strap. "My husband did tell me to be sure to make you welcome, after all."

"Your husband?" he asked, frowning. "That fella outside?"

What is she doing? Mairead started to panic. Persuading them to leave was one thing but convincing them of something that didn't happen was quite another. She wasn't sure her magic would stretch so far.

"You remember, you met him this morning, before he and some of the other men left for the cattle market?"

Then Mairead felt it, the subtle threads of Constance's magic adding to the weave of her own, strengthening it. It was both stronger and more delicate than Mairead's own efforts, so much so that she felt in awe of the other woman. And maybe a little envious.

"Oh yes, of course," the gunman said, shaking his head. "How could I forget?"

"I'm sure he would want me to make sure that you leave our lands safely and in good health. Shall we go?"

Mairead helped her to usher the men from the church, stepping out into the cool, lingering twilight. It was a pleasant evening, the sky clear, the warmth of the day still noticeable beneath their feet.

Fergus hurriedly got to his feet from where he had been sitting on the bottom of the stairs up to the church.

"Our guests wish to leave," Constance said to him, smiling though it did not reach her eyes. "We suggested it would be safer to stay the night, set out in the morning, but they're bound and determined. We've offered to see them to the edge of our land. Would you be so good as to accompany us?"

"Aye, of course, Mistress Gordon," Fergus said, looking both confused and relieved. "Which direction are you heading?"

The leader scratched his head. "I don't rightly recall," he said, frowning.

"Toward Inverness," one of his companions said. "We were to meet up with the rest of the company there."

Fergus nodded. "In that case, we'd be best heading out that way." He nodded over behind the church, out the other end of the village than the road to the Gordon farm. "We can take you overland to the main road to Inverness that way."

They set off. Constance kept up a steady flow of light chatter, laced with her magic, while Mairead spoke only when necessary, focusing on maintaining the flow of her will. By the time they had crossed over fields and a couple of small burns to reach the road, Mairead was nearing her limits. This had been one of the most sustained workings she had ever attempted, and while the magic expenditure wasn't huge, the constant trickle of will was exhausting her.

It was full dark when they saw the men from the Watch off, along the road to Inverness, though the moon was bright and stars filled the sky. Their distant light made it easy enough for travelers to follow the road.

Mairead, Constance and Fergus stood by the roadside, watching until the men were well on their way. Before they passed from sight, Mairead and Constance exchanged a glance, and both sent a push of will after the men, urging them to forget that the village existed and to feel no reason to return.

"How on God's good earth did you convince them to leave?" Fergus asked as they turned for home.

Constance shrugged. "We didn't. They just got it into their heads that it was time to be on their way, and we certainly weren't going to hold them back."

Fergus gave her a skeptical look but said nothing.

"In all the disturbance, I don't believe that I've introduced you. Fergus Murphy, this is Mairead Ferguson. Mistress Ferguson has come to stay with me while Iain and the others are gone. Mr. Murphy is Roisin's father-in-law."

"It's a pleasure to meet you," Mairead said, focusing more on where she was putting her feet than on the conversation. Fergus carried an oil lamp to light their path, but its glow only extended a short distance and traveling over uneven ground was still a challenge.

"The children are with Emily – Mistress Croaker," Constance said. "Hopefully they'll be asleep, and we can just lift them into the cart to go home."

"If the bairns are asleep, you're both welcome to spend the night in my house. I can sleep in the church easy enough, save you disturbing them," Fergus said. "They'll be needing their sleep after the excitement of the day, no doubt."

"They're not the only ones," Mairead said, then flushed when she realized that she had said it aloud.

Fergus laughed softly. "Dealing with the Black Watch is ever a draining experience."

Constance tutted. "We couldn't put you out of your own home. Mistress Ferguson and I can sleep in the church if we decide to stay in the village."

"Not at all," Fergus exclaimed, holding out a hand to first Constance and then Mairead to steady them as they stepped over a small, but lively, burn. "I won't hear of it. I'll be just fine in the church, wrapped in my plaid. You two stay warm in the house. Besides, that way you can have the bairns in with you, if they are still awake."

Mairead straightened up and looked in the direction she thought the village was in. "What's that?"

The others looked too. Fergus frowned. "Is that—"

"Fire," Constance said, dread suffusing her tone. "I think that's a fire."

They set off as fast as they could. The moonlight was not quite bright enough to make it safe to run over the uneven ground, even with the help of the oil lamp. The glow in the distance grew steadily closer, until they drew near enough to smell the smoke and hear the panicked cries coming from the village. Constance broke into a run, stumbling and crashing through a line of trees, before staggering to a stunned halt.

The church was on fire.

Villagers in their nightclothes were already forming into a line, passing buckets of water along from the well, throwing some at the church, while others were soaking the thatch of the nearest cottages.

The front portion of the wooden church building was aflame, the wood catching all the way around the door. The bucket line stopped at the bottom of the steps, and off to the side, Bridie was struggling. A person held each of her arms, while she strained against them trying to reach the building.

A wail warbled into the night air over the sound of the flames and Mairead's stomach dropped with dread, her hands going numb from the horror. There was someone in the building.

Bridie broke free from the people holding her back and bolted up the steps and through the flames into the building, seconds before a resounding crack sounded, as the lintel above the door gave way in the middle, sagging into a V shape that partially blocked the door.

Mairead looked at Constance, who was frozen to the spot, a horrified expression on her face. One of the women who had been trying to hold Bridie back spotted them and ran over.

"We have to do something! Wee Jamie is in there, and Bridie ran in after him."

Constance turned to her, looking utterly stricken. Her hand clawed at the neck of her dress, leaving red marks on her skin.

"Constance! What should we do?" the woman said, grabbing Constance's arm.

Mairead could feel how Constance's energy, her magic, had pulled back tight to her body; she was terrified.

"Help us! Help!"

Mairead dashed to the front of the building and attempted the stairs but the heat was like a wall, driving her back.

"We're going to lose the building!" someone was shouting. "We should focus on protecting the houses!"

"But what about Bridie and Jamie?"

Mairead's breath was coming in shallow panicked gasps, as someone gripped her shoulder and pulled her back, away from the stairs. She couldn't go into the building, but she couldn't just leave them in there to burn. Her thoughts raced, trying to picture the back end of the building. Was there another door, some other way out? Her memories of the inside were fuzzy – when they had been in there earlier, her attention had been drawn entirely to the men from the Watch, and the magic she had been working.

Magic.

Could she get them out that way? The world seemed to have slowed around her; she was still being pulled back from the stairs, had only taken a few steps. Constance was still standing, clutching at her dress, eyes wide with horror. Fergus was moving off toward the well, the next bucket of water had not yet been thrown, and the broken lintel still hung in the middle of the doorway.

If she used magic now, like this, in front of the whole village, there would be no undoing it, no denying what she was. If she were lucky, they would run her out of town. If not, there could be a noose in her immediate future.

"Help!" Bridie screamed from inside.

Mairead squeezed her eyes closed, said a quick prayer, and reached for her magic. She was already depleted from the spell she had woven through the food, but her will responded anyway, rising to meet her. With a last glance at Constance, she threw out her hand, sending the force of her will with it, and pressed the broken lintel upward. It was heavier than anything she had tried to lift with her magic before, and the reciprocal force drove her to her knees.

Cries of shock sounded behind her as the lintel began to visibly lift, but she couldn't spare them any attention. She pushed even more will out, forcing the wood to grind upward farther, shouting with the exertion of it.

Suddenly Constance was at her side, though Mairead hadn't seen her move.

"They need to hurry," Mairead grated out between her teeth. "I can't hold it much longer."

Constance darted toward the building and Mairead raised her other hand, screaming as the weight of the lintel pushed her into the soft ground. Her hands felt as if they were on fire and her skin began to blister and crack. Constance threw a frightened look back over her shoulder, then swept her hands open wide. Mairead felt the magic flow out from the other woman, and in response, the flames separated, making a clear space in the middle of the doorway. To either side, they flickered and writhed as normal, but at the edge of the door, they simply stopped in a straight line, as if meeting an invisible barrier.

"Quickly!" Constance called over the chaos that swirled around them.

Mairead watched, her hands in agony, her shoulders and back shrieking with the weight, as Bridie and a child appeared on the other side of the doorway. Her magic was reaching its limit, she could feel it sputtering and sliding away even as she forced more of it to respond. Just as Bridie and the child stepped into the doorway, her control began to slip, but Constance caught the extra weight and held everything steady, her magic twining around Mairead's own.

They held on while Bridie and the boy at her side slipped out and down the stairs and then both let go, allowing the lintel to crash to the floor. Sparks whirled into the night, spiraling up toward the stars. It was the last thing Mairead saw before she passed out.

Chapter Eight

Mairead

27th August 1745

When Mairead woke, it was to find that she had been placed atop a straw-filled mattress, with thick woolen blankets piled on top of her. Her eyes were crusted shut, and when she lifted a hand to wipe at them, she discovered that her hands were wrapped in thick bandages. Everything smelled of smoke. Her body ached; every muscle complained loudly at what she had put it through the night before.

She rubbed her forearm across her eyes and managed to open them, though the room was fuzzy and unfamiliar; she was none the wiser about where she was or what had happened after she passed out. The fact that her hands were bandaged was reassuring – presumably if they intended to hang her for witchcraft, they wouldn't have bothered treating her burns first.

Her thoughts turned suddenly to Constance. What had happened to her after Mairead passed out? Had her magic been discovered, or had she been able to put it all on Mairead? Would the others from the village believe that Mairead had done it all by herself? What about Elspeth and Janey and Simon? Were they safe? What would happen to them if Constance were discovered and driven out of her home, or worse?

She struggled to sit up, her body objecting to every movement. She had to find Constance, find out just how bad things were.

The door swung open, letting in sunlight and birdsong, silhouetting the person who stood there. Between that and the fact that her vision was still fuzzy, Mairead had no idea who she was looking at.

"Oh, thank goodness you're awake!" a vaguely familiar voice said. "Constance will be so relieved."

"Where am I?" Mairead croaked, her throat so dry it felt like it was sticking together.

The person who had entered strode across the room and lifted something from a table before approaching Mairead.

"Here, have some ale. You'll be as parched as a stone."

Mairead took the cup awkwardly in her bandaged hands and sipped at the warm ale, wishing it was cold water instead, then tried again. "Thank you. Where am I?"

"This is my home. We met yesterday, briefly. My name is Isobel Gordon. It's nice to meet you properly."

Mairead swiped her forearm across her eyes again and her vision began to clear a little. The woman standing beside the bed was middle-aged, wearing a simple but well-made dress and a kind smile.

"Mairead Ferguson," she said. "I hope I didn't put you out of a bed for the night?"

"Don't you worry a bit. I stayed with my daughter last night. And truth be told, there wasn't a lot of sleep for anybody after all that happened."

Sudden panic filled Mairead's chest as she remembered the reason that she had used her magic in the first place. "Bridie! Is she safe? What about the child? Did they—"

"They're fine," Mistress Gordon said, pulling over a stool and perching on it beside the bed. "Well, not fine, but they're alive and they'll recover. They both have quite the cough and young Jamie's arm is quite badly burned. He might need to go to Inverness to see a doctor, but we've done what we can for them."

"Oh, thank goodness," Mairead said, slumping. She was surprised to find tears prickling the back of her tired eyes. It wasn't like her to be so emotional over people she hardly knew.

"No, I believe it is thanks to you," Mistress Gordon said softly. "How did you…"

Mairead took a larger drink of ale to give herself time to think of how to answer. But what could she possibly say that could make this any better? The entire village had seen her use magic; there was no other way to explain what had happened, no way to soften or obfuscate the facts.

"I'm a witch," she said at last. "I was born this way. I swear, I've never made any kind of pact, never met the devil, never swore against God… I just have magic. I didn't ask for it."

Mistress Gordon was quiet for a long moment. "There are divots in the grass, where you were kneeling last night. As if something was pushing you into the ground."

Mairead nodded. "My magic makes things possible that otherwise would not be, but it's not without cost. I used my power to push the lintel back up so that Bridie and Jamie could get out. So, imagine a lever, tipping up at one end to lift something heavy – that weight pushed down on top of me, forcing me into the ground. I'm lucky the earth was soft enough to give, otherwise my legs would have taken the brunt of that force."

"And your hands?"

Mairead looked down at her bandages. "Some of the heat from the lintel traveled back along the line of force to me."

Mistress Gordon looked closely at her, examining her face. "Did you know that would happen? Before you started?"

"Not exactly." Mairead tried to flex her stiff fingers and grimaced at the flare of pain. "I knew there would be a cost, but not exactly what it would be."

"You took quite the risk, exposing yourself like this. You could be reported."

"I know." Mairead held very still. Was the other woman working her way around to telling her she was going to be detained? Taken to the nearest church?

"So why take the risk?"

Mairead lifted her shoulders in a slight shrug and shook her head. "What else could I do? They needed help and I couldn't think of any other way. It all happened so fast, there wasn't really time to try different solutions."

"Let me take a look at these hands of yours," Mistress Gordon said. She leaned over and very gently lifted them. "I've made a poultice that will help with the healing. It should be put on them three times a day."

"What happens now?" Mairead asked, frightened of the answer, but needing to know.

Mistress Gordon paused in unwinding the bandages and looked up at her. "Well now, that remains to be seen. There are some in the village who argued straight away for turning you over to the church, but many thought that unfair given the great service you did for us. A few suggested just sending you away and making that an end to it."

Mairead nodded and tried to blink back the tears that filled her eyes.

"But there are others – more than a few – who think we owe you great thanks, and that we should ask you to stay and make your home with us. Constance being the loudest voice among them, but not the only one by far. The price you paid with your own health makes a strong argument in your favor."

A knock sounded at the door and Mistress Gordon called over her shoulder as she resumed unwinding the bandages. "Come in."

The door opened and Constance stepped inside, carrying Simon on one hip. The girls trailed in behind her.

"You're awake! Thank the Lord. How do you feel?"

Janey ran straight over and climbed onto the bed, settling herself beside Mairead's feet.

"Come down from there, Janey," Constance said, alarmed. "Mairead is ill."

"It's all right," Mairead said, smiling at the toddler. "I'm all right."

Elspeth approached and rested a basket on the side of the bed. "Mistress Croaker sent some bannocks. And honey! They're still warm. And Mama wouldn't let us have any honey until you had some in case there wasn't enough left."

"That was very kind of her," Mairead said, looking up at Constance.

Mistress Gordon turned to Elspeth. "Now, I need to put some medicine on Mistress Ferguson's hands, because they got hurt last night. Maybe while I do that, you could fetch a plate and put some butter and honey on a bannock for her?"

Elspeth nodded shyly and took her basket to the table, making space for Constance to stand beside Mistress Gordon at the side of the bed. "Let me see the burns," she said. "How bad are they?"

Mairead held her hands up. Across both palms ran a thick, red line, blistering in places, the skin cracked in others. Her fingers were largely unmarked but moving them pulled at the skin of her palms and sent a deep lance of pain through the muscles and bone. "It could be worse," she said with a tight smile.

Constance tutted and watched closely as Mistress Gordon applied the poultice. Mairead could feel all the words trapped inside Constance that she was desperate to say but couldn't until they were alone. Most likely starting with, "What were you thinking?" Instead, she let out a sigh and said, "Bridie and Jamie are heading out to Inverness soon, for Jamie to see a doctor. The burn on his arm is bad. Fergus will take them in a cart, get him there faster, though it'll still take two days – they'll have to take care not to jostle him too much. The poor lad is in a lot of pain. Bridie is determined to see you before they leave, if you feel able?"

Mairead thought about it for a moment. Her entire body ached, her limbs felt twice the weight they usually did, and a dull thumping had started up behind her eyes. But she could not stay abed all day, nor could she take up residence in Mistress Gordon's house and hide away from the consequences of her actions. Perhaps it was best to face up to it all just now, get whatever was going to happen over with.

"Of course," Mairead said, swinging her legs over the side of the bed and attempting to get to her feet. As she stood, the room swayed and her vision tunneled. A whooshing noise filled her ears.

"Easy now," Mistress Gordon said, grabbing one arm, while Constance grabbed the other. "Maybe you should get some food in you before we try anything hasty."

Mairead grimaced – she hated being weak – but allowed herself to be pressed back down to sit on the edge of the bed. She really had overexerted herself yesterday. It would take days for her to recover fully. If the villagers decided to send her away immediately, she would struggle to travel in this state.

Elspeth brought over a plate with two warm bannocks, slathered with butter and honey, and Mairead's mouth began to water at the warm and welcome smell of them. She accepted them with thanks and Elspeth gave her a smile, then looked hopefully at her mother.

"All right, on you go. You can share a bannock and some honey with your sister."

The girls both squealed with delight and scrambled over to the table. Constance smiled at them fondly, then glanced at Mairead. "Water?"

"Yes, please."

"Here, let me take the lad for a minute, give your back a break," Mistress Gordon said, reaching for Simon, who was wriggling and gurgling away happily in his mother's arms.

"Thank you," Constance said. She handed him over, as Mairead started to pick the bannocks apart to eat.

The fresh bandages that Mistress Gordon had applied were tighter and wrapped from her wrists to the first knuckle of her fingers, making it a little easier to use her hands than it had been. Her palms pulsed with a hot pain, and any significant movement of her fingers made it spike, so she ate very carefully.

The food and cold, fresh water did much to rejuvenate her and when she tried to stand again, she found that she was not so lightheaded. Constance stood beside her and laid a hand on her shoulder, and from it she felt the other woman's energy flowing into her, bolstering her own, easing some of her weariness and pain.

It would appear that Constance's secret was safe and yet here she was, taking a risk, using her magic to help Mairead. Granted, the risk was small, but the villagers would all be hyperalert to any sign of witchcraft at the moment.

"Are you ready?" Constance asked, studying her face. "You don't have to do this if it's too much."

"I'd like to see them," Mairead said, straightening her back and pushing her shoulders down. "Let's go."

Mistress Gordon stayed inside with the children, which Mairead found herself deeply grateful for. If there were going to be any difficulties, any cries of "Witch," or pelting of fruit, any fear or anger, she would rather the children didn't see it. She had grown fond of them over the short time she had been there and found that their good opinion of her mattered more than she would have anticipated.

They stepped out into the road. Mairead leaned on Constance's arm more than she would like, but her legs felt weak and trembly already. A few people were outside, and all stopped to watch them pass, some looking wary, others merely curious. Mairead had never felt so much like a spectacle in her life. Since she was a child she had done her best not to draw attention to herself, but here she had undone all of that work in one fell swoop.

The scarred and blackened remains of the church loomed ahead of them and the scent of burned wood and smoke lay thick over the village. Very little remained. The building would have to be completely rebuilt. Mairead wondered how and when the villagers would find time to do that. Or perhaps, given that they had no minister, it would just be abandoned, something else used as a communal meeting space when needed.

They reached Bridie's house, where a cart was waiting out front, a little smaller than Constance's with a bench seat at the front. It was yoked to a sturdy, shaggy pony with a rich brown-and-white dappled coat. The pony whickered and Mairead leaned against the cart for a moment, giving her legs at least the semblance of rest. Fergus emerged from the house, carrying a boy of no more than ten years in his arms. The boy's eyes were glassy, and his right arm was bandaged and cradled carefully against his body.

Bridie came out behind them and stopped dead when she saw Constance and Mairead. Then suddenly she was flying in their direction and Mairead was lifting her arms to ward the other woman off if necessary, but then Bridie grabbed her and pulled her into a crushing embrace.

"Thank you. Thank you." Her words were almost lost amongst her tears and Mairead stood there, arms half-raised, confused, until eventually she understood that she was not being attacked and wrapped her arms around Bridie in turn.

After a moment, Bridie pulled away and rubbed at her face with a handkerchief that she then returned to a pocket in her skirt. A coughing fit took her, almost doubling her over before she was able to catch her breath. Constance stepped over to her and rubbed at her back while she took a moment to compose herself.

"Thank you," she said again, her voice still thick with emotion. "You saved our lives. You saved my boy."

"You're welcome," Mairead said. "How are you both? I heard his arm..."

"It's badly burned. He might lose some use of it." She paused, glancing at her son, whom Fergus had placed gently into the back of the cart, cushioned by hides and blankets. "But he's alive. We're both alive because of you. When I ran into that church and the lintel cracked behind me, blocking the door...well, I was making peace with my maker. I don't know how you lifted it. I don't know if it was witchcraft like some people have said, or some other kind of miracle. But I can't believe that any power used to save another at great cost to you can be anything other than a divine blessing. I believe you are a gift from God himself, Mairead Ferguson, and I pray that my friends and neighbors are not too small-minded to see it."

She started coughing again and Mairead just stood there, feeling awkward and useless. The throb started up in her head again, beating in time with the pulsing in her injured hands. She had never felt less like a divine anything in her life.

When Bridie had caught her breath again, Constance asked, "How did the fire start? Has Jamie been able to tell you?"

Bridie shook her head but more in despair than in refusal. "I sent him to fetch the pot you had used to cook for the Watch men," she began. "So that I could get the oats soaking for the morning."

A stab of guilt pierced Mairead's chest and made her gasp. She had forgotten all about the pot in the effort to make the men leave, had just walked away and left it there. It hadn't even crossed her mind that Bridie would need it back to prepare for the next day. It was her fault that the boy had been caught in the fire.

"He said he knocked over a candlestand and the floor caught fire. At first it was small and he...he..." She trailed off, her breath hitching in her chest. She took a couple of deep breaths, cleared her throat and continued, "At first, he was more worried about being in trouble than he was about the fire. He thought he could put it out. He knew the men had taken water in there earlier and thought he might be able to find some. He found a bottle in a cupboard and, thinking it was water, poured it on the fire." She looked at him with haunted eyes, her gaze so full of love and regret that it hit Mairead like a rock to the gut.

"It was whisky," she said quietly. "The flames leapt up; his sleeve caught. He managed to get back, away from the fire, and smothered the flames on his sleeve. My poor brave boy." She looked back at Mairead. "He doesn't remember much after that."

"I'm so sorry," Mairead said at last, the regret that had been choking her finding some release. "This is all my fault. If I had just brought that pot back..."

Bridie shook her head. "And if I had just gone to get it myself instead of sending him. If I had raised him to be less concerned about disappointing me. If I had taught him to run away at the first sign of fire... If, if, if. It happened. It was an accident, and it was no one's fault. Regardless of why he was in that building, you are the reason we both got out of it. We owe our lives to you."

"I hate to interrupt," Fergus said, coming to stand beside them. "But daylight's a-wasting. And it's best for the lad if we cover as much ground as possible before the laudanum wears off."

Bridie nodded and turned to climb into the cart beside her son, then turned back and gripped Mairead's forearm. "I hope you're still here when we return. I don't know how I can possibly repay you, but I'll spend the rest of my days trying." With that she climbed up beside Jamie and lifted his head into her lap.

Fergus nodded to both Mairead and Constance in a friendly enough manner, then climbed up to the bench seat, lifted the reins and clicked his tongue at the pony, who set off at a steady, ambling pace.

Mairead and Constance stood in silence, watching them go until they turned out of sight beyond the last house in the village.

"Will they be all right, do you think?" Mairead asked, the weight of all that had happened pressing down on her at once.

"I hope so," Constance answered, then turned to Mairead. "Will you?"

Mairead gave a surprised laugh. "I hope so," she said, with half a smile.

"Let's get you home," Constance said, offering her arm to lean on. "We can figure everything else out when you've recovered."

Home, Mairead thought. *I hope it is.*

Chapter Nine

Constance

27th August 1745

The room was pitch-black, the moon outside obscured by the clouds that had rolled in that afternoon. Simon snuffled in his sleep and Constance tensed, waiting to see if he would waken and want to be fed or if he would settle again and let her rest. Rest, not sleep, because sleep evaded her this night. No matter how she lay, she was uncomfortable, her body feeling too small to contain all of her thoughts and feelings and worries.

She thought of Bridie and Jamie out there on the road to Inverness with Fergus. She was glad that someone had gone with them – and with Fergus's bad leg and arm, it made more sense for him to go than a more able-bodied adult. But the fact was, they were still down three people who could take on various tasks for the harvest, when their numbers were already depleted. Even thinking in such terms drove guilt deep into her heart.

Simon let out a soft snore and Constance rolled onto her other side with a sigh. She was worried for Jamie and full of empathy for Bridie, but she also had the rest of the village to worry about. A matter that seemed to have escaped the notice of kings and lairds and landowners alike, as they rushed off to wave their swords at each other. Why did all of this have to fall onto her? It wasn't fair. She was ill-equipped to lead the whole village when she had spent most of her life trying to fit in and escape notice. But if not her, then who? Life here was hard, precarious. They had to work as a collective, each relying on the other, or it wouldn't work at all. And it was simply a fact of life that where you had a group of people working together, you must have a person who was in charge, who could make sure that all were pulling together, and everyone's needs were met.

Constance rolled onto her back with a huff, kicking at the covers, which were getting tangled round her legs with all her tossing and turning. Her mind flashed back to the fire, to the moment she had heard Jamie shouting and realized that he was inside. And then she had watched as Bridie dashed inside…the horror of it all had completely overwhelmed her. She hadn't known what to do, had just stood there, watching, her thoughts moving as slow as sap rising in spring. Some leader she had been then. She had been completely useless.

And then Mairead. She had been so brave, so powerful. She had risked so much. To use her magic like that, in front of everyone. Her willingness to risk herself to save people she didn't even know put Constance to shame.

She sighed and scrubbed her hands across her face. Her eyes were gritty, aching with the need for sleep, but her busy mind would not allow her to rest. She was to meet with the villagers again tomorrow, to discuss what was to happen with Mairead, whether she would be allowed to stay or not. Some of them were not comfortable with having a witch living amongst them, never mind that she had just saved the lives of two of their number. The witch trials might be over – for now at least – but there were those who remembered what it had been like, the fear and suspicion cast over whole communities, for where the witchfinders found one 'witch' they often found twenty.

Others had argued for letting her stay though. The fact that two of their own survived because of her actions went a long way in her favor. Add to that the fact that she had been burned, that she had used so much magic that she had collapsed, and had given so much of herself – and perhaps the fact that by collapsing she had shown that her magic had limits, that while she might be more powerful than them, she was also vulnerable – and she had drawn some loyalty and admiration from some of the villagers.

Constance had pointed out that if Mairead had run into the burning building and carried Jamie out, they would be throwing a celebration for her, not discussing sending her away. She had been worried while arguing that if she defended Mairead too loudly, people might turn to her, ask her just what exactly she had been doing standing in front of Mairead at the steps to the church. Why had she made that odd gesture with her hands? Could it be that she defended the witch because she was also one?

The thought made her stomach flip. She was terrified of being accused, but equally guilt-ridden at the thought of leaving Mairead to carry the consequences of their fear alone.

The next morning, she left Mairead resting in the house and took the children back to the village with her. A table had been set up in the middle of the road, with stools brought out to surround it. There was food set out, and the younger children dashed around playing a game while the older ones went about their chores.

The cloud cover lingered but the day was warm enough and it was pleasant to sit outside. Constance wondered what they would do when the weather shifted soon, since they could no longer use the church as a meeting place. None of the homes in the village were large enough to accommodate everyone, and the cattle and sheep would all be moved into barns, so they would be full too.

She shook her head. *A problem for another day.*

Constance sat and settled Simon on the ground at her feet, content with a wooden rattle that Iain had made when she was pregnant with Elspeth. People finished tasks that they were doing and settled around the table, sharing food and drink before getting down to business, as was customary in the village. For all of her fears, Constance did not sense any anger or hostility from anyone, though there were some who seemed wary. She looked around, saw that most people were finished eating, or were merely picking at their food, and suddenly found herself unsure of where to start.

Emily Croaker met her gaze and seemed to understand, for she raised her voice enough to draw attention and said, "How is Mistress Ferguson today? Is she recovering from her ordeal?"

Constance could have embraced the seamstress for, by framing her question as she had, she had started the discussion with kindness and concern for Mairead.

"The burns on her hands will take some time to heal, and she is still weakened by her exertions. She'll need several days' rest, I think, before she'll be somewhat back to her usual self."

"Please do tell her I was asking for her and that I shall pray for her speedy recovery," Mistress Croaker said, stretching across the table to pat Constance's hand.

"I will, thank you." Constance paused for a moment to slice a strawberry and pass a piece down to Simon. Then she looked around the table, meeting everyone's eyes in turn. "I know that some of you have concerns about Mistress Ferguson and her abilities. I understand that it's frightening to have something happen that we can't explain, to have a person in our midst who is capable of unknown feats. It's tempting to send her away, to go back to our lives as we knew them, and to tell ourselves that there is nothing to fear if she is gone. Especially now, when we have so many other things to fear.

"But think for a moment about how we learned about Mistress Ferguson's abilities. She risked her own well-being to save people she had barely even met. She could have done nothing. She could have joined the bucket line, and kept her secret, and instead of coming together in peace this morning, we would be coming together in mourning, to bury our friends. Mistress Ferguson would be safe. Her life, her freedom, have been placed in danger because she chose to save them, no matter what it cost her. Ask yourself if those are the actions of someone you need to be frightened of?"

Silence settled over the table as she finished speaking, broken only by the sounds of the children playing and chickens clucking as they pecked in the gardens around the houses, eating whatever they could find. Simon pulled at her skirt, and she passed him down another piece of strawberry.

"I vote for her to stay as long as she wishes," Isobel Gordon said firmly. "She knew before she acted that she would be injured, and she did it anyway. I think that says a great deal about her character."

"I agree," said Mistress Croaker. "And frankly, we have more important things to be discussing today."

"More important than a witch in our village? Really?" Roisin said, leaning over the table, her voice hard. "What could possibly be more important?"

"How we're all going to eat this winter seems like a good place to start," Mistress Croaker said, raising an eyebrow. "Or were you hoping the food would walk in off the fields and onto your plate by itself?"

Roisin flushed and sat back from the table, crossing her arms across her chest. "Fewer hands to do the work means we also have fewer mouths to feed. So surely the work scales down and we'll manage fine?"

"It's not quite that simple," Constance said with a sigh. "The people who have left are the ones most able to do the work of harvesting food, slaughtering livestock and so on. So, between the men who've been called up, and then the fire, we've lost more than half of the workers, but fewer than a third of the people needing to be fed.

"And that would be bad enough, but it's made worse by not knowing when the men will return. Will they be gone for weeks? Months? Will they all arrive home in the middle of winter, also needing to be fed?"

Roisin paled as she seemed to grasp the enormity of the situation.

"And that's just the food," Mistress Gordon put in. "There are always repairs to be done before winter, thatching to be topped up, fences to mend, before the weather turns. Anything not dealt with before the snow and ice and winds settle in for the season will be in a worse state come spring."

"And what about those men from the Watch?" someone else interjected. "They might decide to pay us another visit and bring backup. Or worse yet, King George's men. If we're branded as Jacobites... well, we're all in danger until the Bonnie Prince or his father takes up the throne."

That set off a babble of panicked talk around the table and Constance pinched the bridge of her nose, where a headache was beginning to form. Still, there had been no real resistance to Mairead staying on, and the conversation had moved to other matters, which was all to the good. Now she just needed to figure out how on earth she was going to feed everyone and keep them all safe until Iain and the others returned.

If they return.

She pushed that thought away. It was the specter that hung over them all, the deep knowledge that even if the uprising went in their favor, it was likely that some of their loved ones would not live to see home again. If the Stuarts lost again, perhaps none of them would return.

Constance stood and waited until all eyes had turned to her. "The days ahead will be challenging," she said, "and that is the only thing we can be sure of right now. But the only way that we have any chance of getting through this is to work together. So, let's turn to the work that needs to be done, and begin to form a plan for how best to approach it."

The following days passed in a blur of work and worry. Each morning and evening, Constance would pour her own magical energy into Mairead, bolstering her body's natural ability to heal. They hadn't talked about what this meant, this newfound honesty between them about what they both were. All Constance knew was that, for the first time in as long as she could remember, there was a person in her life who truly saw her and a space in which she could relax her guard and be herself.

If only she had time to enjoy it.

Each day she rose before dawn and worked until her body could give no more. Exhausted, she would eat with the children and put them to bed, then work some more until at last she fell into bed and slipped in and out of sleep, her worries refusing to let go, even as her body cried out for rest.

Mairead was healing well and, though she couldn't do much in the fields with her hands still raw and recovering, she had taken on much of the childcare and cooking and cleaning the house, though there were some tasks that her hands would still not allow.

The weather turned cooler, the leaves on the trees changed to their glorious riot of autumnal colors, and Constance added the slaughtering of some of the cattle to her worries. It took a degree of both skill and physical strength to slaughter a cow and then to butcher it and prepare the skin and meat, and though she had watched it done, and knew the theory of it, she had never been the one to wield the knife herself and she was not confident that she had it in her.

These were the thoughts she was occupied with when she was crossing the yard outside the house one morning and heard hoofbeats approaching from the direction of the village. She stopped, a feeling of dread beginning to settle in her stomach. That didn't sound like the plodding walk of any of the ponies kept by other villagers. It sounded like a horse, of the type ridden by lords and the like. What new trouble was coming to her door?

Constance moved over to the gate that marked the entrance to her property and peered down the path toward the village. A single horse and rider approached, a young man dressed in wool trousers and a plaid greatcoat, astride a gorgeous chestnut horse, all smooth, sleek muscle and intelligent eyes. Handsome as the beast was, it probably wasn't as well-equipped for Highland life as the sturdy, long-haired ponies they kept in the village.

The young man pulled on the reins as he approached, and the horse halted at her side.

"Mistress Gordon?" he asked, shielding his eyes from the sun, which was just now peeking over the roof of the house behind her.

"Aye," Constance answered. "That's me." *Please don't let this be bad news.*

The man turned and rummaged in his saddlebag. "I have a letter for you," he said. "From Mr. Murphy. He asked me to deliver it on my way to Perth." He straightened and held out a wax-sealed parchment.

Constance stepped forward and took it hesitantly. If Fergus was writing from Inverness, it was unlikely to be with news that all was well, and they were heading home.

"Thank you," she said, though fear was curdling in her mouth. "Can I offer you some refreshment before you continue your journey? There's porridge still warm, or we could cook you up some sausage?"

"That's very kind of you, Mistress, but I must be on my way without delay. I have important messages to carry."

"I wish you a safe journey, then."

The young man nodded to her then clicked his tongue and flicked the reins. His horse set off again at a brisk walk, and Constance stood at the gate and watched until they were out of sight. She looked down at the letter in her hand and sighed, closing her eyes against the weight of concern that settled on her shoulders. She didn't want to open it, didn't want to have to deal with whatever bad news was within. If Jamie's burns had become infected, if he had died because of that fire, she would never be able to forgive herself, for leaving the candles burning when they left, for not cleaning up the wine that had spilled, for freezing in fear when she realized that he was inside…

But ignoring whatever it was would not make it go away. So, she turned and headed back inside, where she could at least steel herself with Mairead's company.

The children were still at the table, eating breakfast, and Mairead was perched on the edge of a chair with Simon on her lap, feeding him porridge that she had cooled for him. She looked up and then frowned.

"Is everything all right?"

Constance shook her head. "A letter from Fergus," she said, holding it up.

They looked at each other and Constance knew that the same dread she felt now moved through Mairead. She blamed herself for what had happened as much as Constance did, though she had risked everything to save Bridie and Jamie.

Please. Please. Constance bit her lip and then broke the seal and unfolded the letter.

2nd September 1745

Dear Constance,

Young Jamie is well. I know you'll be panicking at receiving this letter, and I'm sorry for the fear I've no doubt caused you. The lad's arm is not in a good way, but it is healing. We found a hospital willing to look after him in exchange for Bridie and I working for them, cooking and cleaning. They say with the right care and a bit of luck he might even regain full use of the arm.

There's more you should know. The latest news here is that the prince's army was marching for Edinburgh, though by the time I find someone to bring this to you, it might be that he's reached the city already. We can only pray for the safety of all involved, but if he achieves his goal and takes the capital, then I cannot imagine this will all end soon. The king's forces are said to be moving north, though it may be that they come no farther than Edinburgh.

Some people came into the hospital yesterday, bearing wounds and tales of woe. They were from a small settlement not far from here, smaller even than Kilmartin. They were attacked by a large group of raiders who stole their sheep. When the crofters tried to stop them, it turned bloody. Some of them were killed and their crofts were set on fire. The survivors made their way here. I pray that these raiders content themselves with what they've taken already, or that they come up against the Watch as soon as possible. But you should all know to be careful.

Please keep an eye on Roisin and Samuel for me – I promised Jack that I would keep them safe while he is gone.

Keeping you all in my prayers,

Fergus

Chapter Ten

Mairead

12th September 1745

Mairead was worried. After Fergus's letter arrived, Constance withdrew even further into herself. She was losing weight, her face growing drawn and paler than it should have been given how many hours she spent outdoors each day. Dark circles had formed around her eyes and Mairead wasn't convinced she was sleeping, even after she collapsed into bed each night.

It was clear that Constance could not continue the way she was, but when Mairead tentatively brought it up one evening after the children were in bed, Constance just gave her a dull look and said she would rest when winter came. Guilt niggled at Mairead every time she looked at Constance. How much of the other witch's exhaustion was caused by the healing she had given Mairead twice a day for a week or more after the fire. Fortunately, that was no longer needed; Mairead's hands were still tender, but the burns had healed, and she had fully recovered from the exhaustion caused by pushing her magic to the limit of her abilities.

Mairead lay in bed, a straw pallet that had been made up in the main room of the cottage, against a wall near the hearth, stretching her fingers then curling them into fists. She did these exercises every night, recovering the movement and dexterity she had before the burns. Although the skin had largely healed now, there was still a deep ache in her hands by the end of each day and she had seen enough injuries in her time that she knew how easy it could be to lose function as a result.

Constance had gone through to bed a little while ago, looking utterly exhausted, but every now and then Mairead could hear her moving around or sighing. Mairead lay there, warmed by the banked fire in the hearth, feeling useless. Food that had not been gathered in time was starting to rot in the fields but no matter how hard they worked, Constance insisted that the village was falling further behind.

As Mairead's thoughts drifted in that curious space between waking and sleeping, there was movement in the room, jerking her to full consciousness. She sat up, blinking in the low light. Constance was standing beside the dresser, a dusty, corked bottle in her hand.

"I'm sorry," she said in a soft voice. "I didn't mean to wake you."

"Can't sleep?" Mairead asked, pushing herself up on her elbows.

Constance shook her head. "I thought some of this might help." She held up the bottle and pulled the cork out with a pop. She looked at the door back to her bedroom and then at Mairead. "Care to join me?"

"Whisky?" Mairead asked as thc rich, smoky smell crept across the room.

"Iain likes a drop on occasion," Constance said. She took two small glasses from the shelf and held one out to Mairead, an eyebrow raised in question.

Mairead nodded and reached for the glass. "You must be worried for him. I can't imagine how difficult it is."

Constance snorted but didn't otherwise respond until she had poured generous measures into both glasses and taken a seat between the hearth and Mairead's bed. "Would you think me a terrible person if I told you that I've barely spared him a thought?"

Mairead swirled the whisky in her glass, giving herself a moment to figure out how to answer. When she looked up, Constance was staring back at her, her expression caught somewhere between defiant and fearful. "It's not as if you haven't had many other concerns to fill your mind."

"It's not that I don't care about him," Constance said, sighing. She took a healthy swig from her glass. "I hope that he's safe and well. I do. I want him to survive whatever comes. But I am angry with him too."

"For leaving?"

"Amongst other things." Constance slumped back in her chair.

Mairead shifted her position so that she was propped against the wall, the blankets pulled around her legs. She sipped at her whisky and looked past Constance to the banked fire in the hearth, the embers still letting off heat. She had learned over the years that sometimes the best way to give someone space to open up was to be quiet. To give them time to explore their thoughts and decide how much or how little they wanted to say.

"Iain is a good man," Constance said at last. "He cares about people. Cares about the children. Takes duty seriously. Believes in doing a job well." She took another drink, a smaller one this time. "As far as husbands go, he's a decent one. I'm lucky to have wed him. Only, I never really wanted to wed at all. And now he's gone off to fight, and I'm left here with all of his responsibilities as well as my own and I just…"

"You're doing all that you can and more," Mairead said softly. "No one could ask more of you."

"But it's not enough." Constance shook her head then gulped the rest of the whisky in her glass. "It's just not enough. Ever since the letter from Fergus, I've been waiting for something awful to happen. If those raiders come here, we have no way to defend ourselves. I don't know what to do. I don't know how to keep us all safe." She barked a bitter laugh. "I found myself staring at a scarecrow in the back field this morning and wishing there was some way to bring it to life, just for the extra pair of hands."

"What if there is?" Mairead asked. The beginnings of an idea were taking root in her mind.

"What if there is what?" Constance asked, reaching over to top up Mairead's glass and then filling her own.

"What if there is a way to bring it to life? Or, at least, to give it tasks, if not sentience."

"That's impossible."

"So is holding back flames with nothing but your will, but we both know that happened." Now it was Mairead's turn to look defiant, daring Constance to tell her she was wrong.

Constance broke eye contact first and said nothing.

"We've been dancing around this since we met," Mairead said, keeping her voice low and steady. "But we both know the truth now. We're both witches. You're the most powerful one I've ever met."

Constance laughed

"It's true. Now, I'll not say that I've met loads of our kind, and it's true that I'm far from worldly, but Constance, you have so much power just rolling off you all the time. Have you never noticed how the others in the village all turn to you for advice, and do as you say with barely a question? Truly?"

Constance shrugged, but a small frown began between her brows. "I married the laird's cousin, that's all. Iain has a certain amount of authority, he's the official tenant on the land we all live on, so they're all here by his will. I have authority by association as his wife."

"Do they show Iain as much deference as they show you?" Mairead asked softly.

"Well, of course. I mean..." Constance trailed off, her frown growing deeper. "Not quite as much. No." She got to her feet and started pacing around the room. "I'm not enchanting them, if that's what you're suggesting."

"I know, it's nothing like that. Certainly nothing you do on purpose. It's just that the magic in you is so strong that even those who are not like us can feel it. They sense your strength, and they respond to it."

Constance knocked back her whisky and shook her head. "I won't...I can't accept that."

"You are so powerful that I felt you calling all the way from Argyll. I walked for days, following the beacon of your magic. That's how I came to be here."

"What?"

Mairead looked up at Constance, her gaze steady. Might as well tell her the whole truth now. "I'm not a widow. I've never been wed, it's just a story I use to explain why I'm traveling alone, and to discourage people from asking too much about my past. I'm sorry I lied to you.

"I was in a small town in Argyll before I came here, serving as housekeeper to an old man, a retired magistrate. I meant to move on sooner, but he didn't have long left, and I had grown to care for him, so I didn't want to leave before the end. He died, and the night I eased his passing, I felt you calling. The call was so filled with sadness and loneliness, that I couldn't ignore it. And I have never felt another witch from that far away before. As soon as Callum was buried and his affairs settled, I made my way here. I knew I had to find you."

Constance shook her head. "I don't... How can any of this be true?" She sank down onto the chair again, looking dazed.

Mairead stood and fetched the bottle of whisky from where it sat on the floor by the chair and topped up Constance's glass again.

"I've never met another witch, until you," Constance said, looking up at her, her eyes wide with wonder.

For a moment, Mairead's heart stuttered in her chest, and she wanted nothing more in the world than to hold Constance, and to love her, and to keep her safe and happy as long as they both lived. She swallowed hard and stepped back quickly, putting some distance between them before she did something stupid.

Constance studied her for a moment longer, then sighed and slumped back in the chair again, exhaustion replacing the wonder on her features once more. "Even if all you say is true, it doesn't help us now."

"But it might." Mairead perched on the edge of the other chair, on the far side of the hearth. "I can affect the world with my will, my magic. I can move things without touching them – as the whole village saw with the church – although it's much easier with small things. I can set a brush to sweeping by itself, while I get on with other things and suchlike. Can you?"

Constance nodded thoughtfully. "Aye. Small things. I've never tried anything big."

"Neither have I," Mairead said, leaning forward. "But maybe it's time we did. Maybe we could animate a scarecrow or two and gain a few extra hands. And there's nothing to be lost by trying."

"When though? I can't afford to lose time better spent preparing for winter if this doesn't work."

Mairead got to her feet. "Well, I doubt I'll get to sleep for a while anyway. Shall we?"

It was dark outside. Clouds obscured the sky except for a few small patches where stars peeked through, their light seeming cold and distant. Constance carried a lamp and she and Mairead crossed the yard outside the house arm in arm, stepping carefully in the dark. Constance hadn't wanted to leave the children asleep and unattended, so she went to fetch a scarecrow and bring it back, while Mairead waited within sight and hearing of the house.

Mairead shivered and pulled her cloak tighter around herself, wishing she had taken the time to dress properly rather than just pulling this on over her nightdress and pushing her feet into her shoes without even stockings. The warmth from the fire was fleeing from her already, though the night was mild enough for this time of year.

She stood there, watching the lamp bob as Constance made her way to the nearest scarecrow, and began to wonder if this had been such a good idea after all. Now that she was thinking it through more thoroughly, she was beginning to see flaws in her plan. An owl called from somewhere nearby and Mairead looked for it but couldn't see where it might be perched. She had been fascinated by the nocturnal birds ever since she was a child.

When she turned to look for the lamp again, she saw that Constance was on the way back to her.

We might as well try. If nothing else, perhaps it'll wear Constance out enough that she'll be able to sleep.

"This better be worth it," Constance was grumbling as she approached. "This thing does not smell like fresh-baked bannocks after hanging out here since spring, through Lord knows how many rain spells."

"Oh dear," Mairead said, laughing. "Poor, smelly scarecrow. Let me give you a hand."

Together they propped the scarecrow up so that he was leaning against the fence, then they stood back and studied him.

After a moment of this, Constance nudged Mairead with her elbow. "Well then, what do we do now?"

"I suppose first we try and make it move, and then take it from there?"

"You go first," Constance said with a nervous laugh. "This was all your idea."

For the briefest moment, Mairead thought about calling the whole thing off and just going back inside the house, having one more dram, and calling it a night. But then Constance glanced at her and for the first time in days, there was something resembling hope in her eyes, and Mairead knew that she would do just about anything to keep that look there.

Mairead blew out a short, sharp breath, and shook her limbs, letting go of tension and fear, releasing all other thoughts that were lingering in her mind. It was time to focus. She closed her eyes and reached inside herself for the source of her magic. It was there, waiting for her, as it always was. She opened her eyes and looked at the scarecrow, willing it to move, to stand up straight, instead of leaning against the fence.

At first nothing happened. Mairead could feel the scarecrow, inert, just beyond her reach. She breathed deep and then pushed a little harder with her magic, feeling it sinking into the straw man. There it was; she had the connection now. All she had to do was use it.

Mairead pictured the scarecrow standing up straight and a few seconds later, it did, wobbling slightly. Constance let out a gasp and clapped her hands, laughing in delight. Mairead felt her control start to slip and focused on the scarecrow again, trying to block out her awareness of Constance by her side. She tried to make the scarecrow walk, but it immediately overbalanced and fell onto its face. Constance dashed over, picked it up, and leaned it against the fence again.

This time, Mairead spent more time spreading her will throughout the full body of the scarecrow and thinking through the actual process of walking, the movement from one leg to the other, and then sent that instruction to the straw man. It took one shambling step and then another, falling from foot to foot in the clumsy way of toddlers. Mairead concentrated again and pushed her will further, making the scarecrow come to a halt in front of Constance and bow to her.

Constance laughed and nudged Mairead with her shoulder. "My turn?"

"Have fun," Mairead said, smiling and pulling her will back, as she felt Constance's brushing past her, like a breath on her neck. It raised goosebumps on her skin, which grounded her back in her own body. She was surprised at how tired she was; controlling the scarecrow took a great deal more concentration and energy than keeping a brush sweeping.

Constance was focused entirely on the scarecrow, and Mairead could feel the flow of the other witch's will into the straw man. She was so strong. The scarecrow stumbled over to Mairead and held an arm out to her. She looked at Constance, eyebrow raised.

"We've disturbed his sleep, I think you owe him a dance," she said with a smirk.

Mairead laughed and shook her head, but Constance bit her lip, suddenly looking unsure of herself, and Mairead couldn't bring herself to break this delicate moment of fun between them. She curtsied to the scarecrow and carefully took its arm, allowing Constance to swing them both into a far from graceful dance.

As she let the scarecrow spin her around the yard, she spotted a wisp, floating just above the fence where the scarecrow had been leaning. The dance moved her away and when next she looked, the wisp had been joined by another, the two of them mimicking the movement of the dance.

Mairead laughed and pointed. "Look at that! Aren't they sweet?"

Constance looked over. "Aren't what sweet?" she asked, frowning.

With Constance's concentration broken, the scarecrow's animation fled, leaving it nothing but a sack of straw, hanging limp in Mairead's arms. "The wisps, on the fence," she said, nodding toward them as she tried to haul the scarecrow up and walk with it. "Don't you see them?"

"I don't see anything there at all. What do they look like?"

"Like little dancing flames," Mairead said, coming to stand beside them. "One is a very pale blue color, and the other is orange. You really can't see them?"

Constance shook her head and came over to stand beside her, before taking the scarecrow from her arms and draping it over the fence. "I wish I could. Do you see them all the time?"

"No, not at all. I've only seen them once before, when I was on my way here." Mairead thought of that night and started looking around, peering into the darkness beyond the meager light from the lamp, which sat atop a fence post.

"What are you looking for? Are there more of them?"

Mairead shook her head. "No, just the two on the fence. I thought maybe… Never mind." She still wasn't entirely sure that meeting Nicnevin hadn't just been a dream; it had that same fuzzy, otherworldly quality in her memory as dreams often had.

She watched as the two wisps twirled around each other, rising into the sky, before darting off into the night. She glanced back at Constance, who was looking at her in wonder.

"I've never met anyone else like you," she said.

Mairead felt her neck and face warm as she flushed and hoped that it wasn't obvious in the dark. "I hope that's a good thing."

Extracts from *The Inverness Daily*

15th September 1745

THE YOUNG PRETENDER TAKES EDINBURGH

On 11th September 1745, Prince Charles Edward Stuart walked into Edinburgh unchallenged and, after a brief negotiation with the city leaders, he declared his father, King James III of England and VIII of Scotland, as the rightful ruler of these isles. We are told that the prince has taken up residence at the Palace of Holyroodhouse, traditionally the royal seat of the Stuarts in Scotland, since it was built by King James IV during the time period 1501–1505. It is our understanding that his army is stationed in the city until further notice.

RAIDERS ATTACK HIGHLAND VILLAGES

More settlements in the vicinity of Inverness have reported raids by outlaws who are taking the opportunity afforded by the current state of uncertainty to harass good and honest Highlanders. Livestock has been stolen and houses robbed of what meager supplies they might have. Any who stand up to these raiders have been attacked, their homes burned to the ground, women ravished in front of their children. The new companies of the Black Watch are said to be hunting for these outlaws, though there is every possibility of the Watch having to abandon this task if they are called up by King George II to answer the challenge raised by the Jacobites and their prince.

Chapter Eleven

Mairead

16th September 1745

Mairead sat on a stool in the yard, churning butter and watching Elspeth as she pulled onions and put them into a basket. Mairead would tie the stalks together later so that they could hang in strings. Janey and Simon were with Constance, feeding the animals. Constance was also deciding which ones to slaughter before winter, and how much meat could be stored and preserved, and taken into the village.

Over the last few nights, after the children had been safely tucked up in bed, they had continued their experiments with the scarecrow, but despite the fun they had had with it, it had become clear that this was not the answer to their problems. The straw man was simply too flimsy to pick up tools or carry anything heavier than an empty bucket, and although they had both improved their level of control substantially, there was no dexterity in the scarecrow to perform any kind of delicate or detailed work. Added to that, the amount of concentration needed to maintain control of the scarecrow meant that they couldn't set it a task while they got on with something else – it required their full attention. So instead of reducing their workload, it simply shifted it.

Mairead took her frustration out on the milk as she churned it into butter, a perfect task for the mood she was in. She had watched, helplessly, as the spark of hope she had seen in Constance's eyes had dimmed again, until the other woman had once more retreated into herself, fear and worry overwhelming her. Mairead wanted nothing more than to find a way to lighten her burden.

She glanced up and saw someone walking along the path to the village. She stood and stretched the stiffness out of her back, before approaching the gate to the road. By the time she got there, she could see who approached.

"Elspeth," she called over to where the child was still pulling onions. "Can you please run and tell your mother that Roisin has come to visit? She'll be out with the animals."

Elspeth dropped her basket and dashed off, only to stop halfway across the yard and call back, "Is Samuel coming too?"

"Yes, he is."

"Yes!" Elspeth ran off, braids flying out behind her.

Mairead turned back and opened the gate, welcoming Roisin as she arrived. "Mistress Murphy, how lovely to see you. Are you and Samuel well?"

"Yes, thank you," Roisin said, stopping at the gate. "Is Mistress Gordon here?"

"She's tending to the animals," Mairead said. "I've asked Elspeth to let her know you're here, I'm sure she'll be back soon. Would you like to come in? I can make some tea while we wait."

Roisin gave her a wary look. "I'm not sure that it would be wise to take tea with a witch," she said in a cold voice.

But you think it wise to insult one?

Mairead forced the thought away along with her annoyance. She needed to make allies here. Temper would not help that.

"I give you my word that you are safe here," Mairead said, stepping back and holding her hands up. "I do not wish anyone harm."

"And what is the word of a witch worth?"

Mairead glanced down to where Samuel stood beside his mother, clinging to her skirt. She wondered how much of the journey from the village Roisin must have spent carrying her son, along with the covered basket over her arm, and how she wouldn't have chosen to make that walk today, and to come here where Mairead was, unless it was important. Especially since Constance was due to visit the village in two days anyway. She took another step back.

"If my word is not enough, then consider things logically. If I harbored any evil intent, would I really have exposed myself to save Bridie and Jamie? I could have done nothing, and it all would have been a tragic accident, and no one would have any reason to fear me. That would make it much easier for me to carry out whatever ill intent I had, wouldn't it?"

Roisin *hmmmph*ed and folded her arms across her torso, pointedly looking away.

Mairead sighed. "You're welcome to stand out there and wait if you wish. Or you can come into the yard, and I'll bring out a chair and you can at least take the weight off your feet for a while."

Roisin looked at Mairead and then down at Samuel, perhaps thinking of how she would have to carry him most of the way back to the village.

"Very well." She swept into the yard and past Mairead, then stood in the center of the space, tapping her foot.

Mairead swallowed the desire to curse the unpleasant woman, and headed inside, bringing out a chair and a low stool for Samuel. She placed them carefully and then went back to her churning, choosing to ignore Roisin as far as was possible for the rest of her visit.

Samuel, oblivious to the tension, chattered away at his mother about the sun and the birds and the shapes of the clouds, before getting up and running around the yard, kicking at leaves that had not been swept up yet. Later, Mairead would gather them and add them to the midden, where they could break down and be returned to feed the fields before the spring planting.

Roisin watched her son, and Mairead softened toward the other woman when she saw the look of uncertainty that passed over her face, how her hands tightened around the handle of her basket, when he tripped and stumbled, then caught himself, laughing, and raced off again.

It wasn't long before Elspeth and Janey came running together into the yard, Constance behind them, with Simon wrapped in a shawl at her chest.

"Roisin! Is everything all right? I wasn't expecting to see you until Friday."

Roisin stood and walked to Constance, half of her attention still on Samuel. "I brought you some berries I foraged. I was hoping you might have some milk to spare? Samuel is going through a fussy spell, and I can't get him to eat unless he has milk with everything. Jack is always good at getting him to eat, but Jack isn't here, and who knows when he'll be back, and so I'm running through milk faster than usual because I don't know what else to do to get him to eat, and—"

Constance cut her off, by pulling her into an embrace. "It's all right now, Roisin. Of course you can have some milk."

"What kind of mother am I, that I can't get him to eat?" Roisin wailed into Constance's shoulder.

Mairead looked over to where Samuel and the girls were running around kicking leaves at each other and shrieking with laughter. She might not enjoy Roisin's company but it was clear to see that she doted on her son, and that he was happy and healthy as a result. Of course, that probably wouldn't mean anything coming from Mairead.

"You're a perfectly good mother who is doing her best under trying circumstances," Constance said, stepping back and placing both hands on Roisin's shoulders. "As are we all. Life forces compromise upon us from time to time, and we simply must bend with it. Now let me fetch you some milk. Would you like some tea? Or water?"

Roisin sniffed and dabbed at her eyes with a handkerchief. "No, thank you, I need to get back. I've left fish smoking in the shed, and I need to swap it out."

Constance gave Mairead a questioning look as she passed on the way to the cold store but said nothing. Roisin pointedly turned her back and watched the children play.

Mairead checked the churner – the butter was ready. "Do you need any butter, while you're here?" she asked. "Can't get any fresher."

Roisin glanced over at her and shook her head. "No. Thank you."

Constance came back with two large bottles of milk, handed them to Roisin, and accepted the berries in return. These she placed in a wooden box she had brought with her from the cold store.

Roisin called Samuel to her and Constance walked with them to the gate.

"Oh, I almost forgot," Roisin said, stopping just inside the yard. "A couple of sheep have gone missing. They've probably just wandered off somewhere, but Young Robbie swears up and down that they were safely locked away in the pen at night and gone in the morning."

"He's certain?" Constance asked, dread filling her voice.

"So he says, but it's always possible he miscounted. How careful were you about doing your chores when you were twelve?"

Constance made a noncommittal noise then said, "Have someone else count them in tonight, and let's double-check that the pen is secure."

"I'll let them know," Roisin said. "Thank you for the milk. I'll see you on Friday." She took Samuel's hand and he toddled along beside her as she led him out through the gate.

Constance watched them go for a few minutes, while Mairead tidied away the chair and took the butter round to the cold store. When she came back, Constance was still standing by the gate, her head in her hands.

"Are you well?" Mairead asked, approaching to stand beside her.

Constance lifted her tear-stained face from her hands. "What if the raiders have come? How will we protect ourselves? How do I keep my children safe?"

Mairead reached out and pulled Constance against her, holding her as she cried, just as Constance had done for Roisin a little while ago. Silky strands of hair had come loose from Constance's bun and tickled Mairead's neck and face as she comforted the other woman.

Despite the circumstances, she felt herself reacting to the closeness. She longed to kiss Constance's forehead, to smooth the creases on her brow and wipe all of her fears away. *Oh no. I can't fall for her. I can't.*

"We'll find a way," she murmured, pressing her hands into Constance's back. "I don't know how yet, but we will."

Constance straightened and wiped her tears away then cleared her throat. "I'm sorry."

"You never have to apologize for feeling something," Mairead said.

"I'm frightened," Constance said softly, looking over Mairead's shoulder to avoid her gaze.

"I know. And we'll find a way to keep them safe. Whatever it takes."

That night, as soon as the children were in bed, Mairead sat down at the table and asked Constance to join her.

"I have an idea," she said. "I can't promise that it will work, but I think it's worth trying."

"What's your idea?"

"I think we should call on Nicnevin and ask for help."

"Nicnevin?" Constance asked, disbelieving. "The fae?"

Mairead nodded.

"That's your idea? To call on a character from stories we tell children to keep them from wandering off in the woods?" She laughed dismissively.

Mairead shook her head, trying to push away her hurt at Constance's reaction. "I know it can be hard to believe in something you've never seen. But she's not just a story. She's real. I met her on my way here." *At least, I think I did.*

Constance leaned forward and studied her face as if looking for the joke. "There's no such thing as fae."

"Is that why you have a horseshoe hanging over the barn door?" Mairead said, raising an eyebrow.

"That's just superstition," Constance said, waving it away. "It doesn't mean anything."

"So, you'd be comfortable taking it down then?"

"I..." Constance shook her head. "Not really, no. Iron keeps the animals safe."

"Because it keeps the fae away."

Constance sighed and sat back in her chair. "All right, let's say that she's real and that we can reach out to her. What could she do to help? Why would she care enough to try?"

"She's the Queen of Witches," Mairead said, clasping her hands together on the table to keep from fidgeting. "She's aware of all of us, and our troubles pain her. I think she can be persuaded to help."

"But what can she do?"

"I don't know. Maybe she can ward the village or something. But we won't find out unless we ask."

Constance looked off toward the hearth and gazed at the flames, twisting a loose strand of hair between her fingers as she thought. Mairead could see curiosity warring with caution, and overall, a fierce need to protect her family, all as it crossed her face.

"How would we go about contacting her?"

"We could start by making an offering to her. She told me that she can feel us all, so maybe if we focus our attention on her, she'll feel it and know we want to talk."

"What kind of offering?" Constance asked, sounding suspicious.

Mairead shrugged. "The old stories often say that if you want to appease the fae you should leave milk and honey out for them. Maybe we should start with that?"

Constance got to her feet and fetched a shallow bowl, into which she poured some milk and drizzled the last of their honey. Then she scattered in some dried flowers and herbs, smiling at Mairead. "It seems a queen should have more to her offering than the average fae." When everything had been assembled, she sat back down and said, "Now what?"

Mairead laid her arms across the table, palms up. "Take my hands."

Constance did so, her skin warm against Mairead's, calloused in places but not rough.

"Now try to direct some of your power toward me, to amplify my call. Do you think you can do that?"

"I'll try."

Mairead felt the flow of Constance's power coming into her through her hands and flowing up her arms, making her skin tingle and heart speed up. "Nicnevin, Queen of Witches, two of your daughters beseech you. Please help us to protect our home and the women and children who live here."

Mairead closed her eyes and pushed as much feeling and power as she could behind her words. *Please. Please help us.*

"You called?"

Constance leapt back from the table, breaking the connection, and whirled to face the woman who lounged on one of the chairs by the hearth. Nicnevin sat there, legs crossed, displaying the tattooed vines that wound up one leg and vanished beneath her scandalously short dress. In one hand she held the crispest, greenest apple Mairead had ever seen. The clean, fresh scent of it spread across the room, adding a new note to the usual smells of the house.

Mairead found herself studying the fae admiringly, her otherworldly beauty and raw sensuality overpowering any sense of propriety. Her presence sparked a deep hunger in Mairead that she had no control over.

"My lady, thank you for coming so quickly," she said, rising and moving round the table to stand beside Constance.

"This is…" Constance asked, looking between Nicnevin and Mairead.

"Nicnevin, Queen of Witches, at your service," the fae said with a smile. "And you, dear, are one of the most powerful human witches I've ever encountered. Very interesting indeed."

"I…uh… It's a pleasure to meet you."

"Now, what do you want from me?" she asked before taking a bite from her apple.

"We were hoping you could help us, my lady," Mairead said, looping her arm through Constance's to offer her support. "The men from the village have all gone off to fight and left us without enough hands to get everything ready for winter. We've already come to the attention of the Black Watch and can't be sure that the magic we used to turn their attention away will hold, and now we've had news of raiders attacking other villages in the area while they can't protect themselves."

"That does sound like a lot to deal with." Nicnevin sat forward on the edge of the chair. "What magic were you playing with the other night when the wisps saw you? A living scarecrow?"

"No, not…we weren't playing," Mairead said, taken aback that the wisps reported back to Nicnevin, that she had been keeping an eye on them. "I had thought that maybe we could animate the scarecrows, have them do some of the work, lifting and carrying and so on. And that maybe from a distance, outsiders might believe that it was the village men working in the fields and watching the flocks. That they might make us look a little less vulnerable, a little less like an easy target."

Nicnevin took another bite of her apple and chewed it thoughtfully, tilting her head to the side. "It wasn't a bad idea," she said after a moment. "But it would only work if they had a degree of independence that's beyond human magic."

"Is it beyond fae magic?" Mairead asked hesitantly.

"Nope." Nicnevin stood and tossed her apple core into the air, where it disappeared at the apex of its arch. "Or at least, it is not beyond mine. I can help you, but you're going to need to get the rest of the village involved too. Do you think you can do that?"

"What do you need?" Constance said, sounding sure of herself for the first time since Nicnevin appeared in the room.

"Scarecrows won't do the job; their structure is too weak. You need to build men out of the earth itself. Mud and straw and clay and stone, grass and sticks and moss. Shape them out of this land that you're asking them to help you protect. For each earth man you build, there must be a villager willing to share her life force to animate him and give instructions. You must understand, magic like this is not safe. There are risks, not the least of which is that they will lose a little of their own time, to give to the earth men. For every four days that they live, the person connected to them will lose a day of their own time. That must be clear. There can be no bargain without informed consent."

Constance looked at Mairead, her eyes dark with concern. "What else?" she said, turning back to the fae queen.

"By giving my magic to this endeavor, I too will be bound to these men. Do not use them for anything other than feeding yourselves and protecting what is yours. Any other use of them will taint my magic, and I will not tolerate that. Is this understood?"

"Yes, of course, my lady," Mairead said. "How can we repay you for your help?"

A bargain with a fae was not to be entered into lightly, and Mairead knew it would be a terrible idea to be in Nicnevin's debt with the boundaries of that debt undefined.

"When your current crisis is over and the uprising reaches its end, the two of you will found a safe place for witches. You will build a home for them, where they can learn to control their magic, where they need not fear persecution or death because of the way they were born." Nicnevin stepped forward and cupped Mairead's cheek. "You, daughter, will stop running. You will make sure that there is somewhere in Alba where people like you are welcome. That is the price of my assistance."

"That is no small price to pay," Constance said sharply.

Nicnevin shrugged. "It is no small magic you ask for. Call for me again when you are ready. Otherwise, I wish you luck."

With that, Nicnevin turned on the spot and disappeared in a shower of sparks.

Chapter Twelve

Constance

18th September 1745

"Do you think they'll agree to it?" Mairead asked, keeping her voice low as she scanned the gathered women.

Constance pressed her lips together and thought, not for the first time, about doing away with kings and thrones and all the things that had led to her being in this position. "I don't know."

They had arrived for their scheduled trade then asked everyone who was able to come together for a meeting.

"That's another sheep gone," Roisin said, approaching from the direction of the grazing land beyond the village. "I counted them in myself last night and there's definitely one missing this morning. That gate was secure, there's no way it could have just wandered off."

Constance's heart sped up, and she felt her pulse in her throat. "Raiders," she murmured to Mairead. "We have no choice. We have to get them to agree."

"I'll do whatever you need me to," Mairead said. She took Simon from her and carried him over to sit with the girls, on the low wall around Emily's garden.

Constance thought about the food they had served the Watch men, and the persuasive magic that she and Mairead had served them along with it. Part of her was tempted to use the same approach here, to make the people of the village more amenable to her arguments. What she wanted to do was for the good of everyone, after all. She wouldn't be acting against their best interests... Would it really be any different to a parent overriding a child's insistence on staying up late, when they desperately needed sleep?

But they are not children, and I am not their parent. I do not get to choose for them. No matter how much easier it might be.

Constance had promised herself that she would never use her magic against another, but she had broken that already with the spell on the Watch men, and now the slippery slope beckoned her.

"Will this take long? I've much and more to do," said Catriona McDonnell. "And I know I'm not the only one."

"Well, I may have found a solution to that," Constance said. "Are we all here?"

She looked around at the curious faces. Everyone who wasn't in the fields or with the livestock was here, all waiting for her to explain why she'd called them away from their work. She glanced up at the overcast sky, hoping that the rain would hold until after their discussion.

"I'm not quite sure where to start," she said, looking from face to face and studying them. If this went badly, it might be the last she saw of these people, those she had built relationships with and cared for since her marriage.

"You know we're all here for you," Emily said, giving her an encouraging nod. "Whatever you need."

Constance took a deep breath, and drew on a little of her magic, just enough to bolster her confidence. "When Fergus wrote to tell me they were staying in Inverness, he also told me about a group of people who had come into the hospital where Jamie is. These people were from a village near Inverness, which was attacked by raiders. Raiders who began by stealing their sheep."

A few gasps sounded at that.

"When confronted, the raiders burned down the village and killed some of those who lived there. Only a few survivors made it to Inverness."

"You don't think… Our sheep…"

"We don't know anything for sure, and I don't want to unduly frighten anyone, but I think we have to treat this as a serious threat."

"What are we going to do?" Roisin asked, her voice thick with barely restrained panic. "We have nowhere to go!"

"No one is suggesting we should leave," Constance said, holding her hand up. Small speckles of cold alighted on her forehead as the rain began to fall.

"Surely you're not suggesting we fight them?" Mr. Kinloch shouted. A man long past his prime, he had been left behind by the others and though he could still help out in many ways, he could no longer wield a weapon as he once had.

"Not at all," Constance said. "That would end badly for us, I think. But I may have another solution, to this and to the problem of getting everything done before winter." She paused here and looked around again. The people looking back were frightened and wary, all except Mairead, who looked at her with calm trust. "There's no easy way to say this, and it may not be easy to hear, but I beg of you, if you value our home at all, hear me out."

Frowns and nods came from the group.

"The night before last, I met with someone who has offered us help. Magical help. They said that we can make men out of earth and plants and all of the things that make up Kilmartin, and that these men can be brought to life, to work alongside us and offer us some protection from raiders and the Black Watch, and anyone else we may need some protection from." Someone began to speak, but Constance held up her hand and continued, hoping they would let her get it all out before shouting her down. "Each of these men would be connected to a different one of us, and each of us would be giving a little of our life force to them. In doing so, our own lives will be shortened by a day for every four days that the earth men are with us. I realize that this sounds outlandish, and maybe even frightening, but I do believe that it is our best chance to survive this winter, and this uprising."

She stopped and waited for the outcry, as the raindrops grew heavier and began to roll down her face.

"Have you lost your mind?" Roisin shrieked. "It's bad enough that you expect us to tolerate a witch among us, but now you want us all to participate in witchcraft!"

"I want you all to participate in the protection of this village," Constance snapped back. "No more and no less."

"Mistress Gordon. Constance. We've been friends for a long time, and you know that I trust you," Emily Croaker said, "but you must understand that this is a lot you ask of us. Give us some time to get our heads around it."

"If circumstances weren't so dire I wouldn't ask this of you at all," Constance said, her tone conciliatory. "I have no wish for anyone to participate in anything that makes them uncomfortable. But with these sheep going missing, I fear we have only a small window to take action before it's too late."

"How do we know the witch hasn't put you up to this?" Roisin demanded. "This could all be her plan to weaken us, to put her own creatures in control."

Constance blew out a sharp breath. She had known this would not be easy – she was asking a lot from them after all. But she couldn't let Roisin's voice be the dominant one here, and she would not stand by and allow Mairead to be maligned this way, not when she had risked so much to help them, and Constance had allowed her to take all of the fear and mistrust, while she allowed the village to believe that Mairead had acted alone.

"Mairead, would you be so kind as to wait out past the church?" she said. "I promise it won't be for long."

"Of course," Mairead said, smiling. She sent a subtle pulse of magic toward Constance as she walked away, wordless support. They had talked about the possibility of having to do this.

While she watched Mairead leave Constance considered what would be the best demonstration. Initially, she had thought to lift something without touching it, but the rain had given her another idea. Already, it was making her hair cling to her face and beading in the weave of her woolen wrap.

When Mairead was out of sight, Constance focused her will and sent it out to form a shield around the people standing together in the center of the village, a kind of bubble of energy, which repelled the rain, keeping it from reaching those who stood inside it. It was a subtle form of magic, and one that no one noticed at first.

"Well, what are you waiting for? Why did you send the witch away?" Roisin said, tapping her foot impatiently.

"Mairead is not the only witch in Kilmartin," Constance said, pointedly looking above them.

They looked around, uncomprehending at first, until finally Catriona looked up. Above them, raindrops fell until they met the bubble of Constance's will, then they stopped. Some splashed up, others rolled down the outside until they reached the edge and resumed their fall to the ground.

"Lord save us," Catriona said, pressing a hand to her breast. "What is this?"

"This is my magic," Constance said, somehow keeping her voice steady despite the tremble that shook her from head to foot. "Used to shield you from the rain. Exactly the same way that I used it to help shield Bridie and Jamie from the fire at the church."

They stared at her, some looking horrified, others curious, a few hurt.

"I did you wrong then," Constance said. "And I did Mairead wrong. I was scared, you see. Scared that you would fear me and shun me if you knew what I was. So, I let Mairead carry all of that, and I let you believe she acted alone when she didn't. She acted first and did by far the hardest part – Mairead is a hero. Without her example, I would have remained frozen in fear until it was too late. But she is not the only witch."

"How long…?" Mistress Croaker asked.

"My whole life. I was born this way. I made things float before I could walk." She cleared her throat. "For the last eight years, ever since I wed Iain and came here, you have all known me. In all of that time, I have only ever acted in the best interests of this village. I take my responsibility to you seriously. I am asking you to trust me."

"How can we trust someone who has been lying to us for years?" Roisin spat.

"I have never lied to you," Constance said. "I may not have told you everything there was to know about me, but I have never said anything that is untrue. Do you tell the whole village everything about yourself, Roisin? Do we all know everything that happens in your home and in your head? Can any of us truly say that there are no parts of ourselves that we keep private?"

"I have no secrets that affect the whole village!"

Constance rolled her eyes. Her patience was wearing thin and she had to fight the urge to let the rain fall on Roisin and only her. Being petty would not be helpful. *It might make me feel better though.* "My magic has had no effect on this village until now, when I am using it for your benefit and asking for your help to keep us all safe."

"How can we be sure? How can we trust anything you say?"

"You could try engaging your brain," Constance snapped. "Ask yourself what benefit there is for me in any of this? The answer is none. None! If I chose to do so, I could use my magic to ensure that my family are fed and protected through the winter and leave the rest of you to manage for yourselves. But if you stop reacting and think, you'll realize that I would never do that. That I have always, *always* worked for the well-being of this entire community.

"Now, if none of you want to be involved, that is fine. Mairead and I will do what we can with the skills that we have. But it will not be enough. If the missing sheep really are a sign of raiders, then Mairead and I alone will not be enough to keep us all safe. So that is the choice you make. You can trust me, and we can take steps to protect ourselves and make our lives easier over the coming months, or you can choose to be wary and face whatever comes without magical help."

With that, she withdrew her will into her body and allowed the rain to fall freely on them once more, bringing a few startled gasps and exclamations.

"You must do what you think is right. But don't wait too long to make a choice, or you might find that circumstances overtake us."

She stalked over to the children, lifted Simon in her arms and said, "Let's get Mistress Ferguson and go home, my loves."

The rain kept coming as they traveled home, accompanied by an icy wind for the latter half of the journey. By the time they reached the cottage, they were all soaked through and shivering, and Constance made the decision to take the rest of the day away from work and chores. Her emotions were a storm, and the children were picking up on it and growing fractious themselves. They all needed rest and warmth and time to recover.

As soon as they got inside, she set about heating water, then dragged out the small metal tub they kept for the rare occasions when an indoor bath was needed. Simon got the first lot of water, as he needed the coolest – and she was worried about how cold he looked. As she washed him in barely warm water, then wrapped him in a blanket, Elspeth helped Janey out of her clothes and into the tub. Constance's heart brimmed with emotion at the kindness of her eldest daughter. Mairead carefully added some more warm water to the tub as Constance fed Simon, who was pulling at her dress impatiently. After a quick wash for Janey, and into fresh clothes, it was Elspeth's turn, then Constance pulled a screen around and insisted that Mairead take the opportunity to wash and get warm as well.

At last, she got into the tub herself, her knees pulled up under her chin, the water warm and soothing, as Mairead had topped it up for her. Such luxury. She hadn't had a warm bath since some time last winter, and as she allowed herself a few moments to enjoy it, the tension her muscles had been holding since they set off that morning finally began to ease. She had done all she could. If they decided that her magic made her untrustworthy, then she and Mairead and the children would see out the winter here and when spring came, well. They would just have to wait and see.

As tempting as it was to dawdle until the water was cold, there was still dinner to be made and the children to be tended to. She scooped water up in a cup and poured it over her head and face, letting it wash away her frustration with it. She allowed herself to enjoy the sensations of getting clean, scrubbing soap over her body and through her hair and then rinsing it off.

She stepped out of the tub and roughly dried herself before pulling on a clean shift and kirtle. Together, she and Mairead dragged the tub to the door and tipped it out into the yard. The water joined the puddles from the rain, which was coming down heavier than ever.

The scarecrow they had been practicing with hung limp and sodden over the fence, much of his straw now floating in the puddles that crossed the yard.

"Looks like we got back just at the right time," Mairead said, as they lifted the tub and returned it to its customary corner. "If Roisin had argued much longer, we'd still be out in that."

Constance scoffed, "Roisin would have argued all day if I'd been willing to stand there and argue back." She looked at Mairead and saw understanding in her gaze. "It hurts to be dismissed so, when all I've ever done is help."

As she went to close the door, a flash of light caught her attention and Constance turned toward the path to the village, peering into the early dusk brought by the rain. Whatever it was had disappeared and for the briefest of moments, she wondered if it had been a will-o'-the-wisp, dancing along the path, and her breast filled with awe and wonder.

"Everything all right?" Mairead asked, when Constance stood in the doorway without moving, letting the wind and rain in past her.

Constance closed the door against the weather and turned into the room. "I thought I saw something, but it was nothing." She smiled. "There's a little of the rabbit left. I thought we could have that tonight, with some barley and carrots?"

"Sounds perfect for a night like this."

Constance fetched some carrots and took them to the table, knife in hand, but Mairead stopped her, placing a warm hand over her own.

"Let me."

"Is my cooking really so terrible?" Constance asked with a laugh.

Mairead smiled back, her eyes lighting with humor. "Terrible is a strong word…"

Constance nudged her in the side with her elbow, surprised by how much she enjoyed the closeness of Mairead's body. "And you can do so much better, can you?" she said, hoping her playful tone made her intentions clear.

"Go and sit by the fire and we'll find out."

"Mama, will you tell us a story?" Elspeth asked, tugging at Constance's skirt.

Constance smiled down at her daughter. "What kind of story would you like?"

"One about a princess," Elspeth said.

"Mouse!" Janey cried. "I like mouses."

Constance sat down on the chair by the hearth and waited for the children to settle on the floor in front of her. The two girls moved Simon round so that he was facing her.

"Once upon a time, in a faraway land, there lived a princess. But this wasn't just any princess, she was a mouse princess! Her father was king of all the mice in the land, and even the voles and shrews. All was well for the mice, until one day the rat king—"

A loud thudding at the door interrupted her and made her startle in her chair.

"Who can that be?" she said, frowning, as she got to her feet.

"The rat king!" Elspeth shouted gleefully.

As she crossed the room, Constance couldn't help but imagine a man-sized rat standing on the other side of the door, royal regalia dripping wet. She shuddered, then pulled the door open.

Rather than the rat king, Emily Croaker stood dripping on the doorstep.

"Come in! What are you doing out in that weather? You'll catch your death!" Constance stepped back and gestured for her friend and neighbor to enter.

"Thank you." Emily stepped inside. Her coat hung limp and heavy with water, clinging to her legs. Her gray hair was plastered to her head, so full of rain that it looked almost black again.

"Here, let me take this, warm yourself by the fire." Constance helped the older woman out of her sodden coat and led her to the chair she had recently vacated.

"We'll do it," Emily said without preamble. "At least some of us will. Others were not so willing to listen to reason."

"Have you all been discussing this the entire time since we left?"

"Aye," she said, settling heavily into the chair and leaning forward to warm her hands by the fire. "It has been a trying day."

Constance looked over to Mairead, who still stood at the table, preparing dinner unobtrusively. She glanced up and gave a subtle nod of support.

"I had thought to wait until the rain passed before coming to see you, but at this time of year that could be days hence, and you said that time was of the essence."

"I…yes. Yes, I did. I didn't mean for… Never mind, you'll take dinner with us?"

"That would be lovely, thank you."

"And a dram to take the chill from your bones?"

Emily grinned. "A splendid idea," she said.

Constance busied herself pouring drinks for them all. "So, what happened after we left?"

"I won't bore you with all the discussion and debate that went on – I'm sure you can imagine most of it for yourself. You have eight folk willing to help, to tie themselves to these earth men that you spoke of. Roisin fair ranted on about the wickedness of it all, but the others won't stop us, though neither do they wish to be involved."

Constance handed her a glass of whisky. "Who are the eight?"

Chapter Thirteen

Mairead

19th September 1745

The next morning dawned bright and clear, and Mairead awoke to Janey climbing into bed beside her and peeling her eyelid open.

"It's wake-up time," she said, giggling, when Mairead jerked back, rubbing at her face. "Are you sure?" Mairead asked groggily. "It doesn't feel like wake-up time."

"Birdies are awake," Janey said. "They're singing."

Mairead listened to the chorus of twitters, cheeps and trills coming from outside. "Yes, they are."

"Janey, leave Mistress Ferguson alone," Constance scolded, coming through the front door and taking her muddy boots off.

Mairead sat up with a groan and ruffled Janey's hair fondly. "It's all right. It's wake-up time."

Mistress Croaker had spent the night, taking the girls' bed, while they shared with Constance for the night. As soon as everyone had eaten and the animals had all been tended to, they all set off together for the village, taking Angus and the cart, Mistress Croaker sitting in the cart with the children while Mairead and Constance walked alongside. Though the rain had stopped at some point overnight, the path was muddy, and the wheels of the cart frequently threw up sprays of water from the puddles they passed through.

Mairead was glad of the good pair of boots that Constance had loaned her, even though they were a little loose and she had to wear an extra pair of stockings to keep them from rubbing.

They arrived in the village midmorning, and Mistress Croaker went first to see about her chickens, while Mairead and Constance lingered by the cart. Mairead could feel the tension in the air, the unseen eyes watching them from the homes nearby.

"I don't know how to start," Constance said in a low voice. "What am I supposed to do?"

Mairead looked around, wondering the same thing herself. Nicnevin hadn't exactly left them with clear instructions. "I suppose we start building the men," she said. "Each person willing to participate could perhaps shape their own? At least in part."

Constance seemed to give it some thought and then nodded. "That makes sense. Shaping the creature with one's own hands would surely strengthen the magical bond."

"Why don't we find a space to work and then begin to gather the materials we'll need. Nicnevin said sticks and moss and rocks and all the things that make up Kilmartin."

"There's a field out by," Mistress Croaker said, obviously catching part of their conversation as she rejoined them. She nodded off behind her house. "We've taken the last of the barley from it, so there should be plenty of space."

"Why don't you two take the children and start gathering rocks and so on. I'll round up the others." Constance gave a tight smile then set off down the street.

Mairead thought back to the evening before and the warm baths they had all taken and thought about the fact that they were about to get covered in mud. If only they had waited another night; they might well have need of baths again by the end of the day.

"Come on, children, let's go and play in the mud," she said, lifting Simon from the basket he sat in, in the back of the cart.

Elspeth and Janey gave a cheer and jumped down from the back of the cart, skipping along behind Mistress Croaker, as Mairead brought up the rear. They made their way behind the row of houses and along a path that led between the gardens and the field in question. The sun glinted off a rock that lay beside the path, picking out a pearlescence from within the otherwise smoky-gray stone. Mairead stooped and picked it up. The rock was about the length of her pinkie, wider at one end than the other, with one rough face and one rubbed smooth as if polished. Something about this particular stone spoke to her, and she tucked it away in a pocket in her skirt, before hurrying to catch up with the others.

They entered the field, with the girls chattering away, the sun casting a haze over the ground as the previous day's rain began to evaporate. Here and there, clumps of half-pulled stalks stood, rising from the otherwise empty rows.

"Well then," Mistress Croaker said, with her hands on her hips. "What do we need?"

Mairead shifted Simon on her hip and looked around the field. "Nicnevin said that we would need to build them out of mud and include rocks and plants and all the things that make up Kilmartin."

"Nicnevin?" Mistress Croaker exclaimed. "As in the fae witch? From the old folktales?"

Mairead nodded, biting at the inside of her lip. "Does that change your mind?"

Mistress Croaker let out a long, slow breath. At last, she said, "No. It doesn't. You're not trying to pull the wool over an old woman's eyes, now, are you?"

"Never."

"No. I didn't think so."

They set about gathering rocks and moss and barley stalks and sticks and fallen leaves, building them all into a large pile near the entrance to the field. By the time Constance arrived with the others in tow, a fine film of sweat covered the back of Mairead's neck and trickled down the groove of her spine, beneath her layers of clothing. Simon was old enough to wriggle but too young to hold any of his own weight, so carrying him while gathering supplies was wearing her out much faster than she would have anticipated. She thought of all the times she had watched Constance carrying out various chores with Simon in one arm and found herself even more in awe of her.

When Constance approached and took Simon from her, Mairead rolled her shoulders in relief.

"I see you've made quite the start," Constance said with a nod at the pile.

"We haven't started shaping anything yet," Mairead said, following her gaze. "Just gathering things."

Constance leaned in close and lowered her voice. "She will come, won't she? Nicnevin?"

I hope so. "Of course. She said she would."

"So, how big are we making these things?" Mistress Gordon called, rolling her sleeves up past her elbows.

Constance gave Mairead an anxious look. Her worries pulsed along the line of magic that bound them now, each to the other. Mairead sent calm reassurance back, giving the energetic equivalent of a warm embrace. Constance steeled herself and turned.

"The idea is that these earth men can both carry out some of the work around the village," Constance said, "and that from a distance, they might look like our husbands and brothers and sons, perhaps discourage anyone looking for an easy target. So, we probably want to make them roughly man sized."

Mairead saw the thoughts passing over Mistress Gordon's face, the ribald comment that came to her lips before she glanced over to where Elspeth and Janey were playing, within hearing distance, then bit it back, shaking her head. Mairead chuckled to herself, able to guess the gist of the other woman's thoughts. She might never have been intimate with a man herself, but she had heard plenty of details from friends who had over the years.

Constance clapped, startling her from her thoughts.

"Let's get to work, shall we?"

By the time the sun was nearing the horizon once more, there were ten roughly man-sized figures lying in a row across the field. Their features and shaping were crude, and Mairead worried about whether they would be sufficient for the task. Her back ached as she bent over her own earth man, doing her best to smooth the planes of his face, trying to distract her mind from how much she would like to run her fingers over Constance's face in this manner, tracing every detail until her skin had it all memorized.

"Are you finished?" Constance asked, coming to stand beside her.

Mairead straightened and winced, her spine popping and crackling. "I think so. I don't know." She cocked her head to one side, studying her creation. "It feels incomplete somehow."

Constance glanced over her shoulder to the earth man she had been working on. "As does mine. But I'm not sure we can achieve much more without some guidance from our friend."

Mairead glanced up and down the line of earth men, each with a villager standing beside it. She had been surprised to see Mr. Kinloch was one of the eight who were willing to participate. "You did tell them about the cost, didn't you?" she asked Constance, whose hands and forearms were covered in mud, much like her own. "They know that they'll be giving up some of their own lifetime to do this?"

"Of course," Constance answered, frowning. "I have kept nothing from them."

"Where are the children?" Mairead asked, suddenly realizing that she couldn't see them. Her heart started to beat faster, and she looked around wildly, scanning every dip and corner of the field.

"Be at peace." Constance placed a hand on her arm. The warmth where their skin touched sank into her and soothed the panic, transforming it into desire instead. "They were tired and hungry. Catriona took them to have some food and rest. Her earth man was already finished."

"Do you think this will work?" Mairead asked.

Constance shrugged. "It has to."

Mairead opened her mouth to say something else, though she didn't know what, when she saw Catriona walking toward them, without the children.

She raised a hand as she approached and called, "They're with my mother. She said that just because she can't bring herself to 'perform witchcraft' doesn't mean she's unwilling to help in other ways. The two wee ones are asleep, and Elspeth was looking like she might not be far behind them."

"Is it time then?" Mairead asked, turning to Constance.

"I think so."

While Mairead gathered the group into a circle, Constance fetched supplies they had brought with them from the cart. When the group were positioned correctly, Mairead took the supplies into the center of their circle and poured fresh milk into the bowl they had brought, then drizzled in some honey and added a dram of whisky for good measure.

She returned to her place in the circle and joined hands with the people on either side of her. Constance stood opposite, staring at her, expression intense. Mairead studied her as best she could in the dying light of the day. There was something akin to hunger on her face…longing perhaps. Something unspoken passed between them and Mairead swallowed hard. Could it be? Was there something beyond friendship growing between them? Surely not. Constance was married, after all. Mairead was just seeing what she wanted to see in her expression.

Beside her, Mistress Gordon fidgeted nervously and Mairead pulled her focus back to the task at hand. With a nod to Constance, Mairead sent a pulse of magic around the circle, and Constance did the same. A few of the people in the circle twitched or gasped, as if they had felt it pass through them, but most remained unaware of the power that was building.

"Nicnevin, we beseech you," Mairead called, filling her heart and mind with respect and hope. "Please give us your aid."

The moment stretched out, with nothing to show for their efforts other than the power that was circulating through them, building with each passing. Then between one breath and the next, she was there, standing in the center of the circle as if she had always been there.

"Good day," she said with a smile. "The whisky was a welcome addition. I see you have done as we discussed."

"We have, my lady," Mairead said. She could feel Constance sending a wave of reassurance through the group, who were still standing with their hands joined, except for one person who had gasped and stepped back, bringing her hands to her chest, when Nicnevin appeared. "Are the earth men we have crafted sufficient to the task?"

Nicnevin walked toward her, and Mairead stepped aside to allow her to pass. The fae walked the length of the row of earth men, then turned and came back. "Yes, these will do nicely. Although I feel they deserve a better moniker than 'earth men', don't you?"

"I have been thinking about that," Constance said. "I wondered if we might call them Albans, since they are made from Alba itself?"

Nicnevin nodded slowly. "Albans, yes. I like that. Now. I see that there is one Alban for each of the people gathered here. Let me be sure that you all understand how this will work." She looked over the group. Her gaze came to rest on Constance.

Mairead shivered, as a flash of something passed over her, some fae magic perhaps. Or perhaps it was just jealousy.

"Each one of you will be tethered to one of the Albans. You will be sharing your life force with it, the magic that exists inside each and every living being. For every four days that your Alban is drawing on your life force, you will be giving up a day of your own life, assuming that you die of old age. This magic has no effect on accidents or violence, merely how much power is left to keep your own body running. Do you all understand this sacrifice that you make?"

There were nods and murmurs of agreement from all around the circle.

"Very well," Nicnevin said, when all had answered in some form. "The other thing you must be sure to understand is that this endeavor of yours is drawing upon my magic. Any action taken by your Albans is bound to me as well as to you. They may be used only to protect your village; any act of aggression on their part would taint my magic, and I simply will not tolerate this. If I find you have abused my trust and misused my magic, I will end the spell, and your village will feel my wrath. Be clear that this is a *geis* of some significance."

Mairead's mouth went dry at Nicnevin's use of the word *geis*. The fae queen was making it quite clear that the consequences for breaking her terms would be dire indeed. The villagers seemed more hesitant this time in their agreement, looking to Constance for guidance. She stepped forward, the setting sun making a halo behind her head, granting her a crown of gold.

"We understand and accept your terms," she said in a clear voice, giving the villagers the confidence they needed to agree.

Nicnevin turned to Mairead, who had not spoken. "And you, daughter of magic? Do you agree to be bound by my terms?"

Mairead tore her gaze from Constance and bowed her head. "Of course, my lady. I am yours to command." She frowned at her own words. She had spent much of her life avoiding circumstances that would give another power over her, and yet here she was, giving it freely.

"Then let us begin. Constance, Mairead, come to me."

Mairead looked to Constance, finding herself just as much in need of her leadership as the rest of the people gathered were. Constance walked to Nicnevin's side, head held high, shoulders relaxed, looking for all the world as if she were approaching a friend she had not seen for a time. Mairead pushed down her nerves and followed.

When they reached her side, Nicnevin spoke to them both in a voice pitched for their ears only. "Mairead, your magic will form the foundation of the spell that we work. By agreeing to be part of this undertaking, you are binding yourself to these people and their fate for as long as the Albans live. You will be connected to each and every person here, and you may not leave this place until the spell has been dissolved."

Mairead stepped back, her mind awhirl. She had not bound herself to a single place in all of her adult life; was she really willing to do so now? "Wouldn't it make more sense to use Constance's magic as the foundation? She is already so strongly connected to these people, surely that would lend the spell strength?"

Constance must have sensed something of her panic, for she was frowning and reached for Mairead's hand.

Nicnevin studied Mairead's face; her beauty distracted Mairead. "You have spent much of your life learning to control your magic, to make it solid and dependable, to follow your wishes always. Constance, however, has spent her life attempting to suppress her magic, to force it into a locked box within herself, to allow it to come out only in small bursts when the pressure becomes too great to bear."

Mairead's heart ached at the thought of Constance spending her life hiding, making herself smaller than she was. She deserved so much more.

"As a result," Nicnevin continued, "Constance's magic is wild and unpredictable. She has very limited control over it. Even the call that brought you here those weeks ago was not made with intent. Even now, she does not know how to repeat such an act."

"She's right," Constance said, though her expression suggested that she was far from happy about that. "Any control I've learned over these last weeks has been learned from you."

"So, you see why it must be your magic that serves as our foundation," Nicnevin said.

"How long will I have to stay?" Mairead asked, mind racing. She was in no particular hurry to leave, and truly, if she could see herself settling anywhere, it was here, with Constance. With the villagers' fragile acceptance of who and what she was. But ever since she had left her parents' home, she had built a life that suited her, joining a community for a time but moving on before anyone could get too close, before anyone could hurt her.

Nicnevin shrugged. "As long as they need you."

"I don't know. I…" Mairead looked at Constance, at the naked vulnerability in her eyes, and knew that she could never turn away. "Yes. All right, I'll stay as long as I'm needed. I'll do this."

"Very well. Constance, you have the trust of the village. You stand to my left and lend what power you can. Mairead, stand to my right. You must open your magic to me, and I will shape it to meet our needs."

The two witches took their positions on either side of the fae. Nicnevin waved her hand, and a basket appeared before her, brimming with blooms the like of which Mairead had never seen. The flower heads were large and heavy, covered in an explosion of petals, cream and orange, shimmering with the rainbow gleam of fish scales. The most tantalizing aroma rose from them, filling the air with scents of every good thing Mairead could think of. The heady scents wound through her senses, making her feel almost as if she had been drinking in front of the fire with Constance, a languorous weight pressing down on her limbs.

Nicnevin looked at her, a puzzled expression on her face, then she looked at the flowers. "Ah. I had not considered their effect," she said. "That will not do at all." She placed two fingers in the center of Mairead's forehead, just above her nose, and spoke a word in a language Mairead had never heard before.

The scent of the flowers disappeared as if blown on a breeze, and Mairead's mind cleared with it. "What are they?" she asked, surprised at the slurring of her speech.

"They have no name that you would understand," Nicnevin said, not unkindly. "They grow only in Faery, where they are prized for their beauty. These will form the hearts of your Albans."

Mairead looked at the flowers and found herself mesmerized by the way the petals captured and reflected the dying light of the day. No wonder mortals who strayed into Faery so rarely managed to return home, should all things that grew there have such beauty and power.

"Now, who will go first?" Nicnevin asked, raising her voice to encompass the whole group.

The villagers all looked at each other, nervousness clear in their faces.

"I can go first," Mairead said. She hoped that her own nerves would ease with the taking of action.

Nicnevin shook her head. "You must be last," she said, "to close the spell. It is essential."

"I will go first," Constance said from the fae's other side.

"Very well." Nicnevin turned to face Constance, and Mairead moved with her, being sure to position herself in such a way that the villagers could see past her to what they would be asked to do in a moment.

Nicnevin placed a hand on Mairead's shoulder and said, "Now, you must open to me."

A great fear rose in Mairead, fear not of the fae witch herself, but of the interconnectedness and dependency that was being asked of her. All of a sudden, she felt as if her stays had been drawn too tight, that she could not pull in enough breath. Her panicked pulse fluttered at the base of her throat and for a moment she saw herself fleeing across the open field, heading for the anonymity of Inverness or another town, where no one knew her, or her secrets. She would be beholden to no one. She could do it: travel farther north, maybe even set sail for the islands, wait out the uprising somewhere safe.

Then an image of Constance flashed into her mind, Constance tired and worn down from trying to carry the whole village, Constance making the scarecrow dance with her in the yard, Constance laughing, her eyes sparkling with life and mischief.

I can do what is needful.

Mairead took a deep breath, pulling air into her lungs as if she had been drowning, then opened up her magic. She pictured it unfurling like a flower in sunlight in response to Nicnevin's touch.

"Pick a bloom," Nicnevin said to Constance. "Whichever speaks to your heart."

Constance bent to the basket and selected a flower and when she had straightened again, Nicnevin held a silver dagger with a wickedly sharp-looking blade and a delicately carved bone handle.

Mairead's magic surged in protectiveness and Nicnevin gave her a knowing look.

"She is safe, *a' charaid*, I promise you," the fae said, her voice appearing unbidden in Mairead's mind. Aloud, she said, "Now pluck three hairs from your head and wind them between the petals."

Constance did as she was asked, and Mairead felt Nicnevin pulling upon both of them, winding ribbons of their magic around her own. It brought an odd, draining sensation with it, neither unpleasant nor entirely comfortable.

Nicnevin took hold of Constance's hand and pricked her thumb with the very tip of the silver blade. A bead of crimson welled.

"Press it to the center of the bloom," Nicnevin said.

Constance did as she was bid and gasped in surprise when the inner petals closed over her thumb. Mairead stepped forward, alarmed, but before she could take any further action, the petals opened once more, and Constance raised her hand with a shaky laugh.

"I'm well," she said, meeting Mairead's worried gaze. "All is well."

"Now, take this heart-bloom and stand beside your Alban," Nicnevin said, "and continue to share your will with us while we see to the rest."

Constance nodded then moved away, cradling the flower as carefully in her hands as if it were a baby.

Nicnevin repeated the process with each of the villagers, while Mairead stood at her side, sharing her power, feeling the shape of the weaving that the fae performed. She felt as if she could almost understand how it was done, would almost be able to replicate it herself, but the final twist that Nicnevin brought to the working eluded her. There was some process, some element of fae magic that Mairead just couldn't quite grasp.

She had gotten so lost in trying to figure out how the spell worked, that she was shocked when the time came for her to go through the process herself. She looked down at the basket and blinked in surprise to see that it was still full, although nine other people had selected their blooms from it already.

"You summoned more?" she asked Nicnevin, wondering how she had done that while focusing on the spell. Could she split her will to more than one working at a time?

"Not exactly. Each person must make a choice – therefore the basket will ensure that there is a choice available. Select your bloom."

Mairead spared a glance for the others, who all stood lined up alongside their Albans. They all looked peaceful, filled with wonder rather than the anxiety that had dominated them at the start. She bent over the basket, closed her eyes on a whim and allowed her hands to find the bloom that spoke to them. One made her fingertips tingle when they brushed against the petals, so she carefully scooped that one up and held it loosely in her cupped palm.

She straightened, opened her eyes and turned her face up to Nicnevin, who stood a few inches taller than her. Even when she looked the fae full in the face, her mind could not quite grasp Nicnevin's features, could not really process them beyond 'beauty'. It was quite a bizarre sensation, to be so deeply attracted to someone and so completely unable to describe them.

"Your hand, please," Nicnevin said, holding out her own, palm up.

Mairead placed her hand atop Nicnevin's and watched as the fae witch pierced her thumb with the tip of the silver dagger. The pain was there, the sharp surprise of grasping a rose by the thorn, but it seemed far away somehow and unimportant. Blood welled up and Mairead pressed her thumb to the center of her flower, gasping when the petals closed, and she felt something akin to sucking on the wound. Could a flower really do that, or was something more happening here?

The petals opened and Nicnevin smiled at her. The warmth of her expression made Mairead's toes curl in delight.

"Now, take your place alongside your Alban."

Mairead did as she was bid, meeting Constance's eyes as she passed. There was a flash of something – jealousy perhaps? – but then it was gone, and Constance was smiling at her in encouragement. Mairead wondered if Constance was hurt that Nicnevin seemed to favor her, although she was a less powerful witch.

"You all hold the heart of your Albans in your hands," Nicnevin said so all could hear her. "You must each make a space in the torso of your Alban and carefully place the heart within, but do not cover it until I instruct you to do so."

Mairead knelt by the Alban she had built and placed her free hand upon the center of his torso. The mud was thick, sticky, and full of life. With the channel to her magic still open, she could sense all of the life force within the soil, even things far too small to see. She could feel the traces of life left over in decaying leaves and broken twigs, the tiny fronds of moss, the discarded beetle shells that were somewhere in the mud. She scooped out a hole. The thick rich earth clung to her fingers, filling her with a resigned melancholy over the cycle of life and death and decay and her place in it all.

When the hole was large enough, she hesitated before placing her heart-flower within – it seemed a crime to place a thing of such beauty into the dark mud, but she would do what must be done. When the flower sat within the space, it gave off a faint glow, which she hadn't noticed in the open. The light picked out an earthworm wriggling in the wall of the space. Mairead gently removed it, but as she lifted it over the flower, meaning to place it on the ground of the field, it flipped itself over and off the side of her hand, to land on top of the flower. Those luminous petals closed and when they opened again the worm was gone.

Some of the allure of the flower wore off, its beauty dimmed by the revelation of what it ate.

"Mairead, Constance, please join me." Nicnevin held her hands out, one to each of them.

When they approached, she asked them to kneel on either side of her, and stood with a hand upon each of their heads. She spoke a few words in an unknown language, her voice chiming like the sound of ringing crystal, and a wave of light burst free from her, a dazzling white, woven through with the strong, deep purple of Mairead's magic and darts of red from Constance. The light formed a dome over the whole field, and Mairead felt herself expanding, filled with more energy than her body could house. It flowed through her to Nicnevin, following the shape of the fae queen's will, and Mairead couldn't have stopped it if she wanted to.

She didn't want to.

The feeling was glorious, all-consuming, as if she, as an individual, did not really exist anymore, but lived only as this great outpouring of energy. She could not have said how long this state lasted before the light fractured and poured itself into the heart-flower of each Alban, crackling over and through the men of earth. Gasps and exclamations sounded, and a few people stepped away from their Albans in fear, but all of it seemed so very far away and unimportant.

As suddenly as it began, it was over, and Nicnevin closed the channel between them. Mairead was left panting, on her knees in the mud, feeling incredibly small and empty.

Chapter Fourteen
Constance

"Your Albans will wake with the dawn," Nicnevin said to the group. "There is naught to be done for the night but rest."

Constance pulled herself to her feet and swayed for a moment, lightheaded in the aftermath of the magic. From the looks of it, it had been even harder on Mairead. She was still on her knees at Nicnevin's other side.

"Especially you two," Nicnevin said to the two witches. She offered her hand to Mairead and pulled her to her feet.

Constance hurried to Mairead's side and put an arm around her waist, holding her up. She looked pale and not quite sure of where she was; a spark of anger flickered in Constance's blood. Nicnevin must have taken too much from Mairead, used her too harshly. *How dare she take so much without warning!*

"When the Albans awake tomorrow, they will seek out their maker and will require guidance on what is needed from them," Nicnevin said, studying Mairead and then Constance. "You must be specific in your orders to them – give them a task to accomplish and they will do all in their power to complete it, so be clear about boundaries, if there are any. If you encounter any problems, summon me. Otherwise, I'll be back to check in with you at some point." She looked directly at Constance. "Get her home and take care of her tonight. She needs to recover."

With that, the fae witch disappeared in a shower of sparks. Constance stood in the field, the sky darkening quickly now that the sun had dropped below the horizon. People were milling around, looking a little dazed, as if emerging from a dream. Mairead was leaning into her side, and Constance could feel her trembling.

"Let's get you home," she said softly, then raised her voice so that the others could hear. "We'll meet here at dawn tomorrow, but for now, I bid you all go home. Eat and rest; today has been a lot to absorb for all of us. Tomorrow we will take the next steps together."

Constance started to walk across the field with Mairead, but after a few steps, Mairead stumbled and went to her knees, almost pulling Constance over with her.

"Are you well?" Constance asked, panic rising at the thought of having to face all that lay ahead without Mairead at her side.

"I'm sorry," Mairead mumbled. Her lips barely moved enough to form the words. "I'm just so tired."

"Let me help," Catriona said, approaching Mairead's other side. "Between the two of us, we can get her to your cart."

By the time Constance stopped the cart in front of the house, Mairead had regained a little energy and was sitting up, talking with the children. Constance got them all settled in the house before seeing to Angus and making sure the other animals were all fed.

The children had eaten earlier so were happy enough with some sliced apples and cheese for supper. Mairead claimed not to be hungry, despite not having eaten anything since that morning, but Constance decided not to push her. Instead, she gave her some tea and a piece of honey cake to pick at.

The fire had gone out at some point during the day, and Constance cleaned it all out and got it going again, but the house remained cold, the chill seeping up from the stone floor.

"You can sleep in my bed tonight," Constance said to Mairead after the children were tucked up for the night. "I'll sleep out here."

"It's kind of you to offer, but no. I'll do well enough out here." Mairead's voice was heavy with exhaustion.

"I'm not having you sleep out here, nothing but straw between you and that cold stone floor, on a day when you are already trying to recover from giving so much of yourself for the good of others. Not at all." Constance stood over Mairead, arms crossed firmly across her torso.

"And I'm not putting you out of your own bed when you too spent the day giving of yourself for the good of others," Mairead said, looking up through eyes weighed down with exhaustion.

Constance's pulse thrummed faster, though she didn't know why. "Then we'll share. There's plenty of space."

"I'm...not sure that's a good idea," Mairead said, her voice low and husky.

"Come." Constance held out her hand and waited until Mairead took it. She pulled her to her feet. "There will be much and more to do tomorrow, and you look ready to fall down. We both need rest, so come."

Mairead dropped Constance's hand but reluctantly followed her to the bedroom.

"There's a chamber pot under the bed should you need it," Constance said as they came to stand on either side of the bed. She turned her back and began to undress but looked over her shoulder when she heard Mairead settle on the bed. She was lying on top of the covers, fully dressed.

"I know you're tired, but you'll sleep better if you get into bed properly."

"I'll be perfectly fine like this," Mairead mumbled.

Constance slipped out of her own kirtle and dropped it over a stool between her bed and the children's. "Don't be foolish. Strip down to your shift and get under the covers."

Constance looked away again as she fought with the laces of her stays, but smiled to herself when she heard Mairead get back to her feet with a groan and begin to undress. Constance slid under the covers and lay with her eyes closed until Mairead climbed in beside her, then she leaned over and blew out the tallow lamp on the small table beside the bed.

Mairead was tense, her body stiff, pulled in upon itself as if she were trying to make herself as small as possible.

"You can relax. I won't bite," Constance said, a little hurt at Mairead's sudden distance.

Mairead muttered something that Constance didn't quite catch, but sounded like "It's not you I'm worried about," and seemed to let go of some of her tension, letting her arms fall naturally to her side.

In only moments, Mairead's breathing deepened and her body relaxed as sleep claimed her. Constance lay there, listening to the sound of her breathing and finding herself oddly aware of how close the other woman was. The skin of her forearm tingled where she could feel the heat of Mairead's arm just a few inches away. Something rose in her then, something she had never truly felt before, a kind of longing for closeness, a need to have Mairead by her side always, no matter what shape that relationship took.

Constance had been drawn to people on occasion, had experienced what she thought of as idle fancies, but she had never truly wanted anyone, never longed for their company the way she longed for Mairead. It frightened her and excited her all at once.

Mairead shifted in her sleep; her arm now touched Constance's. Constance lay perfectly still, all of her senses focused on that one spot. She was flushed; her body felt too small to contain the surge of sensation. She lay there, confused and filled with feelings she had no name for, until at last, after a long time, she fell asleep.

At some point during the dark of the night, Constance awoke to find that she and Mairead had turned to face each other, lying almost nose to nose, sharing breath, their hands clasped together, and fingers intertwined.

Dawn already colored the sky when Constance woke to Simon babbling.

"Oh, Lord," Constance groaned, rubbing at her eyes and trying to wake up properly. She glanced over at Mairead, who lay on her back, hair loose and tumbling across the pillow. She placed a hand gently on the sleeping woman's shoulder and shook her. "We're late," she croaked.

Mairead opened her eyes and then screwed them shut against the bar of light coming from the window and lying across her face. "All right. I'm awake." She rolled to the side of the bed and sat up, swinging her legs out.

"You get the children ready, and I'll get Angus and the cart. There are bannocks left from yesterday, we can eat on the way."

They both dressed quickly and Mairead headed to the outhouse, while Constance woke the girls and got Simon changed and dressed. She was helping Janey into a dress for the day when a scream from outside sent her racing into the yard, with a warning to the girls to stay inside.

Mairead stood at the corner of the house, as if she had just come round from the back, and before her were two of the Albans, towering over her, looking much taller than they had seemed lying in the field yesterday.

"What happened? Did they hurt you?" Constance asked, rushing to Mairead's side and taking hold of her arm.

"No. They just startled me." Mairead squeezed Constance's hand where it still gripped her arm. "I'm well. I'm sorry for screaming."

The Albans stood still, waiting. The sun was behind them, casting them in shadow, adding to the sensation of them looming.

Constance's heart finally started to slow, and she let out a shaky laugh. "Well, I hope the others made it to the field in time rather than waking to this." She let go of Mairead and stepped closer to the Albans, studying them.

They were tall, both over six feet, and broad at the shoulder. They still looked much as they had yesterday, made of mud and moss and all the other things Nicnevin had listed, though somehow it all held together. Their faces were crude, pebbles for eyes, sticks marking where their mouths would be. Constance felt their attention on her, as if they were studying her right back. She wondered if they could see somehow, if they could speak, if they could think. If they had souls.

What did we do?

Mairead came closer, looking up at the Albans too. "Good morning," she said, her voice only wavering very slightly to betray her nerves.

The Albans turned their heads to focus on her.

"Can...can you speak?" Mairead asked.

One of the Albans shook its head while the other stayed still.

"Only like this. Only to you." The voice sounded inside Constance's head, causing her to jerk backward in alarm.

Mairead gave her a worried look, but she held her hand up. "I'm well."

The Alban Constance had built was focused on her, as if staring at her through his pebble eyes. "Was that you?" she asked.

He nodded.

"What—"

"He spoke to me," Constance said just as Mairead started to ask. "Inside my head. He said they could speak like that, but only to me."

Mairead looked from Constance to the Albans. "Can you both speak like that, to Constance?"

They both nodded.

"Mama, what are they?" Elspeth said from behind them.

Constance whirled to see the girls standing in the doorway. She opened her mouth to tell them off for coming out when she had told them to stay inside, but then she thought of how long she had been gone, and how much longer it must have felt to them, and really, it was no wonder they had come to see what was happening.

"Go inside just now. I'll be in soon to explain everything."

For a moment it looked as though they would come outside instead of doing as she had asked, but after a brief hesitation, they turned and went back inside.

"What do we do now?" Mairead asked in a low voice. "Nicnevin didn't exactly give us detailed instructions for this part either."

"Are the rest still in the field?" Constance asked the Albans.

"No, they have gone to their makers."

"He says they've all gone to their makers," Constance told Mairead.

A gust of wind lifted her hair, and she pushed it back behind her. She hadn't even had a chance to brush it yet. Only now, standing here, barely awake, with no idea of what the next steps were, did she realize how poorly prepared they were. She and Mairead had been so focused on getting this done, that they hadn't truly thought beyond that goal to how all of this would work.

"Well, I suppose the only thing to do is continue as planned. The others will no doubt be looking to you for some guidance," Mairead said. "We should go to them and figure it out together."

Chapter Fifteen

Mairead

20th September 1745

Something had shifted overnight and Mairead wasn't sure why, but as they traveled into Kilmartin, both sitting at the front of the cart, with the children in the back and the Albans striding along behind them, Constance seemed to keep very close to her, almost leaning into her for comfort.

The children were fascinated by the Albans and sat facing the rear of the cart, watching the earth men move along the track. Mairead couldn't blame them – she kept glancing over her shoulder too. She felt as if the Albans should be less graceful than they were, that they should have a shambling gait, falling from one foot to the other as the scarecrow had done, but instead they moved like humans, walking with as much ease as if they had bones and muscles and sinews holding them up, rather than mud and sticks and moss, which were less than a day old.

"We're probably going to have to find clothes for them," Constance said. "Made of mud or not, it feels immodest to have them walking around naked."

Mairead laughed. "Not that they have anything to show. But you're right, it does feel a tad uncomfortable. And perhaps they will look a little less...other...if they have some clothes on."

"One or two of them, dressed in kilts and plaids, watching over the flocks at night, or seen from a distance tending the fields, might well be enough to discourage the raiders from trying their luck any further here."

"Yes, most likely."

Constance glanced at Mairead and gave her a shy smile, which Mairead returned, finding her eyes drawn to the other woman's lips, wondering how soft they would feel pressed to her own. She pushed the thought away and looked back once more at the Albans.

It seemed curious to her that they could communicate mentally with Constance, but not with her, when, if Nicnevin were to be believed, it was her magic that formed the foundation of the spell. But then, Constance was the more powerful witch and had not been drained so much by the spell, so perhaps that's where the answer lay. They really should have asked Nicnevin more about what they were doing and how it would work before they had gone through with it, but she thought that perhaps neither of them had really expected it to work.

"I can't quite believe that this has happened," Constance said, echoing her own thoughts. "It's so very different to messing around with the scarecrow in the yard."

"Can you feel them drawing on your magic?" Mairead asked, touching her hand to her breastbone, where she could feel the slightest tug.

"A little, yes."

They continued in silence for a while, the day growing duller as clouds blew in to hide the sun. The wind blew steady around them, carrying an icy bite that made Mairead shiver despite her cloak. That wind spoke of winter, and it wasn't far away.

When they arrived in the village, Mairead was surprised but pleased to see that some of the Albans had already been put to work. One was adding thatch to the roof of a cottage, while another walked past carrying a bale of hay in each arm. Constance drew the cart to a halt and jumped down. She turned a slow circle and surveyed the village.

"Good morning!" she called as Mistress Gordon appeared from behind her house, a bucket in her hands. "How do you fare today?"

"Truly, I do not quite know the answer to that question," Mistress Gordon said, glancing nervously at the Albans. "It is surpassing strange to see them moving about the place, but there seems to be no harm in them."

Mairead got down from the cart and joined the other two women, rubbing Angus's nose as she passed. The tough little pony didn't seem to take any notice of the Albans, though she might have thought he would be wary of such unnatural creatures. *But are they unnatural? They're made from nature itself, after all.*

"I'm sorry we overslept," Constance was saying. "I had meant to be here far earlier."

"I think perhaps we should call them together and devise a plan to get the work done," Mairead said. "Nicnevin spoke of being very clear in giving them instructions, so it seems that would be best done together."

"You're right, of course," Constance said. "Shall we ask everyone to gather in the field?"

Mistress Gordon sent the request round, while Constance and Mairead got the children settled with Mistress Croaker, who had offered to sit with them if Constance would fill her in later on the plan for the Albans.

In the field, the villagers and their Albans gathered; Mairead looked at the ring of earth men standing patiently behind their makers and for the first time began to wonder if they had made a mistake. Was there a risk of the Albans turning against them? What would they do if such a thing happened?

The wind gusted across the field, whipping her hair across her face, and she staggered a little against it, thick mud squelching beneath her boot. A hand pressed against her back, steadying her. She glanced over her shoulder, expecting to see Constance, but instead it was her Alban who had reached to offer his support.

"Thank you," Mairead said, taking a step forward to create a little distance between them. The Alban inclined his head to her.

"Thank you all for coming," Constance said, her voice clear. She paused for a moment, to let the chatter come to a halt. "I think it would be wise for us to discuss a schedule of work to be done, and how best to approach it. But first, there is another pressing matter. Nicnevin advised us that we must be very clear in our instructions to the Albans, and it seemed sensible to make sure that we lay some ground rules together, while they are all here, to make sure that the basic instructions are the same for each of them. Now, since it is Mairead's magic that forms the foundation on which they are built, I will hand over to her to set those rules."

Mairead gave Constance a panicked look. They had not discussed this in advance, and she felt rather underprepared. Mairead had gone through her life flitting around the edges of any group she was part of, keeping a distance and then leaving as soon as it felt like people were getting too close. Here, she was being thrust into a central role, and unlike Constance, she was not used to it.

Constance gave her an encouraging nod. Mairead cleared her throat and stepped forward.

"First of all, we would like to welcome the Albans to Kilmartin. This place is a part of you, and you it. We hope you find contentment here, though your stay may be brief." She glanced at Constance again, who was watching her, a faint smile on her face. "We brought you here to help protect this village and all of its inhabitants while the land remains unsafe, and to help us in working the land and preparing for winter. Your primary function here is the protection of the village and its inhabitants. Should we face any threat from outside of the village, we ask you to do whatever is in your power to defend us. Do you understand?"

Each of the Albans nodded.

"We also need your help in planting, tending to the livestock, carrying out repairs and the like. We would ask you to carry out any task given to you by your maker. You may also carry out tasks asked of you by other members of this community, if you are not already occupied." Suddenly, Mairead had an image of a child ordering an Alban to do something that seemed fun but would undoubtedly be dangerous. "You may not carry out any task that would endanger a member of this village, even if asked to do so. If you have any doubts as to the safety of a task, seek out Constance for guidance. Do you understand?"

Once more, the Albans nodded.

"I think that's all from me," Mairead said, looking to Constance. "Do you have anything to add?"

"I think you've covered the basics beautifully. Shall we turn to work planning then?"

With the discussion of who would be doing what starting, Mairead stepped back, happy to carry out whatever tasks were asked of her, and well aware that she didn't have the relevant knowledge to participate in the planning.

She looked across the field, at the empty space where the Albans had lain the day before, and beyond to the hill where the sheep were at pasture, watched over by the older children of the village, the boys who were just too young to have gone to join the fight. No doubt some of them chafed to join their fathers, filled with thoughts of glory and adventure. She prayed they need never see the blood and horror of the battlefield.

The rest of the day passed in a blur of planning and work. Mairead was still drained from the day before and by the time she and Constance gathered the children and headed for home, the sun was low in the sky. She struggled to stay awake with the gentle motion of the cart. Simon was asleep in his basket, and the girls were playing a game that consisted, as far as she could tell, of shouting out random words and then dissolving into fits of giggles.

Constance was humming softly to herself and appeared to be comfortably absorbed in her own thoughts, so Mairead allowed her eyes to drift shut and her thoughts to wander as they would. There was a low murmur at the edge of her thoughts as if from a conversation in the next room. She tried to focus on it, but it was more than her poor, tired mind could manage. Her attention scattered and for a time there were only vague flashes of colors and sounds, pieces of memories, the hardness of the wood beneath her thighs, the warmth of Constance beside her, the scents of horse and soil and decaying leaves.

Some unknown time had passed when Constance let out a small scream and the cart jerked, jolting Mairead fully awake. Angus was rearing up as far as the connections to the cart would allow, and the wood was creaking threateningly. Janey screamed and started to cry, and Mairead twisted in her seat to check on the children. Simon was secure, but the girls were being shaken and rattled around the back of the cart with the pony's panicked thrashing. Mairead reached for them, stretching to grab Janey and hold her steady, but she could not reach Elspeth.

A porcine squeal sounded from somewhere beyond Angus.

"What's happening?" Mairead gasped, as her ribs were bashed painfully off the top of the boards separating her from the children.

"A wild boar burst out of the trees there, right in front of us. It frightened Angus," Constance replied. Her tense tone showed the strain she was under as she fought with the reins in an attempt to settle the pony.

The boar squealed again, followed by a scream from Angus that turned Mairead's blood cold. Wood cracked and the cart listed to one side.

The Albans strode forward, past the cart, and Mairead twisted her neck to see where they were going. Surely they weren't just going to leave them here like this?

One of them scooped up the boar, which squealed and thrashed to no effect, its wicked tusks passing harmlessly through the earth of the Alban's body. The gash it left sealed almost as quickly as it had opened. Before Mairead had grasped what was happening, the Alban had taken hold of the boar's tusks and yanked them, breaking its neck. The beast, which had been full of life and chaos just seconds before, fell silent and limp in the Alban's arms.

The threat removed, Angus stopped thrashing, though still he screamed.

"Is everyone all right?" Constance asked, her breath coming in sharp pants.

Mairead cautiously let go of Janey, who wailed and threw herself at her mother. Elspeth crawled toward them, looking pale and frightened. Simon cried loudly and tried to pull himself to a seated position in his basket.

"Elspeth? Are you well?" Constance asked.

Elspeth nodded. "I hurt my arm and my knee and my head, but I'm all right."

"Let me see, sweetheart," Mairead said, cautiously straightening up and reaching for her.

Elspeth paused to help Simon sit up then came to Mairead for a cuddle. She had a lump on the side of her head, but she was responsive and coherent, so it didn't seem too bad. A bruise was already rising on her knee and shin, and her arm was scratched from some rough piece of wood.

"Oh, pet, you've had the worst of it, haven't you? I'm sorry I couldn't reach you too," Mairead said, pushing the words through a throat thick with emotion. She was surprised to discover how much it pained her to have let the child down.

Constance managed to disentangle herself from Janey and reached for her older daughter, pulling her into a hug. "We're all safe now," she murmured, kissing Elspeth's head beside the lump. "We're safe. We'll get home and get you all cleaned up, all right, my love?"

Elspeth nodded, then buried her face in her mother's shoulder as quiet sobs shook her.

Mairead slid from the cart, wincing as the pain in her ribs and shoulders stretched hot fingers down her back, then she hobbled round to see to Angus. The sturdy pony's foreleg was covered in blood, coming from a gash just above the knee. The boar must have got him with one of its tusks. Mairead shivered, looking at the Albans, who stood together, motionless. One still held the body of the dead boar.

What on earth made it act that way? Why would a boar attack a pony?

Constance came to join her, Simon in her arms and the girls clutching to her skirts. "Oh, Angus," she said softly, when she saw the pony's leg.

"We can wrap it, see if he can walk home on it," Mairead said, already pulling off her short wool shawl. "If we can get him home, we can clean it, treat it. Let him rest for a while."

"He can't pull the cart like that," Constance said. "And even if he could, he broke one of the hitching poles when he was trying to get away from the boar." Constance sighed and closed her eyes, using the hand that wasn't holding Simon to pinch the bridge of her nose. "All right. You strap his leg, and I'll unhitch him from the cart. We can leave it here overnight and come back for anything we need from it tomorrow, figure out what to do from there. It'll be dark soon, so let's hurry."

Mairead worked fast to wrap Angus's leg, trying to send some calming, healing energy into him as she worked. Gradually, his eyes stopped rolling, and his breathing calmed, and when he was disconnected from the cart, he was able to limp forward carefully.

Mairead straightened and looked at the Albans thoughtfully. How much weight could they manage? She had seen one earlier carrying two bales of hay at once, and one of these still stood with a fully grown boar in its arms, as if the weight was no trouble at all. Mairead doubted she could lift the thing, let alone hold it for so long. She suppressed a shudder when her mind flashed to the ease with which the Alban had dispatched the boar, breaking its neck with minimal effort.

"Do you think you would be able to pull the cart back to the house?" she asked the one whose arms were empty. "It's quite heavy."

The Alban nodded to her then walked over and grasped the hitching poles close to the body of the cart, above where one had been broken. With seemingly little effort, it pulled, and the cart began to roll.

"Ha! Wonderful!" Constance clapped, delighted.

Mairead led Angus in his limping walk, while Constance walked beside her, Simon secured to her chest in her shawl, the girls on either side. The Alban with the boar led the group, while the one pulling the cart brought up the rear.

"Well, that was a bit of excitement, wasn't it?" Constance said, sounding oddly cheery for the circumstances. "Still, boar for dinner tomorrow!"

"I wonder what made it behave like that," Mairead said. She looked nervously into the undergrowth between the trees that lined one side of the track here. "I know they can be aggressive if you stumble across their home runs in the forest, but it's not like them to come onto the road. And to attack a pony?"

"It was injured," Constance said, her tone changing from the light, cheerful voice she had used with the children a moment before. "There's a wound on its flank; I had a look while you were dealing with Angus. Someone tried hunting it, looked like. The pain must have maddened it."

Mairead looked into the darkness between the trees again. For the first time she wondered if someone was looking back.

"Raiders?" she asked Constance in a low voice.

Constance gave a small, one-shouldered shrug.

"Do you think they're close?" Mairead asked. "Could they be watching us?"

"If they are, then I wonder what they made of our friends here? If anyone has seen them dispatch a boar without trap nor weapon, then haul a cart a mile or more, I suspect they'll think twice about staying around these parts."

Constance smiled, but it was a cold and predatory look. Mairead was taken aback, but a moment later, Constance looked at her daughters and once more her expression was full of warmth, and Mairead began to doubt it had ever been anything else.

22nd September 1745

My dearest Bridget,

Yesterday we wet the blades of our swords with the blood of the redcoats for the first time, and if that is the best their forces have to offer then the war is won already. Prince Charles had word that they were marching up to take back Edinburgh, so we went out to Gladsmuir to meet them on the field.

Sir John Cope led the enemy, and they chose a ground with marsh lying between the two armies, no doubt thinking to slow us down, but some lad in the prince's party knew of a path through the marsh.

We attacked at dawn, coming at them at speed through the fog, and they broke near as soon as they saw us. I'd kill myself from the shame of it, had I been as cowardly as the men we faced. They say some did not stop running until they reached Berwick.

The prince says this goes to show that our cause is just and favored by God himself. I pray that he is right, and that I am returned to you soon.

Your Loving Husband,
Colm

11th October 1745

Mary,

Please forgive the brevity of this note, my love, I have only a few moments to write it, or the messenger will have to leave without it. We are still stationed in Edinburgh, awaiting the prince's pleasure. I do not know when I will be home. You must prepare for winter without me.

I hope you and the bairns are well and pray to God I return to you soon.

William

5th November 1745

Mary,

We are marching for England. The prince means to take London. Pray for us.

William

Extract from *The Inverness Daily*

25th November 1745

We have received word that Prince Charles Edward Stuart and his forces have taken Carlisle after a three-day siege. The prince is said to have met with civic leaders and then proclaimed his father as king. It is believed that he plans to make for London, there to claim the throne of England as he has already claimed the throne of Scotland.

Chapter Sixteen

Constance

18th December 1745

The Albans were put to work and the women too. Fields were cleared and the winter planting done. Fences and barn roofs were repaired, straw and hay gathered, animals slaughtered, and food preserved. The people of the village grew accustomed to the presence of the Albans very quickly, much quicker than Mairead would have anticipated. No more sheep went missing, which Constance took to mean that the raiders had been discouraged by the presence of the Albans and whatever they might have seen during the incident with the boar.

Mairead and Constance had decided to name theirs, as it felt rude to constantly refer to them as 'the Albans'. Mairead named hers Hamish, while Constance chose Hector. Both Albans performed any task asked of them without complaint and generally to a high standard. Where there were setbacks, it usually came from not being precise enough with instructions. Mistress Croaker spent a week or so adapting clothing for the Albans, dressing them much as would be expected of a Highlander during winter, in shirt and *feilidh-mór* or belted plaid, sometimes with a cloak atop it, though the Albans did not seem to feel the cold as the rest of the village did. Nor did they require sleep, nor food, and they were unaffected by the heavy rains and driving wind that set in not long after their birth, for want of a better term, and continued for several weeks.

Between their enormous strength and their ability to work without rest, the Albans were able to do as much work as twice their number of men, and as Christmas approached and they entered the heart of the winter, far from being behind, the village was well-prepared and had ample provisions to see them through.

One morning, around a week before Christmas, Constance was sitting in a chair by the hearth, tying bunches of greenery together to make decorations for the house, thinking about her grandmother, who had been much on her mind of late. Perhaps unsurprising, given that her grandmother had been hanged for far less witchcraft than Constance had been about in recent months. She glanced over at Mairead, who was currently bending over a cauldron at the hearth, making a soothing syrup for Simon, who had picked up a bit of a cough.

"Someone comes," Hector's voice sounded inside her head.

"Who is it?" she thought back at him.

"The seamstress."

Constance set aside her greenery and went to the door, a smile lighting her face. She opened it in time to see Emily Croaker walk the last few feet of the track from the village and cross the yard to the door. "Emily! How lovely to see you! Come in, come in."

Mistress Croaker stepped inside and removed her cloak, which was beaded with water from the rain.

"I bring news," she said gruffly. "Whether it be good or bad, I leave to your judgment."

Constance caught Mairead's eye and raised an eyebrow. What was this all about? "Well, come and warm yourself by the fire while you tell us," she said.

Emily walked to where Mairead stood, in front of the hearth, stirring a small cauldron that hung over the flames.

"Roisin is gone," she said, turning her back to the fire to look at Constance.

"What? What do you mean gone? You don't mean…"

Emily shook her head. "No, forgive me, she's not dead. She's run off to Inverness. She left a note." She rummaged in a pocket in her skirt and pulled out a piece of paper, which was damp at the edges but otherwise unharmed. She held it out to Constance.

Dread settling like a weight in her stomach, Constance took the note and read it aloud. "To anyone who cares, Samuel and I have gone to Inverness to look for Fergus and Bridie. I cannot in good conscience remain here and be party to the witchcraft and devilment that has taken over this village. I have waited and prayed, hoping that you would all come to your senses and cast the witches out, but things have only gotten worse. May God have mercy on your eternal souls, Roisin."

Constance sat heavily on one of the stools at the table, a roaring sound in her ears, drowning out her ability to think. All this time she had been focused on danger from without – she had never thought to protect them from danger within.

Mairead came to stand beside her, and placed a hand on her shoulder to steady her. The contact broke through the roaring to let her think again.

"When?" she asked. "How long has she been gone?"

"We don't know for sure," Emily said with a sigh. "She's been keeping herself to herself since the Albans came. Distancing herself from the rest of us. So, it took a few days before we noticed that no one had seen her for a while. Catriona knocked on her door yesterday and didn't get an answer, but for all we knew, she was just out walking or the like. We even thought she might have been inside and ignoring it because she didn't want to talk to anyone." She perched on the edge of the chair beside the hearth. "When she still didn't answer this morning, we started to get worried, so Catriona let herself in, and the note was on the table. The ashes in the hearth were cold, so she didn't leave this morning, but we can't really tell any closer than that."

"When was the last time someone saw her?" Constance asked.

Emily shrugged. "We can't say for sure. Best we can tell, four days ago."

Constance rubbed her forehead, thinking. *Four days! She could be there by now.* "We should send one of the Albans after her. If she hasn't made it to Inverness yet, it can bring her home, and we can try and talk some sense into her."

"I know they look almost normal from a distance, love, but you can't have them wandering around where people will see them," Emily said, sounding panicked.

Constance shook her head. "I've been thinking about this for a while. So many of the old stories about witches speak of them being able to change their appearance, or the appearance of their surroundings. What if Mairead and I could do that for the Albans, so they just look like men?"

Mairead squeezed her shoulder. "I don't think it's the right approach, to send one of them," she said gently. "They can't talk to Roisin, reason with her. What would you have them do? Pick her up and carry her home against her will? And what of Samuel? Would you frighten the poor lad that way?"

Mairead had a point, but that didn't make it any easier to hear. Constance stood and began pacing the room. "What other choice is there? None of us has a chance of catching up to her before she reaches Inverness, that's if she's not there already. What would you have me do? Let her go running to the authorities, tell them what we've done here? They could hang us all as witches!" She threw her hands up in frustration. "If we're really lucky, we might be able to persuade them that you and I bewitched the rest of the village into helping and we are the only ones to blame, so it'll be only the two of us who hang."

Sudden wails came from beneath the table, where Elspeth was playing, forgotten and unnoticed when Emily had come in. Constance's anger evaporated and was replaced by shame.

"Ah, Elspeth, love. I'm sorry. Come on out from there."

Elspeth crawled out and ran to her mother, burying her face in Constance's belly. "I don't want you to die!" she wailed.

Constance wrapped her arms around Elspeth and held her tight. "Don't fash, love, nothing is going to happen to me. I was just…being dramatic." She looked up and across the room to Mairead, who looked back sympathetically. "Why don't you go and check if Simon and Janey are still napping, or if I've woken them up with my nonsense? Quiet as a mouse, in case they're still asleep."

Elspeth sniffed and rubbed her sleeve across her face before nodding and heading for the bedroom. Constance covered her face with her hands and sighed. "We can't just let Roisin go and hope for the best," she said in a low voice.

"I can't see that we've any other choice," Emily said, getting to her feet. "Mairead is right, we cannae be dragging her back against her will. That's not who we are. And if reasoning with her was going to work, it would have worked already. Besides, if she left the same day she was last seen, well, even an Alban wouldn't be able to catch her before she reaches Inverness." She moved to the door and wrapped her still-sodden cloak around her shoulders once more. "I'll leave you to the rest of your day. I think all we can do is pray that leaving is enough for her, and she'll keep quiet now. After all, there's a long distance between refusing to be part of what we're doing, and actively wishing harm upon us."

"I suppose you must be right," Constance said with a sigh, going to the door to see Emily out. "Thank you for bringing the news."

When she closed the door behind Emily, she turned around and leaned against it, the wood cold at her back, her hair catching on a rough plank and pulling a small, sharp pain into her scalp. "Would that there was some way we could guarantee she keeps quiet," she said. "I wonder if there is some way to enact a spell on her from this distance."

Mairead frowned. "Distance magic is possible, to be sure. All you need is a proxy and something that belonged to her. But would it be ethical, Constance? Would you really override the consent of someone who has trusted you? Someone who is not trying to harm you?"

Constance thought about it, listening to the flames crackle and pop in the hearth and the rain drumming on the outside of the cottage. "Is it truly any different to what we did with those men from the Watch? They were a threat to the village, and we prevented them from causing us harm. I would do no more to Roisin. Simply prevent her from speaking of what has happened here, keep us all safe from the judgment of outsiders."

Mairead glanced toward the bedroom door, from behind which Simon could be heard coughing. "Why don't we talk about this later?"

"Very well," Constance said, heading to the bedroom to fetch Simon. "But we dare not leave it too long if we mean to act. Otherwise, we risk silencing her after she has told her story to those who would punish us for nothing more than having access to a power that they cannot control."

The rest of the day, a tension hung between the two of them as they went about their tasks. It was clear that Mairead was not entirely comfortable with what Constance had asked of her.

Never mind, she thought as she scrubbed the washing on the board. *If she won't help me, I'll figure out how to do it myself. She's always saying I'm the more powerful witch, anyway.*

It wasn't that Constance couldn't understand Mairead's reluctance; she had made a promise to herself many years ago not to use her magic on other people without their consent, after all. And she had meant it. That was what had brought her grandmother to the attention of the witchfinders, according to her mother.

Constance couldn't remember much, or perhaps she hadn't been aware of the details at the time, having been only around Elspeth's age when her grandmother was taken. But according to the story her mother told, her grandmother had been known for some time as the woman you could go to for help, if you'd had enough children and needed to be sure of no more, or if your husband had a wandering eye and you wanted help to focus it back where it belonged, or if your hens stopped laying, or some other difficulty beset you. While she was helpful, no one thought to call her a witch.

That all changed after she used her magic against someone. Grandmother had a lover. It was an open secret in the town, but since they were both widowed, with grown children, while there were some who disapproved of the arrangement, no one minded overly much. But one day, her lover took it into his head to remarry, only he wanted a younger bride, someone who might still bear him the son his first wife had not. So, he got himself betrothed to a girl in the village who was due to come of age that summer. Constance's grandmother was furious.

She might have been treated kinder if it had been him she went after, Constance thought, as she wrung water out of the clothes, letting it splash into the tub, though some few drops escaped to wet the floor. *People have some sympathy for a jilted lover.*

Alas, her grandmother had taken her ire out on the bride-to-be. She hadn't acted in any way to harm the girl; she had made her fall in love with a young man close to her own age and then used her magic to encourage them both to elope and wed in secret, on the eve of her planned wedding. The girl's mother had found a charm tucked under the girl's bed. After a conversation with the young man's parents, they found a matching charm in a chest of his clothes.

No one thought to look further than the jilted lover. It was enough to turn the town against her, and send her to the gallows, by way of the witchfinder's cruelties.

As far as Constance knew, the young woman and the lad she had married stayed together – their marriage having been conducted before God in a church and so binding – and they lived a happy life together. Certainly, she was likely to have been happier with a husband close to her own age and not one older than her father who wanted her only as breeding stock.

Constance wasn't entirely sure that her grandmother had actually done anyone any wrong, in the end. Not that it mattered; it cost her her life, either way, and Constance's mother had made Constance swear not to follow in her grandmother's footsteps. To stay below notice, to fit in. To live.

Well, she had failed in the first two, but by breaking her vow to herself, perhaps she could still achieve the last. She intended no harm to Roisin at all, despite her annoyance at being put in this position by her, and unlike her grandmother, she was not acting through jealousy or anger. This was self-defense, pure and simple.

The last witch trial might have been twenty years ago, but it remained illegal to be a witch, and the penalty was still death. She wasn't willing to gamble her life, Mairead's life, or those of the rest of the villagers, on Roisin's better nature, if for no other reason than she wasn't entirely sure that the woman had one.

Mairead came inside from checking on the animals as well as Hector and Hamish, while Constance was hanging the last shift up to dry on a rope strung between hooks on opposite walls. The girls were splashing in the water still in the washtub, while Simon was sleeping again, his face flushed. He had a slight fever, but it wasn't so high as to be frightening. Constance prayed it would remain so.

She watched as Mairead hung up her cloak and took off her muddy boots, her manner thoughtful and serious. She walked over to Constance and studied her face for a moment. Perhaps she saw the determination there, because she gave a sharp nod, then said, "All right. Tonight. After the children are in bed."

When the children were finally asleep, Constance emerged from the bedroom to find Mairead sitting at the table with a lamp at one end, and some items for the spell laid out in front of her. She had Roisin's note, a strip of cloth, some sticks and oat stalks and twine, and an unlit candle.

"Are you sure you want to go ahead with this?" she asked as Constance took the stool opposite her.

"I am. I truly believe it's what's necessary to protect this community. But I understand if you don't want to be involved. I can do this myself."

Mairead looked down at the table, and Constance could see her mouth move as she chewed at the inside of her lip. A habit that Constance had noticed she turned to whenever she was thinking deeply or fretting about something.

"No," she said, looking up, the light from the lamp casting her eyes in darkness. "I'll help. But we do the minimum necessary to be safe. Agreed?"

Constance reached across the table and squeezed her hand. "Agreed."

"Distance magic works best if you have something very personal to your target," Mairead said, fiddling with the sticks piled on the table between them. "But we don't want to delay an extra day while one of us goes to seek something out in Roisin's home. So the note will have to suffice."

"Will it be enough?" Constance asked, touching the edge of the paper.

"It should be. She touched it, wrote in her own hand, the words are hers...it should be sufficiently personal to create the bond we need. It helps that she's very familiar to you."

"So. What do we do?"

"First, we tear the note into strips and wind it around these sticks and oat stalks. Then we'll use twine to tie them into a very rough doll figure. It's probably best if you do that, since you know her best. While you're building the doll, you need to keep Roisin very firmly in your mind. You want to focus on building a connection between it and her."

With a nod, Constance got to work, following Mairead's instructions. As she wound strips of paper around sticks and stalks and carefully bound them into a vaguely person-like shape, she kept her mind focused on Roisin: her voice, her mannerisms, her way of moving. She fed a trickle of her magic into the figure, feeling the moment when it became something greater than the sum of its parts. It thrilled her, this feeling of finally having some control over both her life and her magic, not having to hide who she was anymore. It was intoxicating.

"Now what?" she asked, glancing up at Mairead, who was watching her as she worked.

"Take the strip of fabric and wrap it around the figure," she said. "Concentrate on binding Roisin. You need to be very specific – she can't speak or write or in any other manner communicate in any way about the Albans, or any magic use here. Is there anything else we need to include?"

Constance thought it over. That seemed to cover everything but still she had a niggling sense that Roisin would find some way around it. Or worse, that this was all too late, and she had already told someone all that had happened here.

"I can't think of anything else," she said, shaking her head.

While she had been thinking, Mairead had lit the candle. "After you bind her with the fabric, we'll both pour some magic into the working, and then seal it with some wax."

Constance bound the figure with the cloth, concentrating on preventing Roisin from communicating in any way whatsoever about anything that had happened here after Fergus and Bridie left. When she had finished, she held the figure in her hands, and Mairead wrapped her own hands around Constance's. Constance felt her power reacting to Mairead's, a spark and fizzle that somehow drew them together. The sensation grew to fill her as their powers wound around each other, moving through Mairead and then back through her. This was a greater feeling of intimacy than anything she had ever known before, and it left her reeling.

"That should be enough," Mairead said, her voice husky with some emotion that Constance could not name.

Mairead withdrew her hands and lifted the candle, dripping wax on the bound figure to seal the spell. Constance watched, entranced by the deft way her fingers moved, finding herself longing for something she didn't understand.

The combined magic still flowed through and between them both, heady and powerful, making Constance feel like she no longer fit inside her skin, that suddenly not just her life but her body itself, was too small to contain her. She licked her lips, her heart pounding with anticipation over something she could not put into words. She couldn't speak, couldn't give voice to the incredible wonder of what she was experiencing.

"We need to put this somewhere safe," Mairead said. Her eyes seemed huge and dark, as she gazed at Constance with an only previously glimpsed hunger bare on her face.

"On the shelf, up there," Constance managed to answer, nodding at the highest shelf in the room. None of the children would see it and mistake it for a toy up there.

Mairead stood and took the figure to the shelf, stretching on her toes to reach it. Constance moved to help, being an inch or two taller. Their fingers brushed as Constance reached to push it properly onto the shelf and suddenly being so close to Mairead undid her.

They turned, face to face, noses barely an inch apart, staring into each other's eyes and the world disappeared. Nothing existed in this moment, but Mairead's warmth so close, her lips barely a breath away.

Later, Constance would strive in vain to remember who had moved first, but suddenly, somehow, Mairead's lips were pressed against hers, her scent filling Constance's senses. She let her fingers trace the soft skin along Mairead's jaw, then let her lips part. Their tongues met and their magic surged, and Constance was lost, her sense of self completely dissolved in the union.

Part Two

Chapter Seventeen

Mairead

23rd March 1746

The day that Mr. Kinloch died dawned bright and fair, and for the first time in months Mairead could feel a hint of warmth in the air as she and Constance traveled into the village. There was still snow on the hills and in the shaded parts of the forest that skirted Kilmartin, but the track was clear and, on the verge, crocuses opened their bright petals to the sun and daffodil shoots were beginning to emerge.

Mairead sat on the cart and turned her face up to the sun, letting its light bathe her, feeling her blood respond to it in much the same way as the sap would be rising in the trees they passed, some of which were beginning to bud. Mairead loved this time of year; she always felt hopeful and light as the earth around her woke once more from its long sleep.

Hector and Hamish strode along behind the cart, Hector carrying Elspeth in his arms, and Hamish carrying Janey. The girls had taken to riding around in the Albans' arms this way over the winter. At first Constance had been reluctant to allow it, which Mairead understood completely, but eventually they had worn her down with their pleading, and the Albans had promised to take the greatest care.

The day before, a letter had arrived from Fergus, letting them know that young Jamie's arm was healing well, and he should be released from the hospital soon. Roisin had reached Inverness safely just before

Christmas and he had helped her find a job with the hospital too. She liked it there and was of a mind to stay until the rising found its end, one way or another.

There was plenty of work to be done in the hospital, according to his account. People had trickled into Inverness all winter, victims of raiders, or the Black Watch, or even deserters from the prince's army. They could only be thankful that the snows had kept the redcoats stuck farther south, for who knows what havoc they might have wrought on the already-strained Highlands.

He wrote of seeing the Bonnie Prince himself travel through the city on his way to some event or other, all done up in tartan. Some of the soldiers were billeted in Fort George, but he had been unable to find any news of the men from Kilmartin. He thought perhaps they were stationed elsewhere. There was talk of a siege at Fort William, but little was known for sure. He closed by promising to keep them all in his prayers and to write again when they had news of their imminent return.

The letter seemed to have taken a weight from Constance's shoulders, and she had been full of giddy laughter. Perhaps it was the confirmation she needed that their spell to bind Roisin had worked.

Mairead smiled as Constance reached for her hand now, stroking the back with her fingertips and bringing a rush of heat to Mairead's core. Throughout the winter, they had spent as much time together as they could, the monotony of the season brightened by stolen kisses whenever they were alone. They both carefully avoided talking about the future for they knew that sooner or later this space they had carved out for themselves would be taken from them.

Mairead pushed the thoughts away, concentrating instead on sending a pulse of warmth and wonder and wanting through her magic and into Constance, who gasped then gave a soft laugh.

The last few months had been the happiest of Mairead's life and, even though she knew that she couldn't hold onto this, she planned to fully savor every moment that she could.

They arrived in the village around midday, and immediately joined

Mistress Croaker for tea, while Hamish and Hector went off to join their brethren in some task or another. Mistress Croaker brought stools out into the small garden behind her cottage and served them tea in the sunshine, accompanied by thin slices of bannock with dried apple pieces cooked through it. There was little in the way of fresh produce available at this time of year, but they had been well-provisioned for winter, and many of the villagers still had access to dried or otherwise preserved fruits and vegetables from the previous year. The cold, snowy start to the year meant that even these would likely run out before the first crops of spring were ready to harvest.

Still, with the help of the Albans and the hard work of the villagers, the winter had been far easier on Kilmartin than they had expected. Mairead was half listening to Constance and Mistress Croaker debating whether the frozen ground had thawed enough yet to begin the spring planting, and watching Simon crawl about on the ground, playing with a wooden ball, when a shout came from the street on the other side of the house. Exchanging a concerned look, Constance and Mairead got to their feet. Constance reached to scoop Simon into her arms.

They made their way round to the street, where a gaggle of children – Elspeth and Janey amongst them – were still chasing each other around, laughing. Mairead looked around warily for any sign of trouble, her magic coiling in her limbs in preparation, should she need it. Constance's expression was distant, the look she often bore when talking to Hector or one of the other Albans inside her head.

"No strangers have been seen approaching," she said, shielding her eyes and looking around for the source of the disturbance.

"What's going on?" Mairead asked as Mistress Gordon approached from the direction of the burned-out church.

"It's one of the Albans. You'd better come and see."

Mairead followed her, Constance a step behind.

"We set a couple of them to dismantling the church building," Mistress Gordon said over her shoulder as she walked, "before it falls down on someone. It's only a matter of time until one of the more adventurous bairns decides to climb about in there, and who knows how much of the structure was weakened by the fire."

"That was good thinking," Constance said from behind.

They drew up in front of the church and saw that one of the Albans had just stopped, midway through removing a charred board from the wall of the church. It stood, frozen, expressionless and unresponsive.

"How long has it been like that?" Mairead asked, stepping close to it and extending her senses. It felt wrong, like the magic in it was strained or stretching somehow.

"I'm not sure, I wasn't paying much attention until Young Robbie shouted for me to look at it." She paused and looked between Mairead and Constance. "It's not...dangerous, like this, is it?"

Something in the Alban's magic snapped, like a rope frayed to its breaking point, and the ricochet shot through Mairead, driving her to her knees and knocking the breath from her chest. Pain flared, sharp and insistent, on the left side of her breast, shooting down her arm and up her neck to her jaw. She whimpered and sagged to the ground and suddenly Constance was there, cushioning her fall, magic blazing in her eyes.

"Mairead! What's wrong? What's happening?"

"Whose Alban is that?" Mairead groaned, tears leaking from her eyes as she tried to think past the pain.

It released her as suddenly as it had arrived, and Mairead was left with the ghostly ache of it, gasping and disoriented.

A soft pattering sound started as earth began to fall from the Alban, its body losing coherence.

"Malcolm Kinloch's, I think," Mistress Gordon said. "Though truth be told, I have trouble telling them apart sometimes."

There was a wet flump as the body of the Alban gave way completely and collapsed into a pile of mud and other organic matter, losing any sign of what it had been only moments before. Atop the pile, the fae bloom sat, its petals no longer gleaming, but dull and decaying at the edges.

Mairead looked up from where she sprawled on the ground.

Constance knelt beside her, holding her up. "I think he's dead."

Constance insisted on taking Mairead back to Mistress Croaker's to rest while Mistress Gordon went to Mr. Kinloch's house, despite Mairead's protests that she was well. She was well enough to stand and walk and could have helped with Mr. Kinloch, though she still had pins and needles in her arm and neck. Mistress Croaker fussed around her, making her lie down for a while and sitting watch over her, though she no doubt had much better things to do with her time.

"Really, there's no need for this," Mairead said for the third time, after Constance had left to help Mistress Gordon. "I'm sure I'll be perfectly fine in no time at all."

"Really?" Mistress Croaker said, raising an eyebrow. "Had the same experience many times before, have you, to base that assumption on?"

Mairead rolled her eyes. "No."

"Well, then." Her voice softened and she leaned closer. "It may have escaped your notice, but here in Kilmartin we look after our own. And like it or not, Mistress Ferguson, you are now one of our own."

"Thank you," Mairead said, swallowing the pang of guilt at her long-used deception.

She lay there without further complaint, looking toward the door, which stood open to allow the fresh spring air to move through the little house. Mistress Croaker sat in the patch of sunlight, fabric she was stitching upon her lap, spectacles perched on the end of her nose, humming under her breath.

Mairead realized that she loved these people and this place. Not in the heady, passionate way that she loved Constance, but in the quiet, safe way that made this feel like home. For the first time in as long as she could remember, the thought of moving on filled her with a deep sensation of loss.

After a little while she sat up and Mistress Croaker allowed it, though she watched carefully, peering over the top of her spectacles with eyebrow raised.

Constance's voice sounded outside, drawing closer as she approached, talking to someone. Mairead was shocked when, a moment later, she walked through the door with Nicnevin in tow.

Mairead scrambled to her feet, heart thrumming at the sight of the fae. She was never sure if it was Nicnevin's magic or her beauty that was so alluring, but every time she was in the vicinity, Mairead responded the same way. She caught Constance's eye and blushed at the knowing look on her lover's face.

"My lady," she said, inclining her head to the fae.

"I am glad to see you on your feet," Nicnevin said. "Constance told me what happened."

She stepped forward; her aroma of flowers and spices and something that did not exist in this world filled Mairead's nose and made desire surge in her blood. Nicnevin placed a hand on her left shoulder and a cool, soothing energy flowed through her, easing the ache and dispelling the pins and needles.

"Better?" she asked, her voice low, intimate, as if there was no one else present.

"Yes. Thank you, my lady." She felt at once relieved and bereft when Nicnevin stepped back, a subtle smile playing across her lips. "What happened to me?"

"You felt his death," Nicnevin said, taking another step back to lean against the wall. "I am sorry, I had not foreseen that as being a side effect of building the spell that animates the Albans upon the foundation of your magic."

"You could hardly have known that he would die while connected to them," Constance said, as always somehow less affected by the presence of the fae queen, and certainly less deferential in her manner.

Nicnevin just looked at her, a neutral expression gracing her features.

"You knew?" Constance demanded. "You were aware that this would kill him?"

"You all knew the cost of the magic you asked for," Nicnevin answered, her expression still calm but her voice carrying a warning edge. "I made it perfectly clear that for every four days this spell lasts, you each lose a day of your own life force. You all judged that a price worth paying. The spell did not kill him; it merely hastened the demise he was already heading toward."

"You could have warned him against it!" Constance snapped.

Mairead walked over and placed a hand on her arm. "Peace, Constance. If I understand correctly, he'd have been dead by summer anyway. He chose to cut his time short to help us. We should honor his sacrifice for us, rather than squabbling about how it came about."

Constance turned her head away but nodded and Mairead realized that the anger she was aiming at Nicnevin was really guilt aimed at herself.

"You didn't force him," Mairead said softly. "You didn't force anyone. You asked them and then let them make their own decision. This isn't your fault."

Constance cleared her throat and sniffed. "Yes, well. We'll bury him tomorrow."

"I will join you for this custom, if I may?" Nicnevin said. "While I do not grieve his passing, I do respect his bravery and commitment to his community. I would honor that alongside you."

"Very well." Constance sighed. "I think perhaps we should also check with the others that they are content to continue with their participation. Mr. Kinloch's passing may have driven home to them the cost they are paying."

"I think that is wise," said Mairead. "There is something else we must consider – with winter passing, more people will be moving around the Highlands; the risk of discovery is increased."

"But so is the danger in being here without any men," Constance responded. "Fergus's letter suggested that there are many groups on the move who might seek to take advantage of an undefended village."

"Do you think to end the Albans?" Nicnevin asked.

"Perhaps."

"No."

Mairead and Constance spoke at the same time, then looked at each other.

"I do not feel it would be safe to be entirely without them," Constance said, "though I will not attempt to force anyone in the village to participate if they no longer wish to. But Mairead is right, the risk of discovery is increased. We're not on any of the main routes through the area so we do not have frequent visitors, but we do see the occasional pedlar, or traveling minister, or the like. If we could disguise them, it would be safer."

"You could cast a glamour over them." Nicnevin frowned in thought, engaged now in the problem-solving.

"We've been practicing that over the winter," Mairead said, glancing at Mistress Croaker, who still sat on the stool by the door, sewing forgotten on her lap as she listened. "Either of us can change their appearance, but the spell only works as long as the caster is nearby. As soon as the Albans pass out of range, they resume their usual appearance."

"You could try anchoring the spell to them. Focus the magic on an item they can carry with them."

Mairead groaned inwardly. *Why didn't I think of that? The same principle as distance magic.* "Of course! I can see the shape of how that would work now."

"Sometimes it just takes a fresh perspective," Nicnevin said with a smile that sent a tremor through Mairead.

"Thank you, my lady," she said, blushing again.

"Now we just need to think of an object to anchor the spell to," Constance said thoughtfully. "Something small enough to be both convenient and inconspicuous..."

"What about their plaid pins?" Mistress Croaker said, joining the conversation for the first time. "Would metal hold your magic well enough?"

Constance looked between Mairead and Nicnevin for an answer.

"Yes, I believe it would," Mairead said. "But there's only one way to know for sure."

"It should be sufficient to the task," Nicnevin said. "I will leave you to your experiments. Until tomorrow." And with that she disappeared once more in a shower of sparks.

Mistress Croaker gave a gasp, and Constance released a shaky laugh. "I don't believe I'll ever get used to the way she does that."

"I don't imagine she'll be around so much that we get the opportunity," Mairead said, with a pang of regret. "Right. No time like the present. Let's get these pins."

Chapter Eighteen

Constance

24th March 1746

Mr. Kinloch was buried peacefully in the village graveyard, behind the small church, in a plot beside his beloved wife and their children, who had all died in infancy. He was the last Kinloch in the village, with no family left to tend his grave. Constance made a promise to herself that she would keep it tidy, as the man was never anything less than presentable in all the years she had known him.

Only Morag Gordon, Isobel's daughter, wished to withdraw from the working, and after the burial was over, and glasses had been raised to Mr. Kinloch's memory, Nicnevin carefully unraveled her from the magic, allowing her Alban to return to the earth. Constance had asked Hector if the Albans grieved for the loss of their brethren, but this was a concept that he seemed unable to grasp.

"They were, then they were not. That is all."

She supposed that was reasonable, since they had only existed for a period of months. One wouldn't expect a baby of the same age to understand impermanence and loss and grief. It did not cross her mind, then, that they might view human life in much the same way.

Anchoring the glamour spell to the plaid pins worked, and so Kilmartin entered the planting season with eight Albans who looked mostly like normal men, at least when seen from a distance. Close up, the details of their faces tended to blur as neither Constance nor Mairead had found it possible to visualize unfamiliar faces to the level of detail required to be fully realistic.

All they could do was pray that if any strangers came, they'd be able to keep the Albans at enough of a distance that this wouldn't be noticed.

It was April when this was first put to the test, though truly speaking, the lad who came through Kilmartin with the news was far from likely to pay close attention to anything, filled with panic as he was.

Constance was behind the house, planting beetroot in a bed near the road, when Hector's voice sounded in her head.

"A stranger approaches."

Frowning, Constance straightened and made her way round the house to the main gate.

"What kind of stranger?" she asked Hector.

His response felt something like a shrug in her head. *"One alone."*

A few minutes later, a young man came thundering up the track from the direction of the village, his horse looking hard-run. He yanked at the reins and the horse drew to a halt close to where Constance stood at the fence.

"Are you well?" Constance asked. "Do you need aid?"

"Mistress Gordon?" the lad asked in a voice that cracked and squeaked. A youth, really. Barely old enough to be riding around the country alone.

"That's me." She clasped her hands together, trying not to let their tremble betray her fear.

"The folk in yon village begged me stop and give you the news as well on my way past," he said, his horse shifting from foot to foot as he spoke. "Prince Charles Edward Stuart was defeated at Culloden. It was..." The boy faltered, his face paling. "His army was wiped out. The redcoats are sweeping the area for any who escaped the field of battle. Though by all accounts there will be vanishingly few to find." He looked around warily, as if checking to be sure they weren't overheard, then leaned over the side of his horse. "If anyone in the area has any item in their home that might suggest they hold sympathy for the Jacobite cause, it would be well to be rid of it."

"Thank you," Constance said softly, "Do you know anything of survivors? Surely there were some?"

"I'm sorry. I don't know."

"Will you take refreshment? Some water for your horse perhaps?"

"No, thank you, Mistress, but I must be on my way." He straightened and looked over his shoulder then lifted the front of his hat. "Good day to you, and to your husband."

He clicked his tongue and kicked at the horse's sides and took off at a slightly more sedate pace than that at which he had arrived.

Constance turned and saw Hector standing at the other end of the house, watching. So, the glamour worked well enough from that distance then.

"I felt your alarm. Is there danger?"

"No. At least, not immediate. I need to think."

Constance began pacing the yard, her mind racing. It was over. The rising was over, the Jacobite army roundly defeated from what the boy said. Wiped out. What did that mean for Iain and the other men from Kilmartin? Had any of them survived to return home? And what about the redcoats? The boy said they were sweeping the area for survivors. What area? Around Culloden? That was somewhere near Inverness, wasn't it? Not so very far away. Would they come here? When? Oh, dear Lord, she hadn't even asked the boy when the battle happened, so flustered was she by the news.

"Constance? Constance, what's wrong?" Mairead called, as she came running down past the barn. She had been taking the cattle up to the top field to graze. Constance stopped pacing and moved toward her, and Mairead ran into her arms. "What's happening? I could feel you were upset."

This connection, the solidity of Mairead's grasp, the warmth of her body and her heart, all served to ground Constance. She took a deep breath, drawing in that scent that belonged only to Mairead, then placed a kiss on her temple. The coming days would not be easy, but she could get through it as long as she had Mairead at her side.

She looked over Mairead's shoulder and saw Elspeth and Janey coming out of the barn, Simon toddling between them, holding their hands. She released Mairead and took a step back.

"The Jacobites lost," she said, keeping her voice low and speaking fast to try and get it all out before the children got within earshot. "There was a battle near Inverness, the boy who brought the news said it was bad for them. Bad enough that they're saying the rising is over. I don't know if any of our men survived, and the redcoats might be coming."

"They're coming here?"

Constance shook her head. "I don't know for sure. He said they were searching the area for any Jacobites who survived the battle. I don't know if he meant this area, or the area around the battlefield."

"What do we do?" Mairead asked with a worried look over her shoulder at the children. "We could leave. Pack our bags, take Angus and the cart south somewhere. Edinburgh maybe."

"We can't leave the others," Constance answered, though she couldn't say she wasn't tempted by the idea. They had a responsibility though, to the others in the village who had trusted them when they had asked them to. "Simon! Look how well you're walking!"

"Mama, Simon is stinky," Janey said, wrinkling her nose. "He needs changed."

"Oh dear. Let's take him into the house then," Constance said, reaching to take his hand. She started moving toward the house, then stopped and looked back to Mairead. "For now, I think, we must continue as we are and wait for more news. We can discuss this further later."

That night, after the children were in bed, Constance and Mairead sat side by side on the pallet on which Mairead no longer slept. They had taken to sprawling there together in the evenings, limbs entangled, as they spoke on the events of the day, or shared stories of their pasts, or discussed both the theories and practicalities of magic.

"I'm frightened," Mairead said, leaning on Constance, her head tipped back to rest on her shoulder.

"Me too," Constance answered softly, stroking Mairead's hair, twining thick, silky strands of it between her fingers.

Mairead sat up suddenly and turned to face Constance, her expression stricken. "I'm sorry, I've been so shortsighted. You must be so worried about your husband, and I haven't even asked if you know anything about his well-being."

"I don't know anything about the men from Kilmartin. The lad who brought the news barely stayed long enough to tell what he did, and I was so stunned, I never thought to ask him half the things I should have." Constance sighed and studied Mairead's face in the dim light from the hearth. "I wish Iain well. I do sincerely hope that he is not dead but..." She swallowed hard, forcing herself to speak the truth, no matter how challenging that felt. "But I also hope he never returns. These last few months with you, I have found so much joy. You've shown me who I really am, and for the first time in my life I feel truly accepted. I am scared of what might come, scared of the redcoats and what vengeance King George might take on those of us left behind to be punished. But most of all, I am scared of losing you. Of being forced back into a life that doesn't fit, making myself small once more, losing who I am. The woman you have taught me I can be."

Tears glistened in Mairead's eyes, and she leaned forward, cupping Constance's face in her hands and kissing her, deeply.

When they broke apart, Constance scrubbed at her face and got to her feet.

"Where are you going?" Mairead asked.

"I'm going to check and make sure that Iain left nothing in this house that can connect us to the Jacobites. If the redcoats come here, they'll have no cause to mark us as traitors."

"All right," Mairead said, rising to stand at her side. "Tell me what to look for."

20th April 1746

Dear Constance,

I must be brief as my duties in the hospital are pressing. The British Army has taken over the hospital for the treatment of their men following the battle at Culloden, so all we are treating at the moment are soldiers. None who work in the hospital have been allowed to leave – we are told that if we are good and loyal subjects of King George, then surely we must wish to ensure his men receive the best care.

There has been neither sign nor news of the men from Kilmartin, and I fear the worst. No Jacobite soldiers are being brought to us for care. I know not the truth of the matter, but the rumor is that all wounded men on the field of battle were shot where they lay and that any who escaped have been pursued most aggressively.

All of you remain in our thoughts and prayers,

Fergus

Chapter Nineteen

Mairead

1st May 1746

Mairead strolled along the village street, a cup of cider from last year's apples in her hand, when she was joined by Catriona, with whom she had become friendly over the winter. Mairead found Catriona to be intelligent, quick-witted and kind, and had come to value the opportunity to spend time with her.

The villagers of Kilmartin had come together to mark May Day and the turning of the seasons as best they could, though a heavy air lay over them. With no word one way or the other about their husbands, sons and brothers, they could not truly mourn their loss, but with each day that passed without news, the chances of them coming home seemed less and less likely.

"Good day to you," Mairead said with a smile as the other woman fell in alongside her.

"Going somewhere?" Catriona asked, her tone light.

Mairead shook her head. "Just walking. I feel odd. Restless."

They walked in silence for a few more steps, until they came to the empty space where the church used to stand, and beyond it the walled graveyard.

"Do you think they'll come back? Any of them?" Catriona asked, keeping her gaze fixed ahead at the drystone wall ringing the graveyard.

Mairead sighed. "I don't know, but I pray for them, to any god who may be listening."

"Do you think…" Catriona looked down at her hands, which were laced together at her waist, before looking up at Mairead, her eyes wide and full of pain. "Do you think maybe they all died because God is punishing us for our hubris?"

"Hubris?" Mairead asked, frowning.

"For daring to think we had the right to create life where He had no hand in it?" Catriona answered, nodding past Mairead to where one of the Albans was supervising the village children in a game of tug-of-war.

Mairead looked at the Alban and then back to Catriona. "No. No, I don't." She paused, thinking carefully about how to phrase what she said next. "I think, if there is a God at all, then He's likely far too busy to be worrying about the likes of us, and the things we do in order to survive, as long as those things don't harm anyone else. And if He was of a mind to punish us for it, then wouldn't it make more sense to punish us directly rather than punishing the men, who had no part in any of it?"

Catriona looked back at the space where the church used to stand. "I don't know what I'll do if Rab doesn't make it home."

Mairead placed a hand on Catriona's shoulder, offering what little support she could. "You'll get through it," she said softly. "It will be hard, but you'll get through it. And you know you'll have the support of everyone else here."

"Who may be going through the same thing," Catriona said with a laugh that sounded closer to tears than to humor.

"Who better to understand what you're going through?"

Catriona leaned into Mairead for a quick hug then suggested that they wander back down to where a few tables were set up with food and drinks for everyone to share. As they headed out, Mairead spotted Constance, standing still and distant in the middle of the street, head cocked to the side as if listening.

Suddenly she straightened and shouted, "Everyone, come to me! I need your attention, please!"

Mairead hurried to her, thoughts racing. "What is it? What's happening?"

"There are redcoats coming," Constance said, her voice pitched high enough to carry over the crowd. "Six of them have been spotted coming this way from the Inverness side. It seems unlikely that they will be gentle. We need someone to take all of the children and two of the Albans to the bothy up by the eastern pasture. Are there any volunteers?"

"I'll take them," Mistress Gordon said, stepping forward. "I'll do my best to see no harm comes to any of them."

Constance nodded, and with a fearful look handed over Simon, who had been dozing, strapped to her chest with her shawl. "Keep them as quiet as you can. With any luck, when they leave here, they'll follow the road out and never come anywhere near the bothy." She kissed Simon's head then let Mistress Gordon carry him away, her Alban falling in behind her. "As for the rest of us, we've planned for this. We knew it was only a matter of time before they came knocking."

"Remember the plan!" Mairead said, taking over as she felt Constance's fear rise in her, making her falter. "We keep our heads down, speak English if you can, and do nothing to antagonize them. Everyone, fill what buckets you can with water and have them ready in front of every house in case of fire. We want the Albans to be in sight, so it looks as if there are able-bodied men in the village, but we want to keep them far enough away that the oddness of their features goes unnoticed. Understood?"

This was met with various noises of agreement.

"Does anyone need assistance with their part in the plan?" Mairead asked, looking around and meeting the eyes of as many of the villagers as she could. "We stand together."

"Together!" Constance called beside her, her voice a rallying cry to the villagers, helping them to push down their fear and get moving.

By the time the redcoats tramped into the village an hour or so later, the children were safely out of reach at the bothy, there were two buckets of water sitting outside the door of every house, and four of the Albans were visible in the distance, building a wall along the boundary line of a field where cattle were grazing. Some of the women were working inside their homes, while others were planting in their gardens, or feeding chickens that roamed the street.

Constance sat on a stool outside Bridie's house, as it was closest to the church, sorting seeds and tuber shoots into baskets, while Mairead knelt in Bridie's garden, weeding and tidying, as if this were her home, and today was but an ordinary day.

"Good day, gentlemen," Constance said, standing and stepping forward to greet them as a group of six weary-looking men in the distinctive red coats of the British Army appeared at the end of the track where the church used to stand.

"Good day, madam," one of the men answered. "Perhaps you can tell us if we are on the right path for Fort Augustus?"

Oh, thank goodness, Mairead thought, glancing at the straight line of Constance's back. *They're not looking for Jacobites, they're just lost. Maybe they'll take directions and be on their way.*

"I'm afraid you've come a little out of your way," Constance said, her voice betraying no hint of the relief that Mairead could feel flowing along their connection. "From here, you might be best carrying on along this track until it meets a wider road. Take a right there and keep following it north-west. The route is a little longer, it'll cost you extra miles, but it's easier going than the more direct way, through hills and forest."

The man who had spoken sighed and pinched the bridge of his nose. "No wonder this country is so backward, with barely a proper road to be seen," he muttered.

Mairead felt the flare of annoyance from Constance and was careful to turn her own face away lest her anger show.

"Will you and your men take some refreshment before you resume your journey?" Constance asked.

Just go. Mairead pushed her hands into the earth and uprooted a dandelion, which she set aside in a basket for later. They had decided that the best approach was to try and seem as unconcerned as possible – what reason would loyal citizens of the crown have to fear the British Army, after all? – but now that the time had come, that felt like an insurmountable task. *Please, just leave.*

"Thank you, madam, that would be most welcome," the redcoat said. "Captain Paul Sampson, at your service." He removed his hat and gave a brief bow.

"Mistress Ferguson," Constance said, making Mairead look up in surprise. "Constance Ferguson." She glanced over at Mairead, a subtle smile tugging at the corners of her lips. "We have only simple fare, I'm afraid, but we can see you fed and watered before you resume your journey."

"Even simple fare will be an improvement on army rations," the captain said with a smile. He looked around, studying the rows of houses on either side of the dirt track that served as the street. "What do you call this place? Is it even large enough to have a name?"

"It's called Kilmartin, Captain," Constance said, her tone light. "Though as you can see, we have but a handful of families living here. Mairead—" Constance turned to her, smile fixed carefully to her face, "—would you be so kind as to help me see to our guests?"

"Of course," Mairead said, climbing to her feet and brushing the soil off her hands. "I'll bring some stools out, let you gentlemen rest your weary legs."

While Mairead went inside, she could hear Constance talking to some of the other women who were approaching now, making arrangements to provide hospitality to the soldiers. She let herself relax, hoping for a moment that the redcoats would take their refreshments and leave without incident. Surely such things could happen?

She grabbed a couple of stools and carried them out to where the soldiers were milling around. Some looked rather less at ease than others.

"What if they're Jacobites, sir?" one of them was muttering to the captain as they approached. "Wouldn't put it past the rebels to have their women poison us."

If we'd known they were coming, we might have.

"Would you like a seat?" Mairead asked brightly, drawing up to them. She carefully set the stools down and took a step back, keeping a little distance between her and the soldiers. "I can bring you some water, or if you prefer, I can show you where the well is, and you can draw your own?"

"That's a good idea, thank you," the captain said, sitting on one of the stools. "Kendricks, go with this lady and refill all of our canteens from the well please."

The soldier who had spoken as she approached glowered but set about collecting canteens from the others without complaint.

Mairead led him to the well, fear prickling up her spine at his proximity to her back. Perhaps it had been a mistake to offer to take him to the well, out of view of everyone else. She could defend herself against him if she had to, but any such action might put the rest of the village in danger.

"Here you are, sir," she said, walking past the well to stand on the other side, keeping the low structure between them. "Nice and fresh for you."

The redcoat, Kendricks, stared at her and danger crackled in the air. Mairead pushed her will into the space between them, making a wall of it. *I am not interesting. I am not worth the effort. I am no threat to you.*

Kendricks muttered something under his breath – Mairead caught only the words 'bog water' – then set about lowering the bucket into the well. Mairead stayed well back, making sure to give him no cause for alarm as he worked to fill the bucket and then haul its weight back up.

When the canteens were filled, Mairead led him back to the others. A wave of relief washed through her when she came in sight of Constance, who was serving food to the captain.

Keep it friendly. Give them no reason to look closer at us.

"Where are your men?" the captain was asking as Mairead drew close, a note of suspicion in his voice.

Constance nodded toward the field in the distance, where the Albans could be seen working on the wall. "A few of them are over by, building a new wall to keep the cattle from wandering down where we're planting, others are out with the animals at pasture. A few are busy planting."

"And none of them fought in the recent battle at Culloden?" he asked, his tone growing harder.

"A few went off to join the Black Watch when news came that the Young Pretender has raised his standard. We've had no news of them since." Constance paused and cleared her throat, as if briefly overcome with emotion. "I don't suppose you would know, Captain, what might have become of them?"

The captain looked at her, the lines of his shoulders softening with his tone. "I'm afraid not, Mistress Ferguson. The Black Watch are under a separate command structure to my own."

Constance let her shoulders slump. "I thought that might be the case, but I had to ask. It's a hard thing, waiting to hear about loved ones in times such as these."

"I can only imagine. Is your husband one of these men?"

"No, thank the Lord," Constance said with a little laugh. "My husband is building that wall. Our nephew joined the Watch though. His poor mother's heart is sore, waiting for news every day."

Mairead hovered around the edges of the group, keeping an eye on the soldiers as they ate and drank, sending out a constant, low-level pulse of magic. Nothing that would override their will, just a hint that all was well, and they had no reason to be concerned here.

When the redcoats had eaten and drunk their fill, the captain got to his feet and ordered them to get ready to move out. They stood and stretched and shouldered their packs, falling into formation.

Mairead felt almost giddy with relief. They were leaving, just like that! So much worry for nothing. Perhaps the stories of how other villages had been razed to the ground were exaggerated...

The captain turned to Constance and bowed to her. "I thank you for your hospitality, Mistress Ferguson," he said. "Now if you could just fetch your husband for me, I'll have a brief word with him, and we'll be on our way."

"My husband? He...he hates being interrupted while he's busy," Constance stammered.

Mairead's relief fled, tension replacing the giddiness.

"I'll take but a moment of his time," the captain said, "but it would be exceedingly rude of me to accept the hospitality of a man's wife, without ever saying a word of thanks to him."

"Oh please, don't bother yourself with such niceties on our behalf," Constance replied, not quite able to disguise her anxiety. Mairead could only hope that it was more obvious to her than it would be to the redcoats. "We don't stand on so much ceremony around here."

"Still. I must insist," the captain said, his tone growing hard once more. "Unless there is some reason that I cannot speak with him? Perhaps because I might recognize him from Culloden?"

"I'll fetch him now," Constance said. "Though I must warn you, Captain, that my husband speaks no English."

"I am sure you will be able to translate for us."

Constance shot Mairead a worried look as she turned away to fetch 'her husband' from the wall. Mairead's mind raced – how could they make one of the Albans appear to speak? A break appeared in the cloud cover and a shaft of sunlight broke through, falling upon the captain as he stood, hand hovering near the handle of his sword. Tension moved through the other soldiers, their eyes growing more watchful, fingers tightening on the handles of the muskets they carried.

Mairead pulled her magic to the surface. Maybe she could adapt the working that disguised the Albans' appearance to also make it appear one was speaking. Cast her own voice magically. She'd never tried anything like this before, had no idea whether it would work, but trying and failing would put them in no worse position than not trying at all. It would be impossible to pass any of the Albans off as human at close range, especially if they failed to speak.

The moments dragged on though it could not have taken that long for Constance to walk across the field and give the appearance of summoning Hector from the group at the wall. Mairead's magic coiled and writhed through her, uneasy and sparking in response to her fear. She was almost surprised she couldn't see it flaring from her skin; she was so anxious that her magic pushed at the very edges of her control.

At last, Constance returned, Hector following in her wake, a hat pulled down low to cast shadow over his features. He stopped several feet away from the redcoats, who were gathered now in the middle of the street and inclined his head in a bow.

"Mr. Ferguson, I presume?" Captain Sampson asked, stepping forward.

Constance repeated the sentence in Gáidhlig, and Hector nodded.

Mairead focused her will, and muttered a quick prayer to any god who would listen. She shaped the words carefully in her mind and sent them into the world, aiming for them to sound in the air near Hector. Constance frowned, probably feeling Mairead's magic pass her, then jerked, startled. A male voice sounded from Hector, or at least from his vicinity, speaking in Gáidhlig. After a brief moment of confusion, Constance translated for the soldiers.

"My wife tells me you're on your way to Fort Augustus?"

"That is correct. Keeping an eye out for any rebels on the way, of course." The captain stepped closer, and Hector ducked his head more, attempting to keep his face hidden.

We need a distraction.

"You wouldn't happen to have seen any rebels hereabouts, would you?" the captain asked, taking another step forward.

Mairead scanned her surroundings, looking for something – anything – she could use to draw the captain's scrutiny away from Hector. Constance's anxiety as she translated moved along the connection between them, setting a low thrumming in her blood, driving her to do something. But what?

"I asked a question," the captain said, danger radiating from him.

Mairead concentrated and the voice spoke again, followed by Constance translating. "No rebels around here, sir, no. Me and the lads would see them off right quick if any of their like came sniffing round here. We're good, loyal folk as lives here."

"Then why are you hiding your face, sir?"

The captain took another step forward, but this time Mairead's attention was drawn by movement among the other soldiers as Kendricks raised his musket, aiming it at Hector, who stood beside and slightly behind Constance.

"Take your hat off, Hector," Constance said in Gáidhlig, looking between the captain and the Alban, seemingly unaware of the gun aimed her way.

Slowly, Hector removed his hat, revealing his face fully. Mairead blinked in surprise – a scar, which hadn't been there that morning, now worked its way down one side of Hector's face, pulling his lip up in a snarl. Mairead pulled her gaze away to look at the redcoats, who were all either staring at the scar or looking at their feet awkwardly.

Oh, you clever witch!

Constance must have added the scar to Hector's glamour while she fetched him, and Mairead couldn't help but be impressed with her quick thinking. The soldiers were all so distracted by the scar that, with any luck, they wouldn't notice the slight fuzziness to the rest of his features.

"Thank you," the captain said, stepping back. "Might I ask what happened?" He gestured to his own face.

Mairead scrambled for an explanation, wishing she and Constance had had time to coordinate. What sort of injury would have caused a scar like that?

"It was a farming accident when he was a boy," Constance said smoothly. "A sickle hadn't been secured properly when it was hung on the barn wall, and it fell on him as he passed. I'm sure you'll understand that it's made him a little shy."

"Of course. My apologies. Please tell your husband he may replace his hat."

Constance did so, and Mairead breathed out as Hector lifted his arm to put his hat back on. As he did so, his arm brushed against the kilt pin holding his plaid together, knocking it loose. It fell to the ground, the glamour dropping with it.

Mairead threw magic at Hector, reinforcing the glamour, but it was too late. The seconds between the kilt pin falling and her reaction had been enough.

"What in God's name was that?" one of the soldiers cried.

The captain stepped toward Hector again. He drew his sword, the steel ringing as it left the sheath. "What just happened?" he said; the threat of his weapon echoed in his voice.

"I...I don't know what you mean," Constance stammered.

Captain Sampson grabbed Constance by the arm and shook her. "Do not play the fool with me, madam," he hissed through clenched teeth.

Mairead's magic lit a fire in her bones, flaring through her with the rage that came from seeing Constance treated so. Everything seemed to happen in slow motion. Mairead threw out her hand toward the captain, sending a blast of magic intended to knock him away from Constance, but before it hit, Hector reached out and grabbed Sampson's head between powerful hands and swiftly twisted it.

The crunch as the captain's neck broke sounded across the street, the shock of it snapping the other soldiers from their paralysis.

A gun went off and a hole appeared in Hector's shirt. Instead of blood, a trickle of soil poured out. Constance yelped and stumbled back and Mairead turned her magic on the remaining soldiers, sending a blast of force that knocked one of them over at the very second in which he fired his gun. The musket ball went into one of his companions, who fell, screaming, to the ground.

There was more gunfire, Constance screamed, and then Hector was among the soldiers. After that, Mairead could only ever remember flashes of what happened. Blood soaking the sleeve of Constance's dress from where a musket ball had grazed a long fiery line across her arm. The other Albans arriving, some forming a wall between the soldiers and where she knelt beside Constance, trying to stop the bleeding. Screaming from the redcoats. The lifeless gaze of Captain Sampson, lying in the dirt with his head at an odd angle. Mistress Croaker appearing at her side, telling her it was over, they were safe, bringing Constance inside.

Chapter Twenty

Mairead

Mistress Croaker oversaw the cleanup, while Catriona helped Mairead in treating Constance's wound. There was a lot of blood, but thankfully the wound was not deep, and they were able to clean and dress it without too much trouble. Mairead all the while poured what magic she had left into Constance, willing her flesh to knit itself back together without delay.

By the time she had finished, Mairead was trembling and woozy, whether from overuse of magic or shock, she could not say. Catriona got Constance settled on the bed, then insisted that Mairead sit by the hearth and sip some warm tea made with chamomile and lemon balm. Gradually, the trembling subsided, though Mairead still felt as if ice were coursing through her veins rather than blood.

She sat, hunched, staring at the floor, trying to push away the image of Hector grabbing the captain's head and breaking his neck, which pushed its way to the forefront of her mind over and over.

When the door opened and Mistress Croaker came in, Mairead straightened and tried to pull her thoughts into some sort of useful order.

"Is anyone hurt?" Immediately Mairead saw the soldier hit by the musket ball when she knocked his compatriot over, saw the cloud of blood that had puffed from his side, heard his surprised grunt, then the scream when the pain hit. "Anyone from the village, I mean."

Mistress Croaker shook her head as she poured herself a cup of ale and drank it in one go. "Just Constance," she said when she had finished. "A couple of the Albans were shot or stabbed, but they seem to have healed right up, if that's the right term for it."

"The…are they all…" Mairead asked, the words sticking in her throat, the crunching sound of the captain's neck breaking echoing inside her skull.

Mistress Croaker sighed and scrubbed at her face as if trying to scrub the images away. "Aye. All of them. One tried to run. He got a good bit of the way down the track toward Constance's place, but one of the Albans that had been out that way with the sheep got him." She looked away and swallowed. "It…it wasn't pretty."

"I'm sorry," Mairead said, suddenly having to push back tears, though who they were for she couldn't have said. "I'm sorry you've been left to deal with it. Let me take over." She got to her feet and swayed as her vision swam.

Suddenly Catriona was at her side, pressing her shoulder, guiding her back down into the chair.

"Maybe in a moment," Mairead said, hanging her head. She took a deep breath in and let it out very slowly.

"There's no need. The Albans are burying the soldiers as we speak. They've dug a nice deep pit out back in the field they came from. The redcoats and all of their belongings will be covered up soon enough."

"Might it be better to burn them?" Catriona asked, the hardness in her voice at odds with the paleness of her face. "Less likely to be found should anyone come looking?"

Mistress Croaker frowned. "A fire that size would maybe draw attention to us."

"We can plant that field," Mairead said, her heart breaking at the thought that she had to plan how to cover up murder. Or deaths, not murder. It had been self-defense. She had to remember that. "Make sure the pit is really deep, then we can plant oats right over the top of them tomorrow. That way if anyone comes looking, all they'll see is a field in use."

Catriona nodded. "I'll go and make sure it's deep enough."

"The children!" Mairead shot to her feet as she remembered she hadn't checked on the children yet.

"Be at peace, I've already sent someone up to check on them and fetch them back in a little while. Give us time to clean up first."

Constance moaned and shifted in her sleep, Mairead's magic keeping her under for now. Mairead went to her side and smoothed her hair away from her face, murmuring soothing words.

"They were so close to just leaving," she said softly, without looking at Mistress Croaker. "If that kilt pin hadn't fallen when it did…" She let out a deep, shuddering breath. "I have sat at bedsides and eased passings. I have helped to treat people suffering from grievous injuries. I have been no stranger to violence, even. But I have never experienced anything like this before, and I don't know how to make it fit inside my head."

Mistress Croaker crossed the room and laid a gentle hand on her shoulder. "You just have to sit with it. Let yourself feel the things that you have to feel. Eventually it will ease, and you'll realize that it no longer dominates your thoughts as it once did."

"Have you…?" Mairead couldn't think how to tactfully phrase the question.

"Nothing like this, no." Mistress Croaker shook her head and stepped back, perching on a stool behind Mairead. "But I've known my share of grief, and more, and there's only one way through it."

"Grief?" Mairead frowned. "I'm not grieving."

Mistress Croaker gave a soft sigh. "Aye you are, lass. Maybe not for the redcoats, though I'd say that's part of it, a kind heart like yours. Grieving the need of violence? Certainly. Grieving your life such as it was before today? It'll be that too, I'm sure."

Mairead sniffed, tears welling in her eyes. Maybe Mistress Croaker was right after all.

Constance woke up when the children arrived back. The girls were full of high spirits and chatter about all they had seen on their adventure with Mistress Gordon. Elspeth was alarmed when she saw the bandage, but Constance spun them a story of humorous misfortune and soon had both girls laughing, while Simon toddled around the room, hanging onto anything he could reach.

"Why don't you take the bairns home and get some rest," Mistress Croaker said gently, looking fondly at the three worn-out children. "We can take care of anything else that needs done here today. You've had quite enough excitement."

Catriona fetched Angus and hitched him up to the cart while Mairead got Constance and the children settled. Simon sat safely in his basket in the back of the cart, waving a rag bunny around, while Janey curled up on some sacking at his side.

Elspeth looked at her sister then up at Mairead, arms folded in front of her. "She'll be asleep before we're halfway home, no doubt." She climbed into the cart and sat beside her. "Don't you worry, Janey, I'll be here when you wake."

Mairead stifled a laugh. *Little grannie*, she thought, clambering onto the bench at the front of the cart beside Constance and taking the reins from her with a raised eyebrow.

Constance shrugged and then gasped as the movement jostled her arm. She allowed herself to slump to the side and rest against Mairead.

As they set off, Constance spoke, voice pitched low enough that only Mairead could hear. "I love you."

"I'm not sure the children can hear you," Mairead said, twisting slightly to glance over her shoulder, without disturbing Constance.

"Not them." Constance laughed. "You. I love you."

"I..." Mairead's chest filled with an aching joy that was so big she wanted to whoop at the top of her voice and let it soar out into the early evening sky. "I love you too," she said quietly.

By the time they pulled into the yard in front of the little stone cottage, Hector and Hamish were standing outside, one on either side of the door. The scar Constance had conjured had faded from Hector's face, and both of them wore their usual fuzziness around the edges of their features. There was blood on Hamish's sleeve and Mairead's stomach clenched at the sight of it.

Mairead hopped down from the cart and came around to Constance's side to offer her an arm to lean on. "Why don't you take the children into the house, and I'll get Angus sorted and be in shortly?"

Constance nodded, her lips pressed tight together in pain. "Come along, darlings," she said to the children, awkwardly lifting Simon out of the basket with her uninjured arm.

Mairead led Angus toward the barn, where she would uncouple him from the cart and give him a good rub down before feeding him. She was halfway across the yard when she heard Constance calling her. She dropped the reins and dashed for the house, throwing an apology to the sturdy little pony over her shoulder.

She burst in through the front door to find the fire in the hearth crackling away merrily, and lamps and candles lit all around the main room. Nicnevin sat in one of the chairs by the hearth, one leg crossed over the other, revealing enough thigh to set Mairead's pulse racing, even today.

Constance perched on a stool at the table. Simon stood beside her, clinging to her skirts for balance. Elspeth and Janey sat on the other side of the table, Janey staring at the fae with wide eyes filled with wonder, while Elspeth looked somewhat more wary.

"My lady," Mairead said, inclining her head to Nicnevin. "We weren't expecting you."

"Really?" Nicnevin gave a disbelieving look. "You didn't think I would want to know what happened today?"

"Girls, go into the other room please," Constance said, her voice tight with pain. "Take your brother with you please."

"Let me get you some willow bark for that arm," Mairead said, crossing the room to the shelves with such supplies. "Do you want to chew it, or shall I make tea?"

"Both, I think."

Mairead bit her lip. The pain must be bad. She broke a small piece of bark off and handed it to Constance, along with a cup to spit into, and placed another piece in a cup that she took to the hearth. She reached for the ewer of water, intending to pour some into a pot to heat, but Nicnevin clicked her fingers and the cup with the willow bark was suddenly filled with steaming water.

"Well?" the fae queen said, looking pointedly at the bedroom door, which had swung closed behind the children.

Mairead and Constance exchanged a look as Mairead handed over the cup. She sighed and turned back to the fae, settling herself on a stool beside her love.

"We had no choice."

The events of the day took less time to tell than they did to live. When Mairead had finished speaking she felt empty, purged somehow of the awfulness of the day. While she had talked, Constance had sat beside her, sipping at the willow bark tea and occasionally interjecting with a detail Mairead had missed, through it all sending a warm flow of support along the magical bond they shared.

"You are distressed," Nicnevin said at last, studying Mairead as if looking at something that she could not quite understand.

"Of course I am," Mairead answered. "Did you not understand all that happened? The Albans killed those redcoats. All of them. I..." She swallowed hard and then met Nicnevin's eyes. "I think I killed one. Or caused the accident that led to his death, at least. Of course I'm distressed. I'm appalled. How else should I feel?"

Constance reached over with her good arm and took Mairead's hand, lacing their fingers together. "It wasn't your fault. None of it was our fault."

Nicnevin nodded and leaned forward in the chair. "It sounds to me as if you did everything in your power to resolve the situation peaceably. The soldier, this redcoat captain, he was the first to breach the peace between you by grabbing Constance and triggering Hector to act. After that, the rest was inevitable."

Mairead shook her head and looked away, staring at the fire instead of the beautiful fae witch who sat beside it.

"It was self-defense," Constance said softly.

"What about the one who ran away?" Mairead asked, her voice thick with unshed tears. "How was that self-defense, when he was just trying to get away?"

"Do you think he'd have left us alone?" asked Constance. "He'd have gone straight to Fort Augustus and told them all about the village full of witches who killed the king's loyal men. They'd have been back with a whole platoon within days." She shuddered. "You know what would have happened then. None of us would have survived. Not even the children."

The inside of Mairead's nose prickled and she rubbed at it, then let go of Constance's hand and covered her eyes. "How can we be sure?"

Nicnevin crossed the space between them and knelt on the floor in front of Mairead, pulling her hands away from her eyes, leaving her tears exposed for all to see. "When we created the Albans, I told you that if they were misused my magic would be tainted, remember? Well, there is no taint upon my power after today's events. Therefore, the Albans acted only in reasonable defense of you. Otherwise, I would know. You can be assured that, however unpleasant it was, the Albans' actions were necessary for your safety."

Mairead sniffed. "I don't know if I can live with this."

"You can," Constance said. "I'll help you."

"Let me see your wound," Nicnevin said, turning to Constance. "I may be able to heal it for you."

Constance looked warily at Mairead, who nodded. If anyone was going to come looking for the dead soldiers, Constance's injury could only draw suspicion. Especially if they were to see it – any soldier would be able to tell that it was caused by a musket ball.

Constance grimaced as she allowed Nicnevin to unwind the bandage, breath hissing between her teeth when the fae put a little too much pressure on the area around it.

Nicnevin frowned at the angry red wound across Constance's shoulder. "There are traces of iron here," she grumbled. "Not a large amount, but enough that I won't be able to heal this entirely. Iron blocks my power."

"Any help you can give will be gratefully received," Constance said, her words tinged with pain.

Nicnevin placed her hand above the wound and spoke a few words in the unknown language. Her hand began to glow before the light from it sank down into Constance's arm, shining through blood and muscle and bone for a moment, illuminating everything in a muted red.

After a few moments the light faded, and Nicnevin removed her hand. Where before there had been an open wound, now lay a thick silver scar, reminiscent of an injury that was several years old.

The tightness that had lingered on Constance's features since she had awoken suddenly cleared, and a bright smile broke across her face. "The pain is gone! Thank you, my lady."

Mairead didn't miss the fact that Constance had used the honorific for the fae witch. She felt the slightest prickle of jealousy and pushed it away. *Stop being ridiculous. It's not as if your head isn't turned by Nicnevin every time she appears.*

The following days saw a cloud of tension settle upon the village of Kilmartin, as they all waited to see if more redcoats would show up, looking for the ones who were now buried beneath a newly planted field of oats. Mairead found herself increasingly unsettled whenever she was around any of the Albans, but especially Hector. She had come to accept that the violence had been necessary – even the redcoat who had been running away – and that the Albans had acted in defense of the villagers and no more, but the complete lack of feeling they displayed over it sat uncomfortably with her.

It might even be better if they had shown anger for the redcoats. Righteous fury, or whatever soldiers convince themselves to feel on the battlefield. Maybe I could understand them more that way, she thought as she hung washing on the line in the yard.

Hector wandered past carrying a lamb under one arm and Mairead suppressed a shudder. Something in his movements as he walked away made her think that he was aware of her feelings about him. *Do we really still need them?*

When she and Constance were alone that night, sitting at either side of the hearth, she decided to broach the subject with her lover.

"The spring planting seems to be well underway."

"Hmmm," Constance said, frowning at the sewing in her hand. "The Albans have been a great help. They can work so much faster than us."

A log in the hearth popped, making Mairead twitch, startled. "I was thinking that maybe we don't need them anymore."

Constance looked up sharply, dropping her sewing into her lap. "What do you mean?"

"Well..." Mairead paused, all her carefully constructed arguments suddenly gone from her mind as if they had never been there to begin with. "I just...we're in a really good position with the work in the village now. I'm not sure we still need them."

"And who will protect us the next time a troop of redcoats comes through?" Constance asked, sounding exasperated.

Mairead sighed. "What happened—"

"What happened was that they saved all of our lives!"

"They did, and I don't mean to take that away from them," Mairead said placatingly. "But if we're really honest with ourselves about what happened, we have to consider that our lives might never have been in danger in the first place, had the redcoats not seen Hector."

"I can't believe you're saying this!" Constance got to her feet and began to pace the length of the room. "If those redcoats had come into the village and found no evidence of any men in the area, what do you think would have happened? They would have taken one look at us and decided we were all Jacobite widows – which we are, in fact, in case you have forgotten – and they would have decided to have their sport with us. We'd have been lucky if we survived at all, and we most certainly would not have survived intact."

"This was only ever meant to be temporary," Mairead said quietly, pained by Constance's anger. "It wasn't meant to go on indefinitely."

"It was supposed to be until the men came back," Constance said, stopping with her back to Mairead.

Mairead stood and went to her, placing her hands on Constance's shoulders. "What if they never come back? We can't keep the Albans around forever."

"Perhaps not. But we can keep them for a little longer than this." Constance shrugged Mairead's hands off and stepped away. "I'm tired all of a sudden. I'll see you in the morning."

She swept away into the bedroom and though she did not slam the door behind her, Mairead was quite certain that was only to avoid waking the children sleeping on the other side of it.

Chapter Twenty-One

Constance

7th May 1746

Constance jerked awake, her heart pounding in her chest, the pulse at her temples throbbing and threatening to turn into a headache. Mairead shifted in her sleep beside her but did not waken. In the days since their disagreement, Constance had allowed Mairead back into her bed, but things were not yet entirely recovered between them. Constance struggled to sit up, resting her back against the wall. Her arm ached where she had been shot, a hot, searing pain, even though the injury had been healed well by Nicnevin. An aftereffect of her dream, no doubt.

Nicnevin might have healed her arm, but her magic had done nothing to ease the trauma of being shot. Several times a night since it had happened, Constance had dreamed of the moment when Hector's kilt pin fell, and all of the horror that followed. Sometimes in her dreams, the musket ball hit Mairead instead of her, piercing right between her beautiful eyes. Other times, she dreamed that the redcoats had found the children, and she awoke with tears streaming down her face. This last winter had just been one horror after another, and she had never felt so vulnerable in all her life. She was terrified.

That was the thing that Mairead did not seem to understand. The Albans were the only reason that Constance could continue to function through her fear. Redcoats, raiders, the Black Watch…even the shadows of the witchfinders from the past, all felt like threats that surrounded them, just waiting for the opportunity to attack, the second she let her guard down.

Mairead moved closer, her warmth seeping through the chill left by the nightmare. Constance looked at her, watching her eyes move behind the delicate velvet of her closed lids. Ever since she was a child, Constance had known that her life could not be her own – not if she wanted it to last at any rate. She had spent so many years hiding what she was, making herself smaller, marrying Iain for the appearance of normality and the protection that his position brought. She would not say that she had always been unhappy, but until Mairead had come into her life and turned everything upside down, she did not think she had ever been truly happy.

But now, no more secrets kept her isolated. The women of the village knew what she was and while they had varying levels of comfort with it, only Roisin had outright rejected her, and frankly, she was no great loss. For the first time in her life, she could use her magic freely, and instead of submitting to a man she had no great love for, she had been given the gift of Mairead's company, her quick mind and good heart.

When the redcoats came, they had come so close to losing all of that, and more, with only the Albans to stand between them and the loss of all she held dear. How could Mairead possibly ask her to give them up?

The more time that passed since Culloden, the greater the likelihood that the men of Kilmartin would not be returning. And while Constance did mourn for them, she also felt a great, soaring joy at the thought of finally being free. If they kept the Albans around, then what need was there to go back to hiding?

She stroked Mairead's hair back out of her face. It made sense that she didn't understand – she had moved around, living according to her own desires, using her magic as she saw fit for years. She had never had to squash herself into a life that did not fit. But she would understand some day. Constance would make sure of it.

Pushing aside the quiet voice at the back of her mind that cautioned her against it, Constance pushed just a little magic into Mairead, willing her to be more pliable.

In all of the stress of the redcoats' appearance, and then the anxiety of waiting to see if other soldiers would come looking for them, Constance had completely forgotten that Mr. Munroe usually came through Kilmartin in May. Each year, the pedlar would set off from Inverness on the second of May, traveling a winding route down through the Highlands to Stirling, then eventually on to Glasgow, before retracing his steps and passing through again in August or early September.

The pedlar traded in all the towns and villages he passed through and even made a point of visiting a number of individual crofts on his meandering yearly journey. He brought tools, utensils, fabrics, food and even some common medicines and was always willing to trade for anything he thought he'd be able to pass on. He also brought news of the wider world, though it was often out of date by the time it reached them.

In recent years, he had made Kilmartin one of his overnight stops, sleeping with his wagon in Constance and Iain's barn, taking his meals with them.

The day he arrived was warm and bright, the heat almost a weight upon them. Constance and Mairead had taken the children to a spot farther along the stream they had crossed on the night of the fire, where the path of the water widened into a shallow pool. They had all removed their shoes and stockings to wade in the water, while gathering wild greens to add to that evening's meal. Earlier in the day, they had set some fish traps in the deeper water upstream and Constance was hopeful they would find the traps full on the way home.

She climbed out of the water and sat on the grass of the riverbank, allowing her feet to dry in the sun. Constance tipped her head back and closed her eyes. She let the warmth sink into her skin, allowing herself to relax into this rare moment of peace, smiling at the sound of Mairead laughing and splashing with the children.

There had been no more talk of giving up the Albans and the tension between them had passed. For now, in this moment and place, Constance felt as close to fulfilled as she had ever known. Somewhere nearby, crickets sang in the long grass, and birds twittered as they flitted between branches in bramble bushes heavy with flowers.

Constance opened her eyes and watched two white-and-orange butterflies dance in the air above the pool, quickly gaining height when one of the children splashed water that arced too close to them.

The sound of hooves on turf and the sedate creak of a wagon brought Constance to her feet in a flash. She shielded her eyes to peer into the distance, her vision tunneling, her heart in her throat. Her first panicked thought was *the redcoats are back!* But as she waited, pulling her magic to the surface, ready to throw the full might of it against anyone who would cause them harm, she realized that she could only hear one horse. While the redcoats might travel on foot, with one horse to pull a supply wagon or the likes, she could hear no hint of booted feet hitting the ground, no talking or grumbling, not even the shift of weapons or fabric.

Whoever approached was coming alone.

A few minutes later, their visitor came into view, a beautiful chestnut horse, pulling a covered wagon driven by a dark-haired man on the other side of middle age.

"Ho!" he called, pulling the horse to a halt as he drew close. "Mistress Gordon, it is a pleasure to see you looking so well."

"Mr. Munroe! I had not thought to see you this spring. How are you? How's the family?" Constance called back, walking over to meet him.

Mr. Munroe removed his flat hat and wiped his forehead before replacing it. "Aye, they're well, Mistress. My eldest daughter had another bairn, so she has three of her own now and my youngest was wed over the winter."

"And your son?" Constance asked, glancing over at Mairead, who still stood in the pool with the children, watching warily. She had subtly moved to place herself between the pedlar and the children, and for a moment Constance's heart ached with love for her.

"Died, at Falkirk Muir." He turned his face away and Constance could see the muscles in his jaw working as he fought to control his emotions.

"I am truly sorry for your loss," she said softly. "May God keep him close." She wondered what side the lad had fought on but felt like asking would be to minimize his loss somehow. As if his father's grief could only be justified if his son had died on the 'right' side.

Mr. Munroe cleared his throat and said brightly, "You and the bairns look well. Look how fast the wee lad is growing! He was but a babe in arms when I saw you last."

Constance looked over and smiled fondly at her children. "They grow so fast. The three of them fair keep me on my toes."

"Well, and so they should," Mr. Munroe responded with a laugh. "I see you've got some help with them, for today at least?"

Of course he'd notice that he's never met Mairead around the village before. She gestured for Mairead to join them. "This is Mistress Ferguson, a cousin of Iain's. She's been staying with us over the winter, since her husband passed last year."

"I'm sorry for your loss," he said, bowing his head in Mairead's direction. "Peter Munroe, traveling pedlar."

"It's a pleasure to meet you," Mairead said, hoisting Simon up onto her hip when he started to fuss.

"I take it you're not from this area originally? I'm sure we would have met otherwise, and I'd never forget a pretty face like yours."

With his attention briefly diverted, Constance had time to try and think through the implications of him being here. He knew all the men of Kilmartin and would not be remotely fooled by the Albans. They had to get the earth men out of sight for the duration of his visit. Munroe also knew the rhythms of the village and his visits were usually a cause for everyone to gather – he would notice straight away that the men were gone. There could be no pretense at normal with him.

"Hector?"

"I'm listening."

"I need you to gather all of the Albans and take them to the bothy where the children hid when the soldiers came. I need all of you to wait there, out of sight, until I summon you again. Make sure that you are not seen."

"As you wish."

The mental connection broke and Constance brought her mind back to the conversation at hand. Mairead was telling Mr. Munroe about growing up on a croft in Argyll, and Constance realized that she had no idea how much of the story was true. She knew that there was more to Mairead's past than she talked about and sensed that speaking of it was difficult, so she hadn't pushed. She didn't need to know Mairead's past to know who she was now.

"How is Iain?" Mr. Munroe asked, turning to Constance and breaking her train of thought.

"I..." She sighed and looked around warily, scanning for any signs of unseen listeners. "I don't know." She looked at the ground and allowed herself to recall one of the dreams in which Mairead had been killed in front of her, to fully engage with the horror of it, then looked back up, tears brimming in her eyes. "I think he might be dead."

Mr. Munroe jumped down from the seat on the wagon and wrapped his arms around Constance, pulling her into a bear hug. For a moment, she let herself sob, giving him the reaction he would expect to see, while allowing some of her own tension to flow away with the tears.

"Was he at Culloden?" Mr. Munroe asked gently.

Constance nodded, pulling away and rubbing at her face with her sleeve.

Mairead placed a reassuring hand on her back, a warm gesture from a friend.

"And you've heard nothing since?"

Constance let out a slow breath and shook her head. "Not so much as a letter since he left in August. I don't even know for sure that he was at Culloden." She cleared her throat. "It's not just Iain. Most of the men from the village went off, and none of us have heard anything since. What little news we've had has been from Fergus, who's in Inverness just now."

"What a time of it you must all have had," Mr. Munroe said sadly. "August, you said they left?"

Constance nodded, watching him warily. She knew that the timing of their departure made it obvious that they had gone to join the Stuart forces, but she had no choice but to hope that the pedlar would be sympathetic. And if he wasn't, well…she might have to introduce him to Hector.

Mr. Munroe leaned in close and lowered his voice as if to ensure he wasn't overheard, despite there being no one around to listen. "Rumor has it that some of the rebels escaped the battlefield and are hiding out in the wilds, waiting until it's safe to come home. Perhaps there's still a chance…"

She let her relief show on her face, allowing him to think it was for Iain. "We can hope, at least."

Mairead made a show of bouncing Simon on her hip. "I think this little man is ready for a nap. Shall I take the children home, and you can stay and catch up for a bit longer?"

"No need!" Mr. Munroe said cheerily. "I'm heading to the village anyway. The children can ride up here if you two ladies don't mind walking. I'm afraid there's not much space in the back, otherwise I could give you all a lift."

Constance felt a pulse of alarm coming from Mairead and sent silent reassurance back. "That would be lovely, I'm sure the children would enjoy that," she said with a bright smile.

As Mr. Munroe bustled about getting the children settled on the bench of the wagon, Constance leaned in close to Mairead and murmured, "I've told the Albans to hide until he leaves."

The village women were pleased to see Mr. Munroe. The afternoon passed in a blur of trading and catching up, and if there was an undercurrent of tension in the village, Constance could only hope that the pedlar would put it down to their fear for their men. By the time they were home and Constance was serving up the fish from their traps with wild greens, for the evening meal, she had begun to relax.

Mr. Munroe would spend the night in the barn, then take some porridge with him in the morning before setting off for the next stop on his journey, and by noon tomorrow all would have returned to normal. Or the new normal, anyway.

At least, that was what she thought until a knock at the door interrupted their meal.

Constance stood from the table, dread turning the taste in her mouth bitter. She opened the door to find Catriona pacing back and forth in front of the entrance, wringing her hands.

"Catriona, what's wrong?" she asked, fear uncoiling in her stomach.

"Robbie's missing," Catriona said without preamble. "I can't find him anywhere."

"Come inside, tell us what's happening," Constance said. She took the woman's arm and led her into the house.

Mairead stood and came to Catriona's side as soon as they entered.

"When did you last see him?" Mairead asked, taking Catriona's hand in hers.

"I'm not sure. Sometime this morning." She looked at Constance with haunted eyes. "I thought he was with my mother, she thought he was with me."

"And when did you discover that neither of you knew where he was?"

Catriona pulled her hands free from Mairead and started pacing again, apparently incapable of staying still while unable to account for her son's whereabouts.

"Just after you left to come home. I noticed he hadn't done some things I asked him to take care of this morning, so I went over to Ma's to fetch him home to do his chores and she said she hadn't seen him since midmorning, when she caught him chasing some of the chickens and gave him a telling-off for frightening them."

"Is that the last time anyone saw him?" Constance asked.

Catriona gave an exasperated sigh. "We're not sure what order things happened in, because neither of us paid much attention to the time. I think I might have seen him a bit after that, playing with some other bairns around the space where the church was."

"And you've checked with everyone in the village?"

"No, I came running straight out to you without knocking on my neighbors' doors first. What do you think?"

Constance took a step back, surprised at Catriona's anger.

"I'm sorry." Catriona sighed and took a deep breath. "I know you're just trying to help. I just...I've looked everywhere, asked everyone. I don't know where he is."

"Then let's get looking for him," Mr. Munroe said, standing from the table. He had been so quiet that Constance had almost forgotten that he was there.

"Mairead, can you please stay with the children, while Mr. Munroe and I go to help look for Robbie?" Constance asked.

"Of course." Mairead went to Catriona and gave her a brief, fierce hug. "I pray you find him quickly."

Catriona pressed her lips together and nodded, then turned and headed for the door.

Constance had one last lingering look at Mairead before glancing at each of her own children in turn. Guilt twisted her stomach over the fact that she was grateful that her children were safe, while Catriona's son might not be.

Outside, the sun was making its descent toward the horizon. *Please, God, let us find him before it gets dark.* At that time of year, the sun lingered long in the sky and twilight lingered even longer, but eventually it would become too dark to safely conduct a search.

"What are the others all doing just now?" Constance asked as she caught up with Catriona in the yard, Mr. Munroe just at her back.

"Searching all of the houses, gardens and buildings in the village," Catriona said, heading for the gate at a brisk pace. "We thought maybe he was playing a hiding game and fell asleep or something."

"It's possible that we'll get back and they'll have found him, asleep in a corner somewhere," Constance said. It might be possible, but she couldn't convince herself that it was likely. A boy of twelve wasn't likely to sleep the afternoon away unless he was ill.

"All right. You head back along the track. I'll go through the fields, just in case."

"I'll saddle up Samson and—"

"What?" Constance said, alarm filling her body with spikes. In her mind's eye, she saw the redcoat captain bowing to her. *"Captain Paul Sampson, at your service."*

Mr. Munroe was giving her a strange look and she realized she was clutching at her arm where the band of scarring was the only remaining evidence of the redcoats' visit.

"I'll saddle my horse, Samson, and meet you in the village if you want to go on ahead."

"Oh. Yes. Good idea. Thank you." Constance clasped her hands together to stop herself worrying at her scar.

"Are you quite all right?" Mr. Munroe said, leaning toward her. "You're as white as snow."

"Just lightheaded for a moment. I'm fine now." Constance smiled and though it felt fake to her, as if she were stretching her face in a hideous rictus grin, it seemed to be convincing enough for Mr. Munroe.

"We'll meet in the village then." He turned to Catriona, who was shifting from foot to foot, clearly desperate to race back to the search, but not quite wanting to leave Constance in a weakened state. "Let's get out there and find your lad."

Constance arrived at the village after Catriona, having taken the more challenging route through the fields. She only had to look at the other woman's face to know that there was no sign of Robbie yet.

She quickly took control of the search, sending people out in pairs in different directions from the village. *If only we could use the Albans. One of them with each group would make it so much easier to keep track of where people are and what they've seen.* But while she had been willing to take a chance and trust that Mr. Munroe would not turn them in as Jacobites, trusting that he would keep quiet about the Albans was another matter entirely.

Mr. Munroe offered to ride the perimeter of the Gordon land that Kilmartin was responsible for and otherwise act as a go-between for all the others who would be searching on foot.

Constance thanked him and waved him on his way without thinking too much about it, her mind largely focused on trying to picture all of the land that made up Kilmartin and think of anywhere that Robbie might have gone to sulk if he had been unhappy after being told off by his grandmother, all the while trying to push away thoughts of the sheep that went missing all those months ago.

Constance sat at Catriona's table with a pencil and paper, sketching out the land they had to cover and noting where people had been already as they reported back. She had tried to convince Catriona to stay with her and help her with the coordination efforts, reasoning that she was as likely to endanger herself, racing to find him without any thought to her own well-being. Of course, it hadn't worked, and Constance hadn't pushed the argument, being all too aware of how she would react if it was one of her own children who was lost. They would have to restrain her to keep her from the search.

Shouts sounded outside and Constance flew to the door, barely noticing the stool she had been sitting on clattering to the floor as she raced outside.

Two people came staggering down the street, carrying a limp form between them.

"We've got him," Emily called, panting from the effort of carrying him. "Isobel! He's hurt!"

Isobel Gordon came rushing outside and took charge at once. "Put him down there, the light is better out here for the moment."

Robbie's rescuers placed him carefully on the ground.

"Where's Catriona?" Morag asked. "I'll go and let her know."

"She went to check the derelict croft north-east of here," Constance said, picturing the map and notes on Catriona's table. "He was in the woods out toward my house?"

Morag nodded. "I'll let Mistress Croaker tell you." She turned and started jogging in the direction of the derelict croft.

Constance turned back to where Isobel was kneeling on the ground beside the injured boy, who was drifting in and out of consciousness.

"We found him lying flat out beneath a big oak. His foot was caught between some of the roots at an awkward angle, and there was blood on the tree where his head was lying." Emily stopped and pressed her hand to her chest, giving herself a moment to get her breath back. "It looked like he'd caught his foot and then had a fall because of it, gave his head a knock. He was awake when we found him, but passed out when I pulled his foot free, and he's been in and out since."

"What do you need?" Constance asked Isobel.

"Give me a minute," the healer said, fingers carefully investigating the back of Robbie's head.

"Can I get you some water?" Constance asked Emily, who waved her off.

"I can get some myself in a minute, just you concentrate on the lad."

Constance stood there, feeling helpless, biting the inside of her lip in frustration. At last, Isobel sat back on her heels and looked up at the other two women.

"He's got quite a lump on the back of his head, but his pupils are doing as they should, which is a good sign. I don't think the head injury is too serious."

"Then why is he unconscious?" Constance asked.

Isobel pushed herself to her feet with a groan. "Most likely from the pain. I'm fairly sure the ankle is broken quite badly, though it's so swollen it's hard to say for sure. Let's get him into the house and settled in bed, and we can take it from there."

Constance took Robbie's shoulders and Isobel very carefully cradled his injured leg, while Emily took hold of his other leg. Among the three of them, they lifted him and began moving to the house.

"COME NOW." Hector's voice blared inside her mind, startling her enough that she stumbled and almost dropped Robbie. Another head injury would be all he needed.

"Soon, I'm busy now."

"It is urgent." Hector rarely gave off any sense of emotion but this time his words carried a sense of great stress.

Constance sent a mental picture of what she was doing at that moment, then broke the connection, pushing thoughts of Hector away as she concentrated on getting Robbie safely inside.

They got him onto the bed and when she straightened, her lower back twinged, and she gasped at the sharp shock of it. Carrying a twelve-year-old was quite a bit harder on the back than a toddler, she thought as she pressed on the sore spot.

Suddenly, Hector blasted an image into her mind, pushing past the barrier she had erected to let her concentrate on Robbie. The image was of Peter Munroe, lying on a packed dirt floor with blood covering his face.

Chapter Twenty-Two

Constance

Constance made her excuses and left Isobel and Emily to look after Robbie, rushing out of the house and out of the village. The sun hovered just above the horizon, casting long shadows across the landscape. She walked fast and tried not to look alarmed, but all the while her mind was racing.

What on earth has happened to him?

She had pressed Hector for an explanation, but he would only say that Munroe was alive and reiterate his request that she come now. As she raced toward the bothy, she passed another search pair on their way back to the village.

"We've got him!" she called, waving them over. "He's injured, but Isobel thinks he should recover."

"Thank the Lord," one answered, putting a hand to her chest. "Does Catriona know yet?"

"Morag has gone to find her," Constance answered, watching a distant kestrel hovering over a field in the direction of the bothy. "I'm going to have a quick check on the Albans before Mr. Munroe returns. I'll be back soon."

As she parted ways with the searchers, the kestrel dived, then climbed into the sky once more a moment later. Constance couldn't tell from that distance if the bird had managed to catch its dinner or not.

She saw no one else and arrived at the bothy a little out of breath, and trembling, fear fizzing in her blood. She pushed the door open and entered to find the Albans standing round the walls, motionless, almost completely filling the small room. The space was dim; the only light came in through two small windows. In the middle of the floor, Mr. Munroe lay in a bloody heap.

"Please tell me his horse threw him, and you brought him in here to help him?" Constance demanded, looking at Hector, who stared back at her from features that had lost their definition at the edges. "Tell me you didn't do this to him."

Hector remained implacable. *"You said to make sure we were not seen. This one saw us."*

"Goddamnit! I didn't mean..." She threw her hands in the air. "What happened?"

"He came in. He saw us. We stopped him leaving."

Constance pinched the bridge of her nose and tried to think. She knew she should get down on her knees and check if he was alive. She should do whatever she could to treat his injuries and get him back to the cottage. And then she should figure out how to persuade him to keep quiet about it all. She knew all of that and yet she still stood there, paralyzed by fear.

Mr. Munroe groaned and rolled from his side onto his back. *Well, that answers the first question.*

Constance fell to her knees at his side. Pain shot up her thighs as she hit the floor, exhaustion driving her down harder than she had intended. It seemed only fitting that she should share some of his experience.

"You're all right now. Everything will be fine." She took his hand in hers and held it gently, hoping it would be reassuring.

One of Mr. Munroe's eyes was swollen shut but the other opened, its brightness startling against his blood-covered face. He looked first at Constance and relief colored his features as he squeezed her hand.

"Help," he croaked, his words softened by his split lips.

"I'm here now," Constance said. "I'm going to take care of you."

His gaze moved past her to where Hector loomed behind her, and he began to scream in a high, panicked whistle.

"It's all right," she said, the panic that was clawing its way up her throat tinging her voice. "They won't hurt you, it's all right."

"Get them away from me," he said, trying to push himself across the floor, away from Hector. His head hit the foot of the Alban standing behind him and he scrabbled back to Constance, whimpering and clutching at her. "Run, while you can."

"You're safe," Constance said, catching his flailing hands in her own. "I promise, you're safe."

He stopped struggling for a moment, and looked around, eyes darting from one Alban to another. "What *are* they?"

Constance frowned and looked around at the assembled Albans. "They're Jacobites," she said quickly, hoping he was rattled enough to accept the lie. "Survivors from Culloden. They're hiding from the redcoats until it's safe to make their way home."

Mr. Munroe stared at Constance as if she had lost her mind. "They're not human!"

"What do you mean?" she asked. "Of course they're human." He could only see out of one eye, and he was clearly confused, maybe she could convince him that their fuzzy features were a result of his injuries. Maybe with a little push of magic. She concentrated and sent a pulse of reassurance toward him, along with the same pliability she had been pushing into Mairead.

His panicked features gave no sign of it working. "Look at them! They're monsters!"

Constance made a show of looking around and staring at the Albans. "They're just men. Perhaps they look strange because you hit your head?"

"Strange?!" he cried. "Men made out of mud and sticks and worms are not strange! They're surely some demons sent from hell."

Constance's heart thudded at the base of her throat. *How can he see through the glamour?* She studied the Albans again. If she concentrated, she could see the weave of magic that covered them, but even knowing that it was there, she could not see through it to the reality beneath. To her they looked like Highland men with indistinct faces.

"I don't...Peter, they're just men," she said, once more sending a pulse of magic through her hands and into his. *Believe me. Believe.*

Mr. Munroe turned horrified eyes upon her. "Why are you protecting them? Have they cast some evil spell on you, Mistress Gordon?"

He took his hands from her and tried to push himself to his feet. The Albans moved to block the door but made no threatening move toward him.

Constance couldn't understand why her persuasive magic wasn't working on him, but clearly it wasn't going to solve this problem. Instead, she got to her feet and caught at his arm.

"You're right," she said softly. "They're not human. But they won't harm you, I promise."

"What are they? What's going on here?" he demanded.

Constance took a deep breath. She had to persuade him not to talk about this when he left here. She had to make sure they were all safe. "They're called Albans. They are creatures made of Kilmartin, and they are only here to protect the village and the people in it. They're not dangerous."

She realized her mistake almost before the words were out of her mouth. Mr. Munroe jerked back from her, waving a hand at his misshapen, blood-covered face.

"They're not dangerous? Are you under the impression I did this to myself?"

Constance held her hands up, palms out. "Of course not. I'm sorry. They mistook you for a threat, but it was a mistake, and it won't happen again."

"A threat! I was trying to help find a child of this village. I've never been anything but a friend to you."

"I know. I'm sorry."

He made to move toward the door and the Albans continued to block his path out. "Tell them to let me pass," he growled.

Constance swallowed. "I can't do that, until I know what you're going to do when you leave here."

He turned a furious glare on her. "You think to threaten me?"

"It's not a threat. But I need to know that you're not going to tell anyone outside the village about this. All of our men are gone, and likely dead. There are raiders and redcoats all over the Highlands, doing whatever they will to villages like ours. I cannot cope with another threat on top of that."

"I would never have expected such wickedness from you, Constance Gordon. To think, all these years, I've believed you a good, God-fearing woman."

"Just tell me that you'll never speak of this, and we can all go home. I'll patch you up – or Mairead will if you prefer – and tomorrow you can be on your way as normal." She was almost begging now; she needed him to make that promise, even if she couldn't be sure that he would keep it.

Mr. Munroe drew himself up and set his shoulders, though the movement clearly pained him. "I cannot in good conscience do that."

Constance looked at him, blood roaring in her ears. She stepped over to the Alban who blocked the door. He moved aside to let her pass. She put her hand on the door then looked at Hector, her back to Mr. Munroe.

"Don't let him leave. Ever."

Chapter Twenty-Three

Mairead

Mairead lit an oil lamp and placed it on the table, as night gathered outside. She prowled around the room, trying to find tasks to keep herself busy. She had been sewing for a while, but sitting still was grating on her frayed nerves; she needed to move around while she waited. She had cleaned everything she could without making enough noise to disturb the children sleeping next door and now had moved on to sorting through the shelves and baskets of various household supplies, making a note of anything they needed to replenish or replace, glancing at the door every few minutes.

Why is it taking so long to find him? How far could he have wandered?

Robbie was a nice boy – a bit mischievous from time to time but always caring toward the younger children in the village. She wished she knew what was happening. Catriona must be out of her mind with worry. Mairead shuddered as she thought of how she would feel if one of Constance's children was missing. Quietly, she went to the bedroom door and opened it just enough to peek into the room and reassure herself that they were all sleeping, safe and sound. She watched them for a moment, considering how the children had burrowed into her heart just as deep as Constance had.

She closed the bedroom door and went back to her busywork, trying not to think about the future and the tangled web of her relationship with Constance. There was a certain freedom in surrendering herself to this love, even knowing that it could not last, and sooner or later must end in a broken heart.

Mairead straightened, hearing the soft scuffling sounds of someone approaching the house, trying to be quiet. A moment later, Constance opened the door and stepped inside, looking haunted and pale.

"What's happened?" Mairead asked, rushing to her side. "Couldn't you find him?"

"What?" Constance asked. She looked as if she had been completely lost in thought, and didn't really know where she was or who was speaking to her.

"Robbie – did you find him?"

Constance shook her head, as if trying to clear her thoughts. "Yes. Yes, we found him."

Mairead took Constance by the arm, led her over to a chair by the hearth, and guided her to sit down. Something was definitely wrong.

"Was he…" she asked, fearing the worst.

"He's all right," Constance said, still speaking as if her thoughts were someplace else. "A broken ankle and a knock to the head. He was in the woods between here and the village, looked like he'd caught his foot in amongst some roots then fell and hit his head."

"Then what's wrong?" Mairead pulled over a stool and perched in front of Constance, taking her hands. "Has something else happened?"

Constance pressed her lips together and shook her head again. "It's just been a long day."

Why is she lying?

"I've seen you at the end of a long day before, but this seems like something different. Come on, *mo ghaol*, talk to me. Let me help."

"Mairead, leave it!" Constance snapped, pulling her hands away. She sighed. "I'm sorry. I just need to sleep."

Mairead drew back, hurt. She bit the inside of her lip, worrying at it. "Did Mr. Munroe come back with you?" she asked, getting to her feet and moving away.

"He's in the barn," Constance said, not looking at her. "He said he was going to settle his horse and go straight to sleep."

Mairead frowned, glancing at the door. She hadn't heard a horse when Constance returned. Or another person at all, now that she thought of it. Constance stood and walked over to her. She leaned against her as if she did not have the energy to stand alone. A pulse of warmth and reassurance came across their connection. Mairead pulled Constance closer and placed a gentle kiss on her temple. *Maybe they came back overland, and went straight to the barn. Constance could have carried on to the house by herself.*

"Let's go to bed," Constance murmured, taking Mairead's hand and lacing their fingers together, sending another warm pulse of magic.

Mairead squeezed her hand. "Let's."

Mairead woke later than usual, the sun streaming in through the window and slanting across the bed. Constance was gone from her side and the children were up already. She lay there for a moment, groggy and confused. She felt almost as if she had overindulged the night before, though she hadn't had a drop to drink. Her mouth was dry and tasted awful. With a groan, she got to her feet and pulled her kirtle on over her shift before stumbling out to the main room. Constance and the children were nowhere to be seen, but there was a pot of porridge sitting beside the hearth to keep it warm.

Mairead headed to the outhouse and dealt with her morning needs, before taking some water from a barrel in the yard and splashing her face, trying to wake up properly. The sun was well above the horizon and the day was warm though not yet hot. She could hear cattle in the distance, and closer, the goats and chickens. She stood there for a moment, her mind perfectly blank, until the sound of approaching giggling broke through her stupor.

"There you are!" Constance said, appearing from the other side of the house, the children in tow. "Have you eaten yet? I left you some porridge."

"I saw, thank you. I haven't eaten yet." She splashed another handful of water on her face. "I'm sorry, I have no idea why I slept so late. Why didn't you wake me?"

Constance shrugged. "You seemed to need the rest."

Mairead looked past Constance's shoulder as Hector lumbered into view. "Is Mr. Munroe still here?" she asked, panicked at the thought of the pedlar stepping out of the barn just in time to spot the Alban close up.

Constance shook her head. "He set off not long after first light, before the children were even awake."

Mairead frowned. "I thought he usually stays for breakfast."

"He does," Constance said, turning and heading for the door, Mairead following close behind. "He said something about wanting to get his horse to his next stop in time to see the farrier."

"I'm sorry to have missed him," Mairead said. She blinked as she stepped inside and stood still for a moment to let her eyes adjust to the change in light. "I would have liked to have said goodbye. He seems a nice man."

"Mama, can we stay outside and play?" Elspeth asked from the doorstep. Simon laughed excitedly and pulled at her hand.

Constance flashed her daughter a smile. "Of course, just stay close to the house, in case Simon needs anything."

"I want to make a daisy chain," Janey said, dashing off across the yard.

"Come, eat." Constance caught Mairead's hand and pulled her over to the table. "Are you well? You don't seem quite yourself this morning."

Mairead tried to focus, to bring her thoughts in line. "I feel a little groggy. Confused." She allowed Constance to press her onto a stool at the table and place a bowl of porridge in front of her.

"Maybe you're getting ill," Constance said, frowning and placing a hand on Mairead's forehead. "Do you feel ill?"

"I don't know. Not really? Just not quite right." Mairead took a spoonful of porridge and found that she didn't really want to eat. Even the sensation of the food in her mouth was off-putting. She swallowed with some effort then put the spoon down.

Constance looked on, worry reflected on her face. "I think you should rest today. Just go back to bed, I can manage the chores."

Mairead shook her head, wanting to argue, but her thoughts were slow and fuzzy. "I want to… I want… I'll be…"

"Nope, bed." Constance wrapped an arm around her, helped her to her feet, and guided her to the bedroom with one stumbling step after another.

When Mairead next awoke, Isobel Gordon was sitting perched on the side of the bed, her fingers pressed to the inside of Mairead's wrist.

"Hello, love," she said gently when she noticed Mairead's eyes were open. "How are you feeling?"

Mairead tried to answer but her mouth felt gummed together and her voice cracked when she tried to speak.

"I'll get you some water." Mistress Gordon stood, went through to the other room and hurried back with a cup. She helped Mairead sit up a little and held the cup to her lips, letting her sip at the cool, fresh water within. "Better?"

"Thank you," Mairead said, her voice still croaky. "What's happening?"

"Constance asked me to come and check on you. You've had a bit of a fever, and she was worried about you. How are you feeling now?"

Mairead closed her eyes for a moment and tried to take stock. How *was* she feeling? Heavy. Sluggish and slow. A thudding ache behind her left eye, and a tumultuous stomach. She raised a hand and rubbed at the skin just above her left eyebrow. "Um, my head hurts. And...I guess...I feel a little sick."

"When did this all start?" Mistress Gordon asked, placing the back of her hand against the side of Mairead's neck. Her skin felt cool and dry against the feverish dampness of Mairead's own.

"I'm not sure." She slid back down the bed, her body weighted down by exhaustion. "I'm so tired."

"Just you rest, *a' charaid*. We'll take care of you."

Mairead drifted away to the sounds of a murmured conversation.

She drifted in that odd gray space between sleeping and waking, sometimes hearing voices or the sounds of people moving around the cottage, other times hearing nothing but her own rasping breathing. Colors flickered across the insides of her eyelids, like the sun catching the sparkling scales of a fish darting through water. There was a sense of peace here and she wished she could stay.

The next time she opened her eyes, she thought she might be dreaming. Nicnevin was leaning over her. The fae's long hair fell in a curtain to skim the side of Mairead's face, the otherworldly scent of her filling the space between them.

"Well, hello there, precious one," Nicnevin said, her voice like music. "And where have you been?"

Mairead looked up at her, trying to formulate an answer, but her thoughts kept breaking apart in the face of the fae queen's closeness. It wasn't just her beauty that caused the problem, though she certainly had that in abundance, but the force of her presence, her magic, her very being, was so overwhelming that it took up all of the space in Mairead's mind, leaving room only for worshipful lust.

Nicnevin trailed her fingers along Mairead's jaw, leaving a line of fire in their wake, then pulled back, allowing Mairead to see over her shoulder to where Constance waited by the door, her face tight with worry. Guilt gnawed at Mairead, and she pushed herself up the bed a little, creating more space between her and Nicnevin. Shakily, she managed to sit up and rest her back against the headboard.

The fae queen made a gesture with her hand and suddenly she was holding a small earthenware cup, fragrant steam drifting up from inside it. "Here." She took Mairead's hands and wrapped them around the cup. "Drink this."

The clay was warm, the heat soothing. Mairead raised it to her face and inhaled the steam. Some of the scents were familiar to her, but others were not. She sipped the liquid cautiously; it was warm but not too hot, both sweet and spiced, with a slightly bitter aftertaste.

"It's not poison, I promise," Nicnevin said, watching her with a slightly amused expression, one delicate eyebrow arched.

"It's good," Mairead croaked. "Thank you."

"What is it?" Constance asked from the doorway. "Will it help her?"

Nicnevin's voice was cold when she answered. "It'll certainly do more good for her than you have."

Mairead winced. What had happened while she was unconscious? Constance looked as though she wanted to snap at the fae, but instead she crossed her arms over her torso and turned her face away to gaze out of the window.

"What's happening?" Mairead asked, looking between them. "Why are you two at odds?"

Nicnevin gestured at the cup. "Keep drinking – all of that – and I'll tell you." She glanced over her shoulder at Constance. "Unless you wish to confess?"

Constance pressed her lips together and shook her head.

Mairead sipped at the liquid again, feeling it move through her body, soothing aching and exhausted muscles as it went. It did little to soothe the mounting worry about what she had missed while she had been ill. "Would one of you please tell me what's going on?"

Nicnevin blew out a sharp breath from her nose. "Your illness has been of a magical nature rather than physical," she began. "That's why your human healer was unable to help you. Keep drinking." She paused until Mairead had taken another sip. "What do you remember of your illness?"

Mairead took another mouthful while she thought about it. "I woke up late. Yesterday? And I felt wrong somehow, as if I'd had too much whisky, though I hadn't had any at all." She paused and sipped again at a gesture from Nicnevin. With each sip, she felt a little better, a little more like herself. "Then Mistress Gordon was here, and my head ached. Then I fell asleep again."

"You've been ill for three days," Nicnevin said, waving her hand and summoning an apple from out of the air. She took a small knife from a sheath on her belt and began to cut the apple, handing the first slice to Mairead. "Eat."

Mairead took a bite of the apple and sweet, tart juice exploded across her tongue. It was the best thing she had ever tasted.

"The magic was tainted," Nicnevin said, with a hard look toward Constance, who seemed to shrink in on herself.

"What do you mean?" Mairead asked. "I don't understand."

Nicnevin handed her another slice of apple. "The Albans acted outwith the bounds of our agreement, thereby tainting the magic that powers them. That taint affected both of us, as the main founders of the spell, but it affected you much faster and more severely than me. There were two reasons for that. One is that you are human—"

"Wait, wait," Mairead interrupted, holding a hand up. "What did they do?" She looked at Constance, but Constance turned her face farther away, refusing to meet her gaze. Tears glistened on her cheeks, the sunlight from the window highlighting them in streaks of gold. "Constance?"

"They killed an innocent," Nicnevin said, her anger suddenly filling the room, though she neither moved nor raised her voice.

Mairead sat up straighter on the bed, her mind clear for the first time in days. Weeks, even. "Tell me what happened," she said, anger and confusion writhing together in her heart. "Who did they kill? Constance?"

"It was an accident," Constance said. She still refused to look at Mairead. "They didn't mean to kill him."

"Kill *who*?" Mairead asked. Dread settled in her stomach like a boulder. Was it Robbie? Had they hurt that sweet boy?

Constance mumbled, so quiet that Mairead couldn't make out what she said.

"Who?"

Constance groaned and turned to face her, though she still did not meet Mairead's gaze. "They killed Mr. Munroe."

"Why would they…? After he left here?" Mairead stared at Constance, willing this all to make sense.

Nicnevin sat unmoving. Her gaze drilled into Constance.

"The night Robbie went missing, Mr. Munroe stumbled across the bothy where the Albans were hiding. I told them they must not be seen, so when he went into the bothy and saw them, they tried to stop him leaving. They didn't mean to hurt him, it was an accident." Constance swallowed audibly. Her voice was shaky now. "You know how strong they are. They were just trying to restrain him and…"

Mairead stared at her, feeling sick. *That poor man. He was just trying to help.* Suddenly Mairead remembered how Constance had come in that night, how she had said that he was in the barn. "You lied to me."

Constance closed her eyes. "I just… I didn't know what to do, and I didn't want to drag you into it. It was my instruction that caused this, and I thought I could…I don't know…fix it somehow. And you wouldn't need to know."

"I told you that any misuse of the Albans would taint the magic," Nicnevin said, ice cracking in her voice.

"But it was an accident," Constance retorted, a burst of heat breaking through the despondency that had colored her voice a moment before. "I didn't think it would count. And you never said that it would do this to Mairead."

Nicnevin rose to her feet, her temper flaring. A heavy feeling filled the air, like there was a storm approaching. The fine hairs on Mairead's forearms rose in response to the magic crackling in the air.

"It would not have affected Mairead so severely if you had not been dosing her and diluting her magic with your own." Nicnevin's voice was steady and controlled. She did not shout, and yet it filled the room as powerfully as a roll of thunder. "You are the cause of this harm, Constance Gordon."

Dosing her? "What do you mean?" Mairead asked, anger beginning to kindle alongside grief.

Constance looked at her, tear-filled eyes pleading for forgiveness, or perhaps understanding. She shook her head and moved for the door, as if to flee, but Nicnevin raised a hand and Constance froze, wrapped in the fae's power.

"Your companion here," Nicnevin said, spitting the words out, "has been using her magic to influence you, which diluted your own natural power, and your ability to absorb the taint from this 'accident'."

"That can't be right," Mairead said, worrying at the inside of her lip. "Constance hasn't used her magic on me since I was burned, and that was before the Albans were here. I mean, other than the way that our magic is connected because...but that goes both ways, so I'm affecting her as much as she affects me."

Nicnevin gestured, turning Constance around to face Mairead. "Are you going to tell her, or will I?"

Constance shook her head and closed her eyes; her throat moved as she swallowed.

"Your friend," Nicnevin said, fury tight in her words, "has been using her magic to influence you. To make you more docile and agreeable. To turn you into the companion that she wants, rather than treating you with the respect and reverence that you deserve as an individual."

Mairead's thoughts swirled in chaos, leaving her feeling wrong-footed and off-balance. "No. There must be a mistake. Constance would never do that to me."

"Oh, but she has."

"Constance?" Mairead asked in a small voice. She waited for her lover to defend herself, to say that this wasn't true.

"I'm sorry." Constance didn't even open her eyes, didn't look at Mairead to confront the hurt she had caused.

Mairead pushed herself to the edge of the bed and swung her legs out. She held onto the headboard as she stood, swaying. "How could you?"

Constance didn't answer.

Nicnevin gave Mairead a concerned look. "You need to be careful. I've done what I can to heal you, but you will remain weak for the next few days. You must rest."

Mairead sank back down to perch on the edge of the bed, her legs shaky from only that short stint on her feet. "What happens next? Have you unmade the Albans?"

"Not yet," Nicnevin answered. "I didn't want to manipulate your magic until you were well enough to be part of the discussion. Because consent is important." She glared at Constance.

"Please," Constance said, finally looking at Mairead. "Please don't do this. We still need them."

"Do we?" Mairead asked. "They were supposed to help get us through the winter. Well, they've done that. They've kept us safe. But this can't go on forever. The longer they stay, the higher the likelihood of discovery."

"I will not stand for my magic being used to harm an innocent again," Nicnevin said, her voice severe.

Mairead wondered just how badly the fae queen had been affected by the taint.

"It was an accident," Constance said, pleading. "I swear to you, nothing like that will happen again, I'll be more careful when giving instructions."

"Constance, it's not just that. This was never supposed to be a permanent situation. The longer we keep them around, the more time we're all losing from the end of our lives." Mairead sighed and let her head rest against the wall. Fantigue was washing over her once more, threatening to pull her into sleep again. "All of us who are tied to an Alban have given up months of our own lives now. I'm not willing to give up years."

Constance moved toward her, evidently freed of Nicnevin's influence. She reached out to grasp Mairead's hand.

"Don't touch me." Mairead pulled her hand back onto her lap, closing in upon herself.

Constance's face showed a brief flash of hurt before becoming carefully blank. "There is still so much unrest," she said, fixing her gaze to the blankets on the bed. "There are still redcoats rampaging through the Highlands, not to mention raiders, the Watch, and even fleeing Jacobites. At least let us keep the Albans until things are a little more settled. Until we're safer. Please. *Please.*"

Mairead could feel Constance's fear thrumming along the connection that still flowed between them. If she was honest with herself, there *was* cause to be frightened. There was still every possibility that more redcoats would come looking for the ones now buried in the oat field, and if they did come, they were far less likely to be taken so completely by surprise.

"Please."

Nicnevin looked rather unmoved by Constance's plea. Instead, the fae looked to Mairead. "I am willing to accept the explanation for the taint, though I do not feel that someone who is so careless with her words should be left free to instruct the Albans alone." She sighed. "I will say that the air is still filled with violence and danger. Blood soaks this land, and yet the thirst of the conquerors is not slaked. This village is not yet safe. And so I am willing to allow you to make the final judgment."

"Thank you—" Constance started, but Nicnevin cut her off.

"Not you. Mairead."

The weight of responsibility came crashing down upon Mairead, pressing her into the bed. How could she say no, in light of what Nicnevin had just said? *But how can I live with the guilt if the Albans hurt anyone else? And what of the guilt if I say no and then the redcoats come and hurt people I care about because I left us unprotected?*

"I can't think right now. I'm so tired."

Nicnevin nodded. "You need rest. Sleep. I will return tomorrow, we can speak on this further then." She turned on her heel and was gone in a shower of sparks.

Constance lingered between the bed and the door, the silence stealing all of the air from the room. Mairead longed for the easy comfort she usually felt around Constance, a quiet acceptance of who they both were. At least, she had thought that Constance had accepted her. Now she wasn't so sure.

"I am sorry," Constance said at last. "I never meant for you to get hurt."

"And yet…" Mairead stared at the blanket, rumpled beside her, and idly picked at a loose thread.

"I do love you."

Mairead's throat thickened, and she fought not to cry. "I don't know if I can believe that anymore."

Chapter Twenty-Four

Mairead

11th May 1746

Mairead had considered asking Mistress Croaker or Mistress Gordon if she could stay with one of them for a while, but she had not yet recovered enough to be able to muster the energy to gather her belongings and walk the distance to the village. Instead, she moved back through to the pallet bed made up in the main room of the cottage. Constance had looked deeply hurt by this, which gave Mairead a pang of regret, but she needed some space to figure out how she felt about all that had happened.

Constance managed to keep the children out and busy for most of the time, letting Mairead doze throughout the day, waking only to eat and drink the small amounts of food and water that she could manage. She felt as though her world were collapsing upon itself, and she didn't want to think about what that meant.

So of course that was all she could think about.

When Constance brought the children back to the house for dinner, Mairead turned her face to the wall and pretended to be asleep. Elspeth and Janey both came over and planted gentle kisses on her head, almost bringing her to tears. She hated to ignore them, but she couldn't bring herself to pretend everything was all right when that was so very far from the truth, so she stayed still, waiting quietly for them to go to bed.

"Is this how it's going to be from now on?" Constance asked, coming back through after getting the children settled. She took a seat at the table. "Won't you at least talk to me?"

Mairead stared at the wall, the inside of her nose prickling with unshed tears. "What do you want me to say?" she asked hoarsely.

"I don't know," Constance said quietly. It sounded to Mairead as if she, too, was close to tears. "Scream at me if you have to, throw things even, but please don't shut me out. You're the only person I've ever really felt that I could open up to, be myself with. I can't bear to lose that."

"I felt the same way," Mairead said, still not turning around. "I thought you wanted me just as I am. But it seems I was wrong. That I wasn't quite good enough for you."

"Oh Mairead." Constance threw herself to her knees beside the pallet bed and clutched at Mairead's arm. "I swear it wasn't like that at all."

Mairead looked over her shoulder, not quite willing to turn around yet. "What was it like?"

"I didn't even mean to do it," Constance said, her breath hitching between words as she fought to speak through her sorrow. "You remember you told me how I called out to you before you were here, that I drew you to me? And I didn't even know I was doing it? It was like that. I just wanted you to be happy and to feel comfortable here, with what we were doing, and I wanted it so badly that it kind of spilled into my magic." She stopped talking as sobs overtook her.

Mairead closed her eyes and thought back to when she was a child, to the incident with Millicent Ferguson and how Mairead's own longing had affected the poor girl, without any intention on Mairead's part. She had to remember that while Constance was an adult, and her magic so much more powerful than Mairead's own, she had spent her whole life suppressing it rather than learning to control it.

"I didn't even know what had happened until Nicnevin told me," Constance said when she found the ability to speak again. "I'm so sorry."

"Why didn't you say all of this earlier?" Mairead asked.

Constance scrubbed her tears away and took a shaky breath. "I was ashamed and so frightened for you. And Nicnevin was so angry, I knew she wouldn't listen to me."

Mairead rolled onto her back and looked up into Constance's eyes. "You lied to me about Mr. Munroe."

"I know. I did. I'm sorry for that too."

"How do I know that you're telling me the truth now?"

Constance looked down, bunching the blanket in her hands. "I don't suppose you do. I know I'll have to earn your trust again, but Mairead, please let me. I only lied to protect you. I wanted to keep you from getting caught up in my mess."

She was gazing down at Mairead with such mingled sadness and hope that it almost broke Mairead's heart all over again. *Is this her influencing me with her magic again?* Mairead sighed, the thought driving a blade into her. Even if it was true that Constance had not meant to influence her – maybe even more so if it was – how could they work to rebuild the broken trust, if Mairead could never be sure that her feelings were her own?

"I want to believe you. I do."

"But?"

"But I don't know how to be sure that I don't feel that way because you're influencing me with your magic." Mairead looked away.

For a moment, the only sound was the fire crackling in the hearth and the evening songbirds filling the sky outside. Far away, cattle lowed to each other. On other evenings, these sounds had been the background to some of the deepest peace Mairead had ever known.

Constance sniffed. "What if...maybe there's some kind of way to block my magic from affecting you. So that even if it does spill out accidentally, you'll be shielded from it. We could try at least?" She looked hopefully at Mairead. "Maybe Nicnevin knows a spell that would do the trick? Or even...you can bind me, if that's what you need. If that would make you feel safe with me again. I'll let you bind me."

That was the thing that finally broke the last of Mairead's defenses. If Constance would offer to be bound, would truly hand over so much of her power to Mairead, then surely she must mean everything else she said.

Mairead reached out to her and grasped her hand. "All right. Let's try a shield of some sort."

She did not go to Constance's bed that night, but when Nicnevin arrived the next day, she agreed to keep the Albans around until life in the

Highlands was closer to normal, as long as the rest of the villagers agreed. Nicnevin taught her a charm she could use to deflect any magic aimed at her and showed her how to anchor it to her person, so that it would be a constant source of protection to her. When she was shielded, she could not feel Constance the same way that she had before, was not sure of how her lover was feeling at any given moment, and it felt as though a piece of her was missing.

Still, it would protect her from any unwitting influence, or any further dilution of her magic.

Over the following days, she found herself falling back into the patterns that she and Constance had built between them, working around the house and the land, visiting the village, spending time with the children. It was almost as it had been before, except for the fact that she could barely bring herself to look at Hamish and Hector as they worked in the fields or plodded past carrying equipment. She knew it wasn't really their fault – they did only what they had been made to do. The responsibility for the death of Mr. Munroe, and indeed the redcoats, lay firmly on her and Constance.

It was a heavy burden to carry.

Mairead would be in the middle of some chore, when an image of Captain Sampson or one of his men would enter her mind, and the whole horrific incident would play through in her mind until she felt like screaming. Or she would think of Mr. Munroe and how lovingly he had spoken of his family. It pained her that they would never know what had become of him; he just wouldn't return home when they expected him. They would spend the rest of their lives waiting for him to walk in the door, but he never would.

Constance had told her he was buried out behind the bothy, his horse set free to wander the hills, and his wagon broken down for firewood. All while Mairead had been fighting off the consequences of his death.

Mairead did not doubt that Constance had worried about her, had done everything she could to care for Mairead during those days of magical illness. But she couldn't help but be left a little uneasy by the cold collectedness that allowed Constance to cover up the pedlar's death at the same time. As far as Mairead knew, none of the other villagers had any idea that he hadn't gone on his way, happy and safe.

When they were together, Constance would hover nervously around Mairead, obsequious to the point of making Mairead uncomfortable. The wound of the lies still sat between them, denying them the easy familiarity to which they had become accustomed. Mairead wasn't sure how to step past it – or whether she truly wanted to. For the first time since she arrived in Kilmartin, she began to wonder if the time to move on was approaching.

May rolled into June, and with the approach of the solstice came a letter from Fergus with more news from Inverness. Villages all across the Highlands were being burned to the ground, redcoats using any excuse to punish the Highlanders for the fear and humiliation that had been meted out to them by the Jacobites up until Culloden. The prince was said to still be hiding out somewhere, planning to make another attempt, or so the king's army claimed as justification for their violence. Fergus and Bridie were planning to return to Kilmartin after the solstice, though Roisin might not join them. She had taken a liking to city life.

No news had been heard of the men of Kilmartin. Fergus feared they must be given up for lost.

The night after the letter came, Constance seemed small, frightened, and her apparent grief weighed upon Mairead. For all she might not have freely chosen to marry Iain, Mairead knew that Constance cared for him – if for no other reason than that he was the father of her children, whom she adored beyond reason. No doubt she was also grieving for the other men of Kilmartin, her friends and neighbors ever since she wed and came here to live. It could not be easy to learn that they were likely all dead.

"How are you holding up?" Mairead asked softly, when she noticed Constance staring off into space. "Is there anything I can do for you?"

Constance turned a haunted gaze upon her. "Hold me?"

Mairead crossed to her side in three quick strides and wrapped her arms around the other woman, pulling her close. Constance sagged against her, as if she had been using the very last of her strength to remain standing. Her face felt hot against the side of Mairead's neck, and she was trembling.

"Oh, my love," Mairead murmured, the last wall between them collapsing under the force of Constance's need. "I'm here. I'm here."

She led Constance over to the pallet bed and they sat on it, side by side. She kept murmuring soothing words into Constance's hair, holding her and rocking with her, Constance's grip around her tight and panicky.

"Don't leave me," she said, her voice cracking. "Please don't leave me."

"I'm not going anywhere," Mairead answered. "I'm right here."

"I don't know what I'm supposed to do now. I don't know how to tell the children that..." She clung tighter.

Mairead had never seen her so vulnerable. Constance always wore this impenetrable armor, always seemed calm and in control, but here, now, she was finally letting herself truly be seen.

"I don't even know if we'll be able to stay here," Constance continued. "The cottage, the land, it all belongs to the laird, and we only had tenancy because Iain is – was – a distant cousin. They might put us out without Iain here. Or there might be a new laird. How will we all... Iain was... They were... *All of them*? How can they all be gone?"

Mairead rocked with her, cupping her face in one hand, caressing her cheekbone with her thumb. "We'll figure it out. I'll be here. I'll help you. You won't be alone."

Constance kissed the side of her jaw, tentatively at first, but with a growing hunger when Mairead allowed it. She trailed kisses along the line of Mairead's jaw, to her ear, then down her neck, flicking her collarbone with her tongue.

Mairead grasped her head, her fingers tangling in Constance's thick, silky hair, as she pulled her into a kiss. The loneliness and longing and fear that had filled her ever since the redcoats came, all of it gave way under the tide of need that filled her in that moment. Lost in their physical connection, Mairead dropped the magical shield between them. All of Constance's emotions – her fear and sadness and shame and longing and need – poured into Mairead and she was swept away in it.

Mairead groaned as Constance's tongue teased at her lips. She needed to feel Constance's skin against her own, like she needed air to breathe. The clothing between them, separating them, was suddenly intolerable.

She started to pull at Constance's clothing, unlacing her kirtle, and Constance quickly reciprocated, taking the lead as she so often did these days. She pushed Mairead down onto her back and sat astride her hips, leaning in to kiss her again as she pulled the side of Mairead's kirtle apart and slid her shift down over her shoulder, exposing her breasts.

Mairead's breath hitched, and she bit down on her lip as Constance bent and took one achingly erect nipple into her mouth, while teasing the other with her fingers.

So lost in each other were they, that neither of them heard the door to the cottage open, or noticed when someone entered and stood, staring at them. Not until he spoke.

"Constance? What in God's name is going on here?"

Constance jerked away from Mairead as if she had been slapped. "Iain?"

Chapter Twenty-Five

Constance

3rd June 1746

"Iain?" Constance said again, not quite able to accept what she was seeing. Suddenly she became aware of the fact that she was sitting astride Mairead's hips, both of them in a partial state of undress. She jerked to her feet, pulling her shift up, trying to cover herself.

From the corner of her eye, she saw Mairead sit up and pull her own clothing into place, cowering back a little against the wall.

"Would you care to explain to me why a man should come home from war, only to find his wife in a state of wantonness with another woman?"

Constance stared at him, words only slowly fighting their way through the shock. "I…I thought you were dead."

And from the look of him, it might have been a close thing. He stood there in a shirt and trousers that had surely seen better days, one arm held against his body in a sling. From the blood that stained the shoulder of his shirt, Constance assumed that was where his injury lay. He was drawn and pale, a good deal thinner than he had been when he left Kilmartin, and there was a thick streak of white in his beard, which had not been there before.

"So, you jumped straight into bed with another? A woman, no less?" His voice was rising, anger and hurt thrumming beneath his words.

Mairead curled in upon herself, but Constance felt her own temper rising to meet his. "Well, maybe if you'd bothered to send word, a single letter to let me know you lived, then I wouldn't have thought you were dead!"

Iain's body seemed to puff up, his anger growing to fill the room. "Oh aye, while we were making our way across the country, dodging redcoats and fighting for our lives, we had plenty of time to write home and make sure that our wives don't start rutting like animals with the first whore who comes along!"

"Don't you dare speak about her like that," Constance said, a furious fire lashing through her veins.

Simon began to cry in the bedroom, his infant wails drifting through to cut the tension between them.

"I'll check on him," Mairead said quietly. She got to her feet and began to skirt the edges of the room.

"No, ye'll no'. Constance can do it. The boy needs his mother, not her whore." Iain spoke without taking his eyes from Constance.

Her magic flared in response to the anger and fear roaring through her. Iain being back could ruin everything, take away all of the happiness she had found during his absence. She felt cornered, a hunted animal with cliffs at her back and only death in front of her. Before she knew she was going to do it, a whip of magic flicked out from her, lashing into Iain and knocking him from his feet.

"Go to Simon," she said, glancing at Mairead. "Make sure the children don't come out here until Iain and I have had this out. Please. They shouldn't see this."

Mairead nodded. "I'm sorry," she said softly.

Iain groaned from where he lay on the floor.

Constance took two steps to Mairead, and caught the back of her head, pulling her into a kiss. "I'm the one who's sorry," she said when she broke away. Iain was pushing himself up to sitting, his face tight with pain. Mairead hurried into the bedroom and Constance hoped she would be able to settle Simon before the girls woke. Their father's homecoming shouldn't be colored by this.

"Come outside with me," she said, reaching out to help him up. "Please, before we wake the children."

He cringed back from her extended hand. "What did you do to me?"

Constance sighed, much of her anger expended with the lash of magic. "I didn't do anything to you. You fell over."

"I did not." Iain pushed himself along the floor, backing away from her. "You, you pushed me, or… I don't know what you did, but I know it was you."

Constance pinched the bridge of her nose. Suddenly she was exhausted. How had she managed to make such a mess of everything?

"Do you have need of me?" Hector said in her head. *"You are alarmed."*

"Not yet. But stay close. I may yet require your protection."

"Come outside with me," she said aloud. "I'll tell you everything."

She kept a careful distance between them as Iain got to his feet, though she didn't miss the way that he swayed for a moment when he stood, or the way his breath hissed between his teeth in pain, his free hand rising to rub at his injured shoulder. His anger might make him more inclined to lash out, but his injuries definitely limited the amount of threat he posed to her.

"Lead the way," Iain growled after a glance at the closed bedroom door.

Constance moved past him and out into the yard, the hairs on the back of her neck standing up at the thought of having him behind her. He posed less threat than he otherwise might have, but not none.

Outside, the sun was behind the hills to the west, but twilight lingered long, and there was still more than enough ambient light to see by. She walked a short distance from the house then turned to face him.

"I'm sorry you found out this way," she began. "A lot has happened while you've been gone. Much is changed."

"That would seem to be an understatement," Iain said. Much of the anger had left his words, leaving behind a deep hurt.

"We thought you were all dead." Constance looked past him at the house. Simon had stopped crying, and she could see the faint shadow of Mairead moving past the window in the bedroom.

"Most of us are," Iain said with a weary sigh. "Only four of us made it back."

"You mean there are three more men sneaking into the village in the middle of the night?" she asked, panic flaring bright, filling her mouth with the taste of metal.

"Aye," Iain said, a hint of the anger returning. "Will they all find their wives in the state I found you?"

"All Albans, hear me!" Constance shouted inside her head. *"There are men of Kilmartin returning home this night. Do not harm them! They are not a danger to us!"*

"One man detained." The voice of one of the village Albans sounded in her head. He sent a mental image of a man lying face down on grass, the Alban using a knee to pin him to the ground.

"Constance, would you pay attention to me?" Iain said, sounding frustrated. "I'm speaking to you."

Constance held her hand up, asking him to wait. *"Turn him over."*

The Alban did so, allowing Constance to see through his eyes as he did. The man on the ground was Catriona's husband, Rab. *"Let him go. He's one of us."*

The Alban stood, releasing the man.

"Please go to the bothy. All of you, except Hector." And then, to Hector alone, *"Come to me, but stay on the far side of the barn from the house, until I call for you."*

"Constance!" Iain snapped, moving as if to grab her.

She stepped back sharply. "I'm here, I'm listening." She clasped her hands in front of her, not sure if she wanted to ask or not. "Who else made it back? You, Rab and…?"

"John and Seòras. The others…" Iain looked away, swallowing hard. Then he frowned. "Wait. How did you know about Rab? I didn't tell you."

Constance's heart sank. There was no way she would be able to keep her secrets – at least one of the Albans had been seen, after all. Everything she had worked for was coming crashing down around her and she had no idea how to save it. Her freedom, her life with Mairead, all of it was about to be snatched away and she would be shoved back into the too-small box that she had lived in before.

"I'm a witch," she said, her voice breaking on the word.

Iain stared at her, anger, hurt and fear all wrestling across his face. "You're going to have to say that again," he said. "I don't think I heard you right."

"You heard right," Constance answered, stepping toward him, her hands held up to show that she meant no harm. "A lot has happened these months you've been gone."

Iain started to pace back and forth, cradling his injured arm against his body. "I don't know what to say to you. I feel like I don't even know you. Is there anything of the woman I married left in you?"

Constance pushed her hands through her hair, sighing in exasperation. If only he knew what she had lived for all the years they had been married, how the woman he knew was only ever a tiny part of her, a fabrication needed to keep her safe.

"All of this was in me all along," she said quietly. "I've been a witch since I was a child."

Iain shook his head. "So, you've been lying to me since the day we met?"

"I never meant to." Constance took another step closer to him, filled with an unexpected melancholy. She might never have loved Iain, but neither had she ever hoped to hurt him. "I…do you remember I told you how I was close to my grandmother when I was a child, and how heartbroken I was when she died?"

Iain winced in pain and rubbed at his shoulder again. "I remember. But what does this have to do with anything?"

Constance took a deep breath and let it out slowly. She might as well tell him the truth now. All of it. "She was a witch. She was hanged for it. My father had the chance to take on a croft not long after and we all moved away. My mother…she was so frightened that the same thing would happen to me. She taught me to hide my power, to make myself smaller. She made me swear to tell no one what I was, to keep me safe. And that's how I've lived for so very long. Hiding in plain sight, terrified of being discovered."

"But now?" Iain asked, beginning to soften a little. "What magic did you use to find out Rab has returned?"

Constance felt like her heart would beat out of her chest, so anxious was she. She could try to play it all down, tell him she had picked it up from his mind or some such, hope that Catriona's husband did not get a good look at the Alban who had restrained him before it took off, hope that it had gotten away without anything to give away what it was. Or she could tell him the truth – all of it – and hope that they could find some way through all of this to a better future for them all.

"Hector? Would you come out here please?" She was trembling as she called him, though her voice did not betray her.

"Who is Hector?" Iain asked, his voice going hard once more. He reached for her and grabbed her arm, pulling her to him. "Did you betray me with a man as well as a woman?"

Constance yanked her arm back and scrambled away from him. "Hector!"

She felt him approach from behind her, crossing the yard in his lumbering way. Iain reached for the knife at his belt.

"You won't need that," Constance said hastily. "Besides, it wouldn't do you any good."

In the twilight, his face in shadows, the fuzziness around Hector's features would not be clear to Iain – in fact these were probably ideal conditions for passing the Albans off as humans. One last thought urged her to pretend that the Albans were other fleeing Jacobites simply passing through on their way home. Instead, she slowly reached up and unpinned Hector's kilt pin.

The glamour dropped, leaving him standing there in his true form – a man shaped from the earth of Kilmartin, standing there as if he had every right to be there.

"May the Lord have mercy on our souls," Iain said, horror tinging every word. "What is it?"

"This is Hector," Constance said, fiddling with the kilt pin to avoid looking at Iain. "We had some trouble with the Black Watch. And then there were raiders stealing sheep – they burned villages up by Inverness. We were vulnerable and frightened. So, we made Hector and a few others. We call them Albans. They helped with the harvest, and they protected us when the redcoats came."

"You've usurped the power of God, Constance. How could you?"

"What are you talking about?" she spluttered.

"Only God can create life. Have you no shame?"

Constance laughed, incredulous. She couldn't help herself. "And was it God gave birth to your children? I believe you'll find that I was the one to create those lives."

Iain shook his head, peering past Constance to where Hector stood, placid, awaiting further instructions.

"That's different," Iain scoffed. "That was a gift given by God. Not this…this abomination!"

"And where do you think my magic comes from?" Constance demanded, forcing herself to keep her voice low, even though she wanted to scream at him in frustration. "I was born this way, no choice was given to me. Surely that must come from God?"

"And if God had aught to do with it, then why would He have allowed His church, His ministers, to put so many witches to death these years gone by? If He hadnae approved, surely He would have put a stop to it?"

Constance sighed and pinched the bridge of her nose. It was clear there would be no reasoning with the man, despite having called him husband for the last eight years. She had known, really, that there wouldn't be. He was both stubborn and obedient to those he considered his betters – not truly capable of thinking for himself in matters like this.

"What happens now?" she asked wearily, her eyes once more drawn to the bedroom window, behind which waited everything she held dear.

Iain shook his head. "I don't rightly know." He gave a disbelieving laugh. "This was hardly the homecoming I had anticipated."

"I know. I am sorry for that." She reached out, gently touching his arm. "I have cared for you these past years," she said gently. "But it is clear that things can't continue as they were before. We must find a way to move forward that does no harm to our children."

"Aye. You're right." Iain stared off into the gathering dark and Constance didn't press him.

Behind her, Hector waited, a looming shape that filled her with a sense of calm. Having Hector by her side gave her options, gave her protection. She let her gaze wander up to the sky, where the stars were just beginning to show. She felt clean. Purged of all of her secrets. For good or for ill, in this moment, she was as truly and completely herself as she had ever been.

"I'll not turn you in," Iain said at last. "While it certainly seems that I don't know you as well as I thought I did, I cannae believe you've any harm in you. I believe that you did what you did to protect yourself. But it must stop, Constance. You must be rid of these things, these Albans."

"All right," she said, mind racing. "It'll take a bit of time to sort out, but we can do that. They were only meant to keep us safe until our men returned anyway, so if you're back then we no longer have need of them."

"You can send your strumpet in there on her way as well. I cannae say it'll be easy, but I'll do what I can to forgive you, put this behind us. You put your woman and your magic away, and I'll accept you once more as my wife. Everything can go back to the way it was."

Constance's heart fell. There was no way she could go back to the way things had been before. She would rather die than climb back into the box she had lived in before the rising. "Iain, I don't think you understand."

"Understand what?"

"I'm not asking for your forgiveness. I'm sorry that I hurt you, that you've been caught up in all of this, but there will be no going back to the way things were."

"I think you'll find you'll do as you're told," he growled. "Did you not vow before man and God to bind your life to mine until death? To submit to your husband as a good Christian woman?"

"I have submitted more than enough for one lifetime. There is no submission left in me." Constance stepped back, moving closer to Hector. "I am willing to let go of the Albans, but I won't be sending Mairead away and returning to your bed like a good little wife. I'm sorry, but I won't."

Iain looked at her with fury blazing in his eyes, but he made no move toward her. Constance felt the mood between them shift though, her magic coiling in her limbs, waiting to be used should she need it.

"Fine," Iain said through gritted teeth. "Then you and she can pack your things and leave Kilmartin. I'm a gentle man and I'll tolerate many things, but I willnae have you living with her in my home, humiliating me before all and sundry."

"This is my home too!" Constance protested. "These are my friends, my people as much as yours. If it hadn't been for me, looking after this village, keeping everyone safe while you were off playing at soldiers, there might not even be a village left for you to come back to!"

"These are my terms, woman. Either you send her away and return to your duties as my wife, or you leave with her."

"Very well. I'll pack everything up tomorrow and we'll go. I'll need Angus and the cart, to carry the children and their clothes and what have you, but I'll send you money for them both once we're settled somewhere and I can find work."

"You misunderstand," Iain said, his voice flat. "You won't be taking my children with you."

Constance jerked back as if slapped. "Iain, no. Of course I'm taking the children."

"You are not. They will be staying here, with me. You want them, you get me too; you don't get to be a mother, unless you also choose to be a wife."

"You can't keep my children from me!"

"I can and I will."

"How will you even raise them without me? You can't possibly do everything by yourself."

"There are plenty of widows in the village now. Good Christian women who'll need work now that their men are gone."

Horror rose in Constance's heart, filling her with ice. How could he do this? How could he hurt her so? Her children were everything to her. Her thoughts whirled. Could she go back, for the sake of her children? Could she give up Mairead, and all of her magic, and everything that felt real and true about herself, so that she could be with her children? Could she live without them?

"Iain, I can't leave them. You can't ask that of me."

"Enough!" he roared, stepping toward her, rage radiating from him in waves. "I am the wronged party here. You do not get to set all the terms, woman!"

Constance's own anger rose once more, fury burning through the icy fear. Her magic crackled over her skin, lighting her in an eldritch storm. "No." Her voice snapped with power, taking on tones that felt alien to her.

"You will do as you are told!" Iain shouted, his face red, spittle flying from his lips.

"Never. Again." Constance lashed out with her magic, sending Iain flying into the side of the house. A sickening crunch accompanied the impact.

Iain lay, unmoving, crumpled against the stone wall. Constance waited, her magic primed, sure that he would get back up, and that he would really come after her this time. The door opened, and Mairead rushed out into the yard.

"What's happened? I heard shouting and a thud..." She trailed off as she turned toward the house and saw Iain. She hurried to his side and bent beside him.

Constance wanted to call out to her to be careful, to stay back, but the words stuck in her throat, her body tense and mind awhirl.

"Constance," Mairead said, looking at her with slowly dawning horror. "What have you done?"

Chapter Twenty-Six

Mairead

Mairead crouched beside Iain, his blood staining her hand. The back of his head had caved in from the force with which he hit the wall. His eyes were open and glazed, staring sightlessly at the night sky. Above them, a crescent moon was moving out from behind the barn.

Constance stood beside Hector, her magic slowly draining away into the ground. The Alban waited, still and impassive.

"What…what happened?" Mairead croaked. Horror filled her mouth and throat, making it hard to speak. She had cast a bubble of quiet over the bedroom so that the children would not wake to hear their parents arguing – it had worked, blocking out everything until the last moments, when they both began to shout. Thankfully it had been muted enough for the children to sleep through.

"He… I…" Constance shook herself as if trying to come out of a daze. "I didn't mean to hurt him."

"He's more than hurt. Constance, he's dead."

"He threatened to take the children from me," Constance said, her voice flat and oddly emotionless. "He gave me a choice – give you up, give magic up, and go back to the way things were, or leave with you and never see my children again."

Mairead got up and went to Constance's side. "Did he grab you or something? Did Hector try to protect you? Is that how this happened?"

"No, it, it was me," Constance stammered. She was shivering, even though the night was warm.

Mairead put an arm around her and pulled her close. "You said you didn't mean to hurt him. Was it an accident? Did he do something to you first?" Mairead scrabbled for some explanation for what had happened that wouldn't mean that Constance had just murdered her husband. If it was self-defense, if he had tried to hurt her…

Constance shook her head and finally turned her haunted gaze to Mairead, meeting her eyes for the first time since she'd stepped outside.

"I was angry. I lashed out without really thinking."

"Constance please, tell me he grabbed you and you pushed him away. Make this make sense."

Constance shook her head. "No, he grabbed my arm before that, but when it happened, he was just shouting at me, and I was shouting back and then…"

"Were you scared of him?" Mairead asked quietly. *Please let her have been scared. If she thought she was in danger, even if she wasn't truly, this can still be explained.*

"No." Constance straightened, pulling away from Mairead, her usual aura of calm control reasserting itself. "I wasn't frightened. I was furious."

Mairead covered her face. It was murder then. A crime of passion, perhaps, but a crime nonetheless.

"We have to get rid of the body," Constance said slowly, as if thinking aloud. "Before the children wake. We can claim that he never made it home. No one else saw him here. The other men who returned with him won't know for sure that he made it to the house. And Catriona's husband saw an Alban, so we might get away with convincing them that there were strangers in the area."

"What? No!" Mairead grabbed Constance's hand. "We can't cover this up. You've killed someone!"

"Well, there wouldn't be anything *to* cover up if I hadn't," Constance snapped. She blew out a sharp breath through her nose. "Do you want me to be hanged?"

Mairead stepped back from her. What had happened here? This wasn't the Constance she knew. "Of course not! We can explain that it was an accident, that you were arguing and things got out of hand."

Constance looked at her as if she were a fool. "Do you really think anyone will believe that his injuries could possibly have been accidental?"

Mairead looked back at Iain's body, thought of the way his skull had collapsed at the back. Constance was right. The force required to cause those injuries could only be understood as accidental if you knew about the magic she could wield – but apparently could not control.

"All right," she said with a sigh. "I'll help you cover this up. I'll lie for you."

"Thank you. First we have to—"

"No," Mairead broke in. "First we have to agree conditions."

"What do you mean, conditions?" Constance sounded annoyed and impatient.

Mairead was very conscious of time passing, all while a dead body lay at their feet. While it was unlikely that visitors would come along at this time of night, one of the children could wake and come looking for them at any moment.

"He can't just disappear," Mairead said, talking fast, and keeping an eye on the bedroom window for any sign of movement from within. "It's not fair on the children to never know what happened to their father, always wondering if he'll show up some day." She couldn't help but think of poor Mr. Munroe's family. She couldn't bring them any knowledge of their father, but at least she could do this for Iain's children.

"What do you suggest?" Constance asked.

"Have Hector take him out into a field somewhere and leave him there. Let it look as if he was attacked before he got home. You said other men returned with him, yes?"

Mairead's mind was racing now, trying to figure out the best way to protect Constance from what she had done.

"Three more. Two from the village and one from an outlying croft."

Mairead nodded. "Tomorrow, we pay a visit to the village. When we see the men who've returned you can ask them about Iain, do they know if he survived and so on. When they discover that he never made it home, they'll go searching for him and hopefully find his body." She looked sharply at Constance. "If you hope to convince people of your innocence, you must show the expected degree of fear for his safety and mourning when his death is discovered."

"You don't have to tell me to act," Constance said witheringly. "I've been doing it my whole life."

"Well, you're not doing it very well right now," Mairead answered. "You don't seem to feel any remorse at all for what has happened here."

Constance looked away, her mouth drawn into a tight line. "I wasn't aware that I was required to act for you too."

Mairead's heart ached. She stepped closer to Constance and caught hold of her hand. "I don't want you to act for me. I'm just…this is a lot to take in."

Constance let out a shaky breath and nodded. "I'll play the right part. Is that your condition?"

"Not the only one, but perhaps Hector can move the body now, while we discuss the others. And we need to clean away the blood and any other trace that Iain was here."

Constance instructed Hector on where to take the body, while Mairead fetched a bucket of water; a dark stain marked the stone of the wall where Iain's head had collided with it. She stepped inside to fetch some rags and a lamp so that she could see properly to clean, and stopped for a moment standing by the table. Her body began to tremble, and her gorge rose – it was only an act of will that kept her from vomiting.

It was too much. All of this was too much. She loved Constance and wanted more than anything for the other woman to be free and at peace. But ever since the day the redcoats came to Kilmartin, things had felt out of control. There had been too much death, too much fear. And too much lying. Mairead wondered if Constance would have told her the truth of what happened to Iain if she hadn't come upon the immediate aftermath. Or would she have lied as she had about poor Mr. Munroe?

This had to stop. Mairead had reached her limit.

She lit an oil lamp and took it outside, along with a handful of rags to scrub the blood from the wall. Iain's body was gone, and Constance was standing alone in the middle of the yard, her arms wrapped around her torso as if she were trying to hold herself together. Mairead set the lamp down on the step and dropped the rags into the bucket of water, then went to Constance and pulled her into an embrace.

"It'll be all right," she murmured against Constance's hair. "We'll get through this."

"I'm so scared," Constance said, beginning to cry quietly. "I'm always so scared."

Mairead tightened her grip, letting Constance lean on her. What Constance had said was true – she lived in constant fear, never feeling that she had any choice or control over her own life. Mairead understood that Constance's mother had only been trying to keep her daughter safe by teaching her that everything was a risk, and no one could be trusted, but it had left her terrified all the time. And in possession of a great source of power that she could not control.

After a few moments, Constance pulled back and wiped at her face. "I never loved him," she said, her voice still thick with tears, "but I never wished for this."

"I know."

"What were your other conditions?"

Mairead took a deep breath. "We need to let the Albans go."

"They had nothing to do with this!" Constance exclaimed. "Why punish them for my mistake?"

"It's not punishing them. The rising is over, the men have returned."

"Three of them!" Constance threw her hands up and Mairead flinched back, then tried to cover her instinctive reaction by turning toward the house and moving to clean the blood away. "Three men, possibly injured, aren't exactly enough to keep us safe."

Mairead took a rag from the water and wrung it out before beginning to scrub the wall. She did not look at Constance as she spoke. "I don't believe that you will ever feel safe enough to let them go. People are moving around the Highlands again, it's too risky to keep them. We can't have another situation like what happened with Mr. Munroe. And how do you think the men who've returned will feel about them?"

"Well, there are more Albans than there are of them, so does it really matter? They'll just have to get used to it."

"So, whoever is strongest – or controls the strongest – gets to make the decisions?"

Constance didn't answer for a moment and Mairead paused in her scrubbing, still not looking at her.

"Isn't that how the world works?" Constance said at last, her voice closer than it had been when last she spoke.

"Should it be?" Mairead asked quietly.

Constance groaned. "Fine. We'll unmake them. I've told Hector to hide with the others after his current task. We can summon Nicnevin and do whatever needs to be done in the morning. Is that acceptable?"

"Yes." Mairead lifted the lamp to inspect the wall. In the dark, it was hard to tell if the stone was just wet or still stained. "There is one more thing."

"What more could there be?" Constance scoffed. "Unless you want me to give up magic too?"

Mairead didn't answer but got to her feet and slowly turned around.

"Tell me you're joking."

Mairead looked at her most beloved, the woman whom she had given everything to. "Just for a while," she said sadly. "Just until you've learned more control."

"No," Constance said, then louder, "No!"

"You are the most powerful witch I have ever met," Mairead said, wanting to move closer, to offer comfort, even as she must cause pain. "But your fear controls you."

"So, what, you're going to make me powerless and more afraid? You're going to punish me for an accident?"

"I'm not trying to punish you. I'm trying to help you."

Constance gave a disbelieving laugh. "Help me! How exactly is taking away my magic helping me?"

Mairead's heart was pounding, and she was startled and dismayed to realize that she was a little afraid of Constance. "You lost your temper and killed a man. What happens if you lose control like that again? What if one of the children is in the way of it next time?"

"I would never!"

"And until tonight, I'm sure you thought you would never hurt Iain. Please, Constance, please think about what I'm saying. I don't want you to give it up forever, just until you learn how to control it better."

"And how am I supposed to do that?" Constance asked flatly. "How do I learn to control what I can't use?"

Mairead swallowed. This was going to be the hardest part to convince her of. "Let me bind you. We can release the binding a little at a time, so that you have a chance to learn control without being so dangerous if you slip."

"And what if I can't learn control? Will you just keep my magic locked away forever?"

"That won't happen. I'll help you learn, you won't be alone in dealing with this."

"Who decides when I'm controlled enough? You?"

Mairead faltered. She hadn't really thought that far ahead yet.

"You want me to trade living under Iain's rules for living under yours? You want me to give up everything I've gained these last months?"

Mairead moved closer. "It's not like that and you know it's not. Constance, I love you and I will always support you. But I won't cover up another death for you if you lose control again. You're asking too much. I can't stand aside and watch while you endanger people."

"I can't believe you're asking this of me. That you, of all people, would decide to control me."

"I'm not trying to control you!" Mairead fought to keep her voice low although her exasperation was rising. "I'm trying to help you control yourself!"

Constance stayed silent for a moment, her jaw working as though she was fighting the words that wanted to come. "I think it's time you moved on," she said at last. "You can pack your things tomorrow and be on your way."

Mairead felt something snap in her, a brittle crack where her heart had been. She wasn't a fool – she had gotten herself romantically entangled with a married woman, she had known it couldn't last forever and would likely end with her heartbreak. But to be tossed aside like this, over a disagreement, after everything they had been through together, everything she had done for Constance…

She pushed away her anger and hurt, to be dealt with later, when she was alone. "If that's what you want, then I'll go," she said calmly. "But I won't leave until the Albans have been unmade and your magic has been bound. That is the price for my complicity in covering up the manner in which Iain died."

Mairead felt magic crackling in the air and knew that Constance was drawing power to herself.

"You think you can dictate terms to me?" Constance demanded, her voice filled with a low fury.

Mairead pulled on her own power, throwing a shield up around herself. "If you would take some time to think about this calmly and clearly, you would see that I'm trying to protect you. You and the children."

"By threatening me?"

"Constance, you're leaving me with no choice!"

Constance lifted her hand toward Mairead and threw a wave of magic at her. It hit her shield so hard that it drove her to her knees, surrounded by magic powered by Constance's rage, which sparked and crackled across her shield. Even now, pushing all of her power into protecting herself, she could not quite believe that Constance had actually attacked her. Was this what had happened to Iain?

"I trusted you!" Constance screamed, her power lifting her off the ground until she floated a foot in the air. Her hair streamed out behind her and her clothes snapped around her as if buffeted by wind, though the night was still.

"Constance, stop!" Mairead pleaded. She had no desire to fight back, and no real idea how to. Not to mention the fact that Constance was considerably more powerful than she was. If it came down to power and aggression, Mairead would be quickly defeated.

Constance threw more power at her, and Mairead's shield shrank, growing closer to her body. "You're just like him!"

Mairead cowered before her lover, with no idea of what to do. This was proof that binding Constance would be the right thing to do; she had far more power than even Mairead had suspected and had no qualms about using it to get what she wanted. But even now, crouching and panting with the effort of maintaining her shield, Mairead understood a little of Constance's actions. Having spent her whole life terrified of discovery, forced into an unwanted role, all she could see now was all or nothing – either she could have her life of magic with the Albans and no one telling her what to do, or she could be shoved back into her box, made to hide and pander and tend to everyone else first for as long as she lived. She could see no middle ground. If Mairead could just break through her anger and fear, perhaps she could show her that compromise was possible. That she need not lose everything.

Mairead's body ached from the strain of holding the shield against such an intense assault. Still weakened by the tainted magic caused by Mr. Munroe's death, she knew that she wouldn't be able to hold out much longer. She needed to bind Constance now – at least enough to break off her attack and give her time to calm down enough to see reason. But she didn't have the strength to hold the shield and perform the binding at the same time.

She closed her eyes and centered herself, pulling as much magic as she could into her core, ready to be used. Then she stood and dropped the shield.

Constance's magic hit Mairead like a runaway horse, but she screamed and leaned into it, aiming everything she had at Constance. She focused her mind on the image of her endless supply of love for Constance as a wide ribbon of energy that she wrapped around the other witch, pressing her power down, back into her.

For a moment, it worked. The force of Constance's attack reduced, and she drifted to the ground, landing gracefully on her feet. Mairead pushed harder, calling upon every moment of connection they had shared, every joy she had felt in the other woman's presence, and weaving it into her working.

Constance looked at her, her eyes filled with pain. She dropped her attack.

"I'm sorry," she said, crumpling to the ground, gasping. "I'm so sorry."

Mairead brought her shield up again as she approached, but it was a weak, flimsy thing that would do her no real good if Constance decided to attack again.

"You do love me!" Constance wailed. "I could feel it all through your magic."

"I do." Mairead dropped to her knees beside Constance. "I love you so much. That's the only reason for all of this."

Constance tentatively reached for Mairead. "Can you forgive me?"

Mairead took her hand. "Of course."

Constance looked up at her. "I hope you'll forgive me for this too. Sleep."

The final word was accompanied by a push of power and Mairead knew no more.

Chapter Twenty-Seven

Mairead

4th June 1746

Mairead regained consciousness slowly. The first thing she was aware of was a lump in the straw mattress beneath her, digging into her shoulder blade. She tried to roll onto her side, away from the discomfort, but her body would not respond to the command. That realization brought with it a faint panic, but it felt very far away from this space where she drifted. Behind her lay darkness and peace: no body, no people, no pain. Ahead of her lay something huge and grief-filled and she did not want to face it yet. So, she drifted here, between the two.

It couldn't last forever, though, and after a time the world began to intrude more upon her space. The lump beneath her grew increasingly uncomfortable, and she became more aware of the pain that hummed through the rest of her body. Her head thumped viciously as she drew closer to wakefulness. A raven cawed harshly somewhere nearby, bringing surges of pain with it. She could not yet remember what had happened before she slept and she shied away from the knowledge, knowing somehow that it would bring dreadful and unwanted change with it.

Her aching head grew in stature, taking over her interior world until her stomach surged each time the pain did. It was only a matter of time before she was forced to roll over and hang her head over the edge of the mattress to vomit onto the floor.

There was no more hiding after that.

When her stomach finally settled enough for her to straighten, Mairead raised her head and looked about the room through eyes that were blurry and watering. She was on the pallet bed in the main room of the Gordon cottage. The light coming in through the window at the front of the house was bright – midday at least, she thought, maybe later. Something else didn't seem right, but the pain that had lain somewhat dormant while she slept was now clamoring for her attention and making it very hard to think.

Mairead slumped back down onto the mattress for a moment. The smell of her vomit would not let her rest; she would have to get up and deal with it, but everything hurt so much that the effort involved in even that simple task seemed Herculean. She wondered if this was the sickness from the tainted magic returning. She pressed her forehead to her arm – no fever. That was a good sign.

She forced herself to her feet, standing on trembling legs as the room swam around her. Flashes of memories were popping into her head, but she pushed them away, not ready yet to face what had happened.

She stumbled to the outhouse and took care of the necessary, then went to fetch a bucket of water to clean up the mess inside. The bucket was not in its usual spot by the well. She staggered around looking for it, knowing in her gut that finding it would break down the walls in her mind, revealing whatever had happened to leave her in this state. She paused for a moment by one of the rainwater barrels, considering abandoning the bucket to its fate, and just going to lie down in the hay loft of the barn for a while. She could clean later.

But no, she couldn't leave it there for the children to find or for Constance to clean. That wouldn't be fair. She walked back round to the front of the cottage, trailing her hand along the wall for support. She stopped in her tracks when she saw the bucket, sitting beside the doorstep, where she had left it last night. Her gaze went straight to the spot on the wall that was slightly darker than the rest.

She sank to her knees as the previous night all came flooding back to her. The dry grass tickled and prickled at her legs as her mind swam with images. Her heated reconciliation with Constance, Iain's interruption, finding him lying at the base of the wall, dead. Constance. *Oh, God, Constance.*

Constance had attacked her with magic. Twice.

Mairead wailed, pouring her grief out to the sky, before catching herself and biting her own wrist to stifle her pain. *How could she?*

Mairead knelt there, still swaying, every inch of her body and soul aching from the events of the night before – both from the overexertion of her magic, and from Constance's betrayal. She had no idea what to do. Did Constance think it was over, that she had won and there would be no more discussion about it? Did she still expect Mairead to pack her things and leave? What about the Albans?

Her head ached as if her brain were pressing against the inside of her skull. She bent over, retching once more, though there was nothing left for her stomach to eject. The sun beat down on her shoulders, warm even through the thin layer of white clouds that stretched across the sky. Somewhere, the raven cawed again, the sound harsh and grating.

Mairead leaned forward, placing her hands flat on the ground, feeling the warmth that the grass and soil had soaked up already. All of this was just too big to manage. *One step at a time. You've found your way through every other hard thing in your life before now, and you'll find your way through this. Just take one step, and then another.*

She nodded, steeling herself, then got to her feet once more, every muscle squealing in protest. Slowly, trembling the whole time, she took the bucket from the doorstep, emptied it, fetched fresh water, and went inside to clean up the floor.

This time, as she looked around the room, she saw what was different, what her brain had refused to recognize before. Most of the dishes and utensils and food supplies were gone. The furniture was all still in place, but most of the smaller belongings had been taken. Mairead set the bucket down and walked on wooden legs into the bedroom. The wardrobe doors stood open, revealing only empty space inside. The blankets and sheets from the bed were gone, along with the children's toys. All except for one little rag rabbit that lay half kicked under the bed the girls shared.

Mairead sank to the bed in a daze. They were gone. Not just out somewhere, but gone.

It was late in the afternoon and the sun had passed its zenith when Mairead emerged once more from the cottage. Her body still ached all over, but the headache had subsided to a dull thud, and she had managed to keep both food and water down. On her back, she carried a bundle made from her traveling cloak and containing her few belongings – both those she had arrived in Kilmartin with and some small items that had come from her stay here. She shaded her eyes and looked toward the barn and the fields beyond, wondering what she should do about the animals. It wasn't their fault that Constance had killed her husband and then run off, leaving all of her responsibilities behind. But it wasn't like Mairead could just stay here and run the farm.

She shook her head then crossed the yard to the gate, where she stopped again. She looked in both directions. Her pained heart pulled at her to leave the way she had arrived, alone and unnoticed, but she knew that she couldn't. Not yet at least.

Constance might have run out on her responsibilities, but Mairead could not bring herself to do the same. There were people she had to say goodbye to, and the Albans to be unmade. She turned toward the village and began walking along the track, her eyes on the ground in front of her, her mind carefully empty, her heart numb.

She went first to Mistress Croaker's house. When she knocked on the door, she had believed that she had slipped back into her old ways, had drawn enough of the cloak of 'Mistress Ferguson' around her to be able to keep everything inside. She hadn't decided yet what she would say about Constance and Iain, but she would say that it was time for her to move on and somehow convince them all it was time to unmake the Albans. She didn't think it would take too much persuasion, with the men returning home.

When Mistress Croaker swung open the door, she gave a surprised smile and exclaimed, "Mistress Ferguson! What a lovely surprise!" She paused then, peering closer at Mairead. "Oh dear, you don't look very well. Come in, have a seat."

She stepped back and bustled around, leading Mairead to a chair and clearing away the fabric that was piled up on it. The table had more fabric laid out, scissors resting on top, and a lamp at each corner so that the seamstress could see what she was doing.

"Sit down, dear, you're very pale. I'll put on some tea."

All of Mairead's walls dissolved in the face of the older woman's simple kindness and she struggled not to weep. "I'm sorry," she said, covering her face. "Please don't let me put you to any trouble."

Mistress Croaker harrumphed. "After everything you've done for this village, nothing would be too much trouble." She set a kettle over the hearth to heat and tipped dried herbs and leaves into a couple of cups. "Now then, what's happened? Have you and Constance had a row?"

Mairead's mind filled with the image of Constance rising off the ground as she sent a magical attack at her. "Something like that."

"I thought that might be the case. This morning was the first time I've seen her without you since you arrived, near enough."

"You saw her this morning?" Mairead looked across the table to the hearth, where Mistress Croaker stood, waiting for the water to heat.

"She came by with the children, said that they were going away for a while, what with Iain coming home."

Mairead made a noncommittal noise.

"Going to visit her mother, she said. Iain needed the rest after everything. And you can hardly blame him." Mistress Croaker took the kettle and poured water into the cups, fragrant steam rising into the air. "She said he was going to tidy things up at the cottage and meet them on the road. Pity not to see him before they go."

"Did she mention why he didn't want to come into the village and see everyone before they left?" Mairead asked carefully.

"No, not really. I got the impression it was maybe just that he wasn't ready. War can be a terrible thing and not all scars it leaves are on the outside. But I suppose you would have more of an idea, having seen him last night." Mistress Croaker brought the teacups to the table and set one gently in front of Mairead. "I thought maybe that was what had set the two of you at odds? Him coming home and the pair of them rushing off and leaving you to take care of the farm, with only the Albans for help."

Mairead gave a tight smile. "Not quite. She didn't actually ask me to look after anything, she suggested that it was time for me to move on."

"What? That is surprising indeed."

They sat in silence a moment, sipping carefully at the hot tea.

"I can't speak for Constance, of course," Mistress Croaker said at last, "but I rather suspect that she did not mean that. And even if she did, she does not speak for the rest of Kilmartin. You would be very welcome to stay here, with me, for as long as you like. And I believe there are others who would feel the same way."

Emotion swelled in her chest. "Thank you. That means a great deal to me."

"I suppose Iain told you that some of the others came back with him?"

"Three others?"

"That's right. Four in total. Out of near thirty who left…" She trailed off, staring into her teacup. After a moment, she shook herself and forced a smile. "Still, John thinks some more might have escaped and scattered into the mountains. There's still a chance of more stragglers coming in."

"I hope that anyone still out there manages to find their way home," Mairead said quietly.

"May the Lord bless them and keep them." Mistress Croaker leaned across the table and lowered her voice, although there were only the two of them in the little one-room house. "Do you know where the Albans went? They all seem to have disappeared last night."

"I think Constance told them to hide in the bothy," Mairead answered, praying they were still there. "But the Albans were part of what we argued about, so I can't say for sure that they're still there."

Mistress Croaker nodded, as if something had been confirmed for her. "You wanted to get rid of them?"

Why was it so hard to say, now that the time had come to begin persuading people? "Yes," she said after a beat. "It's not so much that I want rid of them – I've gotten rather used to having them around – but it was never intended to be a permanent arrangement, and we're all paying a steep price to keep them."

"You more than most?"

Mairead shrugged. "Not in the sense of the life force used, that's the same for each of us. But they are a constant drain on my magic and that is…tiring. Add to that the fact that more people are moving around now, and the likelihood of them being discovered goes up. And I worry about misunderstandings."

Mistress Croaker frowned. "What kind of misunderstanding?"

"A village man who has managed to survive Culloden, somehow stays hidden and makes his way across the mountains while avoiding redcoats, arriving in the village late at night as those last night did… If the Albans came across one such as that, might they not take him for a threat?"

"Aye," Mistress Croaker said, looking concerned. "Aye, they might at that. I hadn't considered that."

"I only thought of it after Iain arrived so late last night," Mairead answered, inwardly wincing at the deception that her words implied. "I think it's time to let them go."

"And Constance disagreed? Even with Iain home?"

Mairead nodded and pressed her lips together.

"Can Constance power Hector with her own magic instead of yours?"

"I mean to ask Nicnevin that very thing."

"Well, I won't say they've not been a big help," Mistress Croaker said, pushing herself to her feet with a groan. "But I believe you're right. Now, do you mean to seek agreement from everyone else involved? Or will you just do as you need?"

Mairead sat back and sighed. "I would prefer to have everyone's agreement, but the fact is that I can't go on like this. And if I'm to leave Kilmartin, I must sever the magic anyway. I don't know exactly how far my influence extends, but it certainly doesn't cover huge distances."

"I think this may be a situation in which it is better to seek forgiveness than ask permission. Why not go and be about your task just now and then stay the night here? Perhaps a hearty meal and a good night's sleep will help you to see your path clearer tomorrow morning."

"You are a very wise woman," Mairead said with a fond smile.

"Wisdom is merely knowledge in addition to age," the seamstress said, winking.

Mairead left her to her work and headed out to the bothy, waving to people as she passed. She really had come to love Kilmartin, to feel at home here. It pained her to be leaving, especially under these circumstances.

It was only after she had reached the bothy and discovered all of the Albans except for Hector that she realized she hadn't brought anything with which to summon Nicnevin. No milk or honey, nothing of value at all.

She couldn't face the thought of traipsing back down into the village only to drag herself up here again – everything still ached, and she was so weary it was a challenge just to put one foot in front of the other.

With a sigh, she sat on the floor in the middle of the bothy and tried to think of an alternative offering. As she gazed at the packed dirt floor, trying to get her sluggish mind to work, she noticed that the patch she was staring at was darker than the rest of the floor, and wet-looking. She pressed her fingertips to it, and they came away with traces of blood on them. She stared at it, uncomprehending for a moment, until she realized that this was where Mr. Munroe had discovered the Albans. This must be his blood.

She scrabbled to her feet, scrubbing her hand against her skirt, horrified. Now that she had recognized it for what it was, she could see many traces of blood, all over the floor. This was not consistent with the version of events that Constance had told her. *Oh God, did she lie about that as well? Was anything she said ever true?*

Mairead's eyes darted around the interior of the small building, her breath coming in shallow gasps. She had to get out of here. She couldn't breathe. Her vision turned hazy as she staggered toward the door. Hamish reached out to steady her and she recoiled, horrified at the thought that he might have been party to whatever violence was visited upon poor, kind Mr. Munroe. She bounced off the door, setting her head to thumping again, then somehow managed to get it open and stumble out into the fresh air. A fine drizzle had started while she was inside and for once she was glad of the rain; the water cleansed the stain of that place from her skin and grounded her in herself once more.

She stood there for a moment, face tilted to the sky, letting the cool mist of water bead into droplets on her skin, running down the creases in her face. How had everything got so out of hand so quickly? She fumbled in the pocket of her skirt, pulling out a handkerchief which she used to wipe Mr. Munroe's blood from her fingertips. She looked at the traces of blood on it with disgust, and thought of throwing it away – she already carried the weight of his blood metaphorically, she had no desire to be sullied with it in reality too – but she couldn't bring herself to make a mess. With a sigh, she pushed it back into her pocket. Her fingers traced over something hard and she pulled out the smoky gray stone she had found the day they made the Albans. The iridescence inside the stone caught the light, despite the clouds filling the sky from one end to the other.

Mairead looked at it, frowning. She had been sure it was on a shelf back at Constance's cottage the last time she saw it. She supposed she must have picked it up when she packed the rest of her things earlier in the day, but she didn't remember doing it. She turned it this way and that, admiring the colors hidden inside. It wasn't much, but perhaps it would serve…

Mairead held the stone up on the palm of her hand and tilted her head back again, closing her eyes and thinking of the fae queen. "Nicnevin, I don't know if you can hear me, but I need you. I'm sorry, I only have this stone to offer to you, but I hope you will see the beauty in it just as I do and accept this humble gift."

"You called?" The fae queen's voice was drolly amused rather than offended.

Mairead lowered her head and opened her eyes, blinking rain away from her eyelashes. Nicnevin stood in front of her, seemingly completely dry despite the drizzle, no water beading in her hair as it was in Mairead's. The stone was no longer resting on her palm, but was on Nicnevin's.

"Something is wrong," Nicnevin said, frowning, a statement rather than a question. She closed her hand around the stone and when she opened it again the offering was gone.

"I need to unmake the Albans," Mairead said without preamble. So deep in grief was she that for the first time she found herself completely unaffected by the fae's presence. "I think we made a terrible mistake. I. I made a terrible mistake."

Nicnevin stepped closer and placed a hand on Mairead's arm, sending warm, soothing energy into her. "Tell me everything."

So Mairead did. All of it came pouring out – how Iain had come home and caught them in a compromising position, how she had gone to settle the children while he and Constance had argued, how she had found his body, her fight with Constance, all of it. She even told her of the blood she had found in the bothy and her suspicions regarding Mr. Munroe. Nicnevin listened without interrupting, just occasionally sending another pulse of soothing energy.

Part of Mairead wanted to pull away from that – she had been influenced quite enough by others' magic of late – but it was easing the ache in her muscles and the ache in her heart, and at the moment a little comfort was welcome.

When she had finished, Nicnevin straightened and looked past her shoulder at the bothy where all of the Albans except Hector waited. Mairead suspected that wherever Constance was, Hector would not be far away.

"We can unmake the Albans, as soon as you are ready, but first you must get consent from each of their makers. As with their creation, their uncreation must be done with consent."

Mairead sighed. Another complication, another delay. "What if they won't agree?"

Nicnevin nodded at the bothy. "Tell them of what was done here. That is likely to persuade them."

"What about Hector?" Mairead asked. "Constance's Alban. She's not here to consent, and wouldn't anyway."

Nicnevin shrugged. "At the moment, we must let them go."

"So, what, she can go on using my magic as the foundation of her Alban indefinitely? What about *my* consent?"

"Until she breaches the agreement, there is little I can do," Nicnevin said, not without regret. "My magic is bound in rules and conventions, and if I act against those, it weakens me. That is why I was so clear about the agreement when we began."

"Wasn't the agreement breached when Mr. Munroe was killed?" Mairead asked, desperately trying to find some way out of this.

"Perhaps. What happened was definitely enough to cause a taint in the magic, which affected both of us. But can you say for sure that Constance had any hand in it beyond covering it up? Can we be sure that the Albans did not act on their own to eliminate a perceived threat before she came upon the scene?"

Mairead thought through everything she knew or thought she knew about what had happened. "No," she said at last, with some reluctance. "I have no evidence that she was complicit. But what about Iain's death?"

Nicnevin shrugged, a delicate movement of her shoulders. "You said that she did that herself. It reflects poorly on her character, but it does not affect the agreement."

Mairead groaned.

"We can, however, dissolve the Albans that are here, with their makers' consent. Call me when you've spoken with them, and I will come."

Chapter Twenty-Eight

Mairead

Mairead could see the small cluster of houses that defined the center of Kilmartin when she came upon Catriona, running toward her and waving.

"Mairead!" she called, panting. "Mistress Croaker said you were out here." She came to a halt a few feet away and took a moment to catch her breath.

"Is everything all right?" Mairead asked, panic rising in her once more. "Is it Robbie? I'm sorry I haven't been by to see how he is, things have been—"

Catriona broke in, shaking her head. "Robbie is well enough. Mistress Gordon has taken good care of him. It's his father. I think he's dying."

"Let's go." Mairead pushed herself into a stumbling trot in the direction of Catriona's house.

As they went, Catriona explained that her husband had come home late last night, and that he had a wound in his leg, which was festering. She had cleaned it as well as she could, and this morning Mistress Gordon had come in to see him, but even though she'd applied a poultice to the area, he had developed a fever and begun to rave about things that weren't there.

"Mistress Gordon says that if the poison is in his blood now then there's little she can do. That he might have a chance in a hospital, but we probably don't have time to get him to Inverness. And even if we did, he's as likely to be shot by the redcoats as treated."

They had reached the door to Catriona's house and she paused, reaching out to touch Mairead's arm. "I don't know how your magic works, but if you're able to help him…"

"I'll do whatever is in my power," Mairead said, wondering just exactly what that might be. She reached for her magic and realized just how depleted she still was, her reservoir dangerously low.

They stepped inside and the smell hit Mairead straight away. There was no doubt about it, the poison was spreading through him as they spoke. Mairead hurried to the box bed in the corner, where Catriona's husband lay, firelight gleaming on his sweat-slicked skin. He appeared to be sleeping – or unconscious – and Mairead glanced at Catriona for permission before carefully peeling back the blanket that covered him. He wore a long shirt that left his legs bare. The injured one was wrapped in a fresh white bandage, which was already beginning to stain with blood and pus.

"How long since the injury?" Mairead asked. "Was he able to tell you?"

"He wasn't entirely sure," Catriona said, lighting a lamp and bringing it over so that Mairead could see better. "It was after Culloden. Some of them got away and were hiding in an abandoned barn. He's not sure how many days they were there. Then the redcoats came." She swallowed hard and perched on a stool beside the bed, taking her husband's hand in hers. "The redcoats set the barn on fire then lined up, guns at the ready, to shoot anyone who tried to escape. Only there were more Jacobites hiding out than they had expected, and Iain convinced them all to rush the soldiers. There was a battle, Iain was shot in the shoulder, Rab got a bayonet in his leg. Half of the men who'd been hiding with them died."

Mairead knelt on the floor next to him and reached out with all of her senses, the magical ones as well as the more mundane ones. Rab's life force was thin and stretched, hanging on by a thread. It was only really his intense will to live that was keeping him here. His fierce love for his family imbued every strained breath he took. Without ever having spoken to him, Mairead found that she cared deeply about this man. She focused now on his injury; the poison had indeed spread to his blood and was slowly making its way around his body. She could feel the clean, cool area directly on the wound, the herbs and medicines that were in the poultice, fighting to keep him alive. Isobel Gordon knew her craft. There was nothing that Mairead could add other than magic.

She sat back on her heels and looked at Catriona, who gazed back with terror and hope warring in her eyes.

"It's bad," Mairead said softly. "He's beyond any treatment I could suggest. But his will to live is strong. He wants nothing more than to be here with you and Robbie. I might be able to lend him some extra strength to fight."

Catriona nodded, tears spilling from her eyes.

"I'm sorry I can't do more." Mairead reached for her pitiful supply of magic.

"I am grateful to you for even trying," Catriona said. She leaned over and placed her forehead against her husband's. "Come back to me."

Mairead closed her eyes once more and pulled her magic to the surface, pressing her will into Rab's weakening body. She felt him respond, his life force taking in the strength she offered and wielding it in his fight. The aches and weariness in her own body deepened, but she kept pushing everything she could spare into him. She had made so many mistakes in her life, fallen short of her own standards more than she would care to admit, but if she could do this one thing, bring this loving family man home, perhaps that would begin to make up for another good man who had not made it home because of the creatures she had helped to create.

Mairead's head began to feel as if it were being squeezed in a vise, but still she pushed her strength into Rab, helping his body to fight. She thought of Catriona and Robbie and life in Kilmartin, the work and reward of it, the joy of watching his boy grow, and sent all of this to him to bolster his will to fight. At some point, she became aware that her legs were trembling beneath her, but still she pushed. She was no longer sharing her magic, but sending him her own life force itself; if her death brought him back, she found that it was a price she was willing to pay. It seemed a fair way to balance the scales. It crossed her increasingly fuzzy mind that if she died, the Albans would likely go with her, just as Mr. Kinloch's had. That also seemed like a fair way to resolve that problem.

Catriona spoke, her voice sounding panicked, but Mairead couldn't make out the words – they were so muffled and far away. She sent one more push of strength into Rab and then the world tilted, and she was drifting away.

Chapter Twenty-Nine

Constance

5th June 1746

"Mama, when are we going to stop?" Elspeth asked plaintively from the back of the cart. "I'm bored."

"I know, darling. We've got a bit farther to go today before we can stop though." Constance glanced at the horizon, where dark clouds were gathering.

"Do we have to sleep in the cart again?"

"I think we'll look for some shelter tonight," Constance said, eyeing the clouds with concern. "I think there might be a storm on the way. Maybe we'll find a friendly farmer who'll let us sleep in their barn. Wouldn't that be an adventure?"

"I want Mairead," Janey sniffled. "Will she be in the barn?"

Constance sighed, guilt sharp in her breast. "No, she won't be there. Mairead is taking care of our house and the animals, remember? But maybe she'll be able to join us in Edinburgh after a while."

Even after everything that had passed between them, all the things that Constance had done wrong, she still prayed that Mairead might actually forgive her, that maybe there could still be some sort of future for them. That seemed an impossibility right now and the knowledge of what she had lost sat like a boulder on her heart.

Simon started to fuss, distracting the girls as they strove to settle him. Constance glanced to the side, where Hector lumbered along beside them, a hat pulled down low to shade his face. She had adjusted his glamour to include extensive scarring, which she hoped would draw any eyes away from his peculiarity and offer an excuse for his lack of speech. From a distance, she hoped that they would look like nothing more than a family traveling together.

As she turned back to look at the road ahead, Constance thought once more of Mairead, whose magic formed the foundation of the spell that gave Hector life. She wondered if she could take him all the way to Edinburgh, if Mairead's magic would extend that far, or if they would reach some barrier beyond which he could not pass.

She pondered what she would do if that happened; would she turn back and find somewhere else to disappear for a while, somewhere closer to Kilmartin, or would she travel on without his protection?

How did everything get so out of hand? I've made such a mess of things.

The dark clouds ahead filled more and more of the sky, seeming to race toward them. They needed to get off the road and find some sort of shelter as soon as possible. So much for traveling farther today. Constance scanned their surroundings, looking for the nearest likely source of shelter. They hadn't passed any towns or villages all day, and it had been hours even since the last croft. Of course, it didn't help that she had chosen the least-used route that seemed manageable for Angus and the cart, since they were trying to avoid people as much as possible. The track they were on could only just be defined as a track and certainly was not sufficient for the word 'road' to apply. Still, the track had to be in at least somewhat regular use, or it would be more overgrown than it was. And if people came this way regularly then there would be shelter somewhere in the vicinity – the weather was changeable in the Highlands and traveling was not easy, so there were bothies and travelers' rests dotted all over the area.

As they carried on along the track, Constance let her eyes wander over the land to either side, until at last she spotted a wooden shepherd's hut tucked into the lee of a small hill. The day was darkening fast, so she turned Angus straight toward it, leading him carefully over the uneven ground. It was a bumpy ride for the cart, but Simon found each bump and lurch hilarious and soon enough the girls were both giggling with him. As soon as they reached the hut, Constance jumped from the driver's seat and helped the children down, ushering them inside just as the first fat raindrops began to fall.

The hut wasn't large enough for Angus, so all she could do was unhitch the cart and hope he didn't wander too far. Their belongings from the cottage were all tucked inside a couple of large traveling chests, which should hopefully withstand the worst of the storm. She took some food inside and the blankets the girls had been using as nests to sit in and hurried into the hut, Hector just behind her.

The rain drummed hard on the wooden roof, but they were dry and there was space for them all to sleep for the night. Thankfully, it wasn't cold, and though a fire would have been welcome, if only for the comfort it would bring, they had dried meat, cheese and bannocks to eat so did not need one for cooking.

Hector sat in one corner, motionless, except for when Simon started trying to climb up him and he gently set the baby back onto the floor, where he was safe. Constance didn't pay much attention to the Alban as she served up food and escorted the children outside to the back of the hut when nature called.

It was only as she settled them for sleep, listening to the rain still thundering down as she sat, cross-legged, rocking a sleepy Simon on her lap, that she looked at Hector and noticed that something was wrong.

At first, she couldn't put her finger on what had changed, only that something had.

"Hector, are you well?"

There was no response.

"Hector?" she said aloud, keeping her voice pitched low so as not to disturb the half-asleep baby in her arms.

Still the Alban did not respond. Constance frowned and tried to look closer at him in the light of the single oil lamp she had brought inside.

"HECTOR!" she shouted mentally.

Hector gave the barest twitch in response. Constance closed her eyes and reached for the magic that formed his glamour, pulling it down and locking it into the kilt pin. She opened her eyes again and studied him. Beneath the glamour, he was the same earth man he had been since the beginning, though instead of the moist, living mud she was used to seeing, his earth looked dry and cracked. As she watched, a trickle of soil ran down the sloping planes of his face.

Constance placed Simon on the floor, tucked in between his sleeping sisters, and crawled across the hut to Hector's side. Had they reached the edge of Mairead's power? She had assumed that when that happened, there would be a period of weakening as they traveled, signs that they were nearing the limit, and that she would have time to come to a decision. She rubbed her temples and thought. It didn't make sense that this was about distance. Hector had been fine when they first entered the hut, and he hadn't traveled any farther since then, so something else must be the cause of his unexpected decline.

Constance closed her eyes once more and touched the magic that moved through the Alban, animating him. There were three ribbons: her own, Mairead's and Nicnevin's. The fae's magic felt very different from hers and Mairead's, everything about it just subtly wrong to her senses, like looking at the world through spectacles that did not belong to you. It was by far the most precise of the three magics, though, adding the shape and detail to the working. Constance's own contribution felt wild in comparison. The raw power of a waterfall, beside the delicate precision of an icicle.

Mairead's power was the stabilizing influence that wound the other two together, allowing it all to work in tandem. And it was dissolving.

Was I wrong? Have we just gone too far for her to reach us? As she reached for the magic, even more of it slipped away. Constance tried to catch hold of it, cementing Mairead in her mind; perhaps it was possible for her to augment it, or to replace Mairead's working with her own. As she grasped the edges of Mairead's power, horror settled in her gut.

Distance wasn't the problem. Mairead was dying.

Panic filled her, driving any clear thought from her mind and causing her to act on instinct alone. She allowed herself to fill up with all of the desperate love she felt for Mairead, her gratitude over the way that Mairead had helped her to step into herself, and her (possibly foolish) hope for the future, and she pushed all of that along the connection that bound Mairead to Hector.

She felt something as it reached the far end, wherever Mairead was, some sense of her magic sinking into something, being accepted or taken and used in some way, but she was too far away and too inexperienced to control or direct it in any way. All she could do was pray that it would be enough.

Before withdrawing from the working that formed Hector, Constance wrapped a sheath of her own magic around the entire thing, hopefully insulating him and powering him separate to Mairead.

When she pulled her senses back into herself and opened her eyes, Hector was back to normal, the soil that formed his body thick and healthy once more. He looked at her with his head cocked, expression curious.

"All is well?"

"I don't know," Constance answered aloud. "But some things are better, at least."

"Do you require assistance?"

Constance shook her head. "Just watch over us while we sleep."

Feeling empty and somewhat weakened from sending so much energy to Mairead, she lay down beside the children and was asleep within minutes, Mairead's smile dancing across her mind as she drifted away.

The next morning, before they left, Constance spared the time to gather some reeds and other long-stalked plants, which she wound into something resembling a doll shape. Before she tied it off, she went through the chests in the back of the cart, looking for anything that had belonged to Mairead. Lying at the bottom of one was a hairbrush that they both used. She disentangled the strands of hair caught between the bristles, hoping against hope that enough of it was Mairead's for her plan to be effective.

She tucked the little ball of hair into the center of the grass doll, then tied the whole thing off. She tucked it into her dress and throughout the rest of the journey, whenever she had a moment, she sent a burst of healing magic into the doll and hoped that it would reach Mairead.

Chapter Thirty

Constance

30th June 1746

Constance walked quickly, her head down and arms tucked in close to her sides. The Edinburgh streets were crowded and loud, the city so much busier than anything she had experienced before, even in Inverness. Every time she had to step outside her heart raced, every shout and bang, every smell, good or bad, every time someone jostled her as they passed, all of it thundered through her, driving her to panic. In many ways she hated it here, but at least she was free, and no one took much note of her.

She ducked around other pedestrians, doing an awkward little hop to avoid stepping in horse manure, and then dashed through the gate to the pathway leading to the rear door of a large stone townhouse. When she passed into the shade thrown by the side of the house, her shoulders finally started to descend from close to her ears and she began to breathe a bit easier. At least here, the chaos was much reduced.

She made her way past overgrown rose bushes to the servants' entrance at the back and rapped sharply at the door. It swung open to reveal a young man in a valet's uniform.

"Good morning, Mistress Gordon," he said, standing aside to let her in. "Mistress Beecham asked you to stop into her office when you arrived." He closed the door then glanced around and lowered his voice conspiratorially. "She's not in the best mood, so you might want to go straight there, not keep her waiting."

"Thank you, Mr. Henderson," Constance said, inwardly groaning. She stopped only to remove her coat and fix her maid's cap in place before going to the housekeeper's small office beside the kitchen.

The door was open, so she tapped on the frame. "You wanted to see me?"

Mistress Beecham looked up from her papers with a harried expression. "Come in, come in. And close the door behind you."

What have I done wrong now? She had thought herself lucky to find a job so easily on arrival in the city, especially one that paid well enough to allow her to pay a neighbor a few coins each week to look after the children while she was out, but it soon became apparent that it had to pay well, or no one would stay. Mistress Beecham was not just a demanding taskmaster; she was so particular that it seemed she could see dust on the tables and water stains on the silver where others could not. Add to that the fact that the occupier of the house was a colonel in the British Army and the job grew even less appealing.

"It seems our number is once more reduced. Miss Holmes will no longer be employed in the colonel's household."

"That's unfortunate," Constance said carefully.

"It seems the young lady will be getting married to her beau as a matter of some urgency and will be taking up the duties and responsibilities of a wife. And mother."

"Ah." Constance wondered where this was going and why it involved her in any way.

"Can I assume that as a widow with three children already, I do not need to worry about such circumstances occurring with yourself?"

"Certainly not!" *If only you knew.* Constance laughed inwardly at the thought of Mistress Beecham's face if she ever found out that the only lover Constance had any desire for was a woman.

Almost every day in the few short weeks since she had arrived in Edinburgh, Constance considered writing to Mairead and begging for her forgiveness, asking her to join them here. But each time she talked herself out of it. She didn't even know where to send a letter – she had no idea whether Mairead had stayed in Kilmartin or left as soon as she awoke from the spell Constance had placed her under when they fought.

"Hmmm." Mistress Beecham gave her a hard look then gathered up the papers on her desk. "In that case, I am willing to offer you a promotion to under-housekeeper. It comes with a room in the servants' quarters here, although I realize that may not be suitable with the children."

Constance thought furiously. The room she rented in a tenement near the main gate in the city walls was far from ideal – damp and cold, and loud at all hours with streams of soldiers and merchants coming and going. But here, there would be nobody to mind the children for her while she worked, and nowhere for Hector to hide – the building she lived in was next door to one that had been hit by cannon fire during the Jacobite occupation, and was unsafe to live in. Of course, there were squatters, but only the most desperate would take the risk and none of them bothered Hector, who kept to himself.

"Thank you," Constance said after a moment. "I think we're better staying where we are – my neighbor looks after the children while I'm here."

"Very well. You will be required to work an additional two hours per day, regardless of where you live. If you cannot make that work, tell me now, but don't accept the position and then let me down."

"I…I'll make it work." She had no idea how, exhausted as she already was, but unless she could find a way to send Hector out to work, she would be their only source of income for the foreseeable future. "I appreciate your confidence in me."

"Yes, well. See that it is not misplaced. Now get to your duties, you're behind already, and the colonel will be having company for dinner this evening."

By the time she walked home that night, Constance was so exhausted that even lifting her feet felt like a challenge. Hunger gnawed at her belly, as it had ever since they arrived. Between her lack of resources, and the effects of the uprising – not to mention the reprisals of the British Army – there was never quite enough food to go around, and she always made sure that the children had as much as they needed. Which meant she never did. Already, she was wishing for Mistress Croaker's assistance in taking her dresses in; she had lost enough weight that they were beginning to hang poorly.

She missed Emily a great deal. She missed all of her friends and neighbors from Kilmartin, and longed to be back there. For some reason, she had thought that running away would make her free, but all she had really done was trap herself in a different cage. She had run to prevent Mairead from binding her magic, but in doing so she had run to somewhere that she couldn't use it anyway. The city was so crowded that Constance found she was never alone. Even on her daily trudge to and from the grand house she worked in, there were people at every turn. She didn't dare use even the smallest trace of magic where anyone might see her.

At least she still had Hector. As long as he was close, she felt safe. No one could harm her or force her to do anything as long as she was guarded by a being who was impervious to violence, and whose sole priority was to protect her and her children. Nothing short of a mob, anyway.

As she climbed the dark and dirty stairs to the room she rented, she could hear Simon and Janey crying, and Elspeth's voice trying to soothe them. She forced herself to move faster, taking the stairs as quickly as her aching legs could. She stepped inside and stopped short, staring in horror at the scene before her.

Elspeth stood in one corner of the room, Simon and Janey tucked into the corner behind her, as if she was protecting them. Hector loomed at the opposite side of the room, while Mistress Neal, the neighbor whom Constance paid to watch the children, was stretched out across the floor, her neck twisted so that her head was facing the wrong direction. Her sightless eyes stared at Constance as she hurried into the room, closing the door behind her.

"What happened here?" she demanded, looking between the cowering children and Hector. Had he done something to hurt them?

She crossed the room, skirting the neighbor's body, and gathered the children to her. "Elspeth, are you hurt? Are any of you hurt?"

Elspeth looked at her and suddenly the look of defiance on her face shattered and broke down into gasping sobs, which only prompted her siblings to renew their own efforts. She held them all close, rocking and shushing them.

"Hector, what happened?"

The Alban stayed on the other side of the room, as if sensing that she would not tolerate him near the children until she knew what had gone on in her absence. He sent her an image of Mistress Neal hauling Janey's arm so that it was fully extended above her head as the poor girl tottered on tiptoes, then swatting her behind with a thin length of wood.

"Janey, did Mistress Neal hurt you?" Constance asked, her voice gentle, trying to move Janey so that she could see her properly.

Janey only wailed louder and clung to her mother with a panicky tightness.

Instead, Elspeth answered for her, sniffling through her own tears. "Janey was jumping on the bed, and Mistress Neal told her not to, but she kept doing it anyway. So, Mistress Neal pulled her arm like this—" she stretched her arm above her head in demonstration, "—and then hit her with a stick. Janey started shouting for you, then Hector burst in and he…he…" Elspeth trailed off into hitching sobs, burying her face in Constance's side.

"I protected them."

"You went too far. A woman is dead!"

"You said 'Protect the children'. She harmed the child. I removed her."

Constance pulled the children close, her thoughts awhirl. A dead body in her home was a complication she did not need. She felt a white-hot fury toward Mistress Neal for daring to handle her children so roughly; she would never have paid the older woman to watch them if she'd suspected for even a moment she would treat them that way. But one could not argue that she deserved to die for her transgression.

Hector had overreacted and now someone was dead. Thank the Lord she had already warded them and hidden them from Mairead and Nicnevin – if they were able to find her, there'd be no talking them round after this. What penalty would the fae impose beyond unmaking Hector?

"Mistress Neal not wake up," Janey said, finally peeling back enough to look up at Constance. "She hurt me, and Hector hurt her, and now she not wake up."

"I know, my darling, I know. I'm so sorry she hurt you."

"Hector can carry her to bed," Janey said, peeking past Constance to the body, whose face was thankfully turned away.

"She's not—" Elspeth began but Constance cut her off with a sharp look.

"That's a good idea. Hector, please carry Mistress Neal to her own room and put her to bed." She kissed each of the children on the head as Hector hoisted the dead woman in his arms. "I'm just going to help Hector with the doors, all right? Why don't you three sit on the bed, nice and safe until I come back?"

The children climbed onto the bed, Elspeth with a distrustful look; she knew that Constance had just lied to Janey. *I can fix this. I'll figure out how to fix this.*

Constance motioned to Hector to wait while she stepped into the close and made sure no one else was around before opening the door to Mistress Neal's room and guiding him through. She had him place the body on the bed, then stood in the middle of the shabby room, thinking for a moment.

"You wait here," she said at last. "After the children are asleep, I'll tell you when it's safe and then you can drop her body down the stairs. With any luck, people will believe it a horrible accident."

Angus was stabled at an inn just outside the city gates, but if they waited until it was late enough, Hector could pull the cart a few streets without too much risk of getting caught. She left Hector with instructions to barricade the door to Mistress Neal's room until she called for him then returned to the children. Though her body was heavy, and her thoughts slow with the weight of the day, she made some food for the children, then got them ready and into bed. She sat with them all curled into her and spread a cloak of magic around them, gently leading them to forget everything that had happened this day. She sang softly, pressing her magic into them, lulling them into a sleep filled with pleasant dreams from which they would wake in a new home, with no memory of what happened here.

Chapter Thirty-One

Mairead

2nd July 1746

Mairead walked along the street that made up Kilmartin, leaning heavily on the cane that Rab had fashioned for her after she awoke and discovered her new infirmity. It seemed a cruel twist of fate that his leg had fully healed, leaving only a thick rope of scar tissue, while Mairead had lost some use of her own leg. But then, according to Nicnevin, she was lucky to have survived at all. She had overextended her magic so much that the Albans in the village had all collapsed, and she had hovered near death for days. It seemed that the only reason she hadn't crossed that threshold was the fact that when the Albans started to fall apart, Constance had used their connection to send her a surge of magic. Her body used that somehow to find the energy to recover, though not quite as she was before.

Mistress Gordon thought it might be possible that she would regain some use of the leg in time and recommended exercising it whenever she could. So, every morning since she had awoken, she made her slow, painful way up and down the street until exhaustion drove her inside to rest for the remainder of the day.

Mairead paused at the end of the street where the church had once stood, looking beyond the empty space where it used to be to the graveyard where they had buried Mr. Kinloch. Her lower back and hips screamed in pain, no doubt from the odd gait she walked with now, with one leg dragging and barely supporting her weight. In the weeks since Constance had left, Mairead still had not come to a decision about what to do next. The people of Kilmartin had made it clear that she was welcome to stay, and a part of her wanted that so much it hurt: to live somewhere freely, her magic no longer a secret she had to hide, her heart no longer guarded. But Constance had broken that heart, and everything here reminded her of the other woman at every turn.

Leaving, in many ways, seemed safer. Easier. Move on to the next place and the next after that, always more road ahead, her heart safely behind its walls again. Of course, right now she couldn't actually walk to the next town, with this ineffective leg, so the choice was rather made for her at the moment.

As she turned to begin her torturous path back along the street, sparkles filled the air beside her and out of the midst of them appeared Nicnevin.

"Good day," she said, looking Mairead up and down as if assessing her in some manner.

"My lady." Mairead inclined her head in greeting. Nicnevin's presence was as distracting as ever, but she looked as if she was here on a pressing matter. "Is there something I can do for you?"

Nicnevin flashed her a mischievous grin. "I dare say there are any number of things you could do for me, but sadly now is not the time for that." She sighed. "I had hoped to leave you out of this, given that you are still recovering, but it seems I have no choice."

The pain in Mairead's back was a red-hot knot, impinging upon any attention she could give to the fae queen. "I'm sorry, might we sit while we talk? Standing still is not a great deal easier than walking these days."

"Of course, how thoughtless of me." Nicnevin waved a hand, and an elaborately carved wooden bench appeared behind them. It looked almost too beautiful to sit on, the arms and legs shaped into animals, a pattern of leaves and vines running round the edges. "Please, sit."

Mairead looked questioningly at the fae.

"It's from my home." Nicnevin shrugged. "It was the first thing to come to mind."

"Do you have many such beautiful things in your home?" Mairead asked, easing herself down to sit on the bench. Its surface was warm, as if it had been sitting in the sun.

"Perhaps one day I will show you. Though a visit to Faery should not be undertaken lightly as it always comes with a cost. That, however, is a conversation for another day."

"What do you need from me?" Mairead asked, watching a pair of white butterflies dance together over the wildflowers that grew along the wall surrounding the graveyard. She could hear the murmur of voices behind them as people from the village noticed the fae queen in their midst, but she didn't think anyone would disturb them. Most of the others were inclined to keep their distance from Nicnevin.

"The magic is tainted again. The remaining Alban has killed an innocent."

Oh, Constance, what have you done? "Wait, how can she still have Hector when the others all collapsed when I..." She shook her head, pushing thoughts of her near-death away. "And why am I not ill this time?"

"Whatever Constance did when she pushed magic through your connection to keep you alive must also have stabilized her Alban."

Is that why she did it in the first place? Perhaps saving me was simply a side effect of saving Hector.

"As for why you are not ill, I do not know." Nicnevin sighed. "I do not like not knowing. It may be that whatever she did to stabilize the Alban is insulating you somehow from the taint. Or perhaps it is a matter of degree – if we are correct about what happened to Mr. Munroe, it is possible that all of them were involved in his demise. In this instance there is only one, so perhaps only one-eighth of the taint that affected you before. Without honesty and co-operation from Constance, it is likely we will never know."

Mairead watched as the dancing butterflies took flight and disappeared from view. She wished she could do the same. Leave behind her hurt and fear and aching body. "What do you need me for? Surely you can unmake him without me – I didn't really do anything when Morag wanted out after Mr. Kinloch died."

"You're right, I could deal with the Alban alone. But Constance has put a ward in place around them. I can't get close."

"But I can?"

"Perhaps. I do not know for certain, but you have so much of her magic flowing through you, it would take a very intricate working to ward against you. While she has sufficient power, we both know that she lacks the control."

Mairead tipped her head back and closed her eyes, letting the sun warm her face. She longed to be in Constance's arms, safe and loved, and yet she could not stand the thought of seeing her, knowing all that she had done. How cruel life could be at times, making one crave comfort that could only be given by the person who caused the hurt in the first place.

"I'm not fit to travel yet," she said at last, though she hated having to admit to the weakness. "And I don't know if I have enough magic to unmake Hector. I certainly don't have enough to take Constance on. Not that I ever did."

"The longer we wait, the greater the taint will grow. Not to mention the risk of more innocents being killed."

Mairead spread her hands in a gesture of helplessness. "I don't want that any more than you do, but I can't make this body work by force of will alone. If I could, I'd have done it already."

"Why did you risk your life to save that young man?" Nicnevin asked, gazing out over the graveyard and scuffing her bare feet in the grass the bench sat upon.

Mairead thought for a moment before answering. Birds sang in the trees and bushes around them, children laughed somewhere nearby, and yet she felt as if the world were holding its breath waiting for her answer. She couldn't help but scoff at her own hubris. What cared the world whether she lived or died, least of all why she did anything?

"It wasn't entirely a conscious choice," she said slowly. "It was at least in part just instinctive care for a person who needed help. Someone had to try and save him, and I was the one who was there. And it was partly because Catriona is my friend. I care about her. She loves Rab, and I could feel his love for her, and for their son – it was all that was keeping him alive when I arrived – and I didn't want her to lose him."

Silence settled between them as Nicnevin waited and Mairead struggled to find the words.

"It was also because I didn't care if I died."

"She hurt you so much?" Nicnevin asked softly.

Mairead worried at the inside of her lip. "Not just her. Not just that, I suppose."

Again, Nicnevin waited.

Mairead struggled to get her thoughts in order. She had never shared so much of her inner thoughts with someone before, not even Constance, had never been so vulnerable with another person. Why did she feel so compelled to be open with the fae queen beside her? Was it magic? Or just loneliness, finally catching up with her?

She sighed. "When I was young, my father taught me that I would be hurt and rejected for what I am, so I must always hide. And I have done that, moving around, never setting down roots, never letting people get to know me enough to notice that there's something different about me. I have lived in the center of towns and danced in ceilidhs and waulked the wool and taken part in parades and festivals. I've even had a few romantic dalliances. But through all of it, I have always, always been alone."

A playful gust of wind flicked her hair into her face, and she reached up to push it back. "Until Constance. I let her fool me. I let her convince me for a time that there could be a safe place for me. That I could have a home, where I was loved and accepted for *who* I am, and not feared for *what* I am. But so much of our time together was a lie. I don't know what, if any of it, was true. In the end, she cast me aside as soon as I became inconvenient."

Mairead looked at Nicnevin, who was watching her sadly. "I didn't want to go back to being alone, and I couldn't see any other future before me. So, I didn't care if I lived or not, and Rab's life seemed one worth exchanging mine for."

"I too have known despair," Nicnevin said, glancing away. "And I know the challenge to be found in overcoming it. Those who do, have a strength greater than even they know, much of the time. You have given me something of yourself, and I thank you for the trust. It also means that now I can give something to you in exchange."

Nicnevin stood and vanished into a shower of sparks before reappearing no more than a second or two later. In one hand she held a vial of pearlescent liquid, which gleamed like the inside of a shell. In the other, she held some sort of fruit unlike anything Mairead had seen before.

"I have told you before, that the magic of the fae is bound by rules, one of which is that there must always be an exchange. In this case, the gift of your emotional vulnerability is precious enough that it pays in full for these, medicines of the fae realm. Three drops of the liquid every morning and evening, and one segment of the fruit at the same time. I cannot guarantee that they will restore full use of your leg, but they will greatly aid in your recovery and will restore your magic to full capacity."

"You couldn't have suggested this before now?" Mairead asked, holding her hands out to accept the gifts from Nicnevin.

The Witch Queen shrugged. "Emotional connection can only be given, not taken."

"I don't quite know what that means. But thank you."

Nicnevin nodded. "In three days I will return, and we will decide what to do about Constance."

When Nicnevin returned, Mairead was making tea in Mistress Croaker's house, while the seamstress was busily cutting fabric for a new set of clothes for Robbie, who seemed to have grown several inches overnight. Mistress Croaker – Emily, as she insisted that Mairead call her now – was delighted with the new fabric that Fergus and Bridie had brought from Inverness upon their return and had been detailing its advantages at length.

Thankfully, she had just put the scissors down when Nicnevin appeared in the blink of an eye just inside the door to the house, startling both of its occupants.

"It is time," she said, by way of greeting.

"Tea first," Mairead said, setting out another cup.

"There is work to be done," Nicnevin said. "The taint—"

"Is spreading, I know. But first we can drink tea and decide on the best approach."

Mairead looked at the fae queen calmly and implacably.

"Very well," Nicnevin said with a sigh.

"I believe I'll take my tea in the garden, leave you two to talk." Mistress Croaker lifted one of the cups that Mairead had just poured steaming liquid into.

"Please, don't let us put you out of your own home," Mairead said, putting a hand on the seamstress's wrist.

Mistress Croaker waved her off. "I believe a little time sitting out in the sunshine is just what I need right now."

Nicnevin waited until the door had closed behind her, then slumped onto a stool with a sigh. "You are moving around with greater ease, I see."

"I am. Thank you, your medicine has done wonders for me." Mairead turned and walked across the room to demonstrate. She still limped a little, but the cane stood propped beside the door, no longer required. "And my magic has made a complete return. I hadn't noticed how much the Albans had been draining it until now."

"There is still one drain to deal with."

Mairead sighed. "I don't want to do this."

"I know. But you must understand that despite everything, you are still connected to Hector. Any blood that he spills is on your hands and mine as much as on Constance's. We have no choice but to—"

Nicnevin broke off with a gasp and doubled over, clutching at her torso.

"What's wrong?" Mairead asked, moving to her side and crouching. "What can I do to help?"

"The taint," Nicnevin gasped. "He just killed again."

A faint echo of the fae's pain spread to Mairead, but it felt distant, somehow removed.

"We must go. Now." Nicnevin straightened and stood, her eyes flashing with fury, the air crackling around her.

"Where are they?" Mairead asked, reaching for her cane, just in case.

"Far to the south of here, in the city of your kings."

"Edinburgh?"

"That is the place."

"I don't know if I can walk that far. My leg has improved a lot but…"

"We will not be walking," Nicnevin said. "Take my hand and do not let go, no matter what happens."

Mairead looked at her and thought of all the times she had disappeared in a shower of sparks. Was that going to happen now? How could they both travel like that? Hesitantly, she reached a hand out to Nicnevin, noticing as she did that she was trembling. "Is it…safe?"

Nicnevin gave a half smile. "As safe as any magic ever is."

"So, no?" Mairead said with a nervous laugh.

Nicnevin took her outstretched hand and pulled her close, so their bodies were pressed against each other and Mairead's senses were filled with her.

"It will be an adventure," Nicnevin murmured almost against Mairead's lips.

Mairead did not see the shower of sparks that appeared as they vanished.

Chapter Thirty-Two

Mairead

4th July 1746

Time, space, direction, all ceased to mean a thing while traveling with Nicnevin. Mairead clung to the fae as she carried them through a mass of swirling, multicolored clouds. Sights and smells and sounds all became mixed up with each other so that green was the scent of snow, and purple was a child laughing.

Her stomach churned and she closed her eyes against the swirling movement, pressing her face against Nicnevin's shoulder. The skin of her neck was smooth and soft, and Mairead forced her thoughts away from her desire to feel it under her lips.

Suddenly the sensation of movement stopped, and when Mairead raised her head, they were standing together on the grass verge of the main road into Edinburgh. In the distance, the castle brooded over the city, looking down upon the ruins of buildings that had presumably been damaged during the occupation. Even from here, the noise was appreciable: voices raised in greeting, hooves clopping on the stone-lined road, wagon wheels creaking. In all her years of wandering, Mairead had visited the capital only once and had not stayed for long. She vastly preferred the open spaces, subdued colors and farming rhythms of life in the small towns and villages of the Highlands.

"How will I find them in there?" she asked, looking with worry at the crowds of people moving into and out of the city along the road they stood beside.

"How did you find your way to Constance all those months ago?" Nicnevin asked, standing beside her and looking toward the city.

"With a witch stone," Mairead said, remembering how she had used the stone to show her the path that led to the call for help that had drawn her to Kilmartin, looking for a witch in need. "It's back in Kilmartin though, wrapped in my cloak in Mistress Croaker's house."

"Can you not feel her through your connection?"

Mairead bit her lip. Most of the time she sought to avoid brushing up against the connection that she shared with Constance. The pain caused by their ending was just too much to tolerate the reminder. With a heavy sigh, she closed her eyes and focused, reaching for Constance, wherever she was.

"I can feel her. She's somewhere in the east of the city."

"It is likely that she will have cast a glamour over all of them. Will you be able to—?"

"I'll see through it," Mairead said, glancing at the fae. "My second sight is stronger than even Constance's power." She paused and sighed again. "She'll know I'm coming. She can feel me, just as I can her."

Nicnevin looked at her thoughtfully. "Perhaps there is some way that I can cloak your magic, hide you from her..."

"Wouldn't that interfere with the connection, which I'm relying on to find her?"

Nicnevin nodded. "Possibly. Probably."

"Well then, I suppose we shall just have to deal with her knowing I'm here." Mairead looked at the city once more, not entirely sure what she was actually going to do when she confronted Constance.

"I will walk with you as far as I can," Nicnevin said, her voice full of compassion that Mairead almost wanted to push back against.

"How do I unmake Hector?" Mairead asked, stepping down onto the paved road and beginning to walk toward the city.

Nicnevin fell in beside her. "You just unpick the weave of the magic that gives him life. Or, if that fails, simply remove the heart-flower."

Mairead shuddered. "You would not say simply if you had seen him taking on the redcoats." She did not think she would ever forget the sound of Captain Sampson's neck breaking. Or the sight of the puff of dry soil that burst out of Hector when he was shot. Removing the heart-flower without unweaving the magic was unlikely at best. And somehow she had to manage all of that, while the most powerful witch she had ever known tried to stop her.

"I have faith in your abilities," Nicnevin said, a smile tugging at the corner of her lips. "More than you do, I suspect."

"That would not be difficult," Mairead said with a laugh as they passed into the city itself. Buildings rose on either side of them, and the noise suddenly seemed much louder. Mairead's hands went to her ears before she could force them back to her sides, fists clenched tight. The smell of many bodies living in close proximity assaulted her nose and she was reminded of why she hadn't lingered on her last visit, leaving the city after only a couple of days.

Mairead let her gaze wander over the people they passed, not really expecting to discover Constance so soon upon entering the city but hoping for some sort of clue. It took only a moment for her to notice that no one looked at Nicnevin, despite her decidedly eye-catching appearance. Anyone walking near them carefully stepped around her, but none so much as glanced in the fae's direction.

"Why don't they see you?" she asked under her breath, trying to avoid the appearance of talking to herself.

Nicnevin grinned at her. "Humans can only see me when I choose to allow them, as I did in Kilmartin. Most humans, anyway."

They wandered roughly eastward, moving from street to street as necessary. Mairead's heart was drumming as if she'd run for miles as the pull of Constance's magic increased. Her chest was tight and she was breathing in shallow pants. She stepped to the side of the road, into the shadow of one of the tall, stone buildings, and leaned on it for a moment, forcing herself to take several deep breaths.

"You're trembling," Nicnevin said, frowning. "Are you unwell?"

"Am I?" Mairead asked faintly, holding up her hand to see that it was indeed shaking slightly. "I'm... I don't know what I am. Terrified? Excited? Filled with longing and dread all at once? Or maybe I'm picking up some of her feelings. If Hector has just—" she let her gaze dart around to make sure no one was near enough to hear, and then lowered her voice anyway, "—killed someone, then she's probably in a bit of a state too."

"I would not ask this of you if it was not necessary," Nicnevin said regretfully.

"I know. I know." Mairead scrubbed her hands over her face, took another deep breath and pushed herself off the wall.

As they stepped back out into the street, she called her magic up so that it coiled and stretched just beneath her skin. They walked a little farther, Mairead pondering the possibility that Hector might not be in Constance's presence, that maybe she would have the opportunity to face them separately, and if she could find Hector first…

They turned down another street, this one narrower and dingier than the first, when Nicnevin bounced back as if she had walked into a wall.

"This is as close as I can get," she said. "You'll have to do the rest on your own."

Mairead turned back to look at her. "I don't think I can."

"You can." And then, "You must."

Mairead drew in as much air as her lungs could hold and then let it all out in a whoosh, shaking her arms as she did so. "I'll see you when it's over."

As she turned and began walking again, she muttered under her breath, "Unless they kill me."

She drew her magic into a shield and wove it against her skin, invisible armor that would protect her from Constance but not Hector. If he wanted to, the Alban could pick her up and tear her limb from limb without even trying hard. And it would only really protect her from Constance for a short time, as she knew from painful experience.

If she wanted you dead, she's had plenty of opportunity. There's no reason to think that has changed.

Of course, Constance might decide that if it came down to a choice between Mairead or Hector, the Alban was more useful to her. He was definitely more obedient. When she reached the end of the street and tried to focus on which direction the magic was pulling her in, she realized that since crossing the ward, it lay all around her, blanketing her senses. Constance was in the very air here, and there was no way to narrow down a direction.

"Argh!" She groaned in frustration, yanking at her hair. A man who was walking past shot her a disapproving look before hurrying round a corner. Should she go back to Nicnevin and tell her what had happened, how the ward drowned out any finer sense of where Constance might be? They could work together to come up with a solution. Or decide to try again another day.

Are you really going to turn tail and run at the first problem? Are you so scared of her?

Mairead chewed her lip. She *was* scared. She was scared of Constance's power and the chance that this time she wouldn't hold back, she wouldn't just put Mairead to sleep. She was terrified of Hector and the casual way that he inflicted violence upon people as if it meant nothing. And more than all of it, she was frightened of discovering that she was still head over heels in love with Constance and that the other woman had never felt the same way. That it had all been a lie, a tool to manipulate her into doing whatever Constance wanted.

I can't leave. But I can't follow her magic anymore either. So what can I do?

She scanned the street that crossed the one she was on in both directions, looking for inspiration. And then she spotted it. A wide, grassy area with flower beds and benches lay just a block away from where she stood. She strode toward it, determination rising once more.

Constance had brought the children with her to Edinburgh – children who had lived, until this point, on a farm on the edge of a tiny village. Children who loved to be outside, amongst the animals and plants who shared their environment, to whom the city would seem alien and cold, so removed from their home. Constance might have lied about many things, might have used Iain as a disguise and Mairead for her magic, but one thing Mairead knew without a shadow of a doubt was that Constance loved her children. If she was staying anywhere around here, she would bring her children to where they could touch the grass.

She found an unoccupied bench along the main path through this lovely little city garden and sat on it. She briefly considered drawing up a glamour over herself – Constance did not have second sight, and as far as she knew, would be unable to see through a glamour. She would, however, be able to feel Mairead's magic – probably already had, in fact – so it seemed like a waste of her limited resources. Instead, she counseled herself to stillness, settling into as unobtrusive a state as she could.

She let all of her senses, both mundane and magical, wander over this small haven in the center of the city. Couples strolled together, sometimes with a chaperone, sometimes without. Lone men and women hurried through on their way about their work for the day, while families paused and children dashed about laughing and playing.

God, how she missed the children. She had never given any thought to being a mother, but getting so close to Elspeth and Janey and Simon, only to have them snatched away…that hurt almost more than anything else Constance had done.

Mairead stayed in her spot as afternoon dragged toward evening, occasionally stretching to keep her leg from seizing up too much. Nicnevin's medicine had helped it a great deal, but the muscle remained stiff and ached most of the time.

A bell somewhere chimed four, and Mairead began to wonder what she should do if they did not pass this way before night fell. Return to Nicnevin and try again tomorrow? Wander the streets, hoping for some clue, some sign as to their whereabouts?

It was then that she heard a familiar laugh and looked round to see Janey chasing Elspeth along the path, Simon straining along behind them, his chubby little toddler legs pumping beneath him. A woman Mairead did not recognize was holding his hand. Mairead frowned, wondering if Constance had gotten so good at glamours that she had made one Mairead couldn't see through. But no, this woman had no magic, gave off not even the barest hint of it.

Approach the children now or follow them and let them lead me to Constance?

Quickly, before they could notice her, Mairead pulled up a glamour of her own, one designed to encourage eyes to slide away from her, rather than changing her appearance. Such an approach took far less magic and concentration to maintain, and she didn't want to use what resources she had before she was faced with the task she came here to complete.

The woman who was with the children led Simon onto the grass with the girls and stood watching as they played a game that involved one of them standing with their back turned, while the other two attempted to sneak up on them. Her heart swelled with emotion as she remembered watching them play the same game with the village children. *They must be lonely here. What has she told them about why they had to leave their home? What was she thinking, bringing them here?*

She looked at the woman who had brought them here, studying her. A stab of jealousy pierced her breast – was this her replacement? Constance's new lover? *You're jumping to conclusions based on no evidence. And what if she is? Did you come here to stop Constance or to get her back?*

She tasted blood and realized she was chewing at the inside of her lip again. *Don't get distracted. You're here to unmake Hector. That's all that matters.*

The children changed to a new game and Mairead watched as the girls took turns helping Simon to join in. They had such good hearts, both of them. They were so caring toward each other. Mairead wondered if her life would have turned out differently if she had had a sibling. Her mother had lost other pregnancies, she knew, and there had been a baby before her, a boy, who had died in infancy. It had crossed her mind that perhaps her father's hatred of her was in part driven by the fact that she was not the son he had lost.

She shook her head, pushing away such thoughts. What did it matter here and now?

The woman who had brought the children clapped her hands once and called, "Right children, it's time to go. Your mother will be home soon and will wonder where we are."

Janey's face fell, but she made no complaint as Elspeth took both her and Simon's hands and began to walk back to the path, the woman falling in behind.

"Bye grass," Janey said, her voice sad. "Bye flowers, bye trees."

Mairead's heart ached for her. She let them get a little way down the path, then stood with a soft groan, and followed them at a distance. When they left the little garden, she had to move closer as they wound through the foot traffic on the street on the opposite side from where Mairead had entered. Shop fronts lined this street and people milled around; she had to duck around a group of women walking along together – the problem with making herself less noticeable was that no one moved to let her pass.

Up ahead, the children and their companion turned onto a side street and Mairead hurried to follow. She turned into that street just in time to see them turning off again. This time she ran to the mouth of the alley they had turned into, then paused, peering around the corner of the building, until she saw them go into an entrance about halfway down.

After a moment, Mairead set off down the alley until she reached the entrance they had gone through. There was no door, just a passageway into the back of a building. It was dark and smelled of damp and refuse. It angered her to think of the children living somewhere like this, when they should have been back on the farm in Kilmartin, surrounded by people who cared about them. She hesitated, wondering what to do next. The woman had said that Constance would be home soon. Was it better to try and talk her way inside now and surprise Constance when she got there? Or wait until she was home and perhaps get more of an idea of what she was walking into? For all she knew, Constance had beat them here, and was inside already.

She could wait a little, maybe learn something of what to expect.

On the opposite side of the alley was another entrance like the one the woman and children had disappeared into, so Mairead decided to duck in there, and wait out of sight. She lingered in the shadows there, watching the entrance across the way and wondering where Constance spent her days. Presumably she had found some sort of work; she needed money to pay rent and buy food, and there hadn't been much coin in Kilmartin, where most things were bartered for, so she couldn't have brought much with her.

She wondered where Hector was in all of this. Did he wait inside, watching over the children while she was gone? But how would she explain him to the woman with the children? Did she have him hidden somewhere nearby? Mairead nervously looked over her shoulder into the dark interior of the building she was lingering inside. If she could find Hector, separate from Constance, it would be a lot easier to unmake him.

Just as she was considering investigating the surrounding buildings, she heard the scuffing of feet moving along the alley coming closer to her hiding place. She pressed her back against the wall and drew the shadows closer around herself just as Constance came into view, trailed by the Alban. She stopped in the middle of the alley, the lines of her shoulders tense and unhappy. Mairead felt sure that Constance knew she was there and would confront her here, but after a moment the other witch went inside the building where her children waited, Hector following behind.

Mairead moved to follow but some instinct told her to wait, so she stood still, watching. No more than ten minutes passed before the woman who had been with the children left, tucking a small coin pouch into a pocket in her skirt as she went. Mairead tried to ignore the relief she felt at this indication that the woman was just someone Constance paid to look after the children. Maybe she hadn't been entirely replaced yet.

Now. It's time. She tried to summon the courage she needed to go and knock on Constance's door. She still had no idea what to say, what reasoning might possibly work when everything she had tried so far had failed. *If Nicnevin is right and Hector has killed two more innocent people...surely she has to understand now?*

Mairead took a deep breath and checked that her magical shield was still in place.

Constance leaned out of the entrance across the alley and called, "I know you're there. You might as well come in."

So much for hiding. Mairead dropped her glamour and stepped out into the alley. Early evening in June was as bright as midmorning and she could see Constance plainly. She wore a simple black dress and apron, her hair tied back in a modest style befitting a woman of her age and station. So different from the carefree version of her that had danced the scarecrow around the yard, her hair loose and wild, all those many months ago. Her face was drawn and tight and she looked exhausted; like the weight of the world itself pressed down upon her shoulders.

"You felt me when you came home," Mairead said, half question, half statement.

"I felt you as soon as you crossed my wards. I take it Nicnevin is waiting on the other side?"

Mairead nodded.

Constance turned and went inside, not waiting to see if Mairead would follow. She did. What other choice was there?

They walked through the dark and foul-smelling passageway and then down a flight of stairs, lit by two dust-shrouded oil lamps. In the basement of the building, they entered a large room with two tiny windows out onto the street at ground level. Mairead could see feet walking past, a bizarre experience. She felt hemmed in, trapped, by the weight of the building above her.

This must be what it feels like to be buried.

One wall of the room had a built-in hearth and cooking tripod, while the opposite wall had a box bed built in. The children were all sitting there. Elspeth leapt to her feet when she looked up and saw Mairead. They looked at each other for a moment and then Elspeth was clinging to her and Janey joined her and Mairead could not hold back the tears of joy at seeing them again.

"I've missed you," she said, her voice hoarse.

The girls babbled over the top of each other, both excited to share their news. Simon scurried to his mother's side and clung to her skirt, looking at Mairead distrustfully. Hector stood in a corner, quietly looming over the room, though he made no move toward them. Now that she was here with them, the urge to forget everything else and just do whatever Constance wanted so that she could stay with them and be loved and accepted was almost overwhelming.

Constance went to the hearth and started preparing food, while Mairead allowed Elspeth and Janey to pull her over to the bed, where she perched on the edge and let them climb on her and tell her all that had happened since they came here. While she reconnected with them, she set part of her mind to examining Hector's magic. She could vaguely feel the weave of magic that Nicnevin had used to animate him, but it was beneath a sheath of protective magic that Constance had wrapped him in. If she was going to pick apart the magic that animated the Alban, she would need to get through Constance's magic first.

How on earth am I going to do that without disabling her in some way first?

She thought back to the night Iain had died and remembered how Constance had put her to sleep with a touch and a word. Could she do the same? Would Constance even give her the opportunity to try?

"So," Constance said, throwing something into a pot and then turning to face her. "Why are you here?"

Mairead looked up at her, then glanced at Hector. "I think you know why."

"He shouldn't be draining you too much anymore," Constance said, leaning against the wall.

Mairead looked around the room and saw that there was no other furniture, besides a small table by the hearth. No chairs, no shelves, nothing that made this feel like a home.

"I'm glad to see that you're well," Constance said softly. "Although, your leg – did you injure it on the way here? I noticed you were limping."

Mairead sighed and stretched the offending limb.

"Have you got a sore leg?" Elspeth asked.

Mairead nodded. "I do have a sore leg." She looked back at Constance. "No, I didn't injure it on the way here. It happened just after you left."

"I felt—" Constance looked at the children and broke off. "I tried to help."

"I know. Nicnevin says you probably saved me."

"What happened?" Constance asked.

Mairead looked at the children, Constance watching her with a serious expression. "I overextended myself. I was…depleted. Someone was hurt, and I saved them, but it took more out of me than I could spare."

Janey leaned forward and planted a loud kiss on Mairead's knee.

"I kissed it better," she said with a broad grin.

"It's so much better," Mairead said, smiling back at her and trying to force back her tears, though whether they were brought on by Janey's simple affection, or by the reminder of Constance attacking her, she could not say.

Constance had turned back to the fire and stood hunched over a pain she was trying to hide. "I'm sorry."

Mairead's mind flashed back to that night, to Constance crumpled on the ground, saying she was sorry and begging forgiveness. Right before she betrayed Mairead's trust again. How could she possibly believe anything Constance said now?

"Have you come to take us home?" Janey asked.

Elspeth answered before Mairead could. "No, silly, she's come to live with us here."

"I don't like it here," Janey muttered, crossing her little arms over her chest.

"Well now, I think we must wait and see what tomorrow brings," Mairead said, reaching out to stroke Janey's hair. "No one can ever be sure what will happen tomorrow. That's why it's my favorite day."

Elspeth laughed. "Tomorrow isn't a real day."

"Tomorrow can be anything it wants to be!" Mairead gazed at Constance, sorrow and longing wrestling within her anew.

"You'll stay tonight though?" Constance asked. She seemed weary, resigned, and deeply sad.

Mairead had to stop herself reaching for the connection they shared to send a little comfort and healing to the other witch. Who knew what Constance would send back? Better not to give her any ideas.

Chapter Thirty-Three
Mairead

They ate together, a simple meal of a thin broth with scraps of meat and vegetables and a scattering of barley. Before eating it, Mairead did her best to scan it for any magical interference from Constance. It was impossible to be sure, sitting here surrounded by her wards, her magic a steady, pulsing beacon all around them, but she did not think Constance had spelled the food. Having such suspicions in the first place filled her with both guilt and sorrow. Guilt that she should be so mistrusting and sorrow because she had good cause to be.

Through it all, Hector stood in the corner of the room, unmoving but filling the space with an awareness of his presence nonetheless. A part of Mairead's mind kept prodding at the edges of the magic that sheathed him, hoping to find even the smallest gap somewhere that would allow her to catch hold of the weave of magic inside that, the spell that Nicnevin shaped to animate the Albans.

There was nothing. No gap or way through that she could find. Mairead did not believe that she could overpower Constance in a battle such as the one they had the night Iain was killed, and nor did she want to try while the children were here. There was far too much risk of something going wrong and one of them getting hurt.

When their meager meal was over, the children showed Mairead the way to the outhouse, and after she had made use of it, they all did too, Simon included, though he still wore a clout under his little trousers. He was warming to her now and allowed her to hold his hand on the way back to the room they were staying in, though he clung tight to Elspeth with the other hand.

Back inside, she helped them get ready for bed as Constance cleaned up and went to the outhouse herself.

Mairead thought back to the persuasion magic she had used on the men from the Watch, the night of the fire, and wondered if she could use such techniques on Constance without her noticing. Constance had managed to do it to her, after all, diluting her own magic and influencing her decisions. But Mairead had felt so violated when she found out. Did she really want to do the same thing back? 'She did it first' had never really struck her as a reasonable excuse for poor behavior.

As she tucked the children into bed and told them a story about a brownie who would sneak into people's houses, sometimes to cause mischief and other times to help, she realized that magic was not the solution to this problem.

She could not overpower Constance, and did not want to deceive her. The only option left was to persuade her.

The children fell asleep quickly, curled up together on one half of the bed. Mairead stood and began to pace up and down the length of the room, her weak leg aching from all the activity. Her limp was more pronounced than it had been when Nicnevin had arrived in Mistress Croaker's house that morning and she briefly wished for the cane she had left behind. She wondered where the fae queen was now. Had she spent the day lingering where they had parted, waiting for some sign? Or had she gone back to her own realm, giving no further thought to Mairead until the problem was dealt with or not?

"I could try to do something for that. If you want."

Constance stood just inside the door. Mairead hadn't heard her come in and hissed through her teeth as her startled jerk sent a bolt of pain down her thigh.

"Thank you for the offer, but I believe this is as good as it's like to get."

"And you don't trust me to use magic on you. I can't say I blame you. I haven't exactly proven myself worthy of your trust in the past." Her words were matter-of-fact, but her expression disclosed a deep sadness.

"It's not that," Mairead said softly, pushing down the part of herself for which this was true. "Your magic saved my life. If it could have healed my leg too, it would have done so already."

"Is that why you came here shielded against me?" Constance moved away from the door and walked over to the hearth, throwing another bit of wood into the flames.

Mairead moved closer to her, but not so close as to appear threatening. "I wasn't sure of the reception I would receive." Controlling her voice so that it betrayed no hint of the anger she still felt she said, "We weren't exactly seeing eye to eye when last we spoke."

Constance gave a surprised laugh. "That may be a bit of an understatement."

She turned and looked straight at Mairead and for a moment, her guard was down and Constance looked completely lost. Mairead wanted nothing more than to go to her and comfort her, though a voice in the back of her mind reminded her of how many times Constance had manipulated her in the past.

"Why did you come?" Constance asked softly.

Mairead glanced over at the sleeping children and saw butterflies dancing around Elspeth's head. Startled, she moved closer, only to see them fade away. She was performing magic in her dreams. Elspeth was a witch, just like her mother. It made sense – magic often traveled down family lines.

"Does she know?" Mairead asked, nodding toward the sleeping girl.

"I don't think so. Not yet." Constance sighed. "I'll have to figure out how to explain all of this to her. Teach her how to hide. I never wanted that for her."

"In Edinburgh she'll have to hide. Maybe not so much in Kilmartin."

Constance shook her head and turned her face away.

Mairead cast a sound-suppressing bubble around her and Constance to keep the children from hearing this conversation.

"Tell me why the magic is tainted," she said gently, glancing at Hector, still standing in the corner, like a statue.

"I thought... You don't seem sick this time. I thought maybe it wasn't tainted."

"I think whatever you did when I was dying has protected me from it. Nicnevin is feeling it though."

Constance gave a tight smile. "I'm not sure I care quite so much about it bothering her."

Mairead frowned. "All she's ever done is try to help us."

Constance opened her mouth to speak but seemed to change her mind and shook her head before saying, "I don't want to argue."

"All right. Tell me what happened."

So Constance told her how Hector had killed a neighbor woman she had been paying to look after the children because she was rough with Janey. How they had moved here and she had started taking him to the house where she served as a maid and hiding him in a potting shed while she worked. That morning as she walked across the city, someone had attempted to pick her pocket and Hector had knocked them flying into a wall. They had hurried away as fast as they could, but Constance swore the man had been alive when they left him.

Of course, Constance had a history of lying whenever it suited her.

Still, Mairead thought she was likely telling the truth this time. The timing of Nicnevin feeling the death suggested it happened later in the morning, though the fact that Nicnevin felt it at all meant that Hector was the cause whether the death was delayed by a few hours or not.

"You must see that he can't continue like this," Mairead said when Constance had finished speaking. "He's just too dangerous."

Constance stared past her to where Hector still loomed in the corner, his presence spreading a quiet, brooding menace into the room. "He's only seeking to protect us."

"I know. And what happened with the redcoats—"

"You were never comfortable with that," Constance broke in.

"I know. I'm still not. But I do see that it was both necessary and proportional to the threat, no matter how upsetting I might find it all. But death for stealing? For smacking a child? Neither of those deaths was necessary, or proportional." Mairead lowered her voice and took a step closer. "I know you know that."

Constance closed her eyes. "I know. I do. But I need him." Tears leaked from beneath her closed eyelids.

"Why?" Mairead asked, taking another step so that she was close enough to feel the warmth radiating from the other woman's skin. "What do you need him for?"

"I need him to keep us safe. If people think he's my husband, then they'll leave me alone. As long as I have him, I'll never have to submit to being under the control of a man again in my life. No one will be able to force me back into that box."

"As a widow—"

"I know you've used that excuse to keep yourself free," Constance said, her voice thick with emotion. "But as a widow with children – and possession of her husband's land, if we go home – I'll be expected to remarry. Forced, perhaps, so that Iain's land can be passed on."

Mairead thought for a moment, then changed tack. "So do you plan to live with him in Edinburgh? How will you pass him off as human when you're in such close proximity to other people all the time? How will you hide Elspeth's gift, before she learns to control it herself?"

Constance groaned. "I don't know."

"Will you teach her to hide as your mother taught you? To stay small? To marry someone she doesn't love for the protection of their status?"

"No!" Constance sounded horrified at the suggestion. "Of course not."

So, Constance does not want the life she's building. She's just terrified of going back to the life she had. Mairead's mind raced. Logic wasn't enough to overcome fear; she wouldn't be able to rationalize Constance into doing the right thing. She thought of Nicnevin and her medicine, how she had valued Mairead's emotional vulnerability so highly as to warrant such a valuable exchange. Because Mairead kept her walls up, even with Constance for much of the time. There was always a part of her held back, waiting to be rejected, waiting to run when the hurt got to be too much.

Mairead reached out and took both of Constance's hands in hers. Constance tried to pull away, turning her face away, trying to hide her fear and doubts, just as Mairead so often hid inside herself. "Constance, look at me."

The other witch looked at her, meeting her eyes briefly before glancing away. Mairead squeezed her hands and waited. After a moment she looked back.

"What?"

Mairead dropped her shield, placing herself entirely at Constance's mercy. "I love you," she said gently. "I am angry with you, and hurt, and those things will take time to heal, but despite it all, I love you. I know that you feel trapped and frightened and you don't want to go back to the life you had before. But this new life that you're building is just as much of a trap. You *know* that Hector is too dangerous to keep around. You know that Nicnevin will never stop looking for you. And Elspeth cannot possibly be free here."

"Interesting tactic," Constance said, looking away, but still holding Mairead's hands, her skin calloused and dry, but warm and oh-so-familiar. "Is this supposed to convince me to drop my defenses so you can bind me? Or will you attack me instead? Make me pay for what I did to you?"

"No." Mairead shook her head, smiling sadly. "There's been more than enough of that kind of thinking. I will not force you, or trick you, or harm you. I am asking you to do the right thing. I am trusting in your inherent goodness and your love for those children. And I am hoping that your love for me was real and not faked."

"What if I refuse?" Constance asked. "Will you force me then?"

"I vow to you that I will never use magic on you without your consent."

"So, what? If I refuse to let you unmake Hector, you'll just what?"

Mairead hadn't thought this far ahead. She took a deep breath and hoped the answer would come to her as she spoke. It did.

"I'll leave. Not as a punishment, or a threat, but because just as you have the right to choose to live with him, I have the right to choose not to. But I'm still tied to him, my magic is still bound up in him, beneath yours. So each time he harms someone else, I'll return and offer you the same choice. And each time I will honor your decision. But you must be aware that each time this happens, the taint spreads through the magic, to you as well as Nicnevin and me, and your debt to Nicnevin will grow."

Mairead paused and studied Constance, who looked doubtful.

"You should also know, that even though you've found some way to keep her away for the moment, it's unlikely to last forever. Nicnevin is the Fae Queen of Witches. She *will* find some way to get through your wards. The day *will* come when you have to answer to her for breaching the agreement. And the more harm Hector does in the meantime, the worse it's likely to be for you."

Constance pulled her hands out of Mairead's grip and raised them to cover her face. "How did this all get so out of control?" she wailed. "I don't know what to do."

Mairead stood by her side, waiting. She could feel the push and pull of Constance's internal struggle.

"What will she do to me? Nicnevin?"

"I don't know," Mairead said, wondering about the answer herself. What would redress the balance? "But surely it's better to face it before the taint gets any worse. And whatever it is, if you let me unmake him now, I will face it by your side. I will help you in any way that I can."

"Why would you do that for me, after everything I've done?" Constance said, lowering her hands and looking at Mairead with eyes filled with tears. "I don't deserve your help."

"We all deserve help," Mairead said. "Besides, love isn't about what you deserve. I don't know if there's a version of the future where we're together, but I know there isn't one where I don't love you anymore."

"All right." Constance let out a shaky breath. "All right, we'll do this your way. You can unmake him."

Mairead turned to look at Hector, wondering how much of their conversation he was listening to, and how much he had understood. As she turned, she saw a great, ragged, black shadow hunching over Elspeth. She popped the sound bubble and could hear the poor girl whimpering. With the sound, Constance spun toward her daughter.

Mairead raised her hand, gathering her magic, but Constance pressed her arm down.

"It's just a nightmare. I'll deal with this," she said, hurrying to her daughter's side. She knelt on the bed and reached out to smooth Elspeth's hair back, murmuring soothing words as she did so. "It's all right, love, I'm here. Mama is here."

Constance yelped as a blast of magic sizzled and snapped at her, knocking her from the side of the bed and onto the floor. Elspeth's magic was spilling out, uncontrolled, trying to protect her from the creature in her nightmare. Mairead moved to help at the same time as Hector charged out of his corner toward the bed where the children lay sleeping.

"No, Hector, stop!" Constance screamed from the floor. She shot to her feet. "I'm fine, see?"

Hector stopped and looked at Constance, but then resumed his movement toward the bed. Constance threw up her hand and he stopped moving mid-stride, but every line of his body showed that he was straining against some invisible barrier.

"He's not listening to me," Constance said, panting with the effort she was using to hold him. "He thinks she's a threat to me. You have to do it now."

Mairead reached for the magic that powered the Alban, the weave of power fashioned by Nicnevin, but as before she couldn't so much as catch a thread of it beneath the sheath of Constance's power that she used to stabilize him when Mairead almost died.

"I can't reach the spell," Mairead said, hearing the panic in her own voice. "I can't get through your magic to it. You have to drop the shield you have round him."

"That's how I'm holding him back," Constance groaned.

Mairead tore her gaze away from Hector to look at Constance, who was leaning into the magic, with every appearance of pushing a cart uphill. Sweat beaded on her brow, and she was gritting her teeth with effort.

"He's snapped. He won't obey me." Constance gave Mairead a haunted look. "How long will it take to unravel the spell after I drop the shield?"

Panic roared through her mind, making her thoughts distant and slow. She wasn't even entirely sure she *could* unravel the magic. She had planned to convince Constance to lower her wards and let Nicnevin through to do it. She certainly couldn't be certain of figuring it out in the seconds it would take Hector to finish crossing the room to the bed that Elspeth lay in. And Constance was using everything she had to hold him back, she didn't have the control to split her magic like that.

Unravel the spell, or remove the heart-flower. She couldn't do either of those things while Constance's magic was wrapped so tightly around him, but maybe…

"Get ready," Mairead said, her voice steady despite the tremble running through her body. "Drop the shield on three. And be prepared for the possibility that this won't work."

"Mama?" Elspeth asked in a frightened voice. "What's going on?"

"Elspeth, I need you to wake your brother and sister, and go outside, all right? Go as fast as you can and close the door behind you."

"What's wrong with Hector?" Elspeth asked, not moving yet.

"Now, Elspeth!"

Hector pushed forward, managing to put one foot down.

"I can't hold him," Constance groaned.

Elspeth cowered on the bed, still not moving. Hector moved another inch closer. There was no more time.

Mairead pulled all of her magic into her hand, until the heat of it felt like it could burn her. She would only get one chance at this. It had to work. It had to.

"On three!" She took a deep breath and straightened her shoulders, her focus narrowing to one spot on Hector's chest.

"One." She moved so that he was directly in front of her, so that even if he lurched forward, she would still have the right line.

"Two." Sounds deadened, her vision tunneled until all she could see was the spot on Hector's chest beneath which lay the heart-flower.

"Three."

Constance dropped the shield. Hector lurched forward. Elspeth screamed.

Mairead sent the tightest, most focused beam of magic she had ever created straight at Hector's chest. The force of her will sent it shooting across the distance between them with the force of cannon fire.

Dirt and dust exploded behind Hector, followed less than a second later by a wet splat against the wall. Mairead was pulling on more magic to send another bolt, while behind her Constance leapt onto the bed to shield the children with her body. Elspeth was still screaming when Hector began to crumble..

Less than a minute after Constance had dropped the shield, all that remained of Hector was a pile of dirt, a plaid, and a large shirt. On the far wall, the decaying heart-flower was slowly sliding down the rough plaster, leaving a trail of sludge in its wake.

Chapter Thirty-Four

Constance

Constance huddled on the bed, her arms wrapped around all three children. Elspeth was crying softly, while the other two were sleepy and confused. Simon, picking up on his sister's tears, was sniffling, his mouth turned down and ready to cry, though he didn't know why. Janey was sucking her thumb and using the other hand to stroke Elspeth's hair.

They're so caring. All three of them. How did I end up with such kind, wonderful children? I don't deserve them.

Mairead had slumped to the floor and was sitting up, rubbing at the thigh of her bad leg. Constance wondered how much the magic use had cost her, coming so soon after her recent overextension. Had she hurt Mairead again? Caused even more harm, without meaning to?

If she had just agreed to let Mairead unmake Hector as soon as she arrived, it would have been over with before Elspeth had her nightmare. She still couldn't quite believe that he had acted as he had. How had he been able to disobey her? When had she lost control over him?

Mairead said something, but her voice seemed so very far away.

He could have hurt Elspeth. He would have, if Mairead hadn't been here. All because of me, because of my choices.

"Constance," Mairead said, her voice sharper, pushing its way through the fog of her thoughts. "Are you hurt?"

Constance shook her head and pulled the children closer.

"Mama, you're squeezing too tight," Janey said. "I squashed."

"I'm sorry, darling," Constance said, loosening her grip only a little. She listened to Elspeth's soft sobs and thought about removing her memory of what had happened, just as she had done when Hector killed the neighbor who was watching them. Surely it was kinder to make her forget?

But then she thought of Mairead, holding her hands and vowing to never use magic on her without her consent. She remembered her mother and her grandmother, and all of the promises she had made. Promises that were supposed to keep her safe. And maybe also keep other people safe from her.

I swear, I will never again use magic on another person without their consent. She thought then of the redcoats and all of the harm they had inflicted with impunity across the Highlands since Culloden. *Except in the direst circumstances.*

She reached her senses toward Mairead, seeking out the comfort of their connection, almost without thinking about it. It was only when she felt Mairead hesitate in accepting the brush of her magic that she realized what she was doing, and pulled back, ashamed.

She had so much to make up for, so much to make right. Would Nicnevin give her a chance to make it right?

She twitched as she felt Mairead's energy very gently reaching for hers, brushing against her, imparting love and support, before withdrawing once again. Maybe there was still a chance for them. If she did the right thing from now on.

She reached out and touched the magic of the wards she had set against the fae, preventing any from crossing into any part of the city she frequented. She had spent a day traveling around the farthest points from her daily routines and placing spelled rocks in strategic places. She had learned so much about magic from Mairead and Nicnevin; if only she had applied her mind to learning to control herself rather than others.

With a thought, she dropped the wards, pulling the magic that powered them back into herself.

A moment later, Nicnevin appeared in the middle of the room, filling the space with her presence as she always did. Constance gave a soft snort as she understood for the first time that this was part of the reason she was so jealous of the fae. She took up space. She did not feel the need to make herself smaller, to fit in, to prioritize other people's comfort. The way that Mairead looked at her only made things worse.

"You have succeeded in your task," Nicnevin said, looking from the mound of dirt to Mairead, then frowning. "You are injured?"

Mairead shook her head. "No. Just tired. It's been a busy day. How did you get in?"

Nicnevin looked at Constance for the first time since appearing in the room. "I was allowed in."

Mairead twisted round to meet Constance's gaze and gave her a small nod.

"You are in breach of our agreement," Nicnevin said severely. "You have allowed the magic to become tainted. You have lied and manipulated and harmed those around you."

"I have," Constance said. She kissed each of her children on the head then extricated herself from them and stood to face the fae. "I have made mistakes and acted poorly. I am deeply sorry for that, and I'm willing to accept whatever consequences you deem appropriate." She lowered her voice. "Just please, leave my children out of this. They have done nothing."

Nicnevin glared at her, her anger crackling in the air. "I am not like you," she hissed. "I do not harm innocents."

"I'm sorry, I didn't mean to imply you would. I just meant...if you're going to—" she glanced over her shoulder and then looked back at the fae and mouthed "kill me", before resuming her previous volume, "—please don't do it in front of them."

Mairead started pushing herself painfully to her feet. Nicnevin snapped her fingers and Mairead froze in an awkward position. Constance glanced again at the children, who also seemed to be frozen.

"What have you done to them?" she demanded, reaching for her magic before thinking better of it.

"Nothing, I've merely stopped time so that we may have this conversation uninterrupted."

Constance looked past the fae queen to the hearth, where the flames had frozen mid-flicker. "How...?"

"Fae magic. I cannot hold it for long, so do not delay."

Constance looked at Mairead and the children again. Was this goodbye? If Nicnevin killed her now, would Mairead raise them as her own? Would they be safe?

"I'm ready." She swallowed hard, then pushed on. "I know I have no right to ask this of you, but please, can you keep them safe? Elspeth is a witch, so she's one of yours, but please look after them. Or just…shield Mairead. If she's safe, I'm sure she'll take care of the children, somehow."

"You are right, you have no right to ask any boon of me." Nicnevin walked over to her and placed a hand in the center of her chest. "Tell me everything that happened with the Albans – the absolute truth – and then I will decide what to do with you. I will know it if you lie, and it will be the last word you speak."

Constance gasped as little barbs sank into the flesh of her chest beneath Nicnevin's hand, hooking into her magic and pulling it tight.

If she really meant to do the right thing, then this was how it started. She closed her eyes and began to speak, pouring the whole sorry tale out, sticking to the facts and offering no excuses for her choices. When she had finished, the whole thing laid out before her, she found that wrapped around the shame and remorse she felt, there was also a sense of peace, at finally facing up to what she had done.

"Are you going to kill me now?" she asked, surprised to find herself filled with quiet acceptance.

"No." Nicnevin withdrew the barbs from her chest and stepped back, frowning. "Unlike you foolish humans, I do not believe that taking a life in exchange for a life is justice. Nor does it achieve anything. Killing those who are fueled only by violence serves to protect others from them. Killing one such as you, who has the capacity to change… that would only extend the harm you have wrought by causing pain to those who love you."

Constance's head was spinning. "So what happens now?"

"You will live without magic until you have saved thrice as many lives as those taken unjustly by your Alban."

"I'm not a healer!" Constance protested. "How am I supposed to save lives without magic? Why not just say I have to live without magic for the rest of my life, rather than set me an impossible task?"

"The rest of your life will be long indeed, if you do not figure out how to complete the task. You will not experience the peace brought by death until you have paid your debt."

Constance stared at her, completely flummoxed, then shook her head. "I can't. It's not possible."

Nicnevin shrugged. "If you are unwilling to accept my terms then you may travel with me to the Seelie Court and seek their judgment. But beware, they can be capricious. They may decide to imprison you in Faery to redress the balance. Or they may decide to let you go free, but return you three hundred years hence, when all whom you know and love are gone."

Constance shook her head, then looked at Mairead and the children again. However impossible the task Nicnevin had set her, it gave her a chance to be here, with them. She had to take it.

"Very well," she said, getting to her knees in front of the fae queen. "I agree to your terms. Bind me."

The binding did not hurt, as she had half expected it to, and it was over in barely a moment. Nicnevin placed a hand on the top of Constance's head and spoke a few words in that other, musical language that could only be the tongue of the fae. A muffled feeling settled over Constance, as if she were beneath a thick blanket. Everything felt farther away than it should, and there was a feeling of stretching for something that she could not quite reach.

Nicnevin stepped back and time restarted, Mairead completing her move to stand, then frowning as she noticed Constance kneeling on the floor.

She looked from Constance to Nicnevin. "Have I missed something?"

Constance stood, glancing at the children who were animated again and seemingly content on the bed. She realized that for the first time since they were born, she couldn't touch their feelings, couldn't feel their hearts beating along with her own. They felt removed, distanced, and she didn't like it. She automatically tried to extend her senses to Mairead, seeking comfort, but that connection was closed to her also.

Colors were dulled, sounds more subdued, and a whole layer of the world that she had not known she used magic to access was suddenly gone. It was like losing a deep and essential part of herself, something that defined who she was in no less significant a manner than motherhood had come to do.

I don't like this. She trapped her tongue between her teeth, fighting the urge to tell Nicnevin she had changed her mind and would take her chances with the Seelie Court after all. *This is how to make up for everything. You owe them this.*

"We have come to an agreement," Nicnevin said, looking at Constance with an expression that could be read as compassionate.

"And?" Mairead sounded worried now.

"I am to live without magic until I have saved three times as many lives as Hector took," Constance said.

"Only those he took unjustly. The redcoats do not factor into your reparations."

Mairead looked at Constance, concern written across her face. "How will you do that?"

Constance reached for her hand. "I don't know. But I'll figure it out."

"We'll figure it out together. I'll help you." She squeezed Constance's fingers.

"I am afraid that will not be possible," Nicnevin said, waving her hand and summoning an apple from the air.

Always with the apples.

"What do you mean?" Mairead took a step closer to Constance, her body language looking defensive. It was so strange to have to rely on these cues that the rest of the world used, rather than being able to pick up on her emotions directly.

"You have your own obligation to fulfil," Nicnevin answered. "When you asked for my help in creating the Albans, we agreed upon an exchange. Have you forgotten?"

"No, I haven't." Mairead looked between Nicnevin and Constance. "I agreed that I would establish a safe haven for witches, somewhere they could live and learn freely."

"Precisely."

"Why does that prevent me from helping Constance?"

"Because the safest place to do that is hidden away somewhere, away from people," Constance said slowly, as the reasoning dawned on her. "But I'm unlikely to have an opportunity to save nine lives if I'm living away from people."

"Just so," Nicnevin said. "I will leave you to consider the logistics of the way forward. Mairead, when you are ready to leave this city, summon me and I will take you wherever you decide to go."

Nicnevin disappeared in a shower of sparks.

"No. There must be some way round this. I can figure out how to set something up here, in Edinburgh. I'll stay with you."

Constance looked at Mairead, and her heart filled with love. "No, *mo chridhe*. This would not be a sensible place for your witch haven. You should return to Kilmartin. You can use the farm, at least until the laird decides to give it to some other family member. At least in Kilmartin you'll have friends nearby, people who understand about magic and won't demonize you for it. You'll be safe there. Accepted."

"Come with me then," Mairead said, almost pleading. "I can't live in your home without you."

"How can I possibly save nine lives in a village with barely three times that living there?"

"So, what are you going to do? Just wander around Edinburgh, waiting for people to have accidents in front of you?"

Constance sighed and sank down to sit on the edge of the bed, fatigue crashing down upon her all of a sudden. "I don't know. Maybe I can find a hospital to work in, like Fergus and Bridie did. Maybe I could even train as a nurse."

"And what of the children?" Mairead asked, perching beside her and nodding to where the children dozed, wrapped around each other. "Will you pay more strangers to punish them with sticks while you work?"

That remark hurt and Constance wanted to lash out, to defend herself somehow. She would never have knowingly left the children with someone who would punish them in such a manner. But then, that was exactly the point Mairead was trying to make. Here, everyone was a stranger, and she could never be sure. She looked at Elspeth, sleeping now with an arm around Simon, Janey cooried into her side. What would happen to her the first time her magic manifested in front of someone who didn't understand?

"Take them with you," she said, her voice breaking on the words. "Keep them safe."

"Constance, no!" Mairead exclaimed, looking horrified at the idea. "I won't separate you from your children."

Constance bit her lip. She had killed Iain to stop him from taking her children from her, and now here she was, giving them away. But it was the right thing to do. She needed to be here, or somewhere like this, in order to discharge her debt to Nicnevin, but the children should be in Kilmartin, surrounded by people they could trust, who cared about them.

"Please, Mairead. It's so hard to let them go, but it's the right thing to do. Please take care of them until I can come home."

"If that's truly what you wish." Mairead looked into her eyes, studying her.

"It is. But can you stay for a day or two first? Give me a chance to help them understand?"

Mairead looked at the children and Constance saw her own love for them echoed on Mairead's face. "I can do that."

Epilogue

1st September 1749

"Can I feed the goats please, Mama Mairead?" Simon asked, as they stepped out into the yard together.

Mairead smiled and handed him the bucket of vegetable scraps. "Of course. Do you think you can manage the bucket by yourself? It's a little heavy."

Simon hauled it up in both hands. "I'm a big boy."

"Yes, you are." Mairead ruffled his hair, then watched as he waddled off, carefully carrying the bucket.

After he had rounded the corner of the house, she tipped her head back and closed her eyes, letting the warmth of the sun settle over her face like a blanket. This afternoon, she would make a trip into Kilmartin to visit Emily Croaker, both to put in an order for a couple of plain dresses for the new witch who had arrived a few days ago, and to take tea with her friend. Then after the children were in bed this evening, she would need to go through her supplies of herbs and tools and see what she needed from Inverness; Fergus was planning a trip there soon.

But first, there would be morning exercises with the witches who called this place their home now. Mairead had spent the autumn of 1746 building a new barn behind the stone cottage that was Constance's home, and had turned it into a dormitory building to house the witches she had promised to make a safe space for.

With a little help from Nicnevin, she had established wards all around Kilmartin, so that very few people passed through now, and those who did only ever had pure intentions. Inspired by the call that brought her here in the first place, she had also set up a beacon of sorts, calling to witches who could feel it, letting them know there was a haven for them.

She had eight witches here at the moment. Four adult women, one man, and three girls, including Elspeth, whose power continued to grow. Mairead would not be terribly surprised if one day she surpassed even her mother.

The wards pinged at her consciousness, letting her know that someone had passed through. Mairead was curious, but shrugged it off for now. There was work to be done, and whoever it was could only have crossed her wards if they had no malice in their heart.

She headed round to the dormitory barn and the grassy area beside it that she kept clear for exercises. The witches who came here worked on the farm, helped with whatever chores were required, and otherwise contributed their skills to the greater good of Kilmartin. Each shared their knowledge and experience with the group, so that they all could use their magic freely and safely. They were gathering on the grass already, waiting for her to join them.

Today, Mairead was planning to work on some simple healing charms and potions, but as she approached the grass, she was struck by a sense of cloaked power. As if whoever had crossed her wards was hiding themselves in some manner. *Now, what innocent reason would someone have to do that?*

"Someone is coming," she called to the circle of witches waiting for her. "Take no defensive action yet, but be prepared to should the need arise. And remember, we use shielding magic only – anyone attacking another will be removed from our community without exception."

The witches all voiced their agreement, then moved into a huddle, the children tucked into the middle where they would be protected by the adults. Mairead looked around, searching. Simon was sitting on the fence of the goats' paddock, but where was Janey? She stretched her senses, feeling for the girl, when suddenly Elspeth wriggled free from the circle and ran to the front of the house calling, "Mama!"

Mairead followed her, rounding the house just in time to see Constance reach the gate into the front yard.

Elspeth flew into her mother's arms, Simon and Janey appearing not far behind her. Constance fell to her knees and wrapped her arms around her children, tears running freely down her face.

"Oh, look at you!" she cried. "You got so big!"

Mairead hung back, letting them enjoy their reunion, wanting to throw herself at Constance too, but suddenly unsure of how things stood between them. They had exchanged letters frequently during the last three years, and Mairead had taken the children to Edinburgh to visit her twice a year. She had thought that they were making cautious inroads into a romantic involvement again, but why hadn't Constance told her she was coming?

Constance disentangled herself from the children and stood, wiping her face on her sleeve. "I wanted to surprise you," she said, taking a cautious step toward Mairead. "Is that all right?"

"Of course," Mairead said, swallowing against her fears. "This is your home, you can come here any time. Is this...are you just visiting, or...?"

Constance shook her head, smiling. "I'm here to stay, if you'll allow it. Ten days ago, I saved my ninth – and tenth – life. I have paid my debt."

"Your magic has been returned," Mairead said, a statement rather than a question.

"It has. And I heard that there's a haven around here for people like me. May I join your community here?"

Mairead shook her head. "Constance, this is your home. You do not need my permission to stay."

"You are the mistress here, now," Constance said, reaching to trace the line of Mairead's cheek with her fingertips. "I will only stay if you allow it."

"Of course I will," Mairead said. "I've been staying in the house with the children, but I can move into the dormitory with the other witches."

"Please don't," Constance said softly.

Mairead caught the other woman's hand and placed it flat against her face, leaning into it. "I'm glad you're home."

"So am I." Constance leaned in and pressed her forehead against Mairead's. After a moment, she pulled back and said, "Will you show me what you've built here?"

The morning exercises were canceled and the time spent introducing Constance to the other witches who lived here, and showing her around the farm, pointing out things that had changed and others that had stayed the same. As they walked and talked, Constance touched Mairead frequently, as if reassuring herself that she really was there. The children walked round with them, telling Constance seemingly everything that had happened since they had last seen her.

Mairead could feel Constance's magic, and also the tight grip she was keeping on it. It surged and shifted, as powerful as ever. She couldn't imagine what it was like to have it all back, this great reservoir of power, just sitting beneath her skin, after being separated from it for so long.

By midday they had shown Constance just about all there was to see, and headed back to the cottage for some food, before her trip into the village. Constance was eager to see everyone and begin to repair the relationships here – although the one she most wanted to make amends with was Roisin, and she had never returned from Inverness.

As they approached the cottage, Constance asked the children to go on ahead and give her a moment alone with Mairead.

As soon as they did so, she turned to Mairead and looked at her shyly. "There are two things I thought we should discuss, before things go any further here."

Mairead's heart picked up. Was Constance going to ask her to leave? "Yes?"

"First of all, I wanted to ask for permission to kiss you," she said quietly. "I have dreamed of it for so long, imagined myself running through that gate and kissing you until I couldn't breathe, but I'm not sure where we stand and I didn't want—"

Mairead pulled Constance to her and stopped her mouth with her own. The kiss filled her, making her thoughts fuzzy, as the reality of having her love home finally sank in.

Eventually, she pulled away and said, "What was the second thing?"

Constance stood for a moment, hand pressed to her lips, looking dazed. "I have my magic back," she said at last.

"I noticed," Mairead said with a tentative smile.

"You were right. The night with Iain. I have great power but I do need to learn control." She looked down and clasped her hands together, stopping herself from twisting at her fingers. "I don't want to hurt anyone else."

"I'll help you learn. That's what we do here."

Constance looked her in the eye. "I want you to bind me."

"What?" Mairead couldn't believe what she'd heard. Constance had only just had her magic returned to her!

"I want you to do what you said that night. Bind me and release my magic a bit at a time as I learn to control it. Please."

"Are you sure?" Mairead asked doubtfully. "If you think you need to do this to win me back, you don't. We have things to work on, but you don't need to do this."

Constance shook her head. "I'm doing this for me."

Mairead cupped her face. "You don't want to be under anyone's control again."

"Yours is the only control I trust. Will you help me? Please?"

"Yes, I will."

Constance pressed herself against Mairead and kissed her again, not stopping until they were both lightheaded.

"Then let's build something beautiful here."

Acknowledgments

It takes a whole community to bring a book to life, and I'm very blessed to have found a place in that community. I hope you'll spare me a moment more of your time while I thank them.

First of all, my thanks go to Nick Wells for giving me and my odd little books a home at Flame Tree Press. It is an honour and privilege to be published by him. My thanks also to Don D'Auria and Imogen Howson for taking my words and making them prettier. Thank you to Broci for the stunning cover art. I can only hope the words within do it justice. Thanks to Olivia Jackson for all of her efforts to get my books into people's hands, and to all of the other people at Flame Tree who have had a hand in turning my Word document into an actual book.

Thanks also must go to all of the booksellers and event organisers, book bloggers and reviewers, who have included me in their programmes as well as stocking my books and helping me get the word out. You make a huge difference and I'm forever grateful.

In 2023, Tiffani Angus ran a workshop for the British Fantasy Society on Writing Historical Fantasy, and one of the exercises in that workshop gave rise to the idea of the Albans. This book would most likely not exist without that workshop, and I am very grateful to Tiffani.

Speaking of the British Fantasy Society, my life would look very different today had I not joined the BFS in 2016 and I can't imagine being without the community I have met through the Society and its annual convention Fantasycon. Life would be quieter and a great deal emptier. The friends I have made there have shaped me into the writer I am today and this book would not exist without them. In particular, thanks go to the BFS Writing Sprints crew and the committee and volunteers who keep the Society running.

Thank you to David Green, who is a constant source of support and inspiration, and always pushes me to improve.

Thank you to Jenni Coutts for garden centre lunches and being so enthusiastic about this book from the first time I mentioned the idea.

Thank you to Karen Fishwick, Allen Stroud, Charlotte Bond, Stew Hotston, E.M. Faulds, PS Livingstone, Siân O'Hara, Adrian Fletcher, Cameron Johnstone, Annabel Campbell, Omar Kooheji, Neil Williamson, Luke Belcourt and Gareth Hunter for being constant sources of support and enthusiasm for my work and lovely company at conventions.

Finally, my deepest thanks to my family, who spend far too much time having to listen to me talking about whatever corner I've written myself into, and who cheered enthusiastically for me when I finished this book faster than any other I have written.

FLAME TREE PRESS
FICTION WITHOUT FRONTIERS

Award-Winning Authors & Original Voices

Flame Tree Press is the trade fiction imprint of Flame Tree Publishing, focusing on excellent writing in horror and the supernatural, crime and mystery, science fiction and fantasy. Our aim is to explore beyond the boundaries of the everyday, with tales from both award-winning authors and original voices.

•

Other titles by Shona Kinsella:
The Heart of Winter

You may also enjoy:
The Sentient by Nadia Afifi
Junction by Daniel M. Bensen
Keeper of Sorrows by Rachel Fikes
Silent Key by Laurel Hightower
The Widening Gyre by Michael R. Johnston
The Sky Woman by J.D. Moyer
The Guardian by J.D. Moyer
One Eye Opened in That Other Place by Christi Nogle
The Goblets Immortal by Beth Overmyer
Holes in the Veil by Beth Overmyer
Death's Key by Beth Overmyer
The Last Feather by Shameez Patel Papathanasiou
The Eternal Shadow by Shameez Patel Papathanasiou
The First King by Shameez Patel Papathanasiou
Tinderbox by W.A. Simpson
Tarotmancer by W.A. Simpson
The Hatter's Daughter by W.A. Simpson
A Killing Fire by Faye Snowden
A Killing Rain by Faye Snowden
A Sword of Bronze and Ashes by Anna Smith Spark
Idolatry by Aditya Sudarshan
The Roamers by Francesco Verso
Whisperwood by Alex Woodroe
Of Kings, Queens & Colonies by Johnny Worthen

•